Lebriz is dedicated to tw

Enise Ünel Hanımefendi

and

Ayşe Koçer Hanımefendi

LEBRİZ

a novel by

Orvilla Gregg Ünel

Printed in the United States of America

978-1511940542

Cover image: Eastern Beauty by Leon Francois Comerre 1850-1916
Cover design: John Andert

www.lebriznovel.com

YENİKÖY

Four horsemen, led by the heavily mustachioed Haydar, had been riding on the Caucasian plains since early morning. Under the shadow of the Caucus Mountains, they passed an ever-changing terrain of slopes and fields where women gathered tea leaves, men worked crops of wheat, and children helped to harvest lentils and chick peas. They'd been on the road for three weeks and had completed the tour of the first six villages. Their job was to collect taxes, obtain farming reports, and arrange for a share of the crops to be sent to the landowner's manor. With the sun high above, and only one more village to visit, Haydar decided to take a break.

"There's a stream just ahead. We'll take a break there and water the horses," he shouted.

The three young men accompanying him yelled in unison. "Race you! Yah! Yah!"

Haydar slowed his horse to let the dust settle, and followed his three spirited charges. A robust man in his fifties, he arrived at a sparkling stream where the boys had already led their horses to water.

Nejmi, the tallest of the three, was mischievous and self-assured. The son of the wealthy landowner Mustafa, he had inherited his father's dark eyes and jet-black hair. He took off his boots, swaggered toward the river, and with the arrogance of the pampered prodigal son, called out to his cousin.

"Ho, Bedri! We'll be in Yeniköy soon. There will be many girls milling about, hoping for a husband. How many of them do you think you can charm?"

Bedri was sitting on the grassy bank. Cut from the same pattern as his cousin but on a slightly smaller scale, he was painfully shy and blushed as he spoke. "I don't know, Cousin. What about you?"

"You'd better stay away from Sadi's relatives," joked Nejmi, delighting, as usual, in teasing his cousin on the subject of women. "If you don't, none of us will be able to rescue you!"

"I'm pretty sure you will be the one that gets caught first," said Bedri, gathering up his courage and holding his head high. "And if you don't behave yourself, those women will tear you apart and eat you alive!"

Sadi, the third young man, was barefooted by now and knee deep in water. Almost as tall as Nejmi, and just as handsome, with a hint of a beard sprouting on his square chin, he usually positioned himself as Nejmi's rival whenever this kind of banter took place.

"Bedri's right. You're the one who'll get hitched first, brother, you'll see," he shouted, and splashed Nejmi with a handful of cold water.

Nejmi, shocked for an instant, let out a warrior's cry and dove into the stream, clothes and all, to tackle his friend. Sadi laughed and escaped Nejmi's slippery grip.

"It won't be long til the three of us laugh at you at your wedding!"

Nejmi loved a challenge. He grabbed Sadi and tried to dunk his head under water. Sadi, just as powerful, fought back. The two of them went at each other, splashing and wrestling as Bedri stood ashore, cheering and clapping. But not for long. With one swift move, Nejmi grabbed him and pulled him into the water as well. Soon, all three boys were yelping, wrestling, and dunking each other like wild bucks. Wet to the bone, they finally threw themselves on the bank, peeled off their soaked clothes, and laid on the grass to dry themselves under the late afternoon sun.

Haydar watched the boys at play with a wry smile, amazed at how much they'd grown, yet remained the same. As local law and custom demanded, Sadi had been sent to the manor from Yeniköy, the village they were about to visit. He was only seven years old when Mustafa adopted him to be educated and become a companion to Nejmi.

Bedri arrived a short time later. He was the son of Mustafa's older brother and had lost both of his parents to the flu epidemic that coursed through the region. All three boys, practically the same age, grew up as brothers under the watchful eye of Haydar. Now, on the verge of adulthood, they were being initiated to become managers of Mustafa's land. This was the third year the boys accompanied Haydar on these rounds. Over the years, the villagers had come to trust Haydar and to respect Mustafa as a firm but fair landlord. Now they came to admire the young men as well. Many a village mother dreamed of having a daughter marry Nejmi or one of the other boys.

Watching them frolic reminded Haydar of his own youth. He too had been sent to the house of a wealthy landowner as a boy. He and another boy, Ethem, who was Sadi's father, had been raised as companions to Mustafa, just as Sadi and Bedri were to Nejmi.

Haydar snapped out of his reverie as he observed the lowering sun. The boys would be getting hungry. "Come on, boys," he called. "Let's get going. We want to get there before dark."

Bedri and Sadi followed orders without hesitation. Typically, Nejmi was the last to comply. He decided to stay behind to take one more dip. When he turned back and saw Haydar 's stern look, he rolled his eyes and followed the others.

Finally dressed, the boys followed Haydar 's lead toward Yeniköy, the village that had broken Sadi's heart.

Sadi's birth home, situated in the middle of Yeniköy, was bustling with activity. His birth mother Demet was doing everything in her power to calm her houseguest Lana who'd arrived a week ago with her daughter Nesrin. Nesrin had just asked permission to leave the house for "just a little while" and Lana was incensed.

"Under no circumstances," she said. "A girl your age? In a strange village where we hardly know anyone?"

"There are many young people out in the streets Mother," said Nesrin in her gentle, melodic tone. "Boys and girls just like me. I see them from the window. The air is fresh and the flowers are blooming. Everyone is enjoying the outside while I've been stuck in this house for a whole week."

"You should be grateful you're safe here. And you should be thankful to our hosts. How would Demet Hanim feel if a young girl under her charge should venture out and have herself killed?"

Demet was at the ready with some fresh brewed linden tea to calm Lana's nerves.

"You mustn't worry so much my dear," she said. "You're only making it harder for yourself. It's not as dangerous as you think."

"Easy for you to say," said Lana agitatedly stirring her tea. "You didn't live through what we went through. Everyone says there could be another attack soon."

Lana and Demet were connected through distant relatives but had only met last week after Lana and her family came under attack by

Russian bandits and were driven away from their village. As with many other Circassian families who faced the same predicament, she, her husband and five children had set on a three-week journey to Eastern Anatolia, where Mustafa had offered them shelter on his lands. The treacherous voyage strained Lana's already delicate nerves: she got very little sleep while on the road and was always anxious, fearing more attacks. Knowing that arriving in a new town with many strangers would cause her even more stress, Rashit decided to leave her with some acquaintances at Yeniköy to recover her nerves and get some rest. Demet and Ethem were more than happy to host her. Nesrin, being the oldest daughter and the one most likely to keep Lana calm, stayed with her mother as did the family's trusted driver Erdal.

Lana felt relatively safe at Demet and Ethem's home but still could not be consoled. She constantly complained of nightmares and headaches and continued to be anxious over her separation from her husband and children. Erdal the driver was the one who bore the brunt of her complaints.

"How could you allow this, Erdal Efendi," she said. "We should not have been left behind. That road is fraught with danger. What if something happens to them?"

"That's precisely why Rashit Bey wanted you to stay here, Lana Hanim," the driver gently explained, "so that you would be safe and not worry so much."

"How can I not worry? Look. Even my own daughter wants to give me a heart attack."

Nesrin had by now come away from the window and dejectedly sat next to her mother.

"It's alright, mother. I don't have to go."

Demet, who believed the best way to handle Lana was to remain quiet and allow her to voice her anxieties, now decided to speak up.

"I understand Nesrin likes to dance," she said delicately.

"She's a marvelous dancer," Lana declared. "She was the best dancer in the village. Elegant moves, noble posture. No girl can stand up to my Nesrin. And especially with her beauty."

"She is a stunning young lady," said Demet, while admiring the blushing young woman. "I don't think I've ever seen such strikingly beautiful hair. The color is almost indescribable."

"The color of burnished copper," said Lana. "That's how I describe it."

"Burnished copper," repeated Demet wistfully. "You're exactly right. I could not have described it any better."

"People are dancing at town center," pleaded Nesrin. "Young people, and many girls my own age. They dance the kafe in the afternoon. I yearn so much to dance with them."

Lana caressed her daughter's hair.

"Please understand my love. I don't think my heart will take it."

"That's a shame," said Demet. "She would draw such admiration in the village. Men and women both would admire her grace and beauty. What a shame to prevent that."

"Please, Mother," said Nesrin. "Just this once. I want to dance the kafe just once."

Lana was well aware that Nesrin drew the admiration of others wherever she went, and took special gratification to see how other girls envied her. She herself had not been a great beauty when she was young. Clearly, Nesrin had inherited her looks from her father's side, and her grace and intelligence from her mother's. She was proud of her daughter and enjoyed showing her off at any chance she got.

"All right," she said finally. "But just this once. And only if Erdal Efendi will accompany you."

"Thank you, Mother!" Nesrin cried, then quickly glanced at Erdal who was standing at the door. The man nodded with a smile.

"Of course I'll accompany you, Nesrin Hanim," he said. "Nothing would give me more pleasure."

The boys heard the tune from the squeezebox and the clapping of hands as they approached the village. Nejmi grinned at his companions. He and Bedri tapped their saddles to the rhythm. Even Haydar began to nod his head.

"Ho, Sadi. Looks like your father's village is giving us a welcome party," Nejmi said as he slowed his horse. "Let's see what the girls are like!" The animal tossed its handsome black head and pranced as though it sensed there was fun to be had.

Sadi's stomach was beginning to churn but he tried to ignore it. He forced himself to smile and even gyrated a little to the music.

As they reached the clearing at town's center, they saw that many young people, some of them from other villages, had gathered around the well and were clapping and dancing to the ancient rhythm of the Circassian kafe. Everyone was dressed in traditional Circassian costume: the girls wore colorful long dresses over which an embroidered kaftan reached all the way to the ground. Their hair was partially covered by fine lengths of silk. The young men, on the other hand, were dressed in warriors' garb. They sported tight riding pants, soft leather knee-high boots and flaring jackets with kalpaks on their heads.

The group made quite a lively sight. Nejmi scanned the crowd and immediately spotted a young woman in their midst. She was dancing in the middle of the circle, standing on tiptoe and dreamily swaying her arms. Her steps were so smooth that she seemed to be floating. A young man was dancing around her making intricate kicks and moving so fast that his feet were a blur. Shouts and whistles erupted from the crowd every time he made a difficult jump kick. "He's showing off for her," Nejmi murmured under his breath.

Getting off their horses, the four moved closer. Nejmi handed his reins to Haydar and turned to Sadi, indicating the young woman. "Who is she?"

The girl had caught Sadi's eye as well. "I don't recognize her," he replied. "She's not from any of our villages."

Haydar, having noticed Nejmi's interest, chimed in. "She is the daughter of the landowner of an upcountry fief."

"How do you know this?" Nejmi pressed.

"Do you think anything goes by without my notice?" the older man chided. "Those damn Russians."

"Have they been exiled?" asked Nejmi.

"Of course. For all I know, her father is a guest at the manor right now."

Haydar stepped back as the circle widened to include the three brothers. The dancing young man made one final leap toward the boys and, with a flourish, invited Nejmi to join the dance. Nejmi did not hesitate. Tall and arrogant, he crossed his arms in front of his chest and with the slightest of bows, moved into the ring.

With a ramrod-straight back, he lithely made the intricate figures and leaps. Shouts and whistles went up as he did the high jump, touching his toes while in the air. He then boldly held out a hand to invite the young woman to accompany him around the circle.

Nesrin was taken aback to see the hand extended toward her. She caught a quick glimpse of the man's face and noticed how handsome he was, but then turned away. Who was he? She'd never seen him before. Her eyes traveled around the circle looking for Erdal but he was somewhere beyond the crowd. She hesitated for a moment that seemed an eternity. She didn't know what to do. By now, all eyes had turned on her. When the man offered her his arm, she felt she had no choice. She reached over and gingerly touched him. He grinned and led her into the circle, keeping his eyes on her the whole time. She wasn't sure if it was his dark gaze that got ahold of her, or the beat of the drums. Her body swayed and followed his every step like a shadow. He held his head high; she held hers high as well. They both stood erect and the crowd hooted and clapped as they danced the intricate steps of the kafe.

Sadi, just as mesmerized by the girl's beauty, stood at the edge of the circle, watching the couple dance. With her tawny colored hair and glowing, porcelain-like skin, the girl stood almost as tall as Nejmi.

Soon, Sadi and Bedri were invited into the ring and two other young women joined them. They all followed the traditional form of the dance, with the women in line and the men opposite them, circling and giving way, one by one, to do the intricate kicks and leaps.

The dance was over much too soon. Without a word, Nesrin joined the other girls and retreated with them to the side. Nejmi still couldn't take his eyes off of her.

"Sadi, I must meet her," he whispered as other dancers took to the ring. "Find out who she is."

"I'll see what I can do," muttered Sadi with a lump slowly forming in his throat. He could only blame himself. If only he'd been the one to see her first. If only he'd moved sooner. Nejmi was the one who'd invited her to dance, not he. Nejmi swept the girl across the circle, not Sadi. He knew he didn't stand a chance with her. He observed his brother's hungry gaze as it tracked the girl's every move. They both watched her as she joined an older man across the yard, and quickly slipped out to a side street. Sadi glanced at Nejmi and could tell exactly what he was feeling. They had both just experienced the kind of hope they'd never known before. Sadi turned and walked away.

Nesrin was frantically knocking on the door when Erdal caught up with her. Before he could even call out her name, Demet opened the door and Nesrin ran inside, straight into her mother's arms.

"What's wrong?" Lana asked. "What's happened to you?"

"I don't know," said Nesrin between breaths. "Nothing happened."

"Then why are you running? Why are you breathless?"

She turned to Erdal who had entered by now.

"What happened Erdal Efendi? Did someone say something to her? Was someone unkind?"

"Not at all," said Erdal, looking at the girl and smiling. "She danced beautifully. She was magnificent and everyone admired her. I think she's breathless because she's happy."

"Is that why, Nesrin?" asked Lana. "Are you breathless because you're happy?"

"Yes," said the girl, calmer now. She looked at Erdal. "Yes, I'm happy," she said but had no idea what she was really feeling. Was she happy, excited, or terrified? All she knew was that something she'd never imagined had struck her. The man had terrified her, yet when she danced with him, she felt they were one. One body and one mind – united in exhilarating dance.

Is this love? she wondered. Surely this must be what people call love.

Sadi walked down Yeniköy's main thoroughfare observing and remembering his days on these streets as a small boy. Not much had changed. The mud-brick houses, the yards with flower gardens and fruit trees, and the backyards where farmers kept their sheep and goats were still much the same. He watched young children running through the streets, playing hide-and-seek, and remembered how much trouble he'd gotten into for climbing the neighbor's tree and picking the most delicious peach he'd ever eaten. The neighbor, who'd called him a petty thief, was furious and so was his father. As a child, Sadi had sometimes wondered if this was why he'd been sent away. Now, as he walked by the peach tree, he wondered if those peaches would taste as good as they did back then.

Haydar had tethered the horses and joined his childhood companion, now the village headman, Ethem, at the teahouse. This was where the men gathered every afternoon to drink tea, play backgammon, and talk. Many levels of conversation took place, from gossip about a recent wedding to local and world politics, and many problems were also solved. As Sadi approached, he saw that the men were engaged in a serious discussion. He hesitated for a moment, not because he didn't want to interrupt, but because facing Ethem, this man he was expected to call his father, was never easy.

Haydar looked up, noticed Sadi and smiled. "Ho, Sadettin," he said, calling Sadi by his given name. "Come and pay your respects to your father!"

Sadi dreaded the formality of this ritual. He approached Ethem and, as custom required, bent down, kissed his hand and touched it to his forehead. This was a gesture of respect young people were expected to offer their elders. As far as Sadi was concerned, Mustafa was the only father he'd known. It wasn't until three years ago, when he'd first accompanied Haydar to Yeniköy, that Sadi had any contact with his birth family. He felt a stranger among them. Even his mother, whose sweet soapy smell and warm hugs he still remembered, felt like a stranger to him. Entrenched in his memory were those early days at the manor when night after night, as a young boy, he'd hid under the sheets and cried himself to sleep.

Still, Sadi would do as he was told; both Mustafa and Haydar had insisted that he address Ethem as 'Father'. He wished it wouldn't, but that familiar lump in his throat still rose whenever he saw this man.

"Ho, my son," said Ethem. "What a fine man you have grown to be. You are at least a hand taller than when I saw you last year."

Even though he felt it was disingenuous, Sadi was still pleased that this man noticed he'd grown taller. He stood erect and looked directly at Ethem's face. "I hope all is well with you, my mother and sisters," he said formally.

"Yes, we are all well," replied the older man.

Sadi detected a shadow of sorrow in his father's voice. After a brief pause, he turned to Haydar and smiled. "I've been sent to ask about a beautiful guest in our midst. We'd like to know where she's from and who her parents are."

"You mean for Nejmi," Haydar smiled knowingly.

Sadi forced an ironic smile. "Who else?"

Haydar turned to Ethem. "I believe he's talking about Rashit Bey's oldest daughter," he said.

"Yes, I know the family," replied Ethem. "The girl's name is Nesrin. She and her mother are visiting for a few days. I arranged for us all to have dinner at the inn tonight. I will make sure Lana Hanim and her daughter attend as well."

"Excellent idea!" said Haydar.

"Thank you," said Sadi. "This will make Nejmi very happy."

"And what about you my son?" Ethem asked. "Is there anyone who's caught your attention?"

Sadi averted his eyes. "Not yet."

"There are many suitable young women in the village, my boy. You should look around."

Sadi nodded, then quickly took a bow and turned to leave.

"All three of you better get cleaned up and be on your best behavior," Haydar called after him. "Otherwise you know Mustafa will have your skin!"

When Sadi returned to the well, he saw that some young people had stayed behind to continue to dance. Nejmi and Bedri were in the circle opposite each other, one trying to outdo the other with their footwork and leaps. Finally winded, they made a last turn around the circle before leaving the dance. They were both breathing hard and laughing when they saw Sadi.

"Ethem Efendi has arranged for a dinner at the inn. So, if you two don't want to smell worse than your horses, you'd better get a wash," he laughed.

Bedri and Nejmi looked at each other. "We'll show you who smells like a horse!"

Sadi, knowing his friends well, was already halfway to the inn.

The ground floor of the han, or village inn, was one great room with a huge fireplace and a samovar set up in a corner with teacups and glasses. There were four rooms on the second floor, each with four wooden bunks covered with straw. Knowing the men from the manor were coming, Ethem had ordered fresh clean straw to be laid, and water and towels provided. Young boys cared for the horses stabled in the back of the building. Having checked on the horses, Sadi was waiting at the door of the han when the others arrived. They went up to the second floor to clean up, laughing and talking about the upcoming dinner and teasing Nejmi about the beautiful young woman he so wanted to meet.

Bedri and Sadi were already dressed, and Nejmi was toweling off his damp body, when they heard the sound of a horn from the lookouts below.

Downstairs, Ethem buckled his sword and grabbed his rifle. He rushed outside and began to shout orders at the men gathered around him. The villagers had rehearsed this scenario and knew what they had to do. Without a word, the women took cover in the houses as the men readied their rifles and took up their assigned positions in the town center. Another horn blared, this time with even more urgency.

Haydar calmly ordered Bedri to protect the door of the han. He told Nejmi to stay upstairs at the window and instructed Sadi to cover the roof of the stables. Nejmi hesitated for a moment, thinking that Bedri would be left in a vulnerable position, but then decided to follow orders and remain where he'd be in a better position to shoot. The village fell silent except for the barking of dogs.

Within seconds, some twenty Cossacks galloped into town, shouting and whooping wildly. They carried flaming torches and shot randomly at houses. Nesrin cowered behind a wall with her mother. One of the Cossacks threw a torch at the house but it didn't catch. Other houses weren't so fortunate. Two or three houses at the entrance of the village caught fire. The men protecting them had to abandon their weapons to try to put out the fires. Believing they had no real opposition, the Cossacks confidently entered town center.

Suddenly all hell broke loose. Rifle fire exploded from all directions, trapping the Cossacks with no way out. Yells, screams, and the horrible sound of wounded horses echoed through the streets. Five Cossacks were shot immediately. A few tried to turn into side streets but shots fired from rooftops knocked them off their horses. Others made for the road out of the village but were caught in the crossfire there as well.

Nejmi fired freely and ran out of ammunition. From what he could tell, he'd shot at least three Cossacks. He looked down and saw Bedri cowering behind a bush, clinging to his rifle. A Cossack had fallen off his horse and lost his gun. He had a broken leg and was limping over to the side of the street when he and Bedri came face to face.

From the window above, Nejmi shouted, "Bedri, shoot him!" But Bedri hesitated.

The man looked up. "Shoot him, Bedri," shouted Nejmi again.

The man stared at Bedri but then raised his lance, ready to throw it.

"Bedri!" shouted Nejmi one last time. Bedri raised his gun and shot the man in the chest. The man stood for a moment, and then fell face down. The lance he was about to throw fell off his limp hand.

Nejmi, who'd been holding his breath, let out a huge sigh.

Nesrin, peeking through the curtains, cringed at what she'd just witnessed.

"Get away from that window," Lana warned her daughter. "Come here and sit next to me, before they start shooting again."

Nesrin sat next to her mother and reassured her: "It's all right Mama. They will protect us."

Moments later, it was over. An eerie silence reigned, interrupted only by the heavy panting of wounded horses. Leaving his position with his sword drawn, Ethem held up a hand and shouted for caution. He motioned for a group of men to finish off the wounded horses. With their rifles at the ready, the villagers slowly began to leave their cover. All but three of the Cossacks had been killed. Ethem ordered the three wounded to be carried to the han.

Bedri, shaken to the core, flinched each time a horse was shot. Soon, both Sadi and Nejmi were by his side, guiding him indoors and patting him on the back, congratulating him for a job well done.

The young men had never witnessed such carnage before. They'd spent many years training with Haydar, using straw dummies as targets, and had hunted for wolves and deer many times. This was the first time any of them had fired at living men. Shaken and pale, they silently helped other villagers move tables around the great room to form a makeshift hospital for the wounded.

The village barber, who also served as doctor and veterinarian, was called in to treat the wounded Cossacks. Sadi volunteered to help him. He held instruments and gauze, and wiped blood from the wounds. One Cossack who'd been caught in the fierce crossfire had taken bullets through both his legs and throat. He made unintelligible sounds, but Sadi distinctly heard the man mutter the words: "Mama, Mama."

Another man with a head wound wore the blank gaze of a dying man and a strange smile on his face.

When a third man was carried in, Bedri was stunned to see that it was the man he'd shot. He was sure he had killed him, but here he was lying on the table, blood running out of his chest, staring at the ceiling. Bedri stared at the man with mixed feelings. First he felt angry. Why had they carried these dying men in here when they should've been left to die? He watched the blood pooling on the floor beneath the table and realized this was a man's life. Could he feel compassion for this man who'd tried to kill him? *Could I save his life?* he wondered. *Should I hold his hand and comfort him?*

Nejmi noticed Bedri gazing at the man. "He was going to kill you, so you shot him," he said, with chill in his voice. "Let the man die."

Bedri turned and marched out of the room. Haydar saw him running up the stairs, and then started to follow him.

"Don't go up," said Ethem. "The boy must learn to calm himself."

The two older men stood together under a fog of sorrow. It was only an hour ago that they'd talked about the possibility of a Cossack attack. Word had come that the Russians were sending bands of young men to drive the Circassian people from their lands. These youngsters had been ordered to plunder villages and rape and kill their victims, but apparently were not prepared to face any resistance. They'd been sent to their deaths like sacrificial lambs.

Looking across the room, Haydar saw Sadi helping the wounded. Nejmi stood by, his arms crossed, with an indifferent expression on his face. Haydar was struck by the boys' difference in demeanor. How can Nejmi seem so cold, he wondered, when his closest friend can show such compassion?

"Sadi, come over here," he called out. "Take a quick tour of the village and see what kind of damage has been done. Make sure you visit your mother and see if she and her guests are all right. Nejmi, you help with the wounded."

Nejmi begrudgingly uncrossed his arms and looked around to see if there was anything suitable for him to do. Haydar and Ethem were proud of the villagers for putting up such a brave fight. Still, they couldn't be sure how long they'd be able to protect such a vulnerable village against increasing attacks. They knew a plan must be made to prepare for the next assault.

Sadi hurried through the village, surveying the damage. One house had been badly burned and several others were slightly charred. At the end of his tour, he arrived at a house across the square from the inn and knocked softly on the door. When it swung open there stood the woman he called his mother. Demet took one look at her son and tears swelled in her eyes. She gathered him in her arms and in one instant he felt like that seven-year-old boy with a lump in his throat. She kissed him on both cheeks. He inhaled her soapy smell.

"My boy, my dear boy," Demet whispered.

He finally tore himself from her embrace. She took a good look at him and wiped her tears with her apron. She still hadn't forgiven her husband for sending her only boy away at such a young age.

"You've grown so tall. Come in. Sit down."

"I came to make sure that you and your guests were all right."

"We are fine," she said, indicating the two women standing behind her. Sadi looked past his mother and saw Lana and her daughter. He hadn't seen the girl this close before. His heart skipped a beat when she looked at him.

"You must have been frightened," he said, addressing both women but keeping his gaze on Nesrin. Nesrin recognized him as one of the three strange men who had joined the dance. She had heard that they were brothers. The memory of the strange excitement she felt when she danced with the other man was still fresh. How thrilling – yet also how frightening it was. This man seemed gentler than his brother. His gaze was kinder, not as hard. She felt immediately comfortable with him. She couldn't help but smile.

"We thank you for protecting us," she said warmly.

Then, very quickly, her tone changed to one of concern. "I hope no one was seriously hurt."

Sadi was struck once again. What a wonder was that smile that came and went so quickly. What joy he felt in that instant. He stumbled on his words.

"Thankfully only a few burnt hands in the village," he said. "The Cossacks are all killed or wounded."

"We're very glad you're safe, Sadi Bey," said Lana, who was all too aware of the effect her daughter's smile had on the young man. "Won't you come in and have some tea?" she asked. Sadi's gaze now turned away from Nesrin, to her mother.

Sadi was torn. He wanted so much to say yes. He looked at the girl again. By now Nesrin had turned her eyes downward. She didn't dare look at him again.

"I regret I can't stay," he said. "My duty is to return to the han and report the damages."

His heart was pounding when he stepped out onto the street.

"How foolish can you be you imbecile," he chided himself under his breath. "To fall for a girl Nejmi has his eyes set on. You have no chance with her at all."

When he returned to the han, Sadi found tables still laden with mounds of breads, cheeses, and roasted vegetables—all brought over by village women in a display of hospitality. The planned feast had been thwarted by the barbaric attack and the food remained on tables with no one to enjoy it. People stayed huddled in their houses with their families, recovering from the events of the day.

Sadi gave Haydar his report. He said that he'd visited his mother and she and her guests were fine. Nejmi listened intently as he knew by now that Nesrin and Lana were Demet's guests.

"Go take some food to your room," said Haydar. "And make sure

Bedri eats as well. You must all get as much sleep as you can. We will leave before first light."

When the boys entered the room with plates overladen with food, they found Bedri sitting on the bed, staring at the floor.

"Haydar Efendi says you have to eat," said Nejmi, handing him some cheese and a hunk of bread. Bedri bit off a bit of the cheese and nibbled on a slice of bread. Sadi made himself a small plate.

"Did you see her?" asked Nejmi, as he loaded his own plate with more than his share of food. "Did you see the girl?"

Sadi hesitated a moment. "Yes," he said. "She's doing well."

"Good. Isn't she the most beautiful creature you've ever laid eyes on?"

"She certainly is," said Sadi and pushed aside his plate. He'd just lost his appetite.

Bedri, who'd finished his slice of bread, tried to encourage him. "You must eat something, Sadi. We have to remain strong. There could be another attack at any moment."

Sadi said nothing. He wrapped himself in his blanket and laid down facing the wall. The image of the beautiful girl he'd never have, along with the images of the dead Cossacks overwhelmed him. He felt like that little boy again, torn from his home and crying himself to sleep.

Haydar and Ethem stayed up all night and made plans for more defenses, not only for Yeniköy, but for the other six villages as well. At three in the morning, one of the three Cossacks was still conscious.

Ethem approached him. "Who told you to attack Yeniköy?" he asked, leaning low over the wounded man's face.

The Cossack just stared at the ceiling.

"Were you paid for this attack? What kinds of plans are in motion for future attacks?"

Ethem picked up the man's hand, leaned over, and spoke in a low voice. "You are just a boy, like my own son. Tell me why they sent you."

A single tear rolled from the man's eye. Ethem gently wiped it away. The young Cossack and his companions were dead before dawn.

Ethem arrived home in the morning, exhausted and drained of all emotion. All he wanted was to lie down for a few minutes and shut his eyes. His wife, however, had other designs.

"Why can't you let me get some rest, woman?" Ethem grumbled as he kicked off his shoes. "Can't this wait until later?"

"Two youngsters' lives are at stake," said Demet. "Later might be too late. Her father is coming to fetch them tomorrow."

Lana listened intently from the next room. She and Demet had already decided that this was a perfect match and that the two should be paired up. Looking at her daughter's face, she knew the girl was in love with Sadi. Furthermore, when she saw them together, even for that short moment, he could tell he was in love with her too.

"I've never seen her like that," she'd told Demet. "Ever since she came from that dance, she's been transfixed."

Demet was also thrilled with the match. Nesrin would marry the son of a wealthy landowner and Sadi would have a beauty as his bride. They were determined to make this happen.

"This is out of my hands," said Ethem. "You hens think I can make anything happen but there's nothing I can do about it."

But Demet wouldn't give up. "All I ask is that you put a word in. Send Mustafa Bey a message and tell him that these youngsters are made for each other."

Ethem was now really losing his patience. "I will do no such thing. The man is dealing with a war. He's opened his lands for thousands of Circassian refugees. This is not something he wants to think about now."

On the other side of the door, Lana turned to see that Nesrin had entered the room. She waved her daughter away.

"Get out of here," she whispered.

Nesrin left the room but it was too late. She'd heard the whole conversation.

OLD MANOR

During the return trip to the manor, the young men hardly spoke at all. When they stopped to give the horses a break, there was no teasing or jocularity of any kind. Haydar remained somber as well. He knew that the boys had gone through an important initiation—another step toward becoming men. Nejmi was the one least affected by the violence. He and Sadi were both preoccupied with the girl they'd met at Yeniköy. While Nejmi remembered the girl's elegant moves, her delicate body and beautiful hair, all Sadi could think about was her smile.

What a gift, he thought. She gave me a gift with that smile. I'm sure that she likes me. Nejmi doesn't even know her name.

Both brothers wondered where she was right now, and if she was safe. They each had an ache in their heart thinking they'd never see her again.

On the way they saw a number of carriages heading in the same direction. The closer they got to their destination, the more they realized that caravans from nearby villages were heading to Mustafa's manor as well.

"What's going on?" asked Bedri. "Why is everyone going to the manor?"

"I have no idea," said Sadi.

As soon as the big house appeared in the distance, they realized something drastic was taking place. Many villagers were gathered on the grounds and a veritable military camp was being set up. Ottoman soldiers were carrying provisions and erecting tents.

"For the love of Allah," Nejmi gasped.

"It looks like war," muttered Haydar.

The larger tents looked like they were meant to house soldiers; others to serve as offices, kitchens and storage. Servants from the manor ran around trying to assist the soldiers as best they could.

As they approached the grounds, sentries blocked their way to ask questions. When a soldier asked Haydar who they were and what were they doing here, Nejmi shifted on his saddle. Haydar, knowing Nejmi could easily lose his temper, handled the soldier calmly and respectfully.

Once the sentries got their answers, they let the group proceed, only to be stopped by another group of soldiers farther down the road.

These soldiers asked the same questions. "Identify yourselves and state your reasons for coming here."

This time Nejmi couldn't contain himself. "We live here, you fools!" he barked at the man. "My father owns this house!"

The soldier ignored Nejmi and turned to Haydar.

"Don't mind him," said Haydar. "He's only a boy."

The soldier sneered and waved them through.

"How dare you call me a boy," muttered Nejmi. "You humiliated me in front of the man."

Exercising discipline on Nejmi had always been a challenge. Haydar knew that at times like these, the best way to handle him was to come down hard and use Mustafa as a warning.

"Shut your mouth Nejmi," he said, looking straight ahead. "Not another word or your father will have your balls." Nejmi sulked but stayed quiet as the group rode through the checkpoint.

It soon became evident that Circassian villagers and soldiers were also camped on the grounds. They had brought with them their families and as many possessions as they could rescue from their homes. Clearly a massive migration was at hand.

The large double doors of the manor were left open to let people come in and out. Haydar and the boys dismounted. Four stable boys ran from the house to handle the horses, followed by Ümit the butler. "Welcome back," said Ümit. "Mustafa Bey is eager to see you, but he's in a meeting now."

As they entered the house, the boys were dismayed to see many strangers walking about. Their mood brightened slightly when they saw three nice looking ladies descending the stairs. They bowed to them as they walked by. Nejmi's mother, Serra, rushed down the stairs behind the ladies in a flowing robe.

"There you are," she squealed. "My boys! I was so worried about you. We heard such frightening news!"

She kissed the boys one by one. "Are you all right?" she asked. "Is anyone hurt?"

"They were terrific," boasted Haydar. "They fought skillfully and courageously."

"Please be quiet, Haydar Efendi," snapped Serra. "I don't want to hear about that." She looked at the boys. "You must be starving. Have you eaten today?"

"No, Mother," said Nejmi. "We saved our appetite for our return home."

"Good boy," said Serra, then turned to Ümit. "Send some tea and food to the green room at once."

Sighing, she looked back to the boys. "You must excuse me," she said as she rushed off. "I'm drowning in guests."

The green room, with its large windows overlooking the gardens, was the boys' favorite place in the whole house. Bright with sunlight all day, it was wide enough to allow running, chasing, and even tossing a ball. As youngsters, the boys had spent many a day in this room eating, studying, and playing. It was here that they felt the most at home.

The boys had picked their places at the table when they were very young. Nejmi, always entitled, had claimed the chair at the head. The other two sat on the sides, like apostles. Many chairs came and went over the years, but their places at the table never changed. Like their chairs, the boys' personalities were also established early on. Bedri, gentle and more sensitive than the other two, became the peacemaker. He deferred to Nejmi's whims in most respects. Sadi was the one with the smarts. Levelheaded and a quick thinker, he got the boys out of many a jam resulting from boyhood pranks.

Private tutors came to the manor each day. The boys were given lessons in mathematics and the sciences, but most importantly, they were taught the history of the Circassian people. By the time they reached adolescence, they were able to recite many of the centuries-old Circassian fables by heart.

As soon as they entered the room, the four men went straight to the windows to survey the gardens. Soldiers, servants, and strangers were trampling the beautiful grounds. It was heartbreaking especially for Bedri, who'd spent many afternoons assisting the gardener and learning the art of gardening. He couldn't believe that even his roses, tucked away behind some hedges on the southeast corner, had been destroyed.

"Those damn Russians," muttered Nejmi.

"Get away from the window, all of you," commanded Haydar. "Come sit down."

Ümit entered the room carrying a samovar. The family's nanny, Ayshe Abla followed close behind with a tray. An essential member of the household since Nejmi's grandfather first built the house, Ayshe had been nanny for Serra and her sisters, and then for these three strapping young men, whom she treasured more than her life. Her eyes lit up when she saw her boys. She put down the tray and rushed over to hug and kiss them on both cheeks.

"Look at you," she cooed at Bedri. "Look how handsome!" And to the others, "Look how tall you all have grown. *Mashallah, mashallah.*" May God bless.

No matter how old they got, the boys continued to take pleasure in being coddled and spoiled by Ayshe Abla. She held out a bowl of cherry preserves. "Look, Sadi," she said with a lilting voice, "For you. I made it especially for you, because it's your favorite."

It had been a long time since Sadi had outgrown his appetite for cherry preserves but he kissed Ayshe Abla on both cheeks and thanked her. It wasn't often that he was singled out and he relished it without shame.

"Thank you Ayshe Abla," he said. "You never forget."

The tray also held boiled eggs, a variety of cheeses, olives, tomatoes, cucumbers, honey, and steaming hot bread. Nejmi immediately pulled up his chair and started to stuff himself. Ümit poured tea. Ayshe sliced and served cheese. Haydar and the boys all ate with great appetite.

Soon Bedri grew thoughtful. "What do you think will happen?" he asked. "It feels like we're being invaded."

"Be grateful," Haydar replied. "The Sultan's army is here to protect us."

"Who needs the Sultan's protection?" said Nejmi. "We can fight. You saw us. We can take care of ourselves."

"You have no idea what you're talking about," snapped Haydar. "That was nothing. And don't talk with your mouth full."

"Who taught you your manners?" Sadi joked.

Nejmi made a grunting sound and Sadi laughed. Nejmi tossed an olive at Sadi, which Sadi ducked. The olive landed on the floor.

Haydar blew up. "Stop that!" he shouted. "Be serious, for once! You're not children anymore. Start acting like grown men!"

Ümit froze. The boys fell silent. Bedri and Sadi looked down at their plates, trying to contain their laughter. Even Nejmi, although still defiant, looked down.

"Now eat," said Haydar.

Ayshe spooned more food onto Sadi and Bedri's plates and caressed Nejmi's cheek. She knew full well how easily the boy's ego was bruised. Nejmi responded to his nanny's affectionate gesture with another grunt.

The door flew open and Mustafa entered the room. Tall and slim, he was even more handsome than Nejmi. His well-trimmed beard, dark hair, and black eyes set off strikingly against his light skin.

"Good afternoon, gentlemen," he said, his voice hoarse. "It's good to see you back home."

Nejmi jumped to his feet and kissed his father's hand. "Good afternoon, Father."

Mustafa embraced him. "Glad to see you're doing well."

The other boys followed suit, kissing Mustafa's hand and embracing him.

"Remove the plates," Haydar told Ümit, who immediately moved to follow orders.

"Leave it," Mustafa ordered. "I need to talk to all of you, now." Ümit and Ayshe quickly turned to leave the room.

"Shut the door, Ayshe Abla," said Mustafa.

As soon as the door was closed he slumped into Nejmi's seat at the table. "Sit down," he told the others with a heavy brow.

Haydar and the boys took their seats and waited for Mustafa to speak. "Semih Pasha from the palace is visiting," he said gravely. "He's the Sultan's emissary. That's what all the commotion is about. Things are going to change around here."

"What's going on?" asked Nejmi. "It seems so much has happened so fast!"

Mustafa continued. "You all did very well at Yeniköy. I'm proud to have such courageous sons. Villages in other fiefs did not fare so well. Hundreds have been killed. Women and girls were raped, and entire villages burned by the Cossacks. The Sultan has ordered us to retreat."

"To retreat?" said Nejmi. "Why? We can fight them. You know we can. Ask Haydar Efendi. He'll tell you what we can do."

"That small attack was nothing compared to what's to come," said Mustafa. "The Russians are determined to drive us out of these lands."

Sadi was just as outraged as Nejmi. "We won't let them. Tell the Sultan we refuse to leave."

"We will fight," Nejmi said raising his fist. "We won't leave these lands to the Russians!"

"Calm down," said Mustafa. "Our numbers are few. We can't possibly hold off against thousands of invaders and I refuse to let my people get slaughtered!"

"What will we do?" asked Bedri after a short pause. Nejmi and Sadi were still trying to digest the news. "Where will we go?"

"We want to fight," said Nejmi.

Mustafa sighed. "Don't worry, you'll get your chance. Semih Pasha tells me that the Sultan himself was impressed by the reports coming from Yeniköy. You boys proved that we Circassian are fierce fighters. The Sultan is asking us to help secure his borders. In exchange, he will offer us sanctuary."

"Sanctuary?" Sadi asked. "Does this mean we'll leave?"

"Yes. We will leave the manor. We've been offered land where we can settle and be safe. Once there, we will organize our men and then send them to protect the border."

The boys stayed quiet for a moment, digesting the news. It was Sadi who spoke first.

"Who will organize our men?"

"You will. Haydar Efendi will give you instructions on how to proceed."

This was news to Haydar but he took it without a word. He knew what he would have to do.

"Our boys are well trained," he said. "They will do a good job."

"Well they'll have to train a lot of men who know nothing about fighting," said Mustafa. "Many of these farmers have never held a gun." He looked at the boys for a moment to make sure they understood. "Now eat. Get some rest. We have some tough days ahead of us."

He stood, spun on his heels and left the room.

The boys silently stared at space for a moment. Then Nejmi went to the window. "Generations of my family have lived on these lands," he muttered. "I refuse to walk away just because Russia wants our property!"

"We have no choice," said Bedri, joining his cousin at the window.

Sadi remained seated, staring at the wall. "We'll leave nothing behind for them," he said. "We'll make sure of that."

Back at Yeniköy, a carriage arrived carrying Rashit along with Nesrin's four siblings. The family's indomitable servant, affectionately called Nanna, was also with them. Nesrin was overjoyed to see her father and two sisters and ran out to greet them. The younger sister Ayla squealed with delight to see Nesrin while Leyla, the middle sister, looked puzzled.

"What's happened?" she asked. "You look different somehow."

"It's only been a few days," protested Nesrin. "I haven't changed at all."

Lana smiled knowingly. She too knew her daughter was different now. She knew she was in love. She embraced her daughters and her sons, Rafet and Kenan. The boys were famished after a long trip and showed little interest in their mother.

"I'm so relieved to see all of you safe and sound," Lana said. "Demet Hanim and Ethem Efendi have been the most gracious hosts. We missed you but thank Allah, we were kept comfortable and safe."

The family was invited inside where a feast was awaiting them.

"You have my gratitude, my brother Ethem," said Rashit. "We are joyful to be your guests and I regret that we must depart so soon. Tomorrow we will get on the road to go to our new home in Bolu."

Ethem smiled sadly and nodded in acknowledgment. He knew all Circassian families were being displaced, and that his own family would also be soon.

The two families settled in for an evening of feasting, storytelling, and sweet memories. Leyla continued to examine Nesrin questioningly, which made the older girl feel self-conscious. For the last two days, Nesrin had also been enduring her mother's occasional knowing looks.

They must think that I'm in love, she thought. But she wasn't sure if she was in love at all. Is it possible to be in love with more than one person at a time? She wanted to ask. But whom could she ask? The way Nejmi had looked at her, touched her and swept her across the courtyard had been exhilarating. Yet when she laid eyes on Sadi, she felt comfortable and secure.

Her mother hadn't uttered a word, and neither had Erdal. Clearly Lana assumed Sadi was the one Nesrin loved. And perhaps she was right.

It only makes sense that I would love the man with the warm smile and kind face. I believe he loves me as well. It makes sense that I would be in love with him and not the other, she thought, and tried to put Nejmi out of her mind.

The following week was utter chaos at the manor. Six village leaders joined Ethem and Haydar to travel to Anatolia to find appropriate areas to settle their people. The three boys were put in charge of getting the villagers ready for the massive transition. Wagons, carts, anything that could be pushed or pulled, were loaded with household goods, supplies, and personal belongings.

The servants were ordered to sort and pack the furnishings, artwork, and valuables. Serra inspected them as they wrapped her beautiful china and crystal goblets. In the past, she'd have been very meticulous about such things—always keeping an eye on the servants to make sure they didn't break or steal anything. This time, however, she realized that her servants, Ümit, Ayshe Abla, the parlor maid, and others, had been her family. She felt ashamed that she'd regarded them with suspicion at times.

She wandered from room to room reliving her memories. This was the house where she was born. She was the oldest of four girls, and since there was no male heir, her father had bequeathed the house to her husband Mustafa. She always thought she would live the rest of her life and die in this house. But now, as she walked from room to room, she felt she was saying goodbye to old friends.

The carved armoire and oak dressing table had graced her bedroom ever since she was a small girl. She descended the stairs one last time and ran her hand along the banister as she always had. How many times had she run shrieking down those stairs as Ayshe Abla chased her. She was particularly moved as she walked by her father's office and remembered him sitting at his desk, holding court and passing orders. He was always firm but kind. She'd made sure nothing had changed in his office after he died.

She entered the dining room and laid eyes on the large table, generous enough to seat thirty, and the beautifully carved dining chairs. Can any of this be saved? she wondered. The thought of leaving this house was unbearable. How could she ever accept it?

Five days later, Mustafa returned with hopeful news. The village leaders had spotted a fertile area in the northwest edge of Anatolia. They'd said the weather was amenable for farming, the foliage was lush, and the springtime winds were gentle and mild.

"Not to worry, my sweet," he told Serra. "I'm going to build you a house just as magnificent as this one—even better. You'll see."

Serra smiled at her husband but knew that with war at hand, things could not be as bright as he portrayed them to be. Still, she remained dignified and kept a smile throughout the difficult transition. Her heart ached as she watched her beautiful furniture being removed from the house, one piece at a time. The empty rooms looked even bigger than they ever had before. She had to reconcile the notion that without the furniture, it wasn't even the same house anymore.

Everything was organized within a week. Ethem arrived at the manor and brought the whole village of Yeniköy with him. He reported to Mustafa that, according to plan, the village had been set on fire and utterly destroyed. All that was left behind was a pile of smoldering ash.

The villagers had to be carefully managed. While some despaired at having lost their homes, others remained stoic. Ethem and Haydar kept them informed and organized. It was Nejmi, Bedri, and Sadi's job to make sure the people were well fed and that their animals had access to grazing pastures. The boys worked from dawn until late at night, which left no time for their usual bantering.

Haydar was in charge of gathering all the families, along with their animals and belongings, to form a convoy. As usual, the boys were there to help him with this daunting task. The people who were the slowest movers—the sick, the disabled, and the elderly—were placed at the head of the line. This would assure that they'd be well taken care of and no one would be left behind. Following them were the many wagons drawn by oxen, then the herds of animals, and a group of horse-drawn carts. Men and boys rode horses for the most part, while the women, children, and the elderly rode in wagons. Armed men kept pace on either side of the convoy.

Serra, tall and elegant as ever, was dressed in black traveling clothes. She walked slowly down the stairs, running her hands over the banister for the last time. Sobbing female servants followed her. Footmen had already carried her trunks to her private carriage.

She passed through the magnificent carved doors and deliberately trudged down the front steps to the waiting carriage. She tried to maintain her composure. She wanted to set a good example to her loyal servants who were lined up to take their own places in the convoy. She glanced over at Ümit as he opened the door for her. He and another footman, Ahmet, were to stay behind with several other young men. Their job was to perform the final and devastating act of destroying the manor.

Ümit was honored, but also troubled. The manor had been the only home he'd ever known. Burning it down was betraying all that he'd served his whole life. He bent down and clutched Serra's hand. He kissed it tenderly, touched it to his forehead and then looked up at her face.

Serra could hardly contain herself at the sight of this young man shedding such tears. She caressed his cheek and thanked him for his years of service. Ahmet offered her a hand to help her mount the carriage. She was determined to not look back at the house. It wasn't until it lurched to an abrupt start that she finally let go. Tears flowed freely as her carriage became part of the convoy.

Ümit and Ahmet did not wait too long after the carriage's departure to contemplate the job at hand. Ümit surveyed the house for the final time while Ahmet prepared the torches. After descending the front steps, Ümit observed the great front door, which had symbolized the family's hospitality for so many years, and had welcomed so many visitors.

Ahmet began to light the torches.

"Stop!" Ümit shouted.

"What is it?" asked Ahmet.

"Let's take down those doors."

"The front doors?" Ahmet was bewildered. "Why?"

"I refuse to burn them."

With screwdrivers and hammers, the men worked quickly. It took them an hour to unscrew the giant doors, drag them to a safe distance, and lay them on the grass.

Once the doors were loaded on the final wagon, Ümit announced, "Now we're ready."

The convoy had disappeared on the horizon when the two men lit their torches and threw four of them onto the second floor wooden balcony, which quickly burst into flames. They threw five more torches on the east side of the house, where the western winds would feed the fire. The barns and stables were already burning, as were the servants' cottages.

Riding at the back of the convoy, Sadi turned and saw a waft of smoke rising on the horizon. He stopped, unable to move forward. Bedri and Nejmi stopped as well. Soon, the entire convoy was halted. Villagers wailed when they saw the black column of smoke. The three young companions could not bear to look at each other, let alone speak. Nejmi prodded the convoy to move along. Another wail of sorrow arose as the travelers realized that their beautiful manor was gone, and there was nothing left to go back to.

It took the convoy nearly a month to reach its destination. As they traveled through the Georgian lands, they passed through smoldering villages, heavy with the stench of the rotting remains of slaughtered people and animals. Covering their faces, the travelers muttered prayers for the dead, and many shook fists at the barbaric Russians and their Cossack henchmen.

There was no organized Russian force attacking these villages and towns. Small bands of Cossack marauders, more vicious than the ones who had attacked Yeniköy, had been out to destroy them. The devastation was most staggering in larger towns like Batumi. With no one to bury them, the dead remained where they'd been killed: on the streets, praying at mosques, or inside their homes. The entire region was littered with burned-out farmhouses and ruined crops. It became increasingly evident that the Russians were bent on clearing the area of all Circassian and Abazar people. By the time these attacks came to an end, more than a million villagers would be killed. Another half a million people would die of hunger and disease while trying to escape.

Mustafa 's convoy was more fortunate than some of the others. Supplies were carefully rationed and they were well guarded against attacks. They were lucky that no one died of starvation and they weren't hit by any epidemics. Only one old man and two newborns were lost.

NEW MANOR

Attacks by Cossack marauders remained a threat all the way through the journey and even after the convoy reached its destination. Mustafa had made sure the disciplined formation was kept the whole time. The travelers finally set up camp a few miles inland from the Black Sea coast.

Though not as lush and green as their Caucus fields and pastures, these lands were suitable for their animals and crops. Elders, including Haydar and Ethem, staked out areas in the region to establish their individual settlements. Mustafa picked a verdant spot near Tokat to build his new home. Although he had promised his wife a house even more magnificent than the one she'd left behind, he couldn't possibly recreate the memories, worn walls, and ornate staircase of their former home.

The workers began building the new manor at once. It had just as many rooms as the old one, and stood in a beautiful wooded glade. Bedri immediately saw the potential for a lovely garden and couldn't wait to get to work. Serra took temporary abode at a lush tent nearby where she could keep an eye on the construction. It was a comfort to her to see the salvaged items from the manor being installed in her new home.

Serra had also started to cultivate a fresh view of life. She was now in close quarters with the villagers and decided to take an active role in their daily lives. She went out every day to commune with the people, help take care of the sick, and to tend to the pregnant women. For the first time in her life, she experienced the pleasure of selfless service. A few days before the house was complete, two babies were born under her watch. Deeply moved by this experience she returned to the tent and saw, to her astonishment, the carved doors from the old manor being put up in the front of her new house. She had long given up on those doors. She was filled with a profound sense of gratitude and humility.

Nejmi, Bedri and Sadi worked hard toward building the settlements. Whole villages were laid out; houses were built, wells were dug, pastures for grazing cattle and sheep were allocated. Mustafa provided much of the building material and labor was shared among the villagers. By the time winter arrived, none of the families or their livestock would be left without shelter.

The new garden was laid out, tents were struck, and the furniture moved into New Manor. Chandeliers and drapes were hung. The new staircase was beautifully carved, and Serra knew that with time and use it would mellow into the lovely feature she'd adored at the old manor. Sitting at her dressing table in her bedroom, she looked into the mirror and thought about how grateful she was to have all her loyal people around her, and how hard they had all worked to make New Manor a home.

In the late fall, Mustafa summoned Haydar and Ethem to his study. He sat behind his desk and sipped tea while to the two men assured him that the villagers were adapting well and that there were no complaints.

"Excellent," said Mustafa as he rose and walked to the window that overlooked the newly planted garden. "As you know, these lands were granted under certain conditions. The Sultan wants no less than forty men from each village to be sent to guard the borders."

"Of course," said Ethem. "We are prepared."

Haydar nodded in agreement. "The villagers are aware of what they must do."

Mustafa looked earnestly at the two men. "Good. Within a week we must have the first ten men from each village to travel to the border, with at least seventy men staying behind to train and to build barracks. Each group will serve for three months and then the next group will take over. Is that possible?"

"Yes," Haydar assured him. "Our people are ready to make sacrifices. While the men are away, the communities will ensure the crops are sowed and reaped, and that no one goes hungry."

"Excellent!" said Mustafa. "I knew I could count on you. We must get to work at once."

Haydar and Ethem nodded in agreement as they finished their tea.

Mustafa strode over to the table and dropped two extra cubes of sugar in his second glass of tea, then stirred it with a gentle tinkle. "One more thing," he added returning to his desk. "I'd like to discuss the future prospects of our three young blades."

"They are a great asset," said Ethem. "All three of them are well trained and will help train the others. We have Haydar Efendi to thank for that."

"Of course," said Mustafa, looking at Haydar, who smiled modestly and looked into his glass of tea. He wasn't used to being praised but couldn't help but feel proud of the boys and was moved by Ethem's words of appreciation.

"But we must consider," continued Mustafa, "that they are grown men now. Don't you think they should think about settling down and starting their own families?"

"Yes, of course," said Ethem.

"Do you have any suggestions for any of them?" asked Mustafa.

"I was thinking about that very thing yesterday," said Haydar immediately. "Just before the fight in Yeniköy the boys had joined a group of young people dancing the kafe, and Nejmi was enchanted by a young girl from an upcountry fief. She was a lovely thing and he'd asked to meet her. We'd arranged for a dinner at the han, but the accursed Cossacks put an end to that plan."

"Do you know who her people are?" asked Mustafa.

"Yes," replied Haydar. "Rashit Bey and his wife Lana Hanim."

Ethem looked up at the mention of the names. This was the woman who'd stayed at his house, and her daughter the girl his wife had argued for the day after the attacks. He started to say something but Haydar continued.

"The young woman is the oldest of their three daughters. They have lands five or six days ride from here, near the mountains of Bolu."

"Oh yes, I do remember them," said Mustafa. "They also have two sons. They are refined, intelligent people."

"The older girl came to visit Yeniköy with her mother. Nejmi seemed quite taken by her, or more like entranced," chuckled Haydar. "I've never seen a young man under such a spell."

Ethem frowned and stared at the floor. How unfortunate that both boys were smitten with the same girl. He couldn't decide if he should speak up or remain silent.

"I will invite them to visit New Manor in the spring, and make sure they bring their daughters," said Mustafa decisively. "What about the other two, any prospects for them?"

"Bedri is too shy to even look at a girl," said Haydar. "But I believe Sadi is smitten with someone as well."

"Who?" asked Ethem. "How do you know this?"

"I have no idea. I just recognize that vacant look boys get when they are in love!"

"I know who it is," said Ethem, knowing he'd regret it later if he didn't speak up now. "It's the same girl. Both boys are in love with the same girl."

"How do you know?" asked Haydar.

"My wife told me. She said the girl was in love with Sadi as well."

There was a long pause as all three men considered the difficulty of the situation. Haydar looked at Mustafa as though expecting an answer, while Ethem's eyes remained on the floor. Finally Mustafa spoke

"Sadi is younger than Nejmi," he said. "He will have other prospects. As difficult as this is, if Nejmi likes this girl, I will have to favor his desire over Sadi's."

"Agreed," said Ethem, finally.

Mustafa stroked his beard. "However," he said after a moment of contemplation. "There is no need to rush this. The boys will be busy training soldiers for the next few months anyway. And then they'll take turns going to the border. Perhaps in good time, one of them will have a change of heart."

Ethem and Haydar glanced at each other and nodded their heads. All three men were relieved to delay what they knew would be a very difficult choice.

Over the next two months, the three young men remained at the training grounds to prepare the recruits. Many of these village men had never seen a rifle, let alone carry one. Some were adequate swordsmen but none were well trained. Knowing what a disaster it would be to face the Russians with a band of rowdy villagers, Mustafa had stressed the importance of forming an army of well-trained soldiers. He had also maintained that the purpose of these forces was to defend, not to attack. He understood that the loss of life was inevitable but he was determined to keep it as minimal as possible.

Since they'd been so well trained under the watch of Haydar, it fell to the boys to teach the men the skills to fight like proper soldiers instead of hoodlums. It was a big job and there was very little time.

At the end of the first round of training, Mustafa arrived to inspect the troops and to distribute some supplies. With a discerning eye, he watched the men exercise their skills on the field. Some were practicing marksmanship while others were engaged in sword fights. In addition to weapons, he'd also brought cloaks, boots, kalpaks, and various supplies. Even if they're lousy soldiers, at least they'll look like good ones, he thought as he watched the men don their new military garb. He seemed pleased enough when he called his three charges to come to his tent for tea.

"You've done an excellent job, my boys," he said. "And now we must make some decisions."

The boys waited nervously. They knew that only one of them would be selected to lead the first squadron to the border to face the Russians. After three months at the border, the first group of soldiers would return and the next group, headed by one of the other boys, would take their place.

Nejmi, being the oldest, expected to be the first to go. He felt he deserved this honor and that Mustafa would no doubt grant it to him. Sadi, in his usual competitive spirit, was hoping he'd be the one to go first. He knew Mustafa was a fair-minded man who wouldn't discriminate just because Nejmi was older, and the first son. He hoped that in all fairness, Mustafa would designate him to take the leading squadron.

Nobody thought that the peace-loving Bedri would wish to be the first to go but he was hoping to lead the first squadron as well. He saw this as an excellent opportunity to prove to everyone that he was just as tough and courageous as his brothers.

As the boys waited with baited breath for Mustafa's decision, the older man surprised them by pulling out three straws. "It wouldn't be fair for me to make this choice," he explained. "We will leave it to luck to determine who goes first. The shortest straw wins."

Nejmi was not too pleased because this complicated his plan. He was the one to draw the first straw, then Bedri, and finally Sadi. To everyone's astonishment, Sadi drew the shortest straw.

Mustafa held out his hand and smiled. "Congratulations Sadi for being the first one to go. You'll put together your squadron and appoint your officers by tomorrow night. The following day you will be on your way. You must report to the Sultan's headquarters within one week."

"Good man," said Nejmi, rubbing Sadi's shoulder to mask his disappointment. "We'll miss you, you know."

"You'll go with the protection of God," said Bedri. "We will all wait for your safe return."

"The two of you will continue the training." Mustafa addressed the other boys and held out the straws. "The next group of recruits…"

"That's me," said Nejmi, having pulled the middle straw.

"Yes. Your group will leave before Sadi's returns. Now come," Mustafa said, addressing all three boys. "Get ready for dinner at the manor. It's been too long since we've had a proper family dinner."

That evening's dinner was a bittersweet affair. Serra was devastated at the news of Sadi's upcoming departure. She couldn't bear to have her boys in danger, especially after what had happened at Yeniköy. If it were up to her, the boys would get married, settle down, and never go to war. She didn't even care if they were ordinary farmers or carpenters, as long as they were out of harm's way.

She wondered how she'd feel if Nejmi, the child she'd given birth to, were going. Was she actually relieved it was Sadi and not Nejmi? The thought shook her and she felt ashamed. She loved all three boys as her own, as did Mustafa. She knew Nejmi would be next in line and couldn't help but hope the war would be over by then.

Ayshe Abla was the only person who knew how Serra felt. "Why do you worry, Serra Hanim? They're grown men. They're fighters. Nothing will happen to them. Look at how strong they are."

"I don't want to hear that," snapped Serra. "That's what my husband says. How can I be sure nothing will happen to them if they go to war?"

The boys entered the dining hall with Sadi sporting a big grin. Nejmi and Bedri stood aside as everyone congratulated Sadi and offered encouraging thoughts.

Nejmi was clearly envious. "We'll miss you, Sadi," he said, faking a smile.

Bedri was far more genuine. "Yes. We've never been apart before. Who will keep us on the up and up?"

"You'll both be fine, brothers," said Sadi. "I'll be back before you know it, and it will be your turn."

"I should be the first to go," said Nejmi, no longer able to hide his indignation. "It only makes sense. I'm the oldest."

"Only by a few months," noted Sadi.

Nejmi lowered his voice. "Remember what happened at Yeniköy?"

"What are you talking about?" said Sadi, now losing the smile.

"You couldn't stand the sight of blood. You were shivering like a girl and almost got sick to your stomach so Haydar sent you off to check the damage and see your Mother."

"How dare you?" Sadi snapped. "You're being unfair."

"I don't think you're prepared for the challenge," Nejmi argued. "It would be best if you withdraw now, before it's too late."

"I'll be fine. Mind your own affairs. You have your own men to train. You should both go and console our mother."

Nejmi looked at him with the expression that was all too familiar to Sadi. As a child, Nejmi would wear this look whenever he taunted Bedri and Sadi with the fact that Serra and Mustafa were not their true parents. Sadi had learned how to ignore the look but noticed that Serra was gazing at her sons from across the table.

"She's worried sick," he said. "She's your mother, for God's sake. Go sit next to her."

Nejmi gave Sadi a nasty glare before joining his mother.

Serra grabbed her son and kissed him on both cheeks. She looked across the room at Sadi, who was smiling at her reassuringly. Serra smiled trying to hold back the tears.

The villagers had brought food for the event and the evening turned festive. Soon the table was overflowing with lamb, several kinds of rice pilaf, and dishes of eggplant, okra, green beans, and leeks. As usual, Ayshe Abla had made sure all of Sadi's favorite dishes were served. She kept prodding him with lamb chops, "Eat, eat." The evening ended with Turkish coffee and syrupy desserts. Sadi ate voraciously, knowing it would be a while before he had such a feast again.

That night Sadi lay in bed, unable to sleep. He was excited to be going—and was pleased that for once, he took precedence over Nejmi. His brother's remark had angered him and he couldn't help but feel a twinge of pleasure to see the defeat in Nejmi's eyes. For the first time in weeks, he pictured Nesrin's beautiful face smiling at him.

I may never see you again, my lady, he thought. But I'll always carry that smile in my heart.

Nejmi lay awake as well, but it wasn't Nesrin's visage that kept him from sleeping. In fact, he hadn't thought about the girl at all since the trip back from Yeniköy. What kept him awake was the seething resentment he felt toward his father.

How cowardly, he thought, to leave the choice to chance. You should have made the decision, and you should have made the right one. I should be the one going tomorrow, not him. Your cowardly action humiliated me in front of our family.

The next morning, Sadi began to put together his officers and squadron of seventy men. He was careful to select some of the strongest fighters but knew well enough to leave some for future trips with Nejmi and Bedri. He made sure his men were well trained and well equipped. Families and friends poured in from the villages to see their men leave for the borders. They clapped, waved, whistled, and cheered as the proud men rode out. Many tears were shed after they were gone.

Sadi's three-month watch at the border was largely uneventful. A few marauding bands of Cossacks were easily warded off and the men were kept safe. All this news came to families back home with great relief, but Serra continued to worry.

"Every morning I wake up fearful," Serra told Ayshe Abla, "that a messenger is going to gallop up to the manor with bad news. Whenever I see a horseman, my heart rises to my throat."

Ayshe caressed her hand and offered her some tea.

"Don't let your husband see you worrying so much, my dear," she said. "He's always strong for you, so you should be strong for him as well."

Serra tried as best she could to retain a stoic manner while in her husband's presence. Little did she know that Mustafa was just as worried as she. He also tried to maintain a cheery disposition for his wife's sake, but when he received news that a group of the Sultan's officers were on their way to the manor, he became worried. He alerted Ayshe Abla, "Make sure she's busy with one of her causes. Don't let her see the men riding up to the house."

Semih Pasha, an emissary of the Sultan who'd visited the old manor before the emigration, led the group of three officers. The other two men introduced themselves as Serdar Pasha and Orhan Pasha. Mustafa welcomed them, expressed his honor at their visit, and invited them to lunch. The servants were immediately alerted, and the entire staff scurried off to make sure the visitors were properly welcomed and cared for. Haydar and Ethem also came to express their respects.

The men indulged in obligatory small talk over lunch. The officials inquired about their host's families, and whether they had adjusted to their new surroundings. Then they expressed how impressed they were with the Circassian soldiers and how easily the people had become part of the Ottoman territory. Relieved that there seemed to be no bad news, Mustafa relaxed and began to enjoy the men's company. All three Pashas voiced their appreciation of the Circassian people, their history, customs, and character. Mustafa, Haydar, and Ethem nodded graciously to convey their gratitude.

After tea was served, Semih Pasha spoke. "I imagine you must be wondering what brings us here," he said, putting an end to the light banter.

"Not at all," Mustafa replied politely, even though he was more than eager to know the reason for this visit. He knew Haydar and Ethem were also dying to know. "Guests are always welcome at New Manor," he said demurely, "whether there is a purpose or not. We are simply grateful to welcome you."

"We have come to commend you on the performance of the squadron you provided us, and especially of their leader, Sadettin Bey. We are very impressed by the training and courage of the men, but Sadettin Bey especially has risen in our eyes as a leader with superior abilities."

Mustafa, Ethem, and Haydar nodded, smiled and puffed with pride.

Semih Pasha continued. "His strong leadership skills, along with his compassion for his men, are rare qualities, especially from such a young man from the provinces. He has clearly had excellent training himself."

"We are very proud of Sadi, Your Excellency," said Mustafa. "We're grateful for your generous words."

"If I may ask," said Semih, and took a pause.

"Anything, Your Excellency," urged Mustafa.

"Where did Sadettin Bey receive his training?"

"It was solely in the hands of Haydar Efendi," said Mustafa, indicating Haydar who quickly stared down at the floor.

"He's also trained our other two sons, Nejmi and Bedri. As you may know, they will each take Sadi's place when his round is complete. Haydar Efendi has dedicated his whole life to raising and training those boys."

Haydar, not accustomed to such praise, kept his eyes cast down, unable to even look up.

Semih Pasha raised his voice. "May I shake your hand, Haydar Efendi?"

"Get up, Haydar," commanded Mustafa. "This is a great honor!"

Haydar looked at Semih Pasha, as if seeing him for the first time.

"You must be very proud," Semih said as he extended his hand toward him, "for doing such a superior job of training your charges."

"Thank you, your Excellency." Haydar was now standing up straight and taking the man's hand. "I am very proud of all three boys."

"The real reason for our visit," said Semih Pasha, boastfully directing his words at Mustafa, "is to invite your son to be an officer in the Sultan's army."

Ethem gasped.

"God in heaven," muttered Haydar.

"With your blessings, of course," he said to Mustafa.

Mustafa tried to recover from the initial shock. No Circassian had ever been asked to join the forces of the Sultan and as an officer no less!

"We're deeply honored, your Excellency," he said. "I would have no objection at all. But it is for Ethem 's blessing that you must ask. He is Sadi's father."

"I apologize," said Semih. "Sadi Bey told us you were his father."

"I'm his adoptive father," said Mustafa and pointed at Ethem. "His birth father is Ethem Efendi."

"I see. What say you, Ethem Efendi? Do we have your blessing?"

Ethem's face had turned a deep red. He stood upright, trying to hide his utter sorrow at being rejected by Sadi as his father. "Of course," he said. "It's a great honor."

"He will be sent to Istanbul for further training. It will be a while before any of you see him again."

"We will miss him sorely," said Haydar. "But we are very proud of him. May he go with the protection of God and return to us soon."

"Now that that's settled," continued Semih, "we would like to inspect your facilities and observe your methods. His Royal Highness has commanded us to bring him a report."

"Of course," said Mustafa.

Ethem, Haydar, and Mustafa bowed as the Pashas left the room.

"What an honor," said Mustafa, patting Ethem's back, "to go from ordinary border guard to an officer in the Sultan's army! It's an amazing achievement."

"I thought I was just getting to know my son," said Ethem, "but he doesn't even think of me as his own father."

"Don't take it seriously, my friend. Clearly it was a mistake," Mustafa reassured him.

Ethem was inconsolable. "Curses on you, Haydar, for doing such a good job with those boys! Now the Sultan will snatch the other two away. I can only hope that God will grant me some more sweet time with my son."

Haydar couldn't help but chuckle. What an extraordinary day this had been.

The Sultan's men spent two weeks at New Manor observing the second squadron of Circassian villagers in training. At the end of the second week, Sadi and his men returned to a warm welcome. The villagers gathered to celebrate as one squadron returned and Nejmi's squadron left. Sadi left immediately with the Sultan's emissaries to begin his officer's training in Istanbul.

With Sadi and Nejmi both gone, Bedri was left to take over training the third squadron of villagers. For the first time in his life he was without his two friends. Although he'd looked forward to being on his own and making decisions without following the lead of others, he now missed the camaraderie. He hadn't realized how comfortable he was to not be the one taking the initiative. Now he faced a squadron of seventy men looking up to him. Was he wise, strong, and courageous enough to be a leader of men?

The morning after Sadi left, Bedri surveyed the men he was to train. He felt nervous, but tried to look self-assured. Haydar stood beside him and observed him while he addressed his squadron. He spoke eloquently as he told the men what their training schedule would be. He then divided the men into ten practice groups. The men were agreeable, but Haydar wondered how much authority Bedri would be able to assert over them.

Mustafa summoned Ethem and Haydar to discuss the state of affairs. How were the villagers faring now? Were they going to have a full crop this year? What did they think about growing tobacco, which seemed to do well in this climate?

After they finished their tea Mustafa asked, "How is Bedri doing, now that the other boys are gone?"

"I'm not sure," Haydar replied. "He's trying awfully hard to establish his authority but I don't think he's nearly as confident as his brothers."

"Perhaps he's not ready," said Mustafa. "Do you think we should push him or hold him back?"

Haydar sighed. "That's not up to me to decide. I cannot be objective with those boys. All I can say is that Bedri is different from the other two. He has different strengths. He's compassionate and understanding. He makes sure people he's in charge of are well taken care of."

"But is he a warrior?" asked Mustafa.

"That remains to be seen," said Haydar.

"I will let you decide," said Mustafa. "Leading a squadron may not be the right job for him."

"I agree," said Haydar. "I will keep an eye on him."

During the following week, Bedri worked separately with each group in the mornings. He made good use of the techniques he learned from Haydar to train his men in swordsmanship, target practice and wrestling. In the afternoons, the men worked on their own while he went around inspecting and observing.

Three days into the training period, while he was walking by a group engaging in target practice, Bedri noticed a young man of around seventeen struggling with his rifle. He was holding it awkwardly and missing his target. Two men were laughing at him and the boy seemed increasingly self-conscious as the men goaded him, "Go ahead, boy! Try again. You'll do better this time!"

The boy took up the gun and shot again but the bullet fell way below the target.

The men roared with laughter. "You're a child!" shouted one of them. "Go suckle on your mother's tit. You don't belong here!"

The boy was embarrassed but also stubborn. He ignored the men and took up his rifle again. Bedri cringed as he watched. The boy had no technique; he was doing it all wrong. When he missed once again, the men laughed even harder.

Still determined, the boy took up the gun again just as Bedri approached him.

"Stop," said Bedri.

The boy was taken aback by Bedri's tone. He lowered his gun.

"How old are you?" Bedri asked.

"Eighteen," said the boy, blushing.

"He's not eighteen," shouted one of the men. "He's a liar. He's barely sixteen years old!"

"Take a break," Bedri ordered the men. "Don't you have anything better to do than make fun of a poor boy?"

"We're sorry, sir," said one of the men. "It's just that he has no business being here."

"That's up to me to decide," said Bedri. "Now go away." He turned to the boy. "What's your name?"

"Hasan."

"Is it true that you're only sixteen?"

"Yes." The boy looked at his feet. "But I wanted so much to fight. I assure you I'm a very good swordsman. I'm just not a very good shooter."

"Come with me," said Bedri, walking away from the group.

The boy followed him while the men stared. Once they got a distance away, Bedri stopped and turned to the boy.

"You will meet me at sunrise before anyone else is out and about. You will come tomorrow morning and the morning after that and the morning after that. Do you understand?"

"Yes, sir."

"I will train you to be a good marksman and I'll work with you until you're ready. Do you agree?"

"Yes I do, sir, most gratefully."

"Now go practice your wrestling. Are you a good wrestler?"

"Yes! Much better than I am a marksman, I assure you."

"I don't want you to go back to target practice until I tell you to. Now go, and make sure you meet me in the morning."

"Thank you, sir, I will," said the boy, turning to join the wrestlers.

The next morning, Bedri was waiting for Hasan behind the barracks. Eventually the boy showed up, dragging his feet, looking barely awake.

"Look at you," said Bedri. "Did you wash your face?"

"No, sir. I just got out of bed."

"Go over to the well and wash your face. You can't shoot a rifle unless you're awake!"

Hasan washed his face and returned, looking more alert.

Handing him the gun, Bedri said, "Show me how you hold it."

The boy rested the handle of the gun on his shoulder and aimed it awkwardly.

"First," explained Bedri, "you must get into a stance of balance. Your posture and balance make all the difference while holding your rifle on target. If either is off, the gun will wobble and you'll miss."

Hasan gave it a try.

"Your feet should be further apart," said Bedri.

The boy adjusted his stance.

"Good. Now aim and be careful. Pay attention. You must be focused."

The boy followed orders and aimed the gun.

"Now shoot."

The boy shot and missed the mark by at least twenty centimeters.

"You're shooting too low," said Bedri. "You're aiming at the right spot but you're flinching when you squeeze the trigger. You're jerking it too quickly. Next time I want you to imagine it's not a trigger you're pulling, but rather that you're squeezing a block of clay with your fist. Now try it."

The boy tried again, this time with much more focus.

"Better," said Bedri. "Now I want you to practice that, without ammunition, for at least one hour."

For the next week, Bedri worked with Hasan for an hour every morning. At the end of the week, he gathered his men and announced, "We will have a target shooting contest. Who wants to compete?"

Several confident men stepped forward. One of the men who'd been laughing at Hasan turned to his friend. "The boy's been working with Bedri Bey for a few days. Want to see how he does now?"

The friend snorted. "Sure."

The two of them stepped up to the challenge as well.

Ten men had gathered up by now. "That's enough," said Bedri. "Each man has a total of three tries. The man who gets closest in any of his tries, wins."

They each took their turn. There was no question that all of them were competent shooters. Some surpassed the others. Bedri made sure Hasan would be the last to go up.

Hasan took his position, taking extra care to find the correct balance.

Bedri stood behind him and spoke to him in a low voice. "Make sure you take your time."

Hasan got focused and imagined that he was alone.

"Squeeze very soft," said Bedri.

Hasan squeezed the trigger carefully and deliberately. The bullet shot out and hit the bull's eye.

It took the men a second to realize what had happened. Then they burst into hoots and applause. Hasan's next two tries were almost as good as the first. The men shouted and applauded even louder. Even the men who'd made fun of him were hollering.

After the third shot, Hasan turned to Bedri with big grin.

"Well done," said Bedri. "I'm proud of you, Hasan."

Then he turned to the men who'd all gathered around.

"Take this as an example, all of you," he said. "Look what a youngster can accomplish in only one week. All of you have the potential to be better at everything than you are now. I'm proud of all of you, my Circassian soldiers. I will always serve you and support you, as you will always serve our Circassian nation. Let's show the Sultan what Circassian men are made of!"

The men broke into applause.

Haydar had been standing on the side, watching the whole scene unfold. He smiled, turned around, and walked to New Manor.

"Bedri is ready," he said to Mustafa, who stood beside Ethem in his study. "You can have confidence in him now."

"Are you sure?" asked Mustafa.

"I'm sure. He is a true leader of men. I'm confident he will make you proud."

"Excellent!" said Mustafa, as Ethem stood next to him, beaming.

"Let's hope that the Sultan doesn't snap him up like he did Sadi."

The natives of the area had been wary of the newcomers at first. They watched the building of the new villages and training of the border guards with some suspicion. Mustafa was determined to befriend the locals and gain their trust.

In mid-May, when the cherry trees were blooming and nature was in its fullest expression, Mustafa invited the locals to join The Circassians for their annual spring celebration. Mayors from local towns, along with their families, friends, and other prominent persons, arrived with food and gifts. The event was such a success that Mustafa ordered others to be held several times over the summer and made sure the natives felt welcomed. By the middle of summer, some of the local men were even asking to join the Circassian border guards.

The time approached for Nejmi to return and for Bedri to depart for the border. Mustafa's thoughts turned once again to the boys' future and their prospects in marriage. Interestingly, he realized, his dilemma had been solved. Since Sadi was now engaged in the Sultan's army, Nejmi would be the logical choice for the girl.

In the early fall, while the weather was still warm, a messenger galloped up to the house at Bolu. Less than an hour later, Rashit was sitting on the verandah with the letter in his hand, and Lana was anxiously questioning him.

"What does it say?" she asked. "Who is it from?"

"It's from Mustafa Bey," he said reservedly.

"Well what does he want?" she demanded, annoyed as usual at his reticence to share anything of any consequence. "Is he coming to the area for a visit?"

"No," he said, realizing full well the agitation this bit of information would soon provoke. "He's asked us to visit him at his home—New Manor. He wants us to come and to bring our children."

"You mean our daughters."

"The letter says the children."

"He means our daughters," she said, heading inside. "He's only being polite."

Three carriages were arranged within the week to drive the family across the country. The first carriage held Rashit and Lana, along with their three girls. The enthusiastic Erdal was their driver. Their two boys and an aunt and an uncle were in the second carriage, while ladies' maids and Nanna traveled in the third.

Originally from the Upper Caucasus, Rashit was a tall and slender man with hazel eyes. His hair and well-kept mustache were a dark copper tone, matching that of his wife's hair. Lana had grown even heavier since her visit to Yeniköy, but carried herself with such elegance that her girth didn't matter. The boys strongly resembled their father, as did the middle daughter Leyla. Nesrin and her youngest sister Ayla shared the same fine skin and burnished copper-colored hair, and were the beauties of the family.

Nesrin had met the invitation with some curiosity. Perhaps she sensed that her mother's excitement over this trip had something to do with her, but she didn't want to think about that. Instead she occupied herself with girlish games she and her sisters played on long trips. She'd enjoyed traveling with her mother in the past and was happy to have her sisters' company on another venture, when they'd see new lands and meet interesting people.

It wasn't until the third day of the journey, when the family made camp at a small inn by a lake, that Lana finally revealed to her husband what she thought was the true cause of the invitation. Everyone else was either asleep or by the lake, and only Nesrin and Nanna were with her parents in their room.

"Whatever else could it be?" asked Lana impatiently. "Mustafa Bey has three eligible sons and we have three beautiful daughters."

"Doesn't it occur to you that it might be only a social invitation?" said Rashit. "Mustafa and I are well acquainted and I understand he has a beautiful new house where he likes to host relatives and friends. Perhaps he's invited us because he enjoys our company."

"I think you're wrong," said Lana as she caressed Nesrin's cheek. "They were highly impressed with our beautiful Nesrin. I'm sure Mustafa Bey is going to ask you for her hand."

"We shall see," said Rashit gloomily. Like any decent Circassian father, he wasn't keen on the idea of giving away his daughters in marriage, no matter how noble or wealthy the family. Lana, on the other hand, could barely contain herself. What a perfect match this will be, she thought. Our daughter married to the son of a wealthy landowner.

"You'll live like a queen, my love," she told her daughter. "You'll want for nothing and you'll raise beautiful children."

Nesrin, who'd remained quiet through the whole conversation, finally asked in a quiet voice, "Which son?"

"What?" said Lana, startled by the question.

"Which son?" repeated Nesrin. It was now Nanna who held the girl's hand and caressed her cheek.

"I have no idea," said Lana. "What difference does it make? All three of them are handsome, capable, wealthy boys."

"I only met two of them."

"Yes. And I'm sure it will be one of the two."

Rashit mumbled something that no one could understand.

Nanna was now brushing the girl's hair. "Let's get you to bed, my lovely," she said. "Another long day on the road tomorrow."

New Manor shone. A new wing had been built and now there were enough rooms to comfortably host the upcoming visitors. The summer was over and the cool fall winds had brought welcome relief. Friends and relatives of Nejmi's squadron prepared to welcome their men home while they wished a safe return to Bedri's squadron.

As the convoy of three carriages approached, the visitors noticed many people lined up along the road, waving and cheering. Nesrin was excited to see some young men and women dancing the kafe in a clearing near the house. Though not as grand as the old manor, the house was still impressive.

Rashit came out of the carriage first and Erdal helped Lana. The three girls followed. Ümit greeted them and accompanied them up the stairs while other servants, along with Erdal, carried their bags.

Mustafa was waiting for them at the grand entrance and greeted them warmly. "Welcome," he said. "You must be wondering what's going on?"

"What a delightful welcome," beamed Rashit. "Surely it's not all for us!"

"Actually, our son Nejmi is returning from the front," Mustafa said as he caught a quick glimpse of Nesrin. "He and his men should arrive any minute now."

"That explains it," said Rashit. "Sorry for the inconvenient timing."

Mustafa chuckled. "Nonsense. You're here just in time to celebrate with us."

He turned to Lana and the children, "Welcome Lana Hanim," he said. "So nice to see you again. And who are these young people?"

"These are my sons, Rafet and Kenan," said Lana. "And my daughters, Ayla, Leyla, and Nesrin."

Mustafa greeted each child in turn and then held Nesrin's hand.

"Ah, Nesrin," he said with a warm smile. "I've heard what a wonderful dancer you are."

Nesrin blushed and looked down. Lana kept her eye on her daughter, trying to fathom what she was thinking. Nesrin simply remained passive while Lana smiled with pride.

"Serra, they're here!" shouted Mustafa.

Serra rushed down the stairs. "Welcome, welcome," she said and kissed Lana and the children on both cheeks. "It's so nice to see you again."

The crowd grew much louder. Mustafa looked up at Ümit, who stood next to the door.

"They're coming," shouted Ümit. "They're about to turn the corner!"

Mustafa turned and took his wife's hand. He led her out of the front door to stand on the landing. Bedri and the visitors followed them outside. They clapped and cheered along with the crowd as they waited for the first men to arrive.

When Nejmi appeared, sitting erect on his beautiful black horse, the crowd went crazy. Seventy men – all of whom had followed him to the border – were behind him. Every one of them was returning home safe and sound. Nejmi rode up to the house with a wide grin, saluted his father, then turned and saluted the officers of each group of soldiers. Then he ordered his men to dismount.

Women and children—kissing, laughing, and crying—rushed to their loved ones. Nejmi dismounted his horse and handed the reins to a stable boy. He ran up the steps, kissed both of his parents' hands, and gave them each a big hug. Then came Haydar, Ethem, and then Bedri, whom Nejmi embraced with warm brotherly affection. They all told him how noble and proud he looked. The family from Bolu stood aside and watched the reunion with warm smiles.

"Meet our guests from Bolu," said Mustafa to Nejmi. "They arrived minutes ago. This is Rashit Bey, who has been kind enough to bring his family to visit us, and his lovely wife, Lana Hanim."

Nejmi politely shook the hands of the couple. "And these are his children," continued Mustafa. Nejmi nodded at Rashit 's two boys. "Welcome," he said, and then he looked at the girls.

"You might remember Nesrin," Mustafa said with a smile. "I understand you met each other at Yeniköy?"

Nejmi's heart took a leap in his chest. Here was the girl he'd danced with all those months ago. She was standing in front of him, her eyes cast down, looking lovely as ever. He held his breath as he took in the girl's beautiful skin and flowing hair.

"Good afternoon, Nesrin. It's so nice to see you again."

She looked up, and Nejmi almost gasped when he saw her stunning eyes.

"Thank you," she said almost inaudibly. "It's nice to see you as well."

"Welcome to New Manor. I hope you will find it as beautiful and enchanting as it finds you!"

Nesrin blushed and looked away.

Tables had been set up in the gardens and the villagers were preparing yet another feast of roasted lambs and chickens. The women made flatbread, roasted vegetables, and cauldrons of steamed pilaf. The guests from Bolu were happy to join the festivities, which lasted all afternoon and into the evening. Nejmi tried not to stare at Nesrin but was acutely aware of her whereabouts and what she was doing at all times.

Nesrin stayed close to her family while keeping an eye on her sisters. Ayla was shy and reserved like Nesrin, but Leyla was outgoing and sometimes volatile. She had a curious nature and didn't hesitate to start conversations with people she'd only just met. When Nesrin spotted her engaged in conversation with Bedri, she moved to make sure she wouldn't embarrass herself but stopped when she saw Nejmi staring straight at her. He had an amused look in his eye and seemed to be brazenly watching her every move. She blushed and wondered if he was mocking her. Bedri noticed the exchange and gently left Leyla's side while the girl looked sideways at Nesrin and joined her family. Nesrin, feeling her cheeks burning red, followed her sister, vowing that she'd never look at the man again.

Bedri joined Haydar and Ethem who were standing with a group of newly returned soldiers, listening to reports from the front.

Ayshe Abla was plying Bedri with plates of food, and making sure that Nejmi was getting his favorite cuts of lamb. She and Serra hovered over the boys like mother hens. Nejmi, while gently fending off these attentions, still managed to keep an eye on Nesrin and occasionally smiled at her. Huddled next to her mother, Nesrin's discomfort grew. Lana had also noticed the man's unrelenting gaze.

"I hope he doesn't come over here and start talking to me," Nesrin whispered to her mother. "That would be most embarrassing. I wonder where the other son is."

"I understand he's been sent to become an officer in the Sultan's army," said Lana as she returned Nejmi's smile. She herself was now blushing like a young girl. "Nejmi seems nice. He's the first born, you know. The other two are adopted."

By the end of the evening everyone was exhausted. Bedri was to leave with his soldiers early the next morning, so the family excused themselves.

The guests were shown to the three-bedroom guest suite, which was expansive enough to host the whole family. The boys took one room, the parents another, and the three girls took the corner room, isolated from the others. Ayla fell asleep right away. Nesrin also got into bed but Leyla wasn't ready to sleep yet.

"Can I ask you something?"

"Of course," Nesrin replied.

"Are you in love?" asked Leyla.

"What are you talking about? Go to sleep!"

"I see the way Nejmi looks at you. Surely you're aware of it. Don't you think his parents intend to ask for your hand in marriage?"

"I don't know. I suppose so." She still wished the other brother were around but decided not to say anything.

"But are you in love?"

"My heart races when I'm around him, and he's very handsome. But is that love? I suppose I don't really know what it means to be in love."

"I'm in love," declared Leyla.

"What are you talking about?" laughed Nesrin, sitting up in surprise.

"I know what it means to be in love because I'm certain that I'm in love."

"You're only fourteen! Stop talking nonsense."

"Don't you think fourteen year olds can be in love? Our mother was only sixteen when she married our father."

"Where is this coming from? Are you talking about Nejmi's brother, Bedri?"

"Yes," said Leyla, dreamily. "Bedri is so handsome. He's the nicest, gentlest man I've ever met."

"Well he's going off to fight tomorrow," said Nesrin impatiently. "He's got more important things to think about than your silly schoolgirl crush."

"I think he loves me too."

"Go to sleep." Nesrin pulled up the covers and turned away.

Leyla stared wide-eyed at the ceiling, unable to fall asleep.

The family gathered on the grand stairs early the next morning to see Bedri and his squadron off. Leyla watched the men ride away from the window. "Go with the protection of God, Bedri," she whispered. Nesrin shook her head, and with a smile hugged her. "You will have forgotten about him by the time we get back home, my dear little sister."

Once the soldiers were gone, the villagers returned to their homes. The men who'd come back from the border took up their lives with their families, and reassured the others that three months passed quickly and they'd return home before they knew it. The grounds around New Manor became quiet and peaceful again.

In the days that followed, Nesrin and her sisters took long walks in the countryside. Lana spent her days in the friendly company of Serra and other visitors to New Manor. The younger children played games while the ladies visited. Mustafa took Rashit and his two boys to watch the training of the border guards. The young people gathered in the afternoons to dance the kafe, eager to see and be seen.

Nejmi was busy training his men, but whenever he got the chance, he'd show up at town center to join the dancing youths and make sure he had at least one dance with Nesrin. The young couple danced beautifully together but hardly spoke at all.

When they danced together, the movement and rhythm carried Nesrin into a peaceful place in her mind. It was only when they stopped dancing that she'd feel confused. The way Nejmi stared at her with those deep dark eyes made her knees buckle. Was it fear or excitement that she felt?

Orvilla Ünel - 53

She was certain that something powerful was being exchanged between them - something unspoken, beyond words. But she still wasn't sure if it was love.

Almost a month passed when Mustafa and Serra asked to speak with Rashit and Lana. They were sitting in Serra's small sitting room having tea.

"We think you may have also noticed what's happening between Nesrin and Nejmi," said Mustafa. "My wife and I think they make a lovely couple. We hope you feel the same as well. We would like to request your permission for their marriage."

Lana turned to her husband to gauge his reaction. Rashit, although he'd expected this offer, looked somewhat perturbed. To him, at seventeen years old, Nesrin was but a child.

"We don't have a daughter," continued Mustafa with a smile. "If you accept, we'd embrace Nesrin as our own beloved daughter."

Rashit's heart was breaking but when he spoke, he did so with conviction, "Yes, we have noticed that the two young people enjoy each other's company. Of course, having been raised in the Circassian tradition, Nesrin will accept any marriage we decide for her." He looked to his wife as he continued to speak, "But we would still like to be sure that she is a willing bride."

Pleased at his response, Lana concurred.

"Of course, we understand," said Mustafa. "We eagerly await your confirmation of the match." The two men shook hands. "Hopefully, we will soon begin the preparations for an engagement and most joyous wedding."

The next morning, Lana entered the girls' bedroom. "Leave me with Nesrin for a moment," she said to Leyla and Ayla.

Knowing what this was about, the sisters wanted to stay but Nanna shooed them out the door. The girls reluctantly closed the door behind them

Lana sat on the edge of the bed. "You know your father and I want nothing but the best for you, my daughter," she said, taking Nesrin's hand and looking into her beautiful hazel eyes. "Mustafa 's son, Nejmi, would like your hand in marriage. What do you think about that?"

"Do I have a choice?" asked Nesrin, looking away.

"Of course you do. We will not force you to marry him. But we would like you to realize what a favorable match this is." Lana glanced around the well-appointed room. "This is a highly respectable family. They are kind and generous and Nejmi seems quite taken with you. I don't know if we can expect a prospect any better than this."

Nesrin took a pause. She remembered Sadi's smile and the genuine worry in his eyes when he asked if she and her mother were all right. His gentle voice had comforted her and made her feel secure. But now Sadi was gone and this handsome but arrogant man was asking for her hand. Obviously her parents were pleased with the prospect of her marrying into this highly respected and wealthy family.

"Do you want to think about it?" Lana asked, caressing her daughter's hand. "Why don't you sleep on it and decide tomorrow morning?"

"I don't have to think about it," said Nesrin after a moment. " If you and father think it's best, I am willing to marry Nejmi."

Lana squeezed her daughter's hand. "Good. I do believe this is a good match for you, my darling. I'll tell your father right away."

As soon as Lana left the room, Ayla and Leyla rushed back in. Leyla was beside herself.

"What happened? Is it what we think it is?"

Nesrin smiled and nodded her head. Her sisters rushed to hug and congratulate her.

"Soon it will be my turn," Leyla said to Ayla. "And then it will be yours!"

"I don't know," Ayla said. "I don't think I'm as eager as you."

"I don't think anything as exciting as this has ever happened to us," said Leyla. "He's so handsome, Nesrin. You're going to be very happy!"

Mustafa and Serra arranged for a meeting of friends and family at New Manor within the week. Haydar, Ethem and their families, along with the mayor and several village elders, all gathered together in the beautifully appointed salon. The chandeliers, tapestries, and furniture from the old manor gave the room an elegance rarely seen in the area.

The ladies looked exquisite in their embroidered kaftans while the men were especially smart in their traditional Circassian garb. All eyes turned to Nesrin as she entered the room. Few had ever seen a more beautiful girl. She wore a silver and gold embroidered velvet kaftan over her silk gown with a gold belt circling her tiny waist. A misty blue silk veil covered her hair.

Once again, Nejmi was struck by how gorgeous she was.

The mayor, a heavyset man with a drooping mustache, finally spoke.

"Our good friends, we are gathered here to celebrate a joyous announcement: The Honorable Rashit Bey has agreed to a marriage contract between his daughter Nesrin and the Honorable Mustafa Bey's son, Nejmi Bey. I will now perform the ritual symbolizing this happy union."

Nejmi and Nesrin stood next to each other at the end of the salon. Nesrin, her hands clasped in front, looked down demurely while Nejmi stood tall and smiled at guests and family. A small boy was holding a velvet pillow with two gold rings tied together with a ribbon. The mayor took up the rings and put one on Nesrin's finger and the other on Nejmi's.

"I now announce the two of you as promised to each other in marriage," he said, and cut the ribbon with a pair of golden scissors.

Nejmi, smiling even broader, took Nesrin's hand and lifted it to his lips. Nesrin kept her eyes down to the ground.

Much rejoicing followed as people lined up to congratulate the young couple and their parents. Many of the villagers remained late into the night, dancing the kafe and singing traditional Circassian songs. Leyla was the most excited of all; she beamed at each guest with a big smile. Nobody took notice that Nejmi and Nesrin hardly said a word to each other.

The very picture of a shy, innocent girl, Nesrin stayed close to her mother, all the while wondering if she'd made a mistake. Would she feel these doubts if Sadi had been her groom? She stole a glance at her parents and saw how happy and proud they were. They love me and know what's best for me so I must be grateful, she thought. After all he is handsome and the son of a highly respected family. Nejmi, on the other hand, chatted and laughed with his comrades throwing an occasional all-knowing, surreptitious glance at his wife to be.

Rashit and his family departed for Bolu a few days later where, immediately upon arrival, they began preparing for the wedding. For the next three months, the skilled seamstresses of Bolu would sew and embroider tirelessly to assemble the exquisite robes and kaftans for Nesrin's trousseau. Lana and Leyla took great delight in selecting the fabrics and Nesrin tried to appear enthusiastic but was mostly quiet and withdrawn. She was increasingly apprehensive about the wedding but was particularly worried about the henna ceremony, a traditional ritual that every bride had to withstand before getting married.

Typically the henna ceremony would be organized by the leading female figure of the bride's household. Since she was better organized and had more energy than she, Lana wisely put Nanna in charge. All female relatives and friends from both families were invited; Serra traveled from New Manor and was welcomed with open arms.

On the morning of the ritual, Nesrin stood in front of her mirror and dropped her morning robe to look at herself. She saw a tall, slim, almost skinny reflection. She lifted her small well-formed breasts and turned to view her hips and bottom. She blushed at her reflection and wondered if Nejmi would find her pleasing. Leyla entered the room just as she covered herself.

"What do you think happens when you get married?" Nesrin asked Leyla.

Even though she had two brothers, Nesrin had never seen a naked male nor was she at all versed in sexual relations.

"Only good things," Leyla said, enthusiastic as usual. "Getting married is like entering heaven and the children you bear will be your angels."

"You're a silly one," Nesrin laughed.

"Go finish your studies, Leyla," Nanna said as she entered the room. She was carrying a small bowl of hot wax made with sugar, water, and a few drops of lemon juice. "Your tutor is still waiting."

"I hate the violin," groaned the girl, while curiously eyeing Nanna's concoction. "Why do I have to learn how to play something so tedious? I won't ever play the violin once I'm married!"

"Go study," Nanna ordered, and wouldn't stop glaring at Leyla until she left the room. Once Leyla was gone, Nanna placed the bowl on a table and spoke to Nesrin in her soft voice.

"Are you prepared, my sweet?"

"I think so," Nesrin replied.

Nanna vigorously began to knead the substance in the bowl. She would use the hot wax to remove the unwanted hair from Nesrin's pubic area, legs, and armpits. Her short, stout body heaved up and down as she kneaded and muttered a gentle tune. Once she decided it had reached the right consistency, she lifted the sticky mixture out of the bowl and turned to Nesrin.

"Will this hurt?" asked Nesrin, eyeing the wax.

"You have such little hair on your body that it should hurt hardly at all. Now sit back and relax. I'll start with your legs first."

Sent by her parents to serve in Rashit's house when she was a child of ten, Nanna knew Nesrin and the other children better than even their own mother did. Nesrin was "born into my hands," she liked to boast.

Nesrin winced when the hot wax met her ankle, but soon relaxed under Nanna's gentle and knowing touch.

After a moment, she asked, "Nanna, do you think I'm pretty?"

"No, but you are beautiful, my silly girl," Nanna replied with a smile.

"What will happen when I'm married?"

"You will love your husband and be happy." Nanna smeared the sticky substance down the girl's legs and heaved a great sigh. "You will obey your husband and do whatever he says."

Nesrin flinched as Nanna snapped the wax off her soft skin. "My cousin Esra told me that when I get married, my husband will put his maleness inside of me." She watched Nanna closely for a response but got none. "I thought she was joking—I told her she was ridiculous. But now, even Leyla thinks it's true. It's not true, is it, Nanna?"

Nanna was now focusing on waxing under Nesrin's left arm.

Nesrin flinched again as Nanna pulled off the wax. "So it is true?"

"Of course it's true. How do you think children are made? For the love of Allah! Raise your other arm and sit still."

"I don't know if I can endure such a thing," Nesrin said. "What if I pee all over him?"

"You won't pee!" Nanna's laugh made her belly shake. "It might hurt a little the first time, but you'll get used to it. Some women even claim to enjoy it."

Nesrin frowned. "Should I tell my father I don't want to get married?"

"You should count your blessings, my girl," Nanna said. "At least you've seen your intended husband! Many girls don't even set eyes on their men before they marry them. Besides, if it's not Nejmi, it will be someone else. Don't you want to get married and have a family?"

"Of course I do. I want nothing more than to have children."

Nanna smiled. "Remember how afraid you were when you had your first monthly because there was blood coming out of you?"

"Yes."

"You got used to it, didn't you?"

Nesrin nodded.

"Think of it like that. It's part of growing up and becoming a mother. Every woman must endure it."

"Except you," said the girl.

"You're right. I've been fortunate enough to have children to love without giving birth to them. Don't worry too much, my girl. Nejmi is a fine young man. He will be gentle with you."

Nesrin let out a yelp as Nanna pulled off the last of the wax.

"Done!" Nanna stood to help Nesrin get dressed.

As soon as she left Nesrin, Nanna headed to the hamam carrying a lavishly decorated basket under her arm. She had made arrangements with the hamam's management to have all the supplies delivered and the rooms suitably prepared. Her basket—woven with red ribbon and straw—contained all the necessary items for the ritual.

Once at the bathhouse, Nanna examined the front salon to make sure that the fruits, sweets and pastries were all laid out and that the samovar was steaming. She then entered the dressing rooms and found to her satisfaction that the silk bath sheets called *peshtemals*, and the mother-of-pearl inlaid hamam clogs were all neatly arranged. Gifts for the families and their guests were also properly displayed.

Satisfied with the preparations, Nanna undressed, wrapped herself in a peshtemal, and stepped into a pair of hamam clogs. Taking up her basket, she clomped directly to the main bathing room.

Large basins with brass faucets lined the walls. Next to each basin stood several three legged stools flanked by silver boxes holding lavender soap. The dais at the center of the room was large enough to accommodate several guests to be scrubbed and massaged. The entire room—floor, walls, basins, and dais—was made of grey veined white marble.

Nanna quickly took the contents of her basket and arranged them on the dais. She set down seven plates, prepared for the dancers, each with a candle placed on it surrounded by fresh flowers. A large red silk veil, worked in threads of silver and gold, was then placed on the dais, along with a matching pair of mittens. Finally, Nanna arranged a large silver tray that held small bowls containing the henna, a pitcher of lavender water, and another set of mixing bowls.

An ornately carved chair stood in front of the dais, over which she draped a fine silk peshtemal for Nesrin. Her arrangements completed, Nanna hurried back to the dressing room.

Lana, Nesrin, and her two sisters arrived at the hamam next. They situated themselves at the door of the triple-domed building to welcome the many guests—mostly matrons and their daughters—who arrived in carriages. Once all the guests were present, the women retired to the dressing rooms to get ready.

Nanna's next job was to make sure the family group was prepared. She first helped Lana undress and wrapped her in a silk peshtemal. Then she turned her attention to Nesrin. She undressed her, wrapped her in a peshtemal, and reminded her of what she must do during the ceremony. Like all Circassian girls approaching marriage, Nesrin knew she'd face this moment someday.

"Must I take off my clothes and show my body to everyone?" asked the girl.

Nanna's was sympathetic but stern. "Of course you do my darling. It's part of the ceremony."

Nanna still had to make sure Leyla and Ayla were properly attired. They were waiting in the neighboring dressing room.

Leyla, as usual, was impatient and fidgety. "Is Nesrin ready? How does she look?"

"Beautiful," replied Nanna. "Are you two ready?"

"Yes!" Leyla cried. "We've been practicing our singing. Ayla has a beautiful voice but I'm afraid that I don't."

"I do not," said Ayla.

"Yes, you do. You're just too modest to admit it."

Nanna gathered her group. The two girls and Lana and Nesrin put on their clogs and followed her to the main bath chamber.

Many of the guests were already standing around the basins, or perched on stools, wrapped in peshtemals, chatting excitedly. As soon as the family group entered, the women's attention turned to Nesrin. Ayla and Leyla joined a group of giggling girls.

Lana greeted Nejmi's mother Serra, who had traveled all the way to Bolu with Mustafa and Ayshe Abla for this very important ceremony. The two women kissed each other on both cheeks. Lana then went around the room greeting and kissing all the other guests. Nanna led Nesrin to the ornate chair in the middle of the room. Once greeted and welcomed, all the women gathered around her.

Nesrin had seen several other brides perform this ritual, but she hadn't imagined how uncomfortable it would be when she was the center of attention. She sat erect, her heart racing, looking down at the floor. She managed a modest smile when she thought about how boys facing their circumcision ceremonies must feel. She remembered her brother Rafet, laid up on an ornate bed and wearing a white gown, crying from the pain while relatives celebrated around him. She would never forget the miserable look on his face. At least I'm not in pain, she thought.

A group of female musicians took up their instruments to play a traditional Circassian song. As instructed, Ayla and Leyla joined five other girls who each picked up one of the decorated plates. Holding them above their heads, they danced in a circle around Nesrin. The ritual required a somber disposition but Leyla could barely keep herself from smiling. She especially made sure she didn't look at her sister, because she knew that if they looked at each other, one or both would burst out laughing.

The end of the song signaled that it was time for Nesrin to perform the ultimate revealing act. The dancers stopped twirling and lowered their candles. All eyes turned toward Nesrin. Even though she was now seventeen, she thought herself a scrawny little thing, not possessing the full figure of an adult woman. She dreaded having to show her body to anyone, let alone to a crowd of mostly strangers. She stared at Nanna across the room, who gave her a warm, encouraging nod. Then Nesrin stood, untied her peshtemal, and let it slide off her shoulders. The garment fell to the floor like a limp sack, leaving the girl completely exposed.

Some of the women gasped while others were stilled by her beauty. Her skin flawless and fair, her young breasts perfectly formed, and her hair elegantly draped over her shoulders, she looked like a perfectly sculpted statue. The mist rising from the flowing hot water made her look even more perfect and ethereal.

Resisting the urge to cover her breasts with her arms, Nesrin kept her gaze down, averting the eyes examining her. Even Ayla and Leyla, who'd seen their sister naked before, were speechless.

Serra looked at Lana with a smile and a gentle nod of approval. She knew now that she had secured a lovely bride for her son. Lana was proud that her daughter had made such a good impression.

Finally, Nanna walked up to Nesrin, picked up the peshtemal, filled a bowl with lukewarm water, and poured it over the girl's shoulders. She then wrapped Nesrin in the peshtemal and swaddled her tight for a few moments. After she draped a red silk veil over her, leaving only her feet and hands exposed, Nanna sat Nesrin back in the chair.

She lit the candles while two other women mixed henna powder and lavender water in their bowls. They formed balls out of the concoction and pressed them into Nesrin's palms. Next, they wrapped the girl's hands with bands of white cloth and slipped them into the silk mittens.

The musicians resumed playing as the seven girls took up the now burning candles and held them high. Dancing around Nesrin, they began to sing a song that had been sung for centuries to young brides in a society completely dominated by men:

"Oh pretty girl, oh beautiful bride,

It is time to part, it is time to go,

It is time to leave the arms of your mother who loves you so.
Weep pretty girl, weep beautiful bride,
It is time to part, it is time to go,
It is time to be in the arms of a husband you must obey.
Weep, for where he takes you, you must go,
Though it be over mountains and far away."

Overwhelmed by the scents and sounds around her, Nesrin felt she might faint. As soon as the song was over, Nanna escorted her back to the dressing room, pulled off the veil and mittens, took the balls of henna from her hands, and helped her to get dressed.

"Are you all right, my girl?" Nanna asked, concerned by Nesrin's pale complexion.

"Yes, I feel a little better now."

"We must go back out there to face the guests."

"I know," she whispered with a deep sigh.

"You're a beautiful and brave child," Nanna said and squeezed Nesrin's cheek.

She then led her back into the salon where the guests were waiting to shower her with congratulations. Once the bride's mother and future mother-in-law were also congratulated, the women settled down. They spent the rest of the afternoon in the hamam reclining on cushions, drinking tea, eating sweets, and gossiping and singing nostalgic songs.

As soon as the bridal party returned home, Lana ordered Nesrin's trousseau to be loaded on wagons to be delivered to New Manor. The entire family, including Nesrin's brothers Rafet and Kenan, began the five-day journey the next day.

On the day of the wedding, both families and their many friends gathered at the big house. The ceremony was to take place outside, under the stars. Tents were erected and large tables were laid out with ample amounts of food.

The entire village was invited and the people showed up in droves. The mayor of the nearby village, who was to conduct the ceremony, arrived with his family and the head imam, who also brought along an entourage. Lana's brother, Fahri, was to stand as witness.

With garlands of flowers and lanterns hanging from the trees, New Manor looked enchanting. An elaborate dais with a table and five ornate chairs was set up in the middle of the garden. A circular divan with plush pillows had been placed around the platform for the family. Elegant tables with flower arrangements were set for the guests, and a separate area had been cleared in the garden for dancing the kafe.

Servants specially hired for the occasion carried large trays of chicken with a rich walnut sauce, a staple at weddings and special functions. Also offered were roast lambs, delectable vegetables, and mounds of halva for dessert.

Nobody in the crowd could fail to recognize the extent of Mustafa's wealth and generosity. Rashit and Lana were duly impressed. They were convinced that their daughter would be well taken care of, but the prospect of losing her still saddened them.

They were invited to sit with Mustafa and Serra on the circular divan, facing the mayor. Fahri also joined them. The Imam, wearing a huge white turban, wobbled over to his throne-like chair and settled down. Nejmi arrived next, standing erect and dignified in his traditional black Circassian garb.

When Nesrin entered, flanked by her two brothers, a hush fell over the crowd. Her face was covered in rich red silk, but her body exuded a youthful elegance. Her intricately embroidered kaftan revealed a pure white gown underneath, with a red sash around her waist —a symbol of her virginity. Her brothers accompanied her to the third chair and took their places on the divan.

The imam's chant broke the silence. Guests lifted their hands to their waists, palms turned upward in supplication to God. Immediately following the chant, the imam turned to Nejmi and asked: "Nejmettin, do you accept this woman, Nesrin, daughter of Rashit Bey and Lana Hanim of Bolu, as your wife?"

"I do," said Nejmi somberly.

"What do you offer as a bride price?" asked the Imam.

"The bride price is fifty pieces of gold," Nejmi replied.

The imam turned to the mayor. "Do you accept and guarantee this bride price?"

The mayor stood and held out a red velvet purse. "I do."

The imam turned to Nesrin's uncle. "Do you accept the bride price?"

"I do," said Fahri, who then took the purse from the mayor.

The imam turned to Nesrin. "Do you accept this man, Nejmettin, son of Mustafa Bey and Serra Hanim of New Manor, as your husband?"

"Yes, I do," she replied in a barely audible whisper.

"I then pronounce you man and wife!" the Imam announced.

Whistles, shouts, and applause erupted as the small orchestra sprung up a lively tune. Nejmi stood and extended his hand. Nesrin rose and faced her husband. He lifted her veil and she looked directly into his eyes, as though defying the hard gaze that had followed her on those many occasions. He took one look at her and smiled. The penetrating look now seemed one of kindness, even love. She couldn't help but smile back. For the first time, she felt her fears subside. Then he took her hand to lead her to her parents.

Both Nejmi and Nesrin kissed the hands of Lana and Rashit, and touched them to their foreheads in the expected fashion. In turn, the adults embraced them one by one.

Lana wanted so much to feel as though she was gaining a new son, but instead she felt she was losing a daughter. She smiled to mask her aching heart and reached to her daughter's wrist to strap a gold bracelet around it. Nesrin also knew this was saying goodbye to her parents. When Lana next wrapped a gold belt around her waist, Nesrin felt her mother was touching her for the last time. She tried as best she could to hold back her tears and maintain her composure.

Next, the newlyweds joined Nejmi's parents to repeat the same ritual of hand kissing followed by an embrace. It was now Serra's turn to adorn the bride with jewelry. Nejmi beamed with pride as his mother attached another gold bracelet around Nesrin's wrist, hung a gold necklace around her neck, and attached a pair of earrings to her ears. It was now Nejmi's turn to make his offering. Serra gently prodded Nesrin to turn and look at her groom. He was holding a diamond ring that dazzled her with its size and sparkle. He took her hand and slipped the ring on her finger. She felt the warm spark of his touch. It felt oddly comforting, especially because his gaze was now one of wonderment—and, she wondered, maybe love?

He's gentle, she thought. I believe he loves me. She found herself smiling now. Yes, this is right. My husband loves me.

Friends and relatives stood in line to congratulate the couple and present additional gifts. Jewelry equal to the amount of a treasure trove was bestowed on the couple, as well as silver cutlery, vases, and fine porcelain. They were also given a horse, a cow, and a calf from a nearby village. Nejmi's squadron presented him with a fine sword, and village women offered Nesrin hand-woven lace of various sizes and shapes. Mustafa stood aside and proudly observed the people lining up with their gifts. He knew that this was an expression of respect to the man who would one day become their landlord and his bride.

Haydar kept a close eye on the gifts and made sure a young scribe carefully recorded them in accordance to Islamic law. Each gift along with the bride price would stand as a guarantee in case the marriage failed.

Nesrin and Nejmi were invited to the area where youngsters were already dancing the kafe. The dancers immediately formed a circle and surrounded the married couple. The rhythm quickened and Nejmi, in top form, did his signature fast steps and high kicks, which drew ovations from the crowd. Nesrin accompanied her husband with elegant footwork and sweeping arms. His masculine manner was the perfect compliment to her deferential, feminine expression. It was when dancing the kafe that Nesrin felt a natural connection with her husband. While he felt the same way, he was also aware of the primal lust rising inside.

Once the dance was over, the couple joined the wedding table for the feast. The mayor raised his glass of raki—the traditional drink of Anatolia—to propose a toast for a happy, prosperous marriage. Several similar toasts followed, wishing the couple a long-lasting union with many children. It was only the beginning of a long night of eating and drinking raki.

Nesrin had once tried raki but found it intolerable. She'd seen her father enjoy the anise-flavored drink on occasion and was amused to see how jolly he'd get, but she herself didn't care for the taste nor the lightheaded feeling she experienced. Nejmi, on the other hand, had indulged in many a bachelor's night with his brothers drinking "lion's milk," and tonight was certainly no exception. He drank toast after toast, and by the end of dinner he was relaxed, amiable, and noticeably more attentive to Nesrin. When he reached over and touched her hand in front of all the people, she smiled but felt uncomfortable.

The more raki was consumed, the livelier the party became. With each joke, there was laughter and more drink, and with each drink, Nejmi became more demonstrative with his new bride. The women clapped and the men howled when he leaned over and kissed her on the cheek. This was profoundly embarrassing for her. She was almost relieved when, at the end of a very long evening, her brothers stood to escort her and the groom to the bedchamber. Anything, she thought, would be better than being ridiculed in front of so many people. The crowd cheered and shouted as they left, and Nesrin, even more humiliated, still managed a smile.

Nanna followed as Nesrin's aid and chaperone. Nejmi was inebriated by now, and fell heavily on a chair in the sitting room while Nanna took Nesrin to the bath chamber just off the bedroom. She caressed the girl's hair and face to comfort her and to try to convince her that everything would be all right.

"Men behave this way," she said. "It's his wedding night. Don't worry, he will be tame as a kitten in the morning."

But what about tonight? Nesrin thought but didn't dare ask.

Nanna bathed and rubbed the girl with rose water then dressed her in a silk nightgown. "Are you all right, my precious?"

Nesrin paused. "I'm not sure."

"You must try to relax. Enjoy yourself. And don't forget about the nuptial sheet."

"Tell me again," said Nesrin, her eyes distant, as though she was in a dream.

"Once the union is consummated, you must bring the nuptial sheet to the door. I will be waiting for you."

Nesrin spoke softly. "I'm so afraid Nanna."

"I know. But you will get through this."

Rafet and Kenan were sitting with Nejmi in the salon next to the bedchamber. Kenan was especially disgusted with Nejmi's behavior. The man could hardly keep his head up. Rafet took him to the sink and splashed his face with water. This revived Nejmi a little.

"Get a hold of yourself, Nejmi," Rafet warned. "Your bride is waiting for you."

Nejmi slurred his words. "I'm ready for her."

Nanna joined them and surveyed the situation. She and Rafet exchanged looks.

"Is my beautiful bride ready?" Nejmi yelled.

"She is ready," Nanna replied.

Standing up as straight as he could, Nejmi staggered through the door to the bedroom. Nanna took up her place on a chair nearby.

"You boys go along," she instructed Rafet and Kenan.

Rafet looked concerned, but Kenan was seething with anger.

"Don't worry about her," Nanna said. "You both go and join the party."

"He'd better be gentle with our sister!" Kenan took one last angry look at the door, and then strode out of the salon.

Rafet looked at Nanna for reassurance. She nodded at him to indicate Nesrin would be all right.

The brothers joined the party that would last all night and well into the next day.

Nejmi shut the door and looked at Nesrin standing near the bed. Her hair was draped around her shoulders and her silk nightgown revealed her tender bosom. The sight of her made Nejmi crazy with desire. He approached her slowly and touched her arm.

Nesrin was grateful for the tender gesture. She seemed to relax a little. She watched Nejmi take off his shirt and drop it on the nearby chair. He was gazing back at her as he unbuttoned and slipped down his pants. She quickly looked away.

Nejmi stood beside the bed in his underclothes and was overcome. He lifted off her nightdress and revealed her naked body. He paused for a moment, mesmerized by her beauty.

Nesrin, feeling more exposed than she'd ever felt was possible, began to shiver. Without saying a word, Nejmi pushed her back on the bed. She lay naked on her back and shut her eyes. He parted her legs. She held her breath as he mounted her. The stale stench of anise was overwhelming. He thrust himself into her with such pressure that she screamed.

In the hallway, Nanna heard Nesrin's cry and cringed. She shut her eyes tight and blocked her ears, trying to shut out any further sounds.

Nejmi thrust into Nesrin again and again. His teeth clenched, he made a strange animal sound before spilling his seed in her. He rolled off of his bride and lay next to her on his back. He didn't notice she was shaking.

Nesrin wrapped her arms tight around her chest to stop from shivering. She was so tense that she could hardly breathe. She waited for Nejmi to say something. Anything. Did he even know how much he'd just hurt her? He lay motionless for several minutes before he started to snore.

Nesrin felt violated to very depths of her soul, like a used rag that had been cast aside. She wondered if her body had been torn apart. Then she remembered the nuptial sheet that Nanna had strategically placed on the bed. She slowly pulled her body up toward the pillow and stared at the sheet between her legs, now stained with blood. Nejmi was partially laying on it. Her heart raced as she tried to extract the bloodied sheet, horrified that he might wake up and ravage her again.

Nejmi had passed out and didn't seem to notice a thing. He shifted his weight as Nesrin slid off the bed, and began to snore even louder. She pulled on a robe, took the sheet to the door, and quietly cracked it open

Nanna had been waiting for her. Nesrin held out the soiled cloth, her fingers trembling. The old woman took the sheet without looking at Nesrin. Without a word she slowly guided Nesrin to the small bath chamber, gently bathed her and covered her in a fresh gown.

When Nesrin realized she was expected to go back into the bedroom she was petrified. Her eyes stared wildly at Nanna but her childhood protector had nothing to say. Nesrin knew she had to obey. She hung her head and let Nanna lead her back to the bedroom door.

As Nanna closed the door she muttered a short prayer, asking God to help this poor girl and to give her the strength to deal with everything that marriage entailed. She took the soiled sheet to Serra's quarters where both she and Lana awaited proof of Nesrin's virginity. Serra took the cloth and inspected it. Seeing the blood, she folded the cloth and handed it back to Nanna. Lana watched with tears in her eyes.

Nesrin stood silently in the darkened room not knowing what to do next. She couldn't bear the thought of lying next to this man for the rest of the night. Realizing she had no other choice, she approached the bed. She gingerly crept in beside him, making sure her flesh didn't touch his. Then, as softly as she could, she pulled the covers over her body. She lay motionless, overcome by the stench of raki and the terrible racket of his snoring. Tears streamed down her face. She lay awake and prayed for the morning to arrive.

She must have just fallen asleep when she was startled by the touch of Nejmi's hand on her back. She held her breath as he touched her neck and moved his hand down to her breast. A cold chill flooded her body when she opened her eyes to see him staring at her.

"My beautiful porcelain wife," he said. "I've wanted for so long to touch you that I lost control."

His breath was still heavy with the stale stench of alcohol. Nesrin flinched as he started to caress her again. Within seconds she felt completely frozen. She just wanted to get away. The more he caressed her arms, her neck, and her breasts, the more she felt an overwhelming resistance. He kissed her tender nipple but this made her freeze even more.

Nejmi couldn't understand why his bride was not responding to his touch. As his hands explored her soft body his desire intensified. But he was starting to get frustrated. She was his wife—it was her duty to let him take her, whether she wanted him or not. Was it modesty that made her resist him, he wondered? Desire overtook reason and he was on her again.

Squeezing her eyes tight, Nesrin tried not to scream. Minutes later, Nejmi had satisfied himself with a groan and rolled off her once again. She was grateful it didn't last long. Oblivious to her trembling, Nejmi turned away and dozed off again. When he woke, he glanced at her and declared, "I'm hungry as a bear." Getting out of bed, he grabbed his robe and went to clean up.

The following three days and nights were a blur for Nesrin. Her husband's desire for her was insatiable. He took her again and again. For three days, the couple never left the wedding chamber. Food and drink were brought to the sitting room where Nejmi would eat with gusto, then have his bath, and wait for Nanna to bring Nesrin to the bedchamber after she'd bathed her. He expected she would eventually get used to him and even begin to enjoy their union. He wanted his wife to want him as much as he desired her, but every time he touched her, she would freeze. He was at a loss and his patience was beginning to wear thin.

Nesrin could eat nothing. By the second day she felt so weak that she could hardly stand. Her body felt so ravaged that she could barely walk from the bed to bathroom. On the third morning she glanced at the mirror and could hardly recognize herself. Her eyes had purple circles under them and her cheeks were drawn and pale. Nanna insisted that she drink tea with honey and "eat a small bite of bread with some cheese," but the sight of food made Nesrin want to vomit. She looked at Nanna with vacant eyes. "Will it always be like this?"

Nanna caressed her hair and whispered to her. "No, child. If you will try to look upon your husband with affection you may be able to relax, and in time, you will get used to it. But you must be strong and take care of yourself. You are Circassian, and we Circassian women are good, dutiful wives and mothers."

On the third day, Nanna knocked on the door and told Nejmi that his bath was ready. Once he left the room, she escorted Nesrin to the bath chamber. The young woman was now near emaciated. She stooped, looking tired, and defeated.

"Stand up, Nesrin Hanim," Nanna said. "You are going to be presented to your family and guests as the wife of Nejmettin, son of Mustafa, owner and landlord of New Manor! You are the daughter of Rashit Bey of Bolu! You will not slouch about like a common peasant wife."

Nesrin looked at Nanna and saw that even though she seemed strong and unshakable, the old woman was just as helpless as she. Nesrin mustered as much courage as she could manage and sat up.

"You're right, dear Nanna. I mustn't embarrass my parents. I am indeed the daughter of Rashit Bey, and a true Circassian."

"Yes you are, my child. And your parents are proud of you. As am I."

Nesrin wiped the tears with the back of her hand and stood tall. Nanna bathed and dressed the girl with the gentleness of a mother bathing her baby. Still, Nesrin flinched at every single touch. Nanna remained firm, but her heart ached for her dear girl as she prepared her for her presentation.

Three days after the wedding, Lana was feeling more nervous than usual.

"No news for three days," she said to her husband. "And you have us all packed up to return to Bolu. Won't we see our daughter before we depart?"

"You know the custom," said Rashit patiently. "It's on the third day after marriage that a bride is presented to her new family and relatives. I'm sure we'll see Nesrin today."

"Not even Nanna has come out to say anything. I'm worried that something is terribly wrong."

At this moment Nanna entered the room and let the family know that the bride was ready to be presented. Lana tried to read something—anything—in Nanna's demeanor but the woman stood calm and gave no indication at all. Serra and Mustafa joined Nesrin's parents.

When Nesrin first walked into the room, Lana couldn't help but gasp. She immediately took her daughter into her arms. She saw the dark circles that had formed under her eyes, and felt how frail and thin her body had become. Nesrin moved on to kiss her father's hand and then the hands of her in-laws. Lana saw how her hand trembled each time. She glared at her husband, but he remained emotionless, as though nothing was wrong. Next, Nesrin was expected to serve tea to her elders.

As soon as Nesrin left the room, Lana whispered to her husband. "What are you thinking? We cannot leave her like this!"

"What do you mean?" asked Rashit.

"Look at her. She's emaciated. I've never seen her so unhappy."

"My dear, she only just got married. She must adapt to her new life. I'm sure Serra Hanim and Mustafa Bey will not mistreat her, or let her become ill."

Even though he was determined not to show it, Rashit was also struck by Nesrin's appearance and shared his wife's concerns. Annulling the marriage, however, and especially going back on his word against such a respectable family, was out of the question. Whatever the situation was, it had to be endured. In her agitated state, even Lana realized this. She quickly tried to think of a compromise.

"I will not leave my daughter like this," she said, this time speaking loudly. Serra heard her and looked in her direction. Lana whispered now at her husband. "Either we stay, or we leave Nanna behind, to take care of her."

Rashit Bey waited until his daughter came back into the room. She was carrying a tray with glasses of tea and a bowl of sugar cubes. As she quietly served the tea, Rashit observed how much his daughter's hand shook. He watched her serve Nanna a glass of tea.

"Thank you, my child," said Nanna somberly.

Rashit frowned at his wife. She glared at him, clearly expecting him to take action. Rashit turned to Mustafa and Serra.

"If you are agreeable, we would like to have Nanna stay with Nesrin for a while."

Mustafa was also aware of Nesrin's condition. "Of course," he said. "Nanna is welcome to stay."

"Nanna dear, would you mind staying here with Nesrin for a while longer? Her mother and I would be more comfortable if you'd stay to make sure she's all right."

Nanna nodded. "I was hoping you'd ask me to stay. I love Nesrin as though she's my own daughter."

"And you, Nesrin?" asked Rashit. "How would you feel about this?"

"It would be a great comfort Father," Nesrin replied, her voice almost breaking.

"Good. I have no doubt you'll be well taken care of. But with Nanna nearby, perhaps you won't feel so cut off from your family."

A servant entered the room to announce that their carriage was ready.

Lana and Rashit both embraced their daughter. Only by looking at Nanna's kind face was Nesrin able to hold back the tears.

During the following days, Nejmi prepared his men for their upcoming trip to the border while Nesrin, with Serra as her primary role model, learned her duties as a new wife. From watching her, Nesrin learned the intricacies of running a big house. Serra gave her advice on how to deal with the servants (kindly, but never let them forget their place,) how to work with the cooks to prepare menus, and how to shop wisely so that the supplies were purchased at fair prices.

Even though she worked so closely with her, Nesrin would never speak to Serra – or to Mustafa —unless spoken to. Circassian custom required that a bride not speak directly to her in-laws until the birth of her first son. Every evening, after dinner with the family, she retired to the sitting room next to her bedchamber and waited for her husband. Her duties dictated that she never go to bed before him, even if he stayed up long hours drinking, playing cards, and cavorting with his friends.

Serra was not only mentor but also companion to Nesrin. She often invited her to stay when her friends gathered in the family sitting room. Nesrin would stay silent but enjoyed listening to conversation and stories. Other times, Serra would sit with Nesrin in the small sitting room and tell her about her own life. This was when Nesrin learned about Nejmi's childhood, and how he was raised with his two companions Sadi and Bedri.

Serra told her how Bedri's parents perished during the flu epidemic and how, when Bedri came to the family, he was so traumatized that he could hardly speak. "It was the love and companionship of Sadi that helped Bedri to open up."

Serra spoke of all three of her boys with affection but every time she mentioned Sadi's name, Nesrin would feel a pang of regret. What would life have been like if Sadi had been her husband? She wanted to know if Sadi would ever come back but didn't dare ask.

"Sadi was also torn from his family at a young age," Serra told her. "Nejmi's unconditional acceptance of both boys as his own brothers soon led to them all running around the old manor like old friends, playing and laughing together. Although I believe both Sadi and Bedri still carry a bit of that sadness within their souls, it gives me comfort to know that they are loyal and inseparable friends, and that they will always be there to support each other."

Nejmi was baffled. He couldn't understand why Nesrin was so unresponsive to him. Every time he touched her, she cowered like a frightened kitten. He continued to hope that she would warm up to him and learn to accept him with open arms. The more she resisted him, the more he felt himself acting out of anger and desperation. A wife's duty was to obey her husband in bed—at least until she bore him a child. He believed their bedroom activities, even if unpleasant or violent, were required by the rules of marriage. He and Nesrin were obligated to procreate. All he wished was that she come to him willingly, even lovingly, and not be so resistant.

Nesrin, on the other hand, was convinced that Nejmi was a slave to his animal desires and only thought of his own satisfaction. It was inconceivable to her that he'd be so oblivious to how much she feared him. She wondered if he would ever understand or care about how she felt.

A week before Nejmi was due to take his soldiers to the border Nesrin missed her monthly. Nanna, who had been watching her carefully, immediately knew. Nesrin begged her to not tell the family—especially Nejmi—until they were sure.

Bedri returned to New Manor the night before Nejmi was due to leave. His welcome home, if not as jubilant as that of Nejmi, was still festive. It was now his turn to take a break while Nejmi took up guarding the border. The brothers had only one night to spend together.

"How is marriage treating you?" asked Bedri with a sarcastic smile, ready to take up the usual banter. "Women folk got you tamed already, old man?"

Nejmi frowned and looked away, indicating he was in no mood for jokes. "What's the matter, brother?" Bedri asked.

"It's been terrible," Nejmi said. "My wife doesn't love me. She doesn't even like me touching her. Every time I go near her, she cringes and retreats like a scared bird. I don't know what to do."

"Are you kind to her?" asked Bedri.

Nejmi look confused. It occurred to Bedri that Nejmi didn't know the meaning of the word.

"You can't treat her rough and tumble like you treat your brothers," he said. "You need to handle her like a delicate bird. Be gentle. And be patient."

"I tried that," said Nejmi. "Nothing has worked to make her love me. I'm at the end of my rope."

"I see," said Bedri but suspected that Nejmi wasn't entirely telling the truth. He had never thought of Nejmi as sentimental but this time he could see that his brother was genuinely troubled. "You can't make her love you, Nejmi. She'll have to come to it in her own time. In the meantime, you must be patient."

Nejmi leaned down and picked up a rock then flung it across the field. He paused and asked Bedri earnestly: "Will you keep an eye on her while I'm away Brother? Make sure she's all right?"

"Of course. I promise. Go to the border with an open heart."

Once her husband was gone, Nesrin breathed a sigh of relief. She wouldn't have to endure his presence for three months. It was a few weeks later, in her second month, that she started to experience nausea in the mornings. Nanna gave her dry toast and a little mint tea as soon as she woke up. They both agreed that it was time to inform the household of her pregnancy. Serra and Mustafa were both elated to hear the news. This would be their first grandchild. A message was immediately sent to Nejmi, informing him that he was going to be a father.

Bedri, now in the process of training a new group of border guards, spent more time at New Manor. This gave him the excuse to not only keep an eye on Nesrin, but also to spend time with his family. He enjoyed the company of soldiers well enough while away at camp for three months, but he'd sorely missed the companionship of his adoptive parents. Serra and Mustafa were also delighted to be spending time with him.

His young protégé Hasan had now become a loyal servant and friend to Bedri. He showed remarkable talents for leadership, and Bedri even felt comfortable leaving him to train his men while he spent more time with Serra and Nesrin.

Most evenings were spent in the warm comfort of the main salon, while during the day, Bedri made a point of accompanying the women on walks. These afternoon walks helped him remember how much he'd always loved his mother's company and also allowed him to learn more about Nesrin. Each day he found himself growing fonder of her, and

Nesrin felt the same way toward him. She missed her family and two brothers greatly, and Bedri was becoming like a real brother to her.

Both women enjoyed his charming company, his sense of humor and passion for life, and his occasional shenanigans. He would always pick flowers for them during their walks and one time he slipped a grasshopper in the bouquet. When the creature hopped out and nearly hit Nesrin in the face, both women were so startled that they couldn't stop laughing. After that, they were always cautious about accepting bouquets from him, and always laughed nervously when they did.

"You're a mischievous boy, Bedri," said Serra one afternoon in the garden, "and you amuse us so much. Yet you're also charming and gentle. We must really find you a suitable wife."

Nesrin grinned. "I remember you having a nice chat with my sister, Leyla, at my wedding. I believe she was quite taken with you."

Bedri blushed. "How could I ever have need for anyone else when I can spend time with the two loveliest ladies in the world?" he said. "And they are both already taken!"

Noticing how skillfully he averted the subject, especially when Leyla was mentioned, Nesrin smiled. Bedri selected two roses, wrapped their stems with leaves to conceal the thorns, and handed one to each of them.

"Thank you, Bedri," said Serra and kissed him on the cheek.

Nesrin gently squeezed his arm, thankful to know that not all men were as selfish and unfeeling as her husband.

Nesrin flourished under Serra and Nanna's nurturing care over the next few weeks. Bedri's antics and attentive companionship also helped her to finally relax, and even laugh again. She developed a little tummy and was able to keep her food down. As time for Nejmi's return approached, she felt herself become increasingly anxious again. This also meant Bedri would leave and she dreaded the thought of losing him. Her nightmares, which had largely abated, started to come back. Several times she woke up in the middle of the night trembling from a bad dream. Only when she realized Nejmi's side of the bed was empty was she was able to relax and fall asleep again.

Nejmi returned to a traditional festive welcome. When he saw Nesrin he smiled, reached out and caressed her growing tummy. He was excited to see his wife but felt secretly ashamed that her appearance, even though she was pregnant, still aroused erotic desires within him.

Nesrin was moved by his gentle gesture and thought—or hoped—that this pregnancy would improve things between them.

Nanna and Serra discussed Nesrin's fragile time of pregnancy. Nanna reminded Serra that any disturbance, physical or otherwise, could cause her to lose the baby. "Would you kindly approach Nejmi and remind him?" Nanna asked. Serra agreed and pulled Nejmi aside to have a talk with him.

"Please be aware, my son," she said. "Refrain from conjugal visits for the time being so the child is kept safe."

Nejmi was taken aback. He pursed his lips and frowned, feeling humiliated to be approached by his mother on such a subject. He took a pause before he spoke.

"Who do you think I am," he said in an uncharacteristically kind tone. "A monster? Of course I wouldn't touch her while she's pregnant."

"Of course, I know that. Forgive me for mentioning it."

Still, Nejmi could not control his nature. Every time he saw his wife he found himself once again burning with desire. In order to stay true to his promise, he threw himself into training the new squadron and began to sleep in another bedroom.

Recognizing that Serra missed Bedri and their walks, Nejmi returned home in the afternoons to accompany his mother and his wife on outings around the gardens.

Now that they were sleeping apart, Nesrin was not in fear of Nejmi assaulting her. She found that she could sleep and eat well, and to her surprise, she even began to consider Nejmi almost as charming a companion as Bedri.

With a new life growing inside her, Nesrin now looked healthy, even plump, with rosy cheeks and a luminous smile. She was profoundly grateful that the last three months with her husband had passed uneventfully, even pleasantly. She looked forward to Bedri's return—which was coming up soon—not because she would be rid of Nejmi's oppression, but because she missed her dear friend. At the end of her sixth month, she was now wearing loose gowns and preparing for her life as a mother.

Bedri's turn on the border had been relatively quiet. Only a few bands of marauders had put up attacks and were easily warded off. It seemed the enemy had grown reluctant—perhaps because they realized how fiercely the Circassians guarded the borders. At least this was what Bedri and his men presumed.

One evening after the meal, Bedri approached Hasan.

"My brother's wife is due to have a baby within the next two months. I want to offer to take his turn at the border so he can remain next to his wife for the birth of his first child. Will you accompany our men back home while I stay here to meet the new soldiers?"

"No," said Hasan with determination. "The men will be fine. I will stay with you, Bedri Abi."

The two men had grown closer over time so Hasan now addressed Bedri as "abi," big brother, a much more personal address than the respectful "efendi."

Bedri smiled at his friend. "I appreciate that, Hasan."

"Allah willing," said the younger man, "you and I shall never be parted."

When a courier delivered Bedri's offer to New Manor, Nejmi was reluctant at first. He worried it would mean relinquishing his duty and leadership. He was also still resentful that Sadi had been selected to serve in the Ottoman army and he hadn't. And now that he was going to be even more weighted down with the birth of this child, he would never get the chance to prove his deserved esteem as a soldier.

What use would he be if he stayed at home to wait, with nothing to do? There was his mother and Nanna, and other women to wait with Nesrin. Besides, if he didn't go back on the field, he'd forego any chance of being chosen to serve with the Sultan's army. The more he thought about Sadi being given that position, the more humiliated he felt. He was about to turn down Bedri's offer when Mustafa pulled him aside.

"This is the birth of an heir, my son. It's one of the most significant events in our family's history. Don't be foolish. You're the only one who can produce a true heir to inherit our lands. Take Bedri's offer and stay with your wife as she gives birth. Bedri has become a competent leader. Trust him with your men. You will go back to the front after your child is born, proud that you've produced an heir for your family. And the people will be proud of you for that."

Nejmi finally agreed. He escorted his men to join Bedri at the border, at a province called Kars. A week later, he brought home Bedri's garrison and busied himself training them while he awaited the birth of his child.

Taking Nejmi's place as leader of his men proved challenging for Bedri. In spite of his stringent manner, his men had grown fond of Nejmi, and this abrupt shift in leadership was troubling for some of them. Hasan, who'd joined the squadron, became a natural liaison between Bedri and the soldiers. He trained with them, ate, and spoke with them every day, and reported to Bedri his impressions.

A week into the training, Bedri questioned Hasan.

"How are the men doing now? Are they adjusting well?"

"Some of them, yes," said the boy, "but not all. There are men who feel frustrated. Losing Nejmi Efendi has made them lose their confidence."

The words stung Bedri to the core. To think that some men did not trust him saddened him and bruised his pride. But he was wise enough to know that it would take time. He was determined to remain patient and knew he would soon prove to them that he was just as competent a leader as Nejmi.

On a cloudy night three weeks into their rounds at the border, the men were feeling relatively relaxed. The day shift was just leaving their posts, and the night shift was replacing them in the trenches. Aside from a few thieves breaking into camp to try to steal food and other goods, things had been relatively quiet. Any attacks from Cossack marauders over the last six months had proved to be little more than mere scuffles. Like the attack at Yeniköy, the Cossacks suffered more than they gained. The general consensus was that they had, by now, realized the futility of their attacks.

It grew darker and drearier as a storm approached the area. Lightning illuminated the horizon and thunder crashed at a distance.

One of the men nudged his partner. "Did you see that?"

"What?"

"I swear I saw someone run across the hill. There's someone out there!"

"Probably just another thief," said his friend.

"Look, look, another one!"

The two men peered through the darkness to see a shadow cross the hill not far away from them. The wind gusted and another flash of lightning lit up the sky, followed by a huge clap of thunder.

"I see him!"

"We'd better tell Hasan to alert Bedri Efendi," said the first man.

"I don't know. Bedri Efendi is asleep. Do you really think we should bother him?"

"Stay here. I'm going to go tell Hasan."

Minutes later, Hasan was in Bedri's tent.

"Bedri Abi, wake up," he said. "We might have some trouble."

Bedri rushed to join the men who'd been on watch. They all stared into the pitch-dark night and saw nothing.

Lightning flashed again, revealing several silhouettes cowering in the distance.

"There!" Hasan whispered.

"Yes," Bedri agreed. "We must remain calm. Give the three-whistle signal for everyone to ready their rifles."

He tapped the soldier next to him on the shoulder, " move down the line and see that no one is sleeping, and they that have enough ammunition."

"Do you think it's another band of Cossacks?" Hasan asked, his voice betraying his rising fear.

"I don't know," said Bedri with a chill now growing in his chest.

The sky opened up and heavy sheets of rain began to flood the trench.

"For the love of Allah, this is not what we needed right now," Bedri muttered.

Suddenly, there was chaos. Heavily armed men, shooting and hollering, began rushing at them from all directions. Trapped in the trenches, the Circassians were surrounded from both sides. The darkness and heavy rain made it impossible to make out their attackers but an instant flash of lightening illuminated their uniforms.

"These are not Cossacks," Bedri shouted. "This is the Russian army!" He ordered his men to duck deeper into the trenches.

Several Russians, running blindly through the rain, were shot within minutes. But they kept coming. One Circassian fighter took a blow to his arm.

"Hasan, go get the other men!" shouted Bedri.

"No!" Hasan cried out. "I won't leave you. I will fight with you."

"Don't be stupid!" yelled Bedri. "I'm ordering you to go, now!"

Hasan reluctantly climbed out of the trench and ran through the rain toward the barracks. The Circassian men were already awake and taking up arms.

"Quick!" shouted Hasan. "It's the Russians! There's a whole army of them!"

Hasan gathered up all the men and ran back to the trench as a bloody battle was in full force. He estimated that there were many hundreds of Russians, more than enough to overwhelm their squadron of seventy men. In order to take a good shot, the Circassian fighters had to stand above the trench and expose themselves.

Hasan heard Bedri shouting, "Stay down as long as you can! Don't expose yourselves. I don't want anyone to get hurt."

Hasan, panting from the run, felt as though his heart was going to leap out of his chest from fear.

"These are weaklings," Bedri cried out. "We Circassians can take these bastards!"

He reached out from the trench and shot one Russian in the chest, sending him reeling into one of his companions, who was immediately shot by another of Bedri's men. He ducked back down into the trench.

The soldier next to him, seeing Bedri's triumph, stood up and started to scramble out of the trench.

"No!" yelled Bedri. "Don't be a hero, you bastard!"

It was too late. The soldier took a shot in the stomach and fell face down on the other side of the trench.

Bedri, now furious, rose above the trench himself.

Hasan called out to him, "Bedri Abi, stop! Get down!"

But Bedri wouldn't listen. He shot one Russian, and then another. The more he kept shooting the more empowered he felt. Finally out of ammunition, he shouted to Hasan,

"Give me your gun!"

Hasan hesitated. "Bedri Abi, please..."

"Give it to me, you foolish boy," shouted Bedri, straightening up and turning slightly.

Hasan held his gun up to Bedri.

Bedri reached for it just as a bullet struck him in the back. His eyes remained on Hasan as he buckled down and fell into the muddy trench.

Hasan fell to his knees. "No, my God, no."

He leaned over Bedri's lifeless body and was wracked with sobs. He looked up to see the other soldiers watching him. Taking up his gun, he straightened up. "Let's get these filthy bastards!" he yelled.

The men roared with one voice, "Let's get the dirty bastards!"

The fight continued until early hours of the morning. The border guards finally had to retreat but not before making the Russians pay dearly. The results were devastating for both sides but the Russians were the winners.

The Russian invasion of Kars and neighboring Anatolian regions had begun. This was the first of a series of battles that would be known as the Russo-Turkish war.

Days later, Ümit spotted a messenger galloping toward New Manor. He immediately went inside to alert Nejmi.

When Nejmi came outside to greet the rider, he recognized him to be the soldier Hasan. The expression on the boy's face was enough to let Nejmi know what had happened.

"May I see Mustafa Bey and Serra Hanim?" Hasan asked with a raspy voice.

Nejmi nodded and silently led the boy into the house.

Ümit, who had witnessed the meeting on the other side of the door, was already crying.

The family gathered in the main salon. Serra suspected the reason for the meeting and was quietly shedding tears. Mustafa stood behind his wife, a stoic expression locked on his face. Nesrin could not hide the horror that gripped her heart. She was hoping that Bedri wasn't dead, that maybe he was injured. Please God, don't let him be dead, she silently prayed.

Hasan stood in the middle of the room. He now spoke with a clear voice. "Your son died a hero," he said. "He was a martyr who sacrificed himself for the sake of his men. I was the one who should have taken that bullet, but he stood in front of me to shield me from the gunfire."

Audible gasps of "No, oh God, no," went around the room. Nesrin had her hand over her mouth as the tears flowed. Mustafa was shaking his head in disbelief, while Nejmi stood, arms crossed, his face a mask.

Hasan's body shook as tears flowed down his cheeks. "I'm so ashamed," he said. "Bedri Abi should be standing here, not me. I know you will never forgive me. I can never forgive myself."

Serra stood up from her chair and looked at this boy she'd never seen before. She walked to him, touched his cheek, and wiped away his tears. Then she held him. Wracked with sobs, the two of them clung to each other, overwhelmed by their grief.

The ever-staunch Nanna led Nesrin to a chair and made her sit down. "You must be careful of the baby," she told her. Mustafa took Serra and led her to the divan, sat next to her, and wrapped his arms around her. Nejmi remained with the shaken Hasan. Nanna ordered a servant to bring Nesrin some tea.

Soon after Hasan delivered the news, Bedri's men carried his body to New Manor. Nesrin, who was devastated beyond measure, suggested that he be buried in his beloved rose garden. Nejmi thought this a frivolous idea but when Serra also insisted, he agreed. Nejmi also dismissed Mustafa's suggestion that Sadi be informed. "Who knows where he is," he said. "He'll never make it to the funeral. He'll find out in due time."

Because Muslim law required that the dead be buried as soon as possible, a funeral was organized for the next day. Traditionally only men were allowed at the graveside during burial, but Serra wouldn't hear of it. She insisted that she and Nesrin also be present. The two wept quietly as Hasan and another soldier lowered Bedri's body, wrapped tightly in a shroud, into the grave. Mustafa and Nejmi somberly stood aside.

Once the Imam finished prayers, the men, starting with Mustafa and Nejmi, and then followed by Hasan and Bedri's entire regiment, approached one by one and gathered a handful of dirt and threw it into the grave. There were more than seventy men in line and they each paused a few moments to pay their respects. Serra asked Nesrin if she'd like to go inside.

"No mother," said Nesrin. "I want to see the last handful of dirt that will bury our Bedri."

As the procession of men continued, nobody noticed that a horseman arrived at the house, fastened his horse to a nearby tree, and joined the line of men. Nesrin's heart skipped a beat when she saw the dignified looking officer at the end of the line.

"Mother look," she said.

Serra choked when she saw Sadi approach the grave and perform the same ritual. He threw down the dirt, then knelt to the ground, and with tears in his eyes, quietly prayed. When he looked up at his family, he saw that even Mustafa was tearing up.

He approached his adopted father and kissed his hand, and acknowledged Nejmi with a firm handshake and brief hug.

"How did you know, my son?" asked Mustafa.

"I was told soon after the attack," said Sadi. "Thankfully I was on the road to Kars when I got the news."

Serra wrapped her arms around him and sobbed.

"Welcome home my boy," she said. "Your family needs you now."

"I can only stay a few hours," said Sadi.

"Better than nothing," said Serra and caressed his cheek.

Sadi then turned to Nesrin. Their eyes met for a short moment. Noticing that she was pregnant, he smiled.

"How nice to see you again, Nesrin Hanim. My brother is a lucky man."

She was so overcome with sadness that she couldn't speak. By now Ayshe Abla had come out of the house. She kissed Sadi, squeezed his cheeks and started to drag him inside to feed him.

As he walked away, Sadi turned to Nesrin and their eyes met once again. She was sure she saw regret in his gaze.

After devouring a lovingly prepared feast, Sadi mounted his horse and left New Manor. That night, after Nanna had prepared her for bed and she retired to her room, Nesrin sat by her window. It was a moonlit night and she could clearly see the road that had brought Bedri home today and took Sadi away. Her emotions were a jumble as she caressed her raised tummy.

"You're my only hope at happiness in this life, my dear," she whispered to the child she carried inside.

A Russian attack on native soil sent the entire Ottoman military on alert. Troops were sent to the borders and all of the New Manor squadrons were called into action. When Nejmi announced that he would take his men to the border as reinforcements, Serra was incensed. "Don't go!" she ordered her son.

"Stop him!" she shouted to her husband. "I can't bear to lose another child." She pleaded but to no avail.

Nejmi kissed his mother on both cheeks. "I will be back before the birth of my son," he promised. "Don't worry. Allah will look after me."

"Don't go my son. Mustafa, please don't let him go!" she continued to sob.

"He is a man and a soldier my love. We must trust in God to keep him safe," answered Mustafa.

"Allah was supposed to protect Bedri, but he's dead," she cried.

"We must have faith, Serra. Remember, they are my sons too!"

A few days after Nejmi's departure, Nesrin gave birth to a healthy little boy. This was great consolation to the family and distracted them from their grief. Serra smiled for the first time in days as she witnessed the baby come into the world. She'd been there for the labor and remained deeply engaged with the baby for the first days of his life. She found herself using the skills she'd picked up when she'd lived among the villagers during the construction of New Manor. Keeping busy and feeling needed was great consolation to her. According to Nejmi's wishes, the baby was named Jemil.

With a new child on her bosom, Nesrin no longer had time to grieve for Bedri's loss.

She never tired of holding the baby close and marveling at his perfect, tiny hands or the little smile he gave when she sang a lullaby to him. When she took her child out to the garden, she always thought of Bedri, and remembered his bouquets of flowers and gentle smile. She always remained thankful that he'd been a part of her life, even for too short a time.

"I wonder how Leyla took the news of Bedri's death," she asked Nanna one morning as she was preparing to nurse the baby. "She really liked him, you know. I had high hopes for him."

"Don't be so concerned about your sister," said Nanna. "She was saddened, of course, but I hear she's already moved on to a new beau."

"How like her," said Nesrin with a knowing smile, and gazed down at the suckling baby on her breast.

According to Circassian custom, the birth of the first male child symbolized the bride's full acceptance into the fold of the family. This event would be marked by the formal presentation of the child to his grandparents as their rightful heir.

Nesrin had mixed feelings. Like any mother, she was proud of her son and was eager to present him as the legal heir of a great fortune. But she remained bitter about the way the child was conceived and uneasy to have the ceremony in front of so many people. Standing on the dais where her wedding had taken place, she held her child up in front of many guests and villagers. After the initial applause abated, Mustafa spoke in a commanding voice:

"I hereby declare this child, named Jemil, the son and heir of Nejmettin, and grandson of the owner of New Manor, Mustafa. I also declare the wife of Nejmettin, Nesrin, as mother of this beautiful son, named Jemil."

Even though Serra had already been intimately involved with the baby, the ceremonial moment when mother passed the child to the grandmother was a moving one for all. Serra held the baby and wrapped him in a blanket. This was met with more cheering and applause. The child was then passed over to Nanna. Then, Serra and Mustafa presented Nesrin with the usual gifts: a gold bracelet, earrings, and an elaborate necklace. She was now officially a member of her husband's family and would be allowed to address her elders directly, without lowering her eyes.

Nejmi's tour at the border was long and eventful. He and his men fought several battles and suffered many losses. It would be well over a year before Russian troops were pushed back into Georgian territory and Nejmi was finally able to come home to meet his son.

Serra boasted that Jemil was a virtual copy of his father at the same age. At one year old, the little boy was curious and energetic, and was just beginning to walk. Nejmi's return created the usual commotion. There was much noise and jubilation, and when Nejmi first entered the house, Jemil was hiding behind his mother's gown.

Nejmi didn't attempt to talk to or hold his son. Instead his attention immediately turned to Nesrin. She was even more beautiful after giving birth, and the moment he saw her, he felt the great desire course through him again. Nesrin recognized the lust in her husband's eyes and lowered her head. Her body began to tremble. Little Jemil, sensing his mother's fear, took one look at this strange man and started to wail. Nothing could convince him to stop crying so Nanna whisked him away to his nursery. The usual welcome home dinner was subdued that night. Some men hadn't come back, and the loss of Bedri still saddened everyone.

As expected, Nesrin and Nejmi retired to their rooms after dinner. Nanna was on hand to bathe and dress Nesrin in her nightclothes. In her calm and assured manner, she quietly told Nesrin to look with affection upon her husband, reminding her that this was a natural part of married life. She was well aware, however, that when she closed the door, Nesrin was trembling.

Nejmi was gentler with her now, but she couldn't overcome her fear. She still got anxious moments before he thrust himself into her. She tried to remember Nanna's words, but remained uncomfortable throughout the ordeal. All she could do was to pray for it to be over. He seemed to grow even more insensitive to the way she felt. He now accepted it as part of his marriage and decided to ignore her discomfort. He took her at will night after night until, one year and three months after the birth of Jemil, she discovered she was pregnant again.

This meant she wouldn't have to share her bed with Nejmi for almost a year, which came as a relief to her. Mustafa and Serra were delighted at the prospect of another grandchild.

Nejmi, though proud to become a father again, was not at all happy to be delegated to the second bedroom. As before, he threw himself into training new border guards and three new men to be squadron leaders. He made the rounds of the seven villages with his father and Haydar, and renewed his relations with villagers he had not seen since the trek from the old country. The members of his squadron welcomed him to their villages and their homes. By the time another tour of duty was finished, nine months had almost passed.

Jemil, now almost two, was completely fascinated by the prospect of a new sister or brother. He was wide eyed with curiosity.

"Nanna, am I to have a sister or brother?" he asked.

"I don't know, Jemil," Nanna replied patiently. Jemil would not accept that answer.

"Mommy, am I to have brother or sister?" he insisted.

"I don't know, Jemil," answered Nesrin.

Completely frustrated, the little boy pulled at Nanna's skirts. "Nanna, you said the baby was growing in Mommy's tummy. If you lift up her skirt, I'll look and see if it's a sister or brother."

Trying hard not to laugh, Nanna explained that they couldn't see inside a tummy but would just have to wait until the baby came out.

"Mommy, why didn't you look to see if it was a boy or girl before you ate the baby so it could grow in your tummy?" Jemil asked Nesrin.

Nanna had to leave the room to give way to her laughter, while Nesrin hugged Jemil and replied, "I'm sorry, Jemil, but it doesn't matter if it's a boy or girl. I will always love both of you with all my heart."

The new baby came reluctantly. It was after many hours of harrowing labor that a little girl was delivered and placed in Nejmi's arms. She was tiny but it was obvious that she had her mother's burnished copper-colored hair and hazel eyes. When asked what he wanted to name his child, Nejmi shrugged and walked away. It was Nesrin and Serra who decided to give the little girl the ancient Circassian name, Lebriz.

When Nanna gave the tiny girl to Nesrin to nurse, she saw that she was silently weeping. "What is it, my dear child?"

"Oh Nanna, my heart breaks to think what life has in store for this tiny girl that I love so much. God only knows what she will suffer at the hands of men."

The household was still celebrating the birth of the baby when Nejmi left for the border. Serra was elated to have a little girl to endlessly fuss over, and Mustafa was utterly distracted by how beautiful the baby was. It was Jemil, however, who took the most delight in having a new sister. He sat by her crib and watched her sleep and play for hours. As months went by, he grew to adore her even more. She smiled each time he approached her, and delighted him when her tiny hand grasped his finger.

The children thrived and Nesrin felt absolutely complete as a mother. She could not spend enough time with them. She was happiest when she played with them or simply attended to their daily needs. When they got sad or anxious, she was there to hold them and comfort them. She sang them old country ballads and told them ancient Circassian fables. On warm days, she took them on walks in the garden and told them stories about their dear Uncle Bedri, who was a hero and held a tender place in her heart.

When Nejmi returned from the border he found his wife more desirable than ever. Her face was fuller now, her bosom rounder, and her skin was just as fine. Her lips were no longer those of a girl, but of a grown woman. He was also pleased that she'd become more accommodating toward his desires. She no longer feared his touch so much. Although not entirely responsive, she was able to tolerate his advances with more equanimity.

He had little time for the children. His son was still wary of him, and his daughter was so tiny that he could barely hold her for fear she might break. He busied himself training the border guards and visiting the villages. He left the children's education and discipline to Nesrin, Serra, and Nanna, as he saw this as women's work. It was Mustafa who sat in the garden for tea with his wife and watched the children play.

Nejmi continued his tours of duty at the border for the next four years. When Russia and the Ottoman Empire signed a treaty that established permanent borders, the Sultan considered disbanding the border guards and replacing them with the Ottoman army. Nejmi continued to be bitter about not being offered a position and partially faulted Nesrin and the children for holding him back.

If I hadn't let Bedri take my place, I'm certain I could have thrown back the enemy, he thought. Bedri would still be alive, and I'd be an officer!

He stayed out late most nights, drinking raki and playing cards with his friends at the han. When he came home drunk and found Nesrin still waiting for him, he'd sneer at her and mock her for being "such a dutiful little wife." Mustafa noticed the late arrivals and stayed up waiting for him one night. Nejmi stumbled in through the door, barely able to stand.

"Nejmi, you're drunk," said Mustafa. He was well aware of what drink could do to men. "What are you doing? Are you mistreating your wife? We Circassian men do not mistreat our wives and children."

Nejmi held on to the banister and spoke with a lopsided smile. "I'm only following the words of the Imam, dear father. According to him, women are our possessions. They're vessels for our pleasure and for bearing our children."

Mustafa was incensed. He could barely contain his temper.

"The imam is a fool and so are you. If you continue to behave in such a shameful way in my house, I will take steps to stop you! Now go sleep it off and leave your wife alone."

For once, Nejmi went upstairs and walked by his wife without saying a word. He realized he was no longer driven by desire for her. She can go to hell, he thought and fell on his bed.

The villagers met peace with a profound sense of relief. No longer would they have to put their men in harm's way by sending them to the border. Mustafa and Serra also welcomed the news and were glad Nejmi would not have to travel. They saw how he had sunk into a deep depression and had grown detached from his wife and children. They hoped that the end of the war would help ease his troubles. They admired Nesrin and saw how unhappy she was. They loved their grandchildren but imagined that they must crave the presence of their father. In hopes of unifying the family, Mustafa decided they should invite Rashit and Lana to visit New Manor and to finally meet their grandchildren.

Rashit and Lana gracefully accepted the invitation and announced that they would arrive within a month. Nesrin was thrilled at the prospect of seeing her parents.

New Manor glimmered in the summer sun and was once again ready to receive guests. Two carriages arrived, along with a wagon of luggage and supplies. Erdal drove the first carriage, which held Rashit, Lana, and Ayla. Rafet and Kenan had remained in Bolu to take care of their father's holdings and Leyla, recently engaged, stayed behind to put together her trousseau. The second carriage held the servants. They arrived to a welcome that was warm but more subdued than that of their first visit four years ago. It was harvest time and field work kept the youngsters from socializing and dancing the kafe.

As usual, Mustafa and Serra greeted their guests on the steps in front of the house. Haydar and Ethem and their families were also there to greet the visitors from Bolu. When Nesrin saw her parents, she could barely hold back her tears. Her mother had grown noticeably older and Rashit's hair had gone from a distinguished salt and pepper to all white. Lana Hanim also observed the changes in Nesrin. Motherhood had certainly matured her, she thought, but was there something else? Behind the tears of joy, Lana sensed her daughter's sadness.

Following Nesrin, Nanna also kissed and hugged the visitors. This was the family she'd always known. She pulled Lebriz and Jemil to the side and whispered in their ears. Then she sent them, hand in hand, to greet their grandparents. Jemil made a bow, which charmed them to no end.

"Come here, young man," said Rashit, his hazel eyes glittering with pride. "Come shake your grandfather's hand. What a strapping Circassian boy you are."

Jemil kept his head high and shook the older man's hand. But Rashit couldn't resist. He pulled the boy into his arms and gave him a tight squeeze. It was now Lebriz's turn to greet her grandparents. She in turn, also following Nanna's orders, gave an elegant curtsey, which provoked oohs and applause from the group. Lana embraced the child and planted kisses on her cheek. Nesrin smiled from the side. Her children certainly had conquered their grandparents' hearts.

The weather was luscious for the next few weeks, which allowed Nesrin to spend many delightful hours in the garden with Ayla. They reminisced of their childhood, shamelessly gossiped about their sister, and played games with the children. The children's favorite game was hide-and-seek. Jemil would always hide Lebriz behind Nanna's skirts, and then run off to hide himself behind a nearby bush. Nesrin, who was almost always the seeker, would pretend she couldn't find them, and then, to gales of laughter and delight, threw up her hands in astonishment when the children popped out of their hiding places. Serra and Lana heartily joined in the laughter from their seats on the verandah.

For the first time in seven years Nesrin felt happy. Nejmi had left for a final tour of duty, but even when he'd been around, he'd no longer been so insistent on being intimate with her. On the occasions that he had become interested, she was able to better tolerate him and regarded sex as what Nanna had termed "the wifely duty that must be done."

When Mustafa and Rashit returned from a trip visiting nearby villages, they reported that they'd encountered several people who'd fallen ill. Everyone except Nanna brushed off the news as being insignificant. Nanna asked Mustafa what kinds of symptoms they'd observed. When Mustafa listed some of the symptoms—headache, fever, sore throat, and fatigue—Nanna grew quiet.

"What's the matter, Nanna?" asked Rashit.

"I'm afraid it's influenza," Nanna replied. "None of you have seen it the way I have. May Allah protect us all."

Within a week the flu had spread through the region like wildfire. A number of villagers got sick and didn't know what had hit them. Some of them felt ill in the morning and by nighttime they were dead. Others would arrive home after work and were carried out of their house wrapped in a death shroud the next morning. The illness knew no boundaries and it was impossible to predict who would get struck next.

It wasn't long before New Manor was hit by the flu as well. First it was Ümit, the butler. Still vibrant at fifty years old, he fell ill and died quickly. The flu did not discriminate. After it devastated the servants' quarters, it began to infect the family.

Nanna knew all too well that the infection was spread through contact with other sick people, but because there were no early symptoms, it was impossible to tell who was infected.

Haydar and Rashit had spent much time visiting the villages and observing the training of soldiers. They fell ill first. Next, to Serra's great grief, Mustafa became ill. Serra did everything in her power to try to save her husband but his fever would not go down. She ordered the servants to take him outside, where it was near freezing, in the hope that the cold would lower his temperature. When that didn't work, she ordered him wrapped in layers of thick blankets to make him sweat and rid his body of toxins. Mustafa, Haydar and Rashit all died within hours of each other.

Recognizing the need for isolation, Nanna ordered that Nesrin and the children be confined to their family's wing in New Manor.

Nesrin, losing her mind with grief, protested. "What difference does it make, Nanna? Let me be with my family. Let's all be together through this hell."

But Nanna would have none of it. Pushing and wailing, she sent Nesrin and the children to a remote area of the house, locked the doors, and prevented them from being in contact with anyone.

Next it was Lana and Serra who were infected. Followed by them was the all too young and beautiful Ayla. Within one short month, New Manor saw the deaths of ten of its people. A small graveyard was arranged on the south lawn where all of them were buried.

It was a miracle that the disease touched neither Nesrin nor the children, nor the tenacious Nanna. The only other survivor was the ever-loyal driver Erdal, who'd sequestered himself with the horses in the barn.

Nesrin clung to Nanna and her children, not wanting to let them go as far as the next room.

When Nejmi returned New Manor was practically deserted. Once so full of life and family, the house was now empty and silent. He found Nesrin and Nanna huddled with the children in the west wing. His heart broke to see the devastation of his family but, unable to show any vulnerability, he decided to mask his sorrow with a show of strength. At a time when his wife and children needed his kindness the most, Nejmi turned abrupt and cold to those around him. By now, three months after the epidemic hit, infection rates had abated, and people who'd quarantined themselves were beginning to come out.

"Erdal Efendi, go to town and find us a cook and some servants," he ordered. "Jemil, take your sister to the nursery to play. We can't have you children underfoot all day."

Jemil turned to his mother. "I miss my grandparents," he said. "When will they be back?"

Before Nesrin could say anything, Nejmi snapped, "Haven't you told them?"

"No," said Nesrin. "They're much too young to understand."

Nejmi turned to his son. "They're all dead," he said with a gravelly voice. "Your grandparents are dead and you'll never see them again."

Jemil started to cry.

"What's the use of lying?" Nejmi said to his wife. "He will find out sooner or later."

Nesrin wept as she held her boy to her chest. Lebriz, seeing them both so upset, also started to cry.

"Don't be such a mama's boy," Nejmi told Jemil. "Stop crying! Circassian men don't cry. Nanna, get these sniveling children to the nursery, where they belong!"

Soon the news came that Ethem and his entire family had also died in the epidemic. With Bedri dead and Sadi still serving in the Ottoman army, Nejmi was the only one left to handle father's holdings. He felt aggrieved and overwhelmed.

In the meantime, a new Sultan had taken the throne and things were shifting all over the country. When Nejmi learned that the border guards would now be disbanded and that the Ottoman military would take their place, he felt even more bereft. The training of those men and guarding the borders had given him a purpose all these years. He had no idea how he would occupy his time in the wake of such devastation.

In an uncharacteristically selfless move, Nejmi decided to do what he could to support his people. He traveled from village to village to help the people cope with their losses and to provide them with strategies to try to return to a degree of normalcy. He guided villagers to band together, help each other, and become reasonably productive again. He recruited several new servants—many of them women widowed since the epidemic—to help Nesrin and Nanna at New Manor.

The house was scrubbed, cleaned, and aired from top to bottom. It fell to Nesrin and Nanna to sort through and discard some of the belongings left behind by the dead. Some of these personal items carried many sweet memories. Among them were Serra's jewelry and a kaftan she wore at Nesrin's wedding, and Mustafa Bey's old pipe, a gift from an old friend. These and other cherished items had to be either given away or thrown out.

The servants settled in and the little family moved into the big house, reserving the smaller wing for guests. Life slowly settled into a normal routine. The daily hustle and bustle, infused with children's laughter, returned the house to life again.

Nejmi started to frequent the local han again to get the latest news and to socialize with the townsmen. Once again he started drinking and would return home later and drunker each night. Nesrin, keeping with the Circassian tradition, sat alone in her bedroom, and waited for her husband's return, just as before. Occasionally Nejmi would drag her to his bed but most nights he would ignore her and go to sleep.

Almost two years after the epidemic that killed his parents, Nejmi came home one night more inebriated than usual. He grabbed Nesrin by the arm and steered her toward the bed.

"My porcelain wife, my beautiful porcelain wife," he said, slurring his words.

Nesrin turned her head to avoid the stench of his breath.

"You are my beautiful porcelain wife," he said with a sloppy smile. "I need a warm, fuzzy cat in my bed that will spit and claw and purr for me."

Nesrin, about to gag, glared at him.

"I will take a kuma," he declared. "I need a second wife."

Nesrin, horrified, pulled away from him. "Nejmi, what are you saying?"

"Hey, didn't you hear me, my beautiful porcelain wife?" he sneered. "I said I will take a kuma to warm my bed."

"No. You can't do that. No decent Circassian man would bring a kuma to his wife's house!"

"What do you mean 'no'? I will do as I please, woman!"

"If you bring a kuma into this house, you will have to kill me first, or I will kill myself!"

"Ah, my beautiful porcelain wife," he said with his dark eyes narrowing. "I don't have to kill you just to take a kuma. But I will if you insist."

She was mortified. "Nejmi, for the love of Allah and in the memory of all those dear to you, let me take my children and go to my brother in Bolu." She fell to the floor and knelt before him. "I beg of you, let me take the children and go."

Knowing how much his wife adored the children, Nejmi glared down at her with a crooked smirk. "Go if you will, but go alone. The children will stay with me."

She clung to him and wept. "You cannot. I cannot. You cannot do this!"

He pushed her away. "You have until first light. Get out or accept my decision and stay." He stomped out of the room before she could say another word.

Nesrin covered her mouth to keep from screaming, got up and ran through the door in search of Nanna. Nanna had heard Nejmi come home drunk and bellow at his wife, and was waiting for Nesrin in the next room.

"Nanna! Oh Nanna, for God's sake what am I to do? I cannot stay! You know I must go!" She was racked with sobs. "Please, I beg of you to take care of my darlings. I love them so much, but I cannot stay if he brings a kuma to New Manor."

"Oh, my poor child," Nanna said. She was at a loss for words.

"Nanna, please tell me that you understand. You must take care of my babies!"

Nanna's impulse was to shake her into reason. She wanted to tell Nesrin that as a Circassian mother, she had to be strong and withstand any trouble for the sake of her children. No Circassian mother would ever leave her babies behind. But looking at her, she also realized how much Nesrin had suffered. She knew that staying here would only make her life more miserable. She reached down and lifted Nesrin to her feet.

"I understand," she said. "You know I love you as the daughter I never had. And Jemil and Lebriz are dearer to me than life itself. Come, I will help you as much as I can."

Soon Nanna was piling Nesrin's gowns and kaftans on the bed.

"Take these and fill them with your gold and jewelry," she said, thrusting pillowcases at her. "They are yours, as is your bride price, which you must claim when you get to your brother's lands."

In just a few hours, Nanna had wrapped as many of Nesrin's possessions as she could fit into the bed sheets and helped her fill pillowcases with her jewelry of gold and silver. Nesrin looked out the window and saw the carriage that had brought her parents from Bolu waiting in front of the house. It was still draped in the same mourning cloth that had covered it after their deaths. She called to Erdal to help Nanna carry the heavy parcels down to the carriage.

Nesrin slipped a heavy traveling cloak over the black mourning gown she'd worn since the deaths of her parents. She tiptoed into the nursery where Jemil and Lebriz were sleeping. She covered her mouth to stifle a cry as she bent over and kissed Jemil. She ran her hands lightly over his soft hair without waking him up. When she turned to Lebriz she could no longer keep from weeping. The little girl woke and saw her mother bending over her with tears running down her cheeks. She reached up to wipe the tears as Nesrin bent down and kissed her.

Without a word, Nesrin ran from the room, not daring to look back. She climbed into the carriage, so torn with grief that she could hardly breathe. As the carriage drew away from New Manor, a moan erupted from the very depth of her being; it was the haunting cry of a mother who had just lost her babes.

The next morning, when Lebriz awoke, she went directly to Nanna as usual. Nanna was red-eyed from weeping and lack of sleep, but when she saw the little girl, she hugged her to her bosom.

"Nanna, Nanna, I had a dream," said the girl urgently. Nanna couldn't tell if she knew what had happened or if this was an ordinary dream. "What dream did you have?" she asked.

"I want to tell Mommy all about it"

Nanna sat the child on her lap. "Won't you tell me your dream, my little Lebriz," she said, trying to remain as composed as possible.

"We were all playing hide-and-seek, but Mommy couldn't find us, and she began to cry. I told her again and again 'Here we are, Mommy! Here we are!' but she couldn't see us. She just kept crying."

Nanna held the girl close to her bosom. Curses on him, she thought. The drunken monster. No decent Circassian man would treat his wife like that. Mustafa Bey must be turning in his grave. Allah, give me strength to protect my babies.

Nanna gently led Lebriz to the nursery where Jemil was just waking up. He sat up in bed, rubbing his eyes.

"Jemil and Lebriz, come sit with me," she said in as calm a voice as she could muster. "I have something very important to tell you. Jemil, you are quite a big boy now, and you must help me take care of your sister. Your Mommy has had to go away and left the three of us to take care of each other."

Lebriz looked surprised but Jemil stared directly at Nanna. "Did Mommy die like our grandmothers and grandfathers?"

"Oh no, she didn't die. But she had to go away."

"How long will she be away?" asked the puzzled boy.

"I don't know."

Jemil wrapped his arms around Lebriz and hugged her. This seemed to help him fight back his own tears. "Why didn't she take us with her, Nanna?"

"Oh, my dear child, she wanted so much to take both of you with her, but your father would not allow it. He said she must go alone," said Nanna, shedding tears by now. "Jemil, you must be very brave and always take care of Lebriz. The three of us must always love and protect each other."

The boy's lips trembled. "I will try my best to protect you both."

Nejmi woke with a pounding headache and shouted for a servant to bring his tea. He went to the bedchamber he shared with Nesrin to find the bed stripped and her clothes strewn about. It was only then that he remembered the events of the night before. He shook his head and shouted at the top of his voice, "Nanna! Nanna, get in here immediately!"

Shaking with fear, Nanna ran into the bedchamber. When she saw his angry red face, she was sure he was going to hit her.

"Where is she?" he demanded.

"She left in the carriage you sent for her," cried Nanna.

He lifted his hand, but just then Jemil appeared from behind Nanna, grasping the hand of his little sister.

"Father, why didn't you let us go away with Mommy?"

Almost ashamed, Nejmi brought down his hand.

"New Manor is your home, Jemil. I am bringing you a new mommy so you will not miss the old one," he replied sharply.

Jemil's little voice shook as he spoke. "We don't want a new Mommy. We love our own Mommy. We will find her again!"

"Hah!" said Nejmi. "We shall see who you find, you impertinent boy."

He stalked from the room, leaving Nanna and the children sobbing and clinging to each other.

With tears streaking down his face, Jemil looked up at Nanna. "I know that Circassian men don't cry, Nanna. I will be strong and never cry again, but you must help me by being strong too."

"I will also try to be strong, Jemil, but I hurt so much, right here." said Lebriz, holding her hand over her heart.

Nanna dried her eyes. "My darlings, we will all be strong."

A week later, a woman named Serap arrived at New Manor. Shorter than Nesrin, she had black hair, black eyes, and huge breasts that wiggled when she moved about. She demanded that her clothes and boxes be taken directly to the bedchamber Nejmi had shared with Nesrin.

Nanna begged Nejmi to allow her to take the children back to the smaller wing of the house so they would not be underfoot while Serap was getting settled. Nejmi, seeing Jemil's sullen looks and Lebriz' tears, finally gave his permission.

It didn't take Serap very long to settle in. One day she told a servant to bring Nanna and the children to her.

Nanna entered the room with Jemil and Lebriz holding her hands.

"Well, well," Serap said, a mocking smile escaping her fat lips. "So here are Jemil Bey and Lebriz Hanim with their lovely Nanna."

Pinching each of the children's cheeks, she continued, "If you are good and do as I say, we will all be happy. I am your new Mommy now. You may call me 'Mommy'. But if you are naughty, I will tell your father, and he will have you beaten. Do you understand?"

Not expecting a reply, she dismissed them all with an imperious wave of the hand. "Nanna, you may take the children to their own wing. If I wish to see them, I will send for them."

Nanna stood tall, and without a smile or nod, she turned to go. Jemil glared at Serap, rubbed his cheeks, then said in his strongest voice, "You are not our Mommy and you will never be our Mommy!"

"We shall see, you insolent little boy. We shall see!" Serap turned her back to the children and started brushing her hair with Nesrin's silver hairbrush.

That night in bed, Serap did indeed purr like a cat as the insatiable Nejmi buried his face in her voluptuous breasts. He took her again and again. She responded to his every move, whispering, "There has never been such a man, never such a man as my Nejmi!"

A few days later, a courier from the Sultan arrived at New Manor. He was asking for members of the border squadrons to serve in the Ottoman army and was recruiting servants for the palace in Istanbul. It didn't take long for Serap to catch Nejmi at a drunken moment and to convince him that Jemil and Lebriz would become increasingly incorrigible as they grew older.

"This is a great opportunity, my husband," she whispered as she caressed his hairy chest, "and a rare privilege, to send them to be raised in the royal court in Istanbul."

"Do you think the Sultan would have them?" asked Nejmi.

"I have no doubt," said the woman. "Your little girl is stunning and the boy promises to be a strapping young soldier. The Sultan's men will snap them up as soon as we make the offer. You should be proud of them."

"You're right," said Nejmi with a drunken snarl and pulled her down. "Now come here, my naughty cat."

The next morning, Nejmi called Nanna and told her to prepare the children for travel. When Nanna asked where they were going, he would not tell her, nor would he reveal whom the children would be traveling with.

Just before dawn, two strange men rushed into the wing where Nanna and the children were sleeping. Nanna awoke to see the taller of the two men wrapping Lebriz in a heavy blanket while the other man put Jemil's cloak around his little shoulders. When Nanna started to cry out, a short, swarthy man motioned her to be quiet and held a knife to Jemil's throat. She dared not scream. Tears were streaming down her face as she pleaded, "Where do you take my babies?"

A big, tall man, holding Lebriz tight in his arms, replied in a strikingly high-pitched voice, "None of your business."

Nanna waved her hands in desperation as the men began to carry the children off. The swarthy man with the knife turned to her. "Give me their clothes. Hurry!"

Nanna quickly gathered dresses for Lebriz, pants and shirts for Jemil. She put them in a pillowcase and handed it to the man.

"Don't worry," he said. "They will be safe."

Then they were gone.

Nanna stood petrified, frozen in time, as a heavy silence descended upon the darkened room. It was several moments before she started to scream.

İSTANBUL

As the carriage clomped toward dawn, the men sat facing each other, each holding a child wrapped in a blanket and shivering with fear. Jemil was guarded by the short, swarthy man but kept his eye on Lebriz the whole time. As a proper Circassian male, even if only eight, it was his job to protect his little sister. He was determined not to show fear, no matter what. He smiled at her reassuringly and questioned the abductors.

"Who are you?" he asked, his voice cracking just a little as he spoke. "Where are you taking us?"

"We are servants of the great Sultan of the Ottoman Empire," replied the huge man with the squeaky voice, holding Lebriz. "We are taking you to him."

Jemil took a good look at the man for the first time. How strange his voice sounded coming from such a large frame. He had no eyebrows or facial hair and wore a baggy *shalvar* and a black kaftan. A fez ridiculously cradled his large, bald, head. His eyes were a deep blue and held a compassionate but sad expression. Just looking into those eyes, Jemil was almost convinced that this powerful man would not hurt them. Lebriz, shivering with fear and overwhelmed by the heavy lavender smell of the man, began to sob.

The man spoke to her softly and reassuringly. "Don't cry child, it will do no good, and will only make your brother more unhappy." Turning to Jemil he said, "Tell me, boy, what is your name and the name of your little sister?"

"Her name is Lebriz and I am Jemil," said the boy. "I am the grandson of Mustafa Bey of New Manor, owner of seven Circassian villages, granted by the Sultan himself,

"You see?" said the big man to his companion. "I told you these two are special."

The man holding Jemil squeezed him even harder. Jemil felt the hardness of the large curved knife held by the *kushak* wrapped around the man's hefty belly. The man replied in a gruff voice, "Special they may be. Our job is to deliver them safely to the Palace, along with the others."

It was then that Jemil realized there must be other children, perhaps in other carriages close by.

"My name is Haluk," continued the gruff man. "I'm courier of His Majesty the Sultan." He indicated the larger man. "This is Jafer. He is eunuch of the Sultan's Harem."

Jemil had heard the word eunuch before but didn't know quite what it meant. He guessed that the high-pitched voice must have something to do with it.

Haluk continued. "I have spoken with some of the former border guards and was told that you are indeed the heir of New Manor. You will be introduced to the Sultan as such."

The huge eunuch smiled and caressed Lebriz's hair. "Nobody will harm you if you do as you are told," he said.

Jemil sat up a little straighter, giving Lebriz a weak smile.

The swaying carriage finally lulled the two children into a fitful sleep. Haluk gingerly laid Jemil on the bench, while the eunuch continued to cradle Lebriz on his lap. Both children woke with a start when the carriage suddenly came to a halt. Lebriz became aware of her surroundings and immediately started to cry. The carriage door was jerked open and a man in uniform ordered them all to get out. Jemil was overcome with panic but remained under control.

Haluk climbed out of the carriage and Jafer handed him Lebriz, still wrapped in her blanket. Jemil jumped out behind them, determined to stay close to his sister. The carriage shook as Jafer's heavy body stepped out.

They were on a road going through what appeared to be a thick forest. Jemil now saw that there was indeed a wagon carrying a number of youngsters following them. He could see that the wagon was fitted with wooden benches, and the boys and girls, ranging from age nine to fifteen, were seated on opposite sides. The wagon along with their carriage appeared to form a small caravan. Armed horsemen guarded the caravan on both ends.

Jafer took the children by the hand and led them behind a bush. "Now pee," he commanded.

"But I don't need to," said Jemil, his body still stiff with fear.

"Pee now, whether you have to or not. We will not stop later for you and if you soil yourselves, Haluk will beat me. Would you want that?"

Jemil, startled by these words, took a good look at the man. It made no sense that a small, pudgy man like Haluk should beat a big man like Jafer. But he didn't say anything.

"Then I'd be expected to beat you!" Jafer said. "Now pee."

Haluk guarded the girls from the wagon on the other side of the road, while the boys waited their turn to relieve themselves.

Their business done, Jafer led Lebriz and Jemil back to the carriage. He wiped their hands with a damp cloth and gave each of them a piece of bread and cheese. "Eat," he ordered.

Jemil was hungry and devoured his slice of bread quickly. Lebriz delicately nibbled on her piece of cheese. Jafer handed each of them a cup of water and said, "Drink."

When the caravan began to move again, the children heard the young people in the wagon begin to sing. It was an old Circassian tune about leaving home and traveling to unknown lands.

"Who are they?" asked Jemil. "Did you steal them from their beds as well?"

"You are a brave little boy!" said Haluk with a chuckle. "Grandson of Mustafa Bey you are! No, we didn't steal them. Their own parents, like yours, offered them to be servants to His Royal Highness Abdul Hamid. Do you know who that is?"

"He is the Sultan," blurted out Jemil, now with the devastating realization that his father must have decided to send them away.

"That's right," said Haluk. "It is an honor and you should see it as such!"

Lebriz, now somewhat more comfortable and reassured by Jafer's soft touch, huddled closer to him and pulled the blanket up to her chin. Why does this strange man have the voice of a child? she wondered right before she fell asleep.

They traveled for hours. The children slept fitfully. Later that afternoon, they pulled up in front of a han.

The horsemen made camp with their horses around the stables. Jafer, Haluk, and the two children arranged to stay in one room, while the other youngsters were divided into rooms for boys and girls.

For dinner they were served a hearty vegetable soup with bits of lamb, cabbage, and potatoes, along with dark village bread. Jemil and Lebriz were seated at a table with Jafer and Haluk, while the other children, along with their guards, were seated separately. Travel worn and hungry, they whispered softly among themselves.

After dinner, the children were taken upstairs to their room. Jafer laid out their clothes for the following morning, so they could leave at first light. Having been snatched from their beds earlier that day, the children were still in their nightclothes. Lebriz stood in the middle of the room with tears streaming down her face.

Her silent grief touched something in Jafer's heart. "What is it, child?"

"I miss my mommy and my Nanna," she wept. "Who's going to give me a wash?"

Jafer put a hand over his mouth to suppress a laugh as his large belly shook.

"Who are you?" he asked, incredulously. "A princess who has someone to wash her every evening?"

"No, I'm not a princess! I'm just a dirty little girl."

Jafer looked for a moment at the girl's face. He had felt oddly protective of her from the moment he snatched out of her bed, and the whole time he held her while riding in the carriage. Now he even admired for her for speaking up for herself. "Wait a minute," he said, and left the room.

With tears still running down her cheeks, Lebriz looked at her dirty little feet and grubby nightdress.

"Lebriz, it's all right, just go to bed," whispered Jemil. "Please, let's not make them angry, just go to bed!"

"I can't Jemil, I just can't!" she sobbed.

Jafer entered the room where the other girls were staying. He scanned the girls and set his eyes on a tidy girl who looked cleaner than the others. "What's your name, girl?" he called to her.

She eyed the strange-sounding man with suspicion. "My name is Muazzez."

"Did you help your mother with your younger brothers and sisters?" he asked, slowly walking around her to get a better impression.

"Yes," she said, "but it got so crowded at home that my father sent me away to serve the Sultan."

He smiled. "Well, come with me, Muazzez. I have a little girl who needs a big sister to give her a wash."

He led Muazzez back to the room where Lebriz was still standing in the middle of the floor. Even Jemil's pleas had not been enough to make her go to bed without a wash.

Jafer set them up with a large pitcher of water, a basin and a clean towel in one corner of the room. Muazzez set to giving a Lebriz a wash.

"What's your name?" the little girl asked, looking up.

"I'm Muazzez," the older girl replied.

"Mua, Muaz—" Lebriz attempted to repeat her name.

The older girl grinned. "You can just call me Muzzy if you like."

"Thank you, Muzzy, you are very kind." Lebriz reached over to hug the older girl. "My name is Lebriz."

Muazzez, moved by this kind gesture coming from such a small person, squeezed out the towel and delicately wiped the girl's tear-stained face. Later, after she'd finished her work, she took the basin of water to the door and saw that Jafer was waiting.

"I don't know who she is, or why she's here," she said to him, "but she hugged me and thanked me for giving her a wash. No one has ever thanked me before."

"You're a good girl, Muazzez," he said, "and I can see that she likes you. It appears that you have comforted her. You may give Lebriz a wash every evening, if you'd like."

Muazzez smiled and nodded. She had the feeling that this strange man and the little girl would be part of her life for a long to come.

The journey seemed endless. Each day they got up before daylight, ate a piece of cheese and bread, and drank a cup of water. They climbed back into the carriage for another full day on the road to the next han. For nine days they traveled, when Haluk finally announced, "Tomorrow we will be in Istanbul."

This day of travel was different than the others. As they approached the big city the roads got wider and many more carriages were seen traveling to and from the surrounding towns and villages. Jemil and Lebriz had both heard their mother talk about Istanbul and what a marvelous city it must be. Nesrin, who herself had never been there, described the city as the site of many fables and myths, the home of great rulers, superior artists and poets, and aristocratic women who followed all the latest European fashions.

As they entered the city, the children looked out of the carriage windows and marveled at the variety of people they saw. There were yellow-skinned Mongols wearing pointed felt hats and Arabs with huge turbans on their heads. On one prominent corner, they were astonished to see African slaves, all bound together, wearing little more than baggy breeches.

A little further down the road, the children saw fine carriages and people wearing all kinds of dress, with colors and cuts they had never seen before. Their mother had told them that Istanbul was a city of endless diversity and that people from many areas of the world all mingled in its streets.

Lebriz was mesmerized to see the asortment of women and the way they were dressed. There were women veiled in fine silk and others who were completely covered in black burkas, with only their eyes peeking through slits. Astoundingly, at the other end of the street, there were women strutting about with no veil at all.

The han where they stopped that night was much grander than any they had seen before. The meal that evening was not the usual soup and bread, but a feast of real meat with roasted vegetables and yogurt. Some of the children had never seen food like this before. After the main course they also offered fruit, sweet peaches, and apricots.

The owner and his servants, who clearly knew Haluk and Jafer well, welcomed them with a shout, "Ho! Back with another load of gold from Anatolia?"

Haluk grinned. "Plus a couple of rough diamonds."

Well fed, the children slept soundly that night. In the morning after breakfast, several Ottoman soldiers marched through the door of the han, followed by a high-ranking officer. Haluk and Jafer immediately stood erect and greeted the man with a bow.

"Ho, Haluk Efendi," the man said. "Welcome back to Istanbul. I see you've brought us some new recruits."

Haluk proudly indicated the youths that had been riding in the wagon.

"These are some fine boys, Mithat Pasha," he said. "But I'd like to point out to you this young man," he said, holding Jemil's hand. "He is Jemil, grandson of Mustafa Bey of New Manor, the owner of seven Circassian villages granted by the Sultan."

Mithat wiggled his nose as he regarded the boy. "Oh, yes. I've been told of him. A fine-looking boy he is. I will take him to my home where he will grow up with my sons, and then he will attend the military academy."

Jemil opened his eyes wide. "Sir, I won't be separated from my sister. I have promised to take care of her. She is very small and well behaved."

The man wiggled his nose again as he looked at Lebriz, seemingly considering Jemil's request.

Jemil pleaded, "Please sir, she will be no trouble at all."

The man took a short pause then turned to Haluk. "What will happen to the girl?" he asked.

"We will take her to the Imperial Palace," said Haluk.

The man turned to Jemil again. "See? No need to worry. She will be in good hands. I'll have to take you by yourself. There is no place for a little girl at my house."

Even more desperate, Jemil started to plead again, but the man turned and walked away. With tears welling up in his eyes, Jemil turned to Lebriz. "My darling sister, there is nothing we can do." He embraced her and held her to his chest.

Lebriz suddenly realized that Jemil was about to be torn away from her. "Jemil, please don't leave me alone, please!" she sobbed.

Once again, Jemil put on a brave front. He held his sister at arm's length and looked directly into her eyes. "One day I will come back for you," he told her. "I will find Mommy too, and the three of us will be together again. I swear!"

"When?" she cried. "When will you come back for me?"

"As soon as I can," he said, his voice breaking.

Jemil turned to Jafer and stood erect. "Jafer Efendi, I charge you with the care and protection of my sister Lebriz until such time as I may come to take her home to New Manor," he commanded in his child's voice.

Jafer, rather impressed by the authority of this small boy, bowed slightly, held Lebriz by the hand, and replied, "Yes, Jemil, you may count on me. I will take excellent care of your sister."

When Mithat began to lead Jemil away, the girl let out a cry and reached out to her brother. Jafer picked her up and hugged her tightly. She buried her face in his neck, racked with sobs.

That evening, devastated by the separation from her brother, Lebriz returned to the previous night's gloomy room with Muazzez and Jafer. A storm was brewing and rain soon pelted the windows. Thunder rumbled as the rain fell harder. Lebriz sat in a corner, huddled in a blanket, with tears running down her cheeks. Muzzy sat with her, trying to console her. "I'm all alone, Muzzy," she sobbed. "I loved my mommy and she's gone. I loved Nanna and she's gone too. I loved my brother and they've taken him away from me. What am I to do? What's to become of me?"

Lightning lit up the room in a flash. Both girls jumped. Thunder clapped and they heard the neighing of horses as the rain pounded the cobbled streets. Lebriz started to cry harder and Muazzez, only a young girl herself, held the little girl and cried with her.

How cruel Allah can be, thought Jafer, sitting across the room from the two girls. On this day of great grief, He sends us this horrible thunder storm.

He went to Lebriz. "It will be all right, my child. You're not alone. I promised your brother that I would always look after you, and Muazzez will wash you and spend the night with you again."

Lebriz's tears didn't stop, but she took Muzzy's hand and tried to smile. "I promised Jemil I'd be strong," she sputtered, "but I don't feel strong. I just feel like a helpless little girl."

"You will be strong, Lebriz," said Jafer tenderly. "It will take time, but you will be."

Muzzy hugged her tightly. "I will be right here, Lebriz," she said, tucking the heavy blanket around her. "I will help you to be strong." She wiped the girl's face, caressed her hair, and held her until they both fell asleep sitting up against the wall.

Two weeks earlier a similar storm had pelted the small city of Bolu, about 100 kilometers south of Istanbul. In the middle of the night, a man desperately knocked on the door of a well-appointed house.

Inside, the young servant, Ahmet, lay awake in bed, spooked by the violent thunder outside. He heard a knocking at the door but dismissed it as just another trick of the storm. The knocking persisted, and he heard a voice. He pulled himself out of bed and hurried to the front door. "Kenan Bey! Are you home? Please wake up, Kenan Bey!"

Ahmet opened the door to see a man, soaking wet.

"Who are you? What do you want?"

"Please," the man pleaded. "Will you get Kenan Bey, please!"

"I can't do that. He's asleep."

"Please do it," said the man, still standing outside with rain pouring down his face.

"Come inside, out of the rain," said Ahmet.

"No, I'll stay here. I've brought his sister. Please get him for me."

Ahmet shut the door and rushed up the stairs. Minutes later, Kenan was at the door, tying on his robe, followed by his wife Alev, barely awake, also in her nightgown and robe.

"What is it? Who is it?" shouted Kenan as Ahmet opened the door to reveal the wet man. "Who are you?"

The man moved slightly forward into the light.

"Erdal Efendi, is that you?"

The man nodded and looked down. "My God, Erdal Efendi, what are you doing here? Please, come inside."

"Your sister is in the carriage," said Erdal. "She's very weak."

"Why? What is Nesrin doing here?"

"Please help me bring her in. She's sick and she hasn't eaten in days."

Kenan rushed outside, followed by Ahmet and Alev. Erdal opened the door to the carriage, revealing an unconscious Nesrin. The three men lifted her out and carried her inside. Alev led them into the living room and the men laid Nesrin on the sofa.

"Is she alive?" asked Alev. Kenan checked her pulse.

"Yes, she's breathing. Ahmet, get her some tea."

"I will get towels and dry clothes," Alev said as she left the room.

"What happened? What did that man do to her?"

"She will tell you all about it," said Erdal, caressing Nesrin's hair. "My poor Nesrin has suffered so much."

Ahmet brought the tea and Kenan lifted her head to give her a sip. "It's all right, Nesrin. You're safe now. It's all right."

Ahmet took the shivering Erdal to the servants' quarters to give him a pair of dry pants and a shirt. Kenan gave his sister another sip of tea to warm her up. She moaned and tried to open her eyes but quickly fell asleep. Kenan and Alev sat with her all night. After a while, the storm abated and Nesrin slept well into the morning. Erdal slept on a cot in Ahmet's room.

The wagon full of girls traveled the next day through a hilly terrain toward the body of water called the Bosphorus. Lebriz rode in the carriage under the watchful eyes of Jafer and Haluk. Jafer explained to the girl that the Bosphorus was a narrow strait that ran through the city of Istanbul and linked two large seas, the Marmara in the south and the Black Sea in the north.

"It is full of fish and boats and changing tides," he said. "Many artists have painted it, and many poets have been inspired by its beauty, especially at sunrise and sunset."

Lebriz was stunned by the majesty of what she saw. She'd never seen such a large body of water before. In the past, she'd been terrified to see her brother wade in a small river; she was sure he would drown and was thrilled to see him jump out and splash her with water. But this river could swallow you whole, she thought.

They stopped when they approached the ferry docks and Jafer gently lifted Lebriz from the carriage. The girls from the wagon were just as stunned by what they saw. Waves smashed against the wharf, causing a huge vessel to rock back and forth. Noting Lebriz's anxious tug on his hand, Jafer tried to reassure her that the boat was perfectly secure.

"That's a ferry," he explained. "It crosses these waters several times each day."

A loud horn bellowed. The girls screamed and covered their ears. The ferry belched out a huge puff of smoke as it hit the wharf with a thud. Lebriz, mortified by this thing she could only think of as a monster, grabbed Jafer's hand even tighter.

A man emerged from the ferry and threw a plank between the wharf and the boat. Passengers started walking up and down on the plank as the boat was continued to sway on the water.

When Lebriz realized she was expected to walk onto the ferry she was horrified, I can't do it, she thought. I don't want to. She watched the other girls being slowly guided to the boat. Clearly they were just as terrified as she was.

They clung to the wooden railing and gingerly made their way up to the deck of the boat. Finally, when all the girls had climbed aboard, Jafer asked Lebriz, "Are you ready?"

"No, I'm not!" she snapped. "I will never get on that thing. I will stay right here."

"What did you promise your brother Jemil?" asked Jafer.

"I don't remember," said Lebriz, determined to keep her feet on solid ground.

"You promised him you'd be brave. This is your chance to prove to him, and to yourself, just how brave you can be," he said. "I don't want to have to carry you on board, like a baby. I'd like you to go up on your own so that you can see how brave you are. Will you do that, Lebriz?"

Lebriz looked up into Jafer's eyes. They were blue pools of light that were both comforting and sad. Realizing that she could trust him, she slowly nodded her head.

Jafer took her hand and guided her to the plank. She clung to him as they boarded the boat. Once on deck, she looked up and saw a myriad of seagulls, squawking and circling above the ferry. This scared her at first but then she saw one of the gulls suddenly dive straight down into the water like a dart. This surprised her so much that she laughed. The other gulls continued to screech and frantically circle the boat. They were so distracting that she almost forgot to be afraid. The clanging bells and foghorns startled the other girls but Lebriz hardly heard them. She felt a jolt as the ferry pulled away from the wharf, but this didn't bother her. She was mesmerized by the gulls.

As the boat made its way across the strait, Lebriz found herself calmed by the churning waves and the gentle swaying of the vessel. By now, some of the seagulls had left the ferry in pursuit of a fishing boat. She could still see them frenziedly spinning over the vessel. After a few minutes, she let go of Jafer's hand.

All the other girls were huddled together, some of them whimpering with fear. Lebriz didn't understand why she felt so calm, when minutes ago, she was just as afraid as the rest. She was comforted by Jafer's presence, but was glad she wasn't holding on to anyone. Gliding over the water made her feel freer than ever before. A glimmer of happiness flowed through her, and brought with it a sense of hope.

The other girls also calmed down and began staring out the windows. Other ships even larger than the ferry passed them by, traveling in the opposite direction. One blew its horn and their boat blew its horn as well, as though in reply. The gulls, unfazed by the noise, continued to swirl around the boat and follow it like protective angels. A passenger threw a piece of bread in the air and one of the gulls swooped down to grab it, beating the other ones to it. Even the scared girls laughed at the sight, and clapped as the gulls continued to swirl and squawk.

When, in the early afternoon, Nesrin finally opened her eyes, she saw both of her brothers and Alev watching over her. Her older brother Rafet had been summoned that morning. Alev propped her up. "Drink this," she said, offering Nesrin a glass of warm milk. Nesrin tried to speak, but she started to cry.

"What happened to you?" asked Kenan, his one hand gently caressing her shoulder, while the other was clenched into a fist. "What has he done to you?"

All Nesrin could mutter between sobs were two words. "My babies. My babies."

"I'll kill him," mumbled Rafet through gritted teeth. "I'll go over there right now and kill the bastard."

"Nesrin must gain some strength before anybody goes rushing off," said Alev.

The next day Nesrin was composed enough to tell her story. She told her brothers of Nejmi's declaration that he would take a kuma and of his drunken ultimatum after she argued with him. "Dear Nanna helped me gather a few things and Erdal Efendi, God bless his soul, drove me away from that awful house."

"Thank God for Erdal Efendi," said Rafet.

"It was a mistake," said Nesrin, starting to cry again. "I will never forgive myself for leaving my children."

"You did the right thing," said Kenan. "No sister of ours will live under those circumstances. You were right to leave."

"I will go back," Nesrin blurted out. "I will be with my children again. I don't care if there is a second wife in the house. I will endure it. My children need me."

"Do you think he'd ever take you back?" asked Rafet.

"I will beg. I will cry. I will do whatever he wants. He can treat me any way he likes as long as I can stay with my children."

"You're a stained woman now, Nesrin," said Kenan. "There's no place for a wife who abandons her husband and family, you know that. This is your home now. You will live with us."

"But I can't live without my children!" Nesrin wailed.

"We will wait until you feel stronger, then we will all go together to rescue your children," Kenan assured her. "I promise you, we will get Jemil and Lebriz back, and Nanna, too."

Alev took her hand. "Don't cry anymore, my sister. It will be all right. Your brothers will make sure of that."

"Thank you," Nesrin said, now holding back her tears. Her grief was overwhelming but she was grateful to be among family.

YILDIZ PALACE

Small boats and skiffs were rocked by its waves as the ferry approached the dock at Beshiktash. Lebriz was amazed to see how the fishermen stood steady and held on to their lines while their boats were tossed about. The ferry met the wharf with a small thud. Planks were let down once again and the girls were led off the boat and toward a wagon and an opulent carriage. The other girls boarded the wagon while Jafer took Lebriz to the carriage.

"Where are we going?" Lebriz asked, feeling anxious again.

"To a place you could never have imagined, even in your dreams," said Jafer. "Yildiz Palace is the home of His Royal Highness Abdul Hamid."

"The Sultan?" she asked.

"You're a smart one," mused Jafer. "Yes, the great ruler of the Ottoman Empire."

Lebriz felt dread in her heart as they entered the carriage and closed its ornate door. She felt so small, just a girl from a tiny village. What was she to do at a palace?

The small convoy clopped along cobbled streets lined on both sides by tall trees and various buildings made of stone and wood. Lebriz could still catch glimpses of the Bosphorus and the light that sparkled on its waves. This gave her some comfort. She felt she would be all right as long as she could see the strait.

When they reached an elaborate, black steel gate, a uniformed man approached the carriage and peered inside. Jafer gave him a curt nod, and the man immediately ordered the gate opened. Two other men pushed open the heavy inner doors, and shut them after the caravan passed through.

Suddenly there was silence. Only chirping birds and the wind brushing through the cypress trees could be heard. The group traveled down a long garden path, flanked by trees and gracefully organized flowerbeds. They passed by majestic buildings, the likes of which Lebriz had never seen. An enormous fountain, with water sprouting over a carved column, captivated her. The only fountains she'd ever seen had been in the baths, and none of them were as magnificent as this.

I hope that's not where we will be made to bathe, she thought. Bathing in the open air was unthinkable.

The carriage stopped in front of a sturdily constructed, two-story building. The girls from the wagon were ushered out and told to line up in front of its door. Jafer held Lebriz's hand as she climbed down from the carriage.

This was the first time she'd seen all the girls grouped together. She scanned them quickly to find Muazzez. Not seeing her at first, she started to get worried, but then Muazzez's face emerged from behind another girl. Being somewhat taller, Muazzez was accustomed to standing in the back when grouped with girls her age. She moved forward and smiled at Lebriz. They were both happy and relieved to see each other.

Lebriz now turned her attention to the ominous building facing her. From the outside, it looked almost ordinary, especially compared to the other buildings they'd passed. She saw that the windows were latticed and that a heavy steel door guarded its entrance.

"What is this house?" she asked Jafer, the familiar sense of dread once again rising in her throat.

"It's the Sultan's harem," Jafer replied. "This will be your new home. Bid goodbye to Haluk Efendi. He's not allowed to enter this house."

Haluk climbed down from the carriage and gently caressed Lebriz' hair. "Farewell, Lebriz Hanim," he said, addressing her now as though she were an adult. "I hope you will be happy here. I hope our paths will cross again, some day."

The finality of these words worried Lebriz even more. She hardly knew this man but the thought of more loss was unbearable. She turned to Jafer. "What about you," she asked the large man with dark full lips and kind gaze. "Will you leave me too?"

"Never," replied Jafer. "I will always remain with you, just as I promised your brother Jemil."

Soon the doors swung open and Lebriz found herself being ushered in, ahead of the other girls. An imposing black man met them and spoke with the same high-pitched voice as Jafer.

"Ho, what have we here, Jafer Efendi?" he asked, looking Lebriz up and down. "What have you brought us from Anatolia?"

"A treasure, Ali Aga, a treasure to be sure," Jafer bowed, still holding on to Lebriz's hand.

"She's indeed a very small treasure," the man said while examining the girl's face, her fair skin, and striking hair. The scrutiny frightened her and made her feel smaller than she was. She looked at Jafer pleadingly.

Ali Aga chuckled and spoke with a booming voice. "Don't be afraid. No one will hurt you here."

He took a look at the other girls who had also entered through the gates.

"As long as you're good girls," he announced, "and do as you're told."

Jafer squeezed Lebriz's shoulder reassuringly.

"Don't worry," he whispered to her. "He sounds tougher than he is."

Güldane, a delicate young woman with light brown hair and blue eyes, had entered the room quietly. She and a young African woman, Zehar, stood at the side, viewing the new arrivals.

"Take our new girls to the hamam, Güldane " Ali Aga ordered.

Güldane carefully gathered the girls to form a line. Jafer knelt down to Lebriz. She was the smallest of the girls, and clearly the most distressed. Güldane saw this and came up to them.

"Will you introduce me, Jafer Efendi," she said with a melodic tone. "Who is this lovely young lady?"

"This is Lebriz," said Jafer. "She traveled from New Manor in Eastern Anatolia. She is the daughter of a respected landowner there."

"My name is Güldane," said the woman. "I am what is called an odalisque which means I am the chamber maid to Valide Sultan."

"That's the Sultan's mother," said Jafer boastfully. "A position of great importance."

"I'm certain Valide Sultan will be especially pleased to see you," said Güldane, admiring the girl's hair and hazel eyes. "But only if you let me give you a bath and rub you with some scents. Once I do that, you will look even more beautiful than you do now."

Güldane took Lebriz's hand. The girl took one quick glance back to see Jafer nodding and smiling at her reassuringly. Soon she had joined the other girls and was led into the deeper, cryptic recesses of the harem.

The harem was run under the supreme leadership of one formidable woman, the Sultan's mother, known as Valide Sultan. She ruled the harem with an iron fist, and held absolute authority over all decisions. She presided over hundreds of women of all ages, as well as the many eunuchs, teachers, cooks, maids, and gardeners. Nothing went past her and no one entered or left the harem without her permission. Breaking any of the rules of the harem resulted in harsh punishment for the offender and, depending on the seriousness of the crime, could even result in death.

Ali Aga, the head eunuch, was Valide Sultan's most important servant. He watched over all the other eunuchs, slaves, and servants; collected reports from them; and relayed all information, gossip, and happenings to Valide Sultan. He also kept close watch on the girls and women of the harem for any signs of misconduct.

The newcomers were processed and initiated according to Valide Sultan's strict instructions. Upon arrival they were immediately bathed and inspected for lice, physical defects, or disease. Güldane, Zehar, and two other odalisques performed these tasks.

Muazzez spotted Lebriz as soon as they entered the baths. She hurried to stand beside her as the girls lined up to get undressed and inspected. Güldane was walking down the line surveying each girl when she saw that Muazzez, having already undressed herself, was now helping Lebriz.

"Are the two of you sisters?" she asked.

"Yes!" jumped in Lebriz, hoping this would assure that the two girls would be kept together. Muazzez kindly corrected her. "No, but we're almost sisters. Jafer Efendi put me in charge of bathing Lebriz every night before bed. I've grown quite fond of her."

"Who bathed you at home?" asked Güldane.

Lebriz answered, on the verge of tears. "My Nanna bathed me and my mother brushed my hair."

"There, there," said Güldane, her voice softening. "Don't worry. We'll allow Muazzez to bathe you and help you get dressed here as well."

Suddenly a shriek was heard from across the room. Muazzez and Lebriz turned to see a girl with long hair being dragged, fighting and screaming, out of the room.

"What's wrong with her?" asked Muazzez.

"She most likely has lice," Güldane said. "She'll be all right after they cut her hair very short and comb out the bugs."

With a look of terror in her eyes Lebriz immediately reached up to her hair. "Do I have lice?"

Güldane ran her fingers through the girl's hair and inspected her scalp. "You don't have lice, my dear. You are perfect." She then performed the same inspection on Muazzez before moving on to the next girl.

All but two of the girls passed the inspection; aside from the girl with the lice, one girl had a clubbed foot. Deemed unqualified for harem service, she was sent down to the kitchen to be trained as scullery maid.

Once they were inspected and bathed, the girls were wrapped in towels and transferred to another room where the Mistress of the Robes awaited them. She and her assistants carefully measured the girls and a scribe recorded their names and measurements. As soon as this information was processed, the girls were divided into groups according to their size. Bundles of clothes were immediately delivered and disbursed.

Lebriz was anxious when she was grouped separately from Muazzez, but she was soon distracted when the bundles were opened and the clothes were revealed.

The girls were all given a pair of harem pants and a bodice of fine silk. Next, they were dressed in flowing dresses with slits up the sides to reveal the full, colorful harem pants beneath. Lebriz was handed a short vest to wear over her dress, while Muazzez and the other older girls were given knee-high kaftans. They all had a kushak to tie around their waist.

Lebriz thought these luxurious clothes must be for special events, but Güldane assured her that they were everyday clothes and that she'd be receiving another set or two soon.

Another woman entered and announced that she was the Mistress of Hairdressers. She went around looking at all the girls' hair with an air of superiority and disdain.

"Who did this to you?" she cried out at one girl whose hair hung in a single braid.

"I did," said the girl, coyly.

"It's worse than a bird's nest! You have a lot to learn," exclaimed the woman. She then turned and called out, "You all have a lot to learn. I've never seen a more miserable bunch in my life! None of you are in any shape to be presented to the Valide Sultan!"

Her assistants immediately went to work combing, braiding, and arranging the girls' hair.

A young assistant working on Lebriz said, "Your hair is so unusual. How would you describe this color?"

"I inherited it from my mother," said Lebriz. "My Nanna said it was the color of burnished copper."

"Burnished copper," repeated the girl. "Your mother must have been beautiful. Is she dead?"

"She most certainly is not!" Lebriz began to cry.

"Don't cry little girl. I'm sorry I said that. Look, I'll make a special braid. You will look so beautiful, just wait and see."

Sure enough, the woman created a beautifully intricate, multi-layered braid with Lebriz's long hair. The other girls took notice and some of them expressed admiration. Others remained silent, already resentful of Lebriz's beauty and the special treatment she was getting.

The girls were now ready to begin their training in palace life and etiquette. The first phase began with the evening meal. Famished at the end of such a long day, they were escorted to a large room where pillows of various colors were strewn about the floor or placed on divans that lined the walls. Several large wooden disks with short legs were brought in and placed upon clean white cloths. An odalisque named Ferah seated the girls on the pillows surrounding each table and then another large cloth was spread over the disk. Ferah instructed the girls on how to sit properly; they were to cover their knees with the cloth and sit straight up, with their hands folded in their laps. Ferah demonstrated the position and watched carefully while the girls imitated her. A plate, bowl, and spoon were then set in front of each girl and the procession of foods began.

A steaming hot soup was served first. Ferah picked up the bowl and demonstrated how it should be silently sipped. Servants then placed large dishes of vegetables, rice, and meat on the table, and small stacks of flatbread were placed next to each diner. Ferah showed the girls how to use a piece of the flatbread to scoop up the food from the dishes and transfer them to their plates. They were told to eat slowly and deliberately, and to not talk during the meal.

A serving of sweets and piping hot tea followed the main course. Once finished with the meal, the girls were given a bowl of hot water with a slice of lemon to clean their hands. Stomachs full and hands clean, Ferah then showed them how to delicately pull back the cloth to prevent crumbs from falling on the floor.

Finally, the table and cloths were lifted off the floor, and the pillows were placed on divans or strewn about the floor. For the first time in days the girls had a moment to relax and breathe. No longer were they being carted around in carriages, being inspected or washed, or being taught new skills. They started to chat and giggle and tell stories. Ferah brought over a *saz* and one of the girls began to strum a tune. Another girl picked up two wooden spoons and began to clap them to the rhythm. Soon they were all clapping, singing, and dancing the folk dances of Anatolia.

Lebriz, being the youngest, remained on the side for a while but then could not resist. She jumped up, stood on tiptoe, and began to dance the kafe. All eyes turned to her as she captivated Ali Aga and all of the women with her elegant moves. Ali Aga seemed especially pleased.

"A treasure," he murmured. "A treasure indeed."

Güldane and the other girls congratulated Lebriz for how beautifully she danced. Some of them even hugged her.

"Where did you learn to dance like that?" asked Güldane.

"All the girls at New Manor dance," Lebriz replied, "but my mommy was especially good at dancing the kafe."

Friendly chatter continued for a while as the girls wanted to know each other's names and where they came from. The girls also asked questions of Ferah and Güldane, eager to know what their lives would be like in the harem. Ali Aga observed from the sidelines to assess which girls would adjust easily, which of them would be friendly and kind, how many of them seemed smart, and how many would have trouble with the new rules. He followed Lebriz especially closely and observed how delicate and innocent she was.

She's eager to make friends, he thought, but she's going to have trouble. She's much too beautiful and the other girls will always be jealous of her.

He then signaled Ferah, who in turn ordered the servants to prepare the room for bedtime. Beds were taken out of cupboards where they were stored during the day and laid down. A pallet was laid out for each girl with a pillow, a sheet, and down-filled comforter. Güldane instructed the servants to put Lebriz's bed next to Muzzy's.

Before falling asleep, Muzzy spoke to Lebriz in a hushed voice. "I'm told everything will be decided tomorrow, after breakfast. That's when we will be assigned to various duties around the harem."

"How do you know this?" asked Lebriz.

"One of the odalisques mentioned it. Apparently some girls will be assigned to serve Valide Sultan and others will be scattered in various other areas."

"Does this mean we'll be separated?"

"I hope not. But from what I can see, you're prime material for Valide Sultan. I can see it in the eyes of the odalisques when they look at you."

"And you?"

"I'm not sure. But I'm not worried. Either way, we'll always find each other."

"I don't want to serve Valide Sultan if you can't be with me," Lebriz whispered.

"I'm afraid you don't have much choice, my darling. Besides, it's an honor to serve Valide Sultan. It's the most advantageous position possible. You will most certainly become an important odalisque like Güldane, and then possibly even a concubine, and maybe even a wife!"

"A wife?"

"Yes. And if you give birth to the Sultan's son, what will happen then? You might be the next Valide Sultan. That's what!"

"I don't want any of that," cried Lebriz. "I don't like any of that at all."

"You'll understand as you get older," said Muazzez. "Now try to get some sleep."

That night, Lebriz once again dreamt that she was playing hide and seek with her mother and Jemil, but this time it was she who could not find them, and she was crying bitter tears. She woke to find Muzzy kneeling beside her, holding her hand and gently wiping away her tears. How comforting, she thought, to have a friend by my side.

In the morning, the servants flung open the latticed windows and carried in an oversized samovar. As the girls were served tea, other servants gathered up the beds and stored them back in the cupboards. Next, Güldane and Zehar took the girls to the washroom and toilets. They washed up, had their hair brushed and arranged, and dressed in clean clothes. When they returned to the main salon, they found the tables had been set out and were laden with fruits, cheeses, olives, bread, and honey. Egg dishes with spicy sausages were served in small copper-clad skillets. Once again, Ferah instructed the girls on how to eat properly and corrected them if they made mistakes. Finger bowls and small towels signaled the end of the meal.

After breakfast, Güldane instructed the girls to line up against the wall. Lebriz desperately tried to be next to Muazzez, but since they had to stand according to height, she ended up on the opposite side of the room.

Güldane explained how they would be assigned to various duties around the harem.

"Some of you will be taught to sew, some will be trained as hairdressers, and others will serve as servants to the concubines and wives of the Sultan. Only a select few ..." She was interrupted by Ferah who entered the room and whispered something in her ear.

Güldane nodded then turned to the girls again. "Only three of you will be selected to serve Valide Sultan." The girls waited with baited breath as Güldane surveyed the room for a moment and then pointed at each girl in turn. "Hande, Betül, and Lebriz."

Betül was at once delighted, Hande seemed unsure, and Lebriz was nearly devastated. She looked at Muazzez who smiled at her from across the room and indicated that it would be all right.

Güldane glanced at the other girls. "You may all enjoy a walk in the gardens before you're sent away to train for your duties." Then, turning to Betül, Hande and Lebriz, she said, "I'll see the three of you here after your walk."

Zehar accompanied the girls to the harem grounds. The air was fresh and crisp, the flowers were in bloom, and the ponds were glistening with goldfish. Lebriz took little comfort in the scents and beauties that surrounded her on this walk through the meticulously arranged gardens—the first of many to come. Muazzez held her by the hand.

"I'm told I'll be training as a seamstress. I'm happy. It's something I've always wanted to learn."

"I want to be a seamstress," cried Lebriz. "I don't want to be a concubine or a wife or anything like that!"

"Be patient, my sister. You will always be my sister and I will always love you. Don't worry."

After their outing the girls were sent off to various areas of the harem. Zehar accompanied Hande, Betül and Lebriz back to the main salon where Güldane was waiting for them. In preparation for their presentation to Valide Sultan, Güldane taught the three girls how to walk and stand straight with lowered eyes. She warned them to never speak until spoken to, and then to answer questions politely, in a low voice.

Once she felt they were ready, Güldane, along with Ali Aga, accompanied the girls to Valide Sultan's private salon. Another African eunuch, just as impeccably dressed as Ali Aga, in a long black dress coat and pinstriped trousers, stood guard at the ornate doors of Valide Sultan's private quarters. He bowed low to Ali Aga, knocked twice with his cane, and then opened the door. The sound of women's voices with an occasional twitter of laughter could be heard within.

Though smaller than the main salon of the Harem, the room was beautifully furnished. Large mirrors hung on the walls and plush silk rugs covered the marble floor. A divan lined one wall, while luxurious armchairs were arranged in the corners with artfully carved tables beside them.

The rich smell of fresh coffee greeted them as they stepped into the room. Valide Sultan sat in a throne-like chair, surrounded by ladies-in-waiting seated on stools and pillows. The Coffee Mistress was getting ready to serve coffee. The taster—who tasted everything before it was served to Valide Sultan—had just taken a sip when the group entered the room.

Valide Sultan looked at the girls and motioned Ali Aga to approach. The servants retreated as Ali Aga bowed, kissed, and touched the woman's hand to his forehead. Valide Sultan motioned Güldane to approach as well. Güldane performed the same hand-kissing ritual, and then sat on one of the stools.

After surveying the three girls, Valide Sultan commanded Ali Aga to bring forward the girl on the left. The eunuch obeyed. A raven-black-haired girl with black eyes and high cheekbones, Hande had learned her lesson well; she lowered her eyes and moved forward slowly and cautiously.

"What is your name, girl?" asked Valide Sultan.

"They call me Hande, Your Grace."

"Hmmm. We shall call you Zinniye. How old are you Zinniye?"

"I am eleven, Your Grace."

Valide Sultan turned to Ali Aga. "Bring me the next girl."

Ali Aga hurried to Betül, a pretty girl with dark brown hair and a pert upturned nose. A little nervous, she was not as graceful as Hande, her stride hurried and awkward.

Valide Sultan watched her approach, and then waved her hand. "Take Zinniye to Nahire and send this one back to the other girls," she said dismissively. "Now, bring me the little mite."

Ali Aga motioned to Lebriz, who then approached Valide Sultan with great caution. Although she appeared graceful, she was trembling like a leaf.

Valide Sultan looked at the little girl, and in a much kinder tone said, "They tell me you are called Lebriz. How old are you Lebriz?"

"I am six, Your Grace."

"Lebriz is such a pretty name. We shall call you Lebriz. I think you will be a fine friend for Ayshe Sultan, my granddaughter. You may do your lessons together and perhaps you can teach her the Circassian kafe, which I am told you dance very well."

"Thank you, Your Grace," Lebriz kept her eyes lowered. "If I may ask something, Your Grace..."

"Shhhh," warned Güldane. "You may not speak."

"Let her speak," said Valide Sultan, clearly charmed by the little girl. "What have you got to say?"

"I have a friend who takes care of me and gives me baths." Lebriz's voice was shaking.

Güldane spoke reluctantly. "A girl named Muazzez is like an older sister to Lebriz. They've grown very close."

Valide Sultan chuckled. "In that case, bring Muazzez here as well. The two of you will make good company for Ayshe. Muazzez can help you when you need a wash. Now, come kiss my hand and let me see those eyes."

Lebriz stepped forward, took the proffered hand, and with a little curtsey brought it to her lips and then to her forehead. She raised tear-filled hazel eyes to meet those of Valide Sultan. "Thank you, Your Grace," she whispered, lowering her eyes and repeating the curtsey.

Valide Sultan turned to Güldane. "Take Lebriz to Nadide Sultan's apartments and tell her this is a sister and companion for Ayshe Sultan. They are to take their lessons together and share their room with Muazzez."

"Yes, Your Grace," Güldane took Lebriz by the hand.

Valide Sultan turned to the Coffee Mistress. "I'll have that coffee now!"

Ali Aga immediately fetched Muazzez and escorted the two girls, elated to be reunited, to Nadide's apartment. At the door, another black eunuch bowed to them before he rapped twice with his cane.

A female servant welcomed them into a foyer that was separated by heavy curtains from the rest of the house.

"One moment," she said. "I will tell Nadide Sultan that you've arrived."

She disappeared behind the curtains. Some murmuring discussion was heard, then the curtains were pulled open to reveal Nadide's living room.

Nadide was sitting on a divan facing the gardens. On low stools in front of her sat four ladies-in-waiting, each holding a musical instrument:

a lute, a mandolin, a flute, and a tambourine. There was a fresh feeling about the room; the light blue hue of the divans, vases full of bright colored flowers, and large windows that welcomed generous sunlight gave the room a sense of airiness and optimism. For the first time in days, Lebriz felt an ache lift from her heart.

Nadide motioned for them to enter.

Ali Aga approached her and kissed her hand in the traditional way. "We come with greetings from Valide Sultan," he said in French. "We have brought a sister and a companion for Ayshe Sultan. This is Lebriz." He motioned Lebriz to approach.

Nadide looked her up and down and seemed pleased. "Summon my daughter," she told a servant. "And who is this other one?" She asked, indicating Muazzez.

Ali Aga pushed Muazzez forward as he introduced her. "Her name is Muazzez and she is to be companion to the two younger girls. Valide Sultan wishes that the girls share a room and that they take their lessons together."

"Please convey to Valide Sultan my gratitude," said Nadide. "I'm most appreciative of everything she does to improve our lives."

She managed a warm smile then motioned the girls to approach. Both girls bowed low and kissed the woman's hands, just as they'd been instructed.

Suddenly, a chubby little girl with blonde hair, flushed and out of breath, rushed into the salon. She took one look at Lebriz and clapped her hands with delight. "Hello! You're just as short as I am! What's your name?"

Startled by the girl's abrupt approach, Lebriz quietly replied, "I'm Lebriz. This is Muzzy."

Nadide smiled. "Ayshe, these are to be your sisters and companions."

"Oh, I am so happy to have a sister, Lebriz. My name is Ayshe. We shall play games and take our lessons together, and we won't be lonely anymore because we will have each other and Muzzy," the little girl gushed.

Lebriz and Muzzy, who had both kept their eyes lowered, looked up and smiled.

Ayshe addressed Güldane and Ali Aga. "Please tell my grandmamma, thank you. I am so happy to have a sister and a playmate."

"Of course, Ayshe Sultan, we will tell her," replied Ali Aga, with a warm smile.

A bittersweet smile crossed Nadide's face as she lay back on the divan and watched the young girls getting to know each other. A former concubine, Nadide had been sent to the Sultan as a gift from the ruler of a small Balkan state in thanks for sparing the invasion and pillage of the fief. She was blonde and blue eyed and had quickly become one of Sultan Abdul Hamid's favorites. The nights Abdul Hamid invited Nadide to his rooms had produced a daughter, and earned her the precarious position of becoming one of his wives. This role in the harem was uneventful and deadly boring. Any unusual event or excitement was cherished, and the arrival of these two girls, to be companions and sisters for Ayshe, certainly qualified as one. The happiness of her daughter was all that mattered to her.

Educated in western methods, Nadide was fluent in German, Turkish, and Persian, but she usually spoke French with her daughter, as well as with Ali Aga and most of her servants. Her European tastes manifested themselves in her apartment, particularly in the dining room.

The western-styled table was set with fine china, silver cutlery and crystal glasses. Lebriz was accustomed to this type of table from New Manor, but for Muzzy this was a new experience. At dinner, she was told to watch what the others were doing and to do the same. She was confronted with a variety of utensils: forks, knives, and spoons of different shapes and sizes were set in front of her. She found the practice of sipping soup from a spoon highly inefficient compared to holding up the whole bowl to her mouth. She observed that Güldane, who was sitting across from her, used a separate fork and a special knife for the fish course. Once the fish plates were taken away, a course of roast beef, potatoes, and vegetables arrived, and another set of forks and knives were required.

Even Lebriz, who'd been accustomed to using forks and knives, didn't realize different courses required specific sets.

Muzzy, somewhat befuddled through the whole meal, let out a sigh of relief when she saw the fruit course arrive: peaches, her favorite! How many ways could there be to eat a peach? She was astonished to see how Nadide skillfully used a fruit knife to quarter, peel and slice the peach, and then passed the perfectly peeled slices to Ayshe, who smiled and said "Merci beaucoup". Muazzez had no idea where to begin. She picked up her knife and attacked the peach but got no further than poking a large hole into it.

Amused by Muzzy's quandary, Nadide smiled and patiently peeled and quartered peaches for both Muzzy and Lebriz, all along giving them instructions in French, which neither one of the girls understood at all. By the end of the meal the girls had learned how to say, "un petit peu, s'il vous plaît" and "non, merci." When offered their peaches the girls both smiled and said "Merci beaucoup," which delighted Nadide .

The meal ended with the usual finger bowls and towels. Returning to the salon, Nadide was served coffee and the girls drank pomegranate juice with honey. The four musicians returned to their stools and began to play a lilting tune of the Balkans. They also played some sad little ditties which Ayshe and her mother sang. Lebriz, seeing mother and daughter so close, felt a profound longing for her own mother. She fought back her tears and reminded herself of her promise to Nanna and Jemil. "I will be strong, I will be strong," she repeated to herself, over and over again.

It grew late, the musicians left, and the lamps and tapers were lit.

The three girls retired to the bathroom of the apartment where the servants bathed them, pulled their nightdresses over their heads, and brushed their hair. Wrapping themselves in their dressing gowns the girls went back to the salon where Nadide was sitting on the divan.

"Come sit with me, girls," she said, speaking in Turkish now, with a charming accent. "Tell me where you are from and how you come to be here at Yildiz Palace." She looked at Lebriz.

"My grandfather was the Circassian Mustafa Bey, who owned lands and seven villages in Anatolia," began Lebriz. "Two men came at night and stole me and my brother from our beds. When we reached Istanbul a man came to the han and took my brother Jemil away. They brought me here. I promised my Nanna and Jemil to be strong, but I miss them and my mommy so very much that it hurts me here," she explained, holding her hand over her heart.

"Oh, my poor, dear little girl," said Nadide, wiping tears from her own eyes as well as from Lebriz's cheeks.

"Did they steal you away as well, Muzzy?"

"Oh no, my father sent me with the Sultan's couriers to serve in the palace. He told me I was too smart to stay in a crowded village hut, and do nothing but wash my brothers and sisters. He sent me here to make a life for myself."

"How old are you, Muzzy?" asked Ayshe.

"I'm eight, but Lebriz is only six, so Jafer Efendi asked me to help her when we were traveling from New Manor."

"We are all here together for a reason which we cannot understand yet, so we must be sure to make each other happy and help each other be strong," said Nadide. "You are now Ayshe's sisters and my daughters, so let us all be good and kind to each other, always."

The girls each kissed her hand and she kissed them on both cheeks. They bid Nadide "bonne nuit," and went to bed.

When morning arrived, Nadide entered the bedroom with a tiny bell. She went to each girl's bed, tinkled the little bell, bent over and kissed her on the cheek, saying "Good morning, beautiful daughter."

A servant escorted the girls to the bathroom, where they were washed, and then returned to the bedroom where their clothes had been laid out.

When they reached the breakfast table, Nadide was already at her place, waiting for them. They were each served a small glass of hot tea, croissants, egg dishes, and *palatschinken*. "Bon appétit" Nadide said as soon as the tea was served, signaling the beginning of the meal and the start of the day.

Each morning Nadide would present the schedule for the day. After breakfast, a walk in the fresh air was the rule. In good weather, a half hour in the garden, or in rain or snow, a fast walk through the many covered corridors was taken. Various eunuchs would give them their lessons in math, history, and geography, while gifted odalisques would teach them music and dance, French, German, Persian, and help them refine their Turkish.

Ayshe and Muzzy's good nature, enthusiasm, love, and sheer joy for life helped Lebriz adjust to her new life. Although her heart still ached for her dear mommy, Nanna, and Jemil, she was able to laugh and love her newfound sisters and the gracious Nadide.

One morning the following April, a carriage pulled up to the front of New Manor. Driven by the trusted Erdal, it was carrying Nesrin and both of her brothers. Although she had regained her strength, Nesrin's grief and regret at leaving her children still kept her awake at night. She had spent most of her days huddled in a corner of her room, hiding her tears from the others. When they reached the grounds of Nejmi's home, they noticed that the gardens looked untended and that the house seemed deserted.

Kenan got out of the carriage first. "Wait for me here."

"No," said Nesrin. "I'm going with you."

"Let us take care of this, Nesrin," said Rafet, also climbing out of the carriage. "It will only upset you more to see him."

"I'm going to talk to him," she insisted. "You can't stop me. They're my children."

"Let her do it," said Kenan. "She's right. This is her business. Let her take care of it."

Nesrin walked to the door and without a moment's hesitation she banged on it as hard as she could. After a moment, Sevin, the maid, opened it.

"What are you doing here, Nesrin Hanim? You shouldn't be here. The master will get very angry."

"I must see him," demanded Nesrin. "Please bring him to me."

"I'll see what I can do," said the girl. "Please wait here." She showed them into the sitting room off the entrance hall.

A moment later, Serap burst into the room.

"What is this?" she shouted. "Who are you to come barging into my home?"

"I'm Nesrin and these are my brothers. I'm here to see my husband."

"I'm Serap Hanim, Nejmi's wife. You should be ashamed to show your face here. You abandoned your children! What right do you have to come back here and claim to be his wife?"

"Please, please," pleaded Nesrin. "Let me see him. Let me see my children!"

"My husband is not here," said Serap, her voice cold and dry.

"Then we will see Nanna and the children," said Kenan, raising his voice.

"Oh go away! There are no children here, except for the one in my belly! The mad woman, Nanna, is about here somewhere. If you can find her please take her away! I'm mistress of the manor now. Go away or I'll have you driven away by my guards."

"Where are the children, Serap Hanim?" Rafet was calm but firm.

"I don't know and don't care. Now leave!"

Nejmi, obviously drunk, waddled into the room.

"What's this?" he sneered at Nesrin. "Have you come back to your loving husband, my beautiful porcelain wife?"

"I want my children, Nejmi. Please allow me to have my children," she pleaded.

"They were becoming a nuisance so I sent them away. You will never see your children again."

Kenan strode toward him and grabbed him by the neck. "I'll kill you, you drunken lout! What have you done with them? Where are the children?"

Rafet and Erdal held Kenan back.

"It's no use, Kenan," said Rafet. "Let's get out of here."

"Yes, get out, the lot of you," said Nejmi, holding his throat. "You'll never see those brats again! They're dead, for all I know!"

Nesrin let out a cry. Kenan advanced toward Nejmi again but it was Serap who interfered this time.

"Nejmi!" she shouted. "Don't say that!"

"Why not?"

"They're not dead," Serap said to Kenan. "They were taken away. We don't know where."

Nesrin cried out again, this time with relief as Erdal held her shoulders to stop her from collapsing to the floor.

"What about Nanna?" Erdal asked. "What have you done with her?"

"Nothing," said Serap. "The old lady's gone mad. We put food out for her and she eats it like a stray dog, then she runs back into the bushes."

Kenan glared at Nejmi. "My God, how cruel can you be?"

"Get out, all of you," Nejmi yelled, barely able to stand. "Leave me in peace."

Kenan assisted Nesrin out the door. Rafet followed them. Erdal was the last to leave the room. He turned back and took one last look at Nejmi, who was still gasping for breath and having trouble standing. Serap reached over and held him by the arm.

"What a pity, Nejmi Bey," said Erdal. "You're not too long for this world."

"Get out, you peasant," Nejmi groaned, "before I break your neck."

Nesrin was just about to mount the carriage when a shadowy creature sprung out of the bushes toward her. Erdal was the first to spot the figure.

"Ho! Stop!" he shouted as the creature approached Nesrin.

Nesrin turned, startled. "What is it?

The creature lifted her veil to show her face.

"Oh my God, it's Nanna!" Nesrin cried out. The two women embraced.

"God is great," cried Nanna, "for bringing you back to me. Have you found my babies?"

She looked at Kenan, who was standing together with an astounded Erdal and Rafet.

"Has anyone found my babies?"

"Not yet," said Kenan. "But we will. Rest assured of that. Now everyone get in the carriage. Nanna, you will come with us."

"Yes, I will," said the old woman, caressing Nesrin's cheek. "God is great and I surely will go with you."

Serap watched from the window as the carriage drove away from New Manor.

As soon as they returned to Bolu, Rafet and Kenan organized search parties for the children. Messengers, travelers, merchants, and migrants were alerted to be on the lookout for an eight-year-old boy with blue eyes and a six-year-old girl with flowing, burnished copper-colored hair.

First all the townships neighboring New Manor were searched. Then the parameters were widened to include all of Eastern Anatolia and its environs. A hefty reward was offered for anyone with news or sightings of the children.

Nanna and Nesrin were tireless in their search as well. Driven by the inexhaustible Erdal, they visited many cities where they went from door to door, asking if anyone had seen any signs of the lost siblings.

Lebriz, Ayshe, and Muzzy spent their days studying and taking regular outings in the gardens. Each girl excelled in the specific field she'd been assigned to. Ayshe, like her mother, had a talent for decorating porcelain and spent much of her time painting sets manufactured at the Yildiz Palace porcelain factory. Muzzy, who had started out as a seamstress, became particularly good at designing clothes. Lebriz was the scholar and was rarely seen without a book in her hand. She was interested in learning English so an English-speaking eunuch was engaged to give her lessons.

Valide Sultan kept in close touch with the three girls. She would invite them to her rooms for tea and took great delight in hearing about their studies and the games they played together. She referred to them as "my three delightful granddaughters." It wasn't unusual for her to shower them with expensive gifts, which she'd always couch in a delightful little surprise. One time, she gave each girl a crystal bowl full of chocolates. Once the girls began to dig into their treats they discovered the actual surprises hidden within: Ayshe found a ring embedded with an aquamarine, to match her eyes. Lebriz's ring had a pearl surrounded by diamonds, while Muzzy had one embedded with an emerald. The girls were oblivious to the monetary value of these gifts. It was the care Valide Sultan took to tailor each gift especially for each one of the girls that mattered to them the most. They felt great affection for her and indeed considered her their true grandmother now.

The girls' positions as the favorites of Valide Sultan did not escape the attention of other girls in the harem. The special treatment they received, not only from Valide Sultan, but also from Nadide, was beginning to cause envy and resentment in the wider circles of the compound. Lebriz especially drew sharp stares since she was clearly the most coveted of the girls, and a protégé of both Ali Aga and Jafer.

Jafer was Lebriz's main agent and protector. He was the one who vetted her instructors and stood up for her if any of the girls teased her. Increasingly, this friendship became a subject of ridicule and gossip.

One afternoon, Lebriz and Muazzez sat in the garden practicing their French verbs, when Jafer came out with a light sweater for Lebriz. He gently placed the sweater on the girl's shoulders.

"It's getting breezy," he said. "We don't want you to catch cold."

"Thank you," said Lebriz. "I was just starting to get a little chilled."

After Jafer went inside, Muazzez and Lebriz saw three girls walking by. Surprised and delighted to see strangers in this part of the garden, Muazzez smiled and greeted them.

"Hello!"

"Hello yourself," snapped one of the girls in such a surly voice that Lebriz looked up from her book.

"Why not even a hello from the beautiful Lebriz?" snarled one of the other girls.

"Hello," said Lebriz softly, a little taken aback. The girl laughed.

"Look at you, beautiful Lebriz. Everyone says you have copper colored hair," she said mockingly.

"Yes," said Lebriz. "I inherited it from my mother."

"Tell me, are you in love with the eunuch?" the girl asked.

Lebriz was stunned to silence. What did the girl mean? Why would she say such a thing?

"Get away from here, you impertinent creature!" said Muazzez.

The three girls giggled.

"If you're not in love with him, he's certainly in love with you," said one of the other girls. "It's obvious. Everyone is talking about it."

"Who's talking about it?" asked Lebriz, her voice shaking.

"Don't mind them," said Muazzez. "She's making it up."

"What kind of husband do you think a eunuch would make?" said the third girl, and the three of them burst into laughter. Jafer came back out when he heard the commotion.

"What's happening?" he said. "What are you girls doing here? Don't you have somewhere else to be?"

"It's nothing," said Muazzez. "They're harmless. They were just leaving anyway. Weren't you girls?"

"Get out of here," shouted Jafer, sounding more ridiculous than ferocious with his falsetto voice. The girls laughed even harder and sauntered off.

"If those girls ever give you any more trouble," said Jafer as he watched them go, "you let me know and I'll take care of it right away."

Muazzez and Lebriz sat quietly for a moment after Jafer left, trying to digest what just happened. Lebriz was especially disheartened since she'd never been treated that way by anyone. She didn't understand why the girls would resent her or make fun of her. Muazzez, on the other hand, was moved with a profound desire to protect her friend. Just like everyone else, she felt Lebriz was a beautiful and fragile creature, and that she must be sheltered and handled with the utmost care.

"Don't you mind people like that," said Muazzez. "There will always be some who will resent you and hate you. Only because you're better and more beautiful than them and they're jealous."

Lebriz looked away as though her attention had already turned elsewhere. After a moment, she turned her gaze back at Muazzez and spoke cautiously.

"I want to ask you something," she said.

"What is it, my precious? You can always ask me anything."

"What is a eunuch, Muzzy?" Lebriz asked.

Muazzez was astonished to hear the question, but also saddened. Could she really not know, after almost ten years in the harem?

"Don't you know what a eunuch is, Lebriz?" she asked.

"Everyone is always saying it and laughing. Why are Ali Aga and Jafer called eunuchs? Is it because they have strange voices? And is that why they're sad all the time?"

"I'm so surprised," said Muazzez, "that you've grown up in the harem and still don't know what a eunuch is. Valide Sultan says you're too pure for this world, and she's right."

"All right don't tell me then," said Lebriz, now feeling a bit cross.

"Eunuchs are men who have been castrated," said Muzzy almost in a whisper.

"What does that mean?" asked Lebriz, not liking the sound of the word.

"It means their male organs have been cut off."

Silence fell between the two as Lebriz tried to comprehend what she'd just heard.

"Why?" she asked after a moment.

"So that they can't have intimate relationships with women. As children, their organs are cut off, or sometimes crushed with stones. That way, as adults, they pose no danger to women in the harem."

Lebriz covered her mouth to stop herself from crying out. Her eyes welled with tears of horror and sorrow.

"As children?"

"Yes. Five or six years old."

Lebriz couldn't help but let out a cry. Muazzez couldn't remember the time she herself learned what a eunuch was. For her, it had always been a fact of life. She couldn't fathom the devastation her friend was feeling at this moment.

"I'm sorry to be the one to tell you, Lebriz," she said, trying to hold her friend's hand.

Lebriz jerked her hand away as though it was touched by fire. She didn't want anyone to touch her or try to console her at this moment. The horror of what she'd just found out was so devastating that she didn't even want to look at another human.

"It's all right, my dear," said Muazzez. "It's just life. Ali Aga and Jafer are all right."

"How can you say that?" cried Lebriz. "How can anything like that ever be all right?"

"It's their fate," said Muazzez, trying to hold back her own tears. "Just like everyone else, they have their burden to bear. It's their fate."

Lebriz couldn't comprehend how her friend could say such things. She turned around and ran inside.

She remained alone in her room for the rest of the day. She tried to read but had no capacity to focus. At dinner she remained silent except to say "merci" when one of the girls served her food. Nadide and Güldane also remained largely quiet; Muazzez had told them what happened. It was only Ayshe who was oblivious. After a long, silent meal of lamb and bean stew served over piles of steaming rice, Nadide spoke cheerfully:

"Tomorrow is the big day," she announced. "We will go to the palace theater! Have you girls selected your gowns?"

"I know exactly what I'm wearing," chimed in Ayshe. "Mama please can you tell us what the play is about? I do hope it's by Molière. I love Molière so much!"

"It is even better than Molière," said Nadide. "And better than Voltaire or any other famous writer. It is a play by your father, the Sultan."

"Oh," said Ayshe sullenly, daring not to say anything more. She knew as well as everyone that the plays written by the Sultan were always long and boring and not funny at all. It would be another interminable evening at the theater where everyone would clap and pretend they enjoyed themselves.

"I wish …" she started to say against her own judgment.

"You wish what?" asked Nadide.

"I wish …" started Ayshe again, and saw the quick warning glance Güldane gave her. Still she continued.

"I wish," she said, "that my father would continue to translate the works of Molière and Voltaire and Shakespeare. I think those plays are the best."

"Are you saying those plays are superior to your father the Sultan's work?"

"Of course not," said Ayshe, now retreating. "I love going to the theater, and all plays are wonderful. I think going to the theater is the most exciting thing we do. And I know exactly the dress I will wear. And why is everyone else so quiet?" she finally asked exasperatedly.

"I suppose we're all tired," said Nadide somberly. "Why don't we all retire to our rooms for a good night's rest? And girls, make sure you lay out your clothes for tomorrow and inspect them. We don't want any last minute surprises."

The girls dipped their fingers in the bowls of water, wiped them clean with their napkins, and shuffled out of the dining room to head to bed.

Two hours after going to bed, Lebriz still couldn't fall asleep. Muazzez lay awake as well, concerned for her friend.

"You mustn't mention anything to either Ali Aga or Jafer," said Muazzez. "It's embarrassing for them, so it's best not to say anything."

"I don't want to go to the theater," said Lebriz.

"Why not?" asked Muazzez with worry in her voice. "What does the theater have to do with eunuchs?"

"Nothing. It has nothing to do with them at all. It's about the other girls and the ones who can't go. Why are we always the ones who go to the theater and get the best seats and get the prettiest dresses? No wonder they're angry at us."

"Don't be foolish, Lebriz. You can't worry about the others. Besides, turning down an invitation from the Sultan would be the ultimate insult. What would Nadide and Valide Sultan think? Now, be thankful for your good fortune and go to sleep."

The play the next evening was to be performed at the Sultan's opera house at Yildiz Palace. A great fan of poetry, theater, and opera, Abdul Hamid had translated many important works, and hosted many famous European performers at Yildiz. He was also a skilled carpenter: many of the tables, chairs, and cabinets at Yildiz were the product of his royal hand.

Generous and welcoming with guests most of his life, Abdul Hamid had grown increasingly circumspect in his later years. He'd developed a fear of spies and impending attacks, bordering on paranoia. This had caused him to be selective, even when inviting his own wives and their entourage.

The women gathered in front of the harem where carriages were waiting to transport them to the theater, not very far within the grounds. It was a great honor to be invited to witness His Royal Highness's own work of art. Tonight, they looked forward to a military-themed composition appropriately named "The Emperor's Song."

Lebriz, Muzzy, and Ayshe, accompanied by Güldane, decided to stroll down the gardens rather than riding in the carriage. Just as they were leaving, the three girls from the day before came from around the corner. One of them—the mean one, Lebriz remembered—looked especially vicious.

"Where are you all going?" she asked with venom dripping from her voice. "I assume you're all going to the theater."

"Leave us alone," said Muzzy.

"Don't you both look so pretty," sniggered another girl. "Especially beautiful Lebriz. Lebriz who dances so elegantly. Lebriz, Lebriz, Lebriz."

"We're sick of hearing about Lebriz," sneered the girl in front, pulling out a pair of scissors and grabbing a lock of Lebriz's hair.

Lebriz screamed, "Jafer Efendi!"

"No!" cried Muzzy, leaping at the girl.

She knocked the girl away with the lock of hair still grasped in her hand. The girl slashed out with the scissors, cutting a gash in Muzzy's arm and stabbing Lebriz just above the knee, before she fell to the ground.

Ayshe screamed, "Jafer Efendi! Jafer Efendi!"

Jafer ran out of the house to see the three girls running away. Ali Aga also ran out. Jafer went directly to Lebriz, who was seriously shaken but not badly wounded. Ali Aga immediately went to Ayshe.

"Are you all right, Ayshe Sultan?"

"Yes," said Ayshe. "They wouldn't dare touch me. Please make sure Muzzy is all right."

Muzzy was bleeding but her wound was not very deep. The eunuchs escorted all four of them to Nadide's apartments. They were all in shock but it was Jafer who looked like he could have a heart attack.

"My dear child, my dear girl. How dare they hurt her!" he muttered continually. The fear of any harm coming to her had jolted him to realize how deeply he cared for this little girl. She was the child he never had and he knew that he'd gladly break the neck of anyone who tried to hurt her.

When Valide Sultan and Nadide returned later that night, they were worried.

"Where were the girls? They never came to the theater. Were they lost?" asked Nadide.

"They were not lost," said Ali Aga, bowing at her. "Please come inside."

"What happened?" demanded Valide Sultan and barged in before Nadide. The three girls, still shaken, were lined up on the couch, holding hands with Güldane hovering over them.

When they were told of the attack, Nadide gasped in horror and rushed over to see if her girls were all right. Valide Sultan remained quiet for a moment seething with anger. She wasted no time.

"Gather those girls and bring them to me right away," she ordered. "Pull them out of their beds and drag them over here at once!"

It was after midnight by the time the offending girls were gathered and brought to Nadide's apartments. They hadn't been given a chance to get dressed and were in their nightgowns. Valide Sultan gathered the girls along with Ayshe, Muzzy, and Lebriz in the room.

"Are these the girls who attacked you?" she asked.

"Yes they are," answered Lebriz hesitantly, already fearing for the girls' fate. The three guilty girls sat huddled together, shaking like leaves.

"Bring me the Mistress of the Hairdressers," Valide Sultan ordered.

The girls realized what their punishment would be and threw themselves at the feet of Valide Sultan, crying and screaming for mercy.

As soon as the Mistress of the Hairdressers arrived, Valide Sultan bellowed:

"Cut off their hair and shave their heads!"

Then she turned to Lebriz, Muzzy, and Ayshe. "And the three of you watch!"

Lebriz, in tears now herself, and just as fearful as the girls, protested.

"No I don't want to stay. I'm tired. I want to go to bed."

"No," said Valide Sultan with a gentle but commanding voice. "These girls harmed you. You will sit here and watch them being punished."

Muazzez held Lebriz's hand as the servants held down the girls and shaved their heads. Once the deed was done, the girls were made to stand in front of everyone. All three of them with bare heads looked alike and it was hard to distinguish them at first. They stood there rubbing their heads as though trying to hide their nakedness. Lebriz tried to make out their features when she noticed one girl staring at her with tears rolling down her cheeks. She then recognized her as the one who spoke with such disdain and mocked her. But now Lebriz only felt sorry for her. She wanted to reach out and console the girl and assure her that her hair would soon grow back and that all would be forgotten. But then she heard Valide Sultan's formidable voice once again.

"Had you dare touch Ayshe Sultan," she said, her voice deeper than usual, "I should have had you executed immediately!"

Lebriz gasped at those words and the girls sobbed even harder.

"But I will be lenient with my punishment," continued Valide Sultan.

"All three of you will be given to the soldiers to play with and do what they wish. When they are finished with you, you will be sold to the brothels."

An gasp rose across the room. Lebriz didn't know what brothel meant, but she could tell it was something horrible. Even Güldane, who always remained stoic, had a look of terror in her eyes.

"No!" Lebriz cried out.

Jafer immediately shushed her. "Be quiet," he said.

"Take them away," ordered Valide Sultan.

The girls were quickly shuffled out of the room. Lebriz wanted to throw herself at Valide Sultan's feet and plead for the girl's forgiveness but she didn't dare. The old woman looked especially formidable and Jafer also was quite scary. Then she heard Jafer speak in a tone Lebriz had never heard before.

"Very good, Valide Sultan," said the eunuch with an ice-cold voice. "Death would have been too quick. This way they will suffer for the rest of their lives. A fitting punishment for anyone who would hurt our dear girls."

Lebriz didn't sleep that night, or the night after that. It was two days before she could leave the building and go for a stroll with Muazzez in the gardens. After wandering around aimlessly all morning, she made her way to the scullery where Jafer was helping servants stock up for the week's meals.

"What happened to those girls?" she asked, her exhausted voice shaking with dread. "Have they been given to the soldiers like Valide Sultan ordered?"

"I don't know," answered Jafer, his own voice also sad.

"If they haven't, will you please speak to Valide Sultan and beg her to forgive them? And if they've been sent, will you please ask her to bring them back?"

"There is nothing I can do, Lebriz Hanim Those girls got what they deserved."

"How can you say that, Jafer Efendi, knowing what you've been through yourself? Muzzy said what happened to you was your fate. Was this punishment those girls' fate as well?"

Jafer paused. This was a conversation he'd always wanted to avoid.

"No, my precious girl," he said softly. "They committed a wrong and deserved their punishment. My lot had nothing to do with anything I did. It was beyond my control. Therefore mine can be called fate while theirs can only be called hell."

Lebriz was once again struck by the coldness that came out of this otherwise gentle and kind man.

It was now ten years since Nesrin and Nanna came to live in Bolu and they still hadn't found any leads. Rafet, who'd been so determined at the beginning, was starting to suggest that the search was futile. This infuriated Nesrin but she kept her thoughts to herself. After all, her brothers had sheltered her, fed her, and consoled her at times of despair. She was grateful for their care but giving up the search was unthinkable.

She and Nanna continued to knock on doors and ask questions. Over time their quest shifted; no longer were they asking about two small children. Now they searched for a young man of eighteen with blue eyes and a slender woman with long, strikingly beautiful hair.

"Do you think her hair is the same color, Nanna?" asked Nesrin once.

"How can you doubt it?" said the old woman, caressing Nesrin's hair. "She has her mother's hair and that will never change."

These moments of tenderness made Nesrin realize how grateful she was to have Nanna at her side. Without her, she certainly could not have maintained hope.

It was Alev who suggested that the children might have been taken to Istanbul. "I've heard that many wealthy families recruit youngsters from villages to serve as servants in their homes."

"Don't you realize what a vast city that is?" asked Kenan, when Nesrin suggested she'd like to travel to Istanbul. "It will be worse than searching for a needle in a haystack. I will organize a search party," he said.

"I want to go as well," said Nesrin.

"They will eat you alive," Rafet countered. "Let the men do the searching. They'll let you know as soon as there's any news."

Nesrin relented, but she had already invested all her hopes in finding her children in Istanbul. In the meantime, she turned her attention to the family's youngest members. She and Nanna had become caretakers of Kenan's two young boys, and Nesrin had grown especially fond of the younger boy, Batur, who reminded her so much of Jemil. She played hide and seek with them, just as she did with her own children. Her heart broke every time she found little Batur in his hiding place and held him in her arms.

"I found you, my baby," she'd whisper to him. "See? I told you I'd find you and I did."

The boy would shriek with joy, break away, and run off to hide again.

It was on one of those afternoons when Nesrin was pretending to search for Batur when Kenan entered the house and called her name. She knew the boy was hiding under the stairs with bated breath, thrilled at the prospect of being found, but her brother's voice stopped her cold.

"Come to the drawing room," he said. "I have some news."

Minutes later she was facing her brother as he held out a piece of paper with a shaking hand.

"Look at this," he said. "It's from Jemil."

Nesrin felt her heart rise up to her throat. She felt dizzy; she could barely stand. Had she really heard those words, "from Jemil"? She held the paper but her eyes welled with tears and she couldn't read it.

"What does it say?" she asked, holding on to a chair to steady herself. "Is he all right?"

"He's all right," said Kenan, also with emotion. "He's with the Imperial army. He's been deployed to Iznik."

"To Iznik," she repeated, realizing it wasn't that far away at all.

"He's a corporal. He says when he can steal a few hours he will pay his uncle a visit."

Nesrin tried to catch her breath.

"Does he know I'm here?"

"He has no idea."

Nanna had entered by now, followed by Alev.

"Did you hear that Nanna?" said Nesrin, choking back her tears. "My boy has been found. We've found my boy!"

Nanna held Nesrin. Kenan pulled Alev close to him. Little Batur had come out of his hiding place. He stood in a corner, watching Nesrin and Nanna clutch each other and cry.

As chief eunuch of the harem, Ali Aga had a special relationship with Sultan Abdul Hamid. Every morning, after the sovereign had his breakfast, Ali Aga would join him in his offices where Abdul Hamid answered correspondence, met with his secretaries and chamberlains, and received reports from his spies. His paranoia growing by the day, the Sultan had shaped Yildiz into a self-sustaining compound. He'd built a private farm, a small artificial lake, a stable, workshops, a theater, cemeteries and an aviary—all enclosed within the impenetrable walls of a fortress. He was a lonely man with almost nobody he could trust except his mother—to whom he paid weekly visits to convey his respects—and the eunuch Ali Aga.

Ali Aga had the privilege of accompanying the Sultan on his walks every afternoon. During these walks, Abdul Hamid wanted to hear everything that happened in the harem. He took special interest in reports of rivalries and catfights among the women and eunuchs, which he invariably found amusing. Ali Aga's reports also included episodes of misconduct and immoral behavior. It wasn't unheard of for the Sultan to order a woman drowned or a eunuch hanged based on an unfavorable report from Ali Aga. While aware of the weight of his responsibility, Ali Aga also realized his influence over the sovereign's opinions and point of view. On this particular afternoon, he brought up a delicate subject.

"Have you been observing, Your Majesty," he asked, "what a lovely young woman Ayshe Sultan has grown to be?"

Ayshe had lost her baby fat by now and was blond, tall, and slender.

"Oh yes," said Abdul Hamid, with his crooked smile. "She was visiting my mother when I was there a month ago. I always knew she would be a beautiful girl."

"And what about her friends?" inquired Ali Aga. "Have you noticed them as well?"

"Her friends?" asked the Sultan. "You mean the companions Nadide took under her wing?"

"Precisely," said Ali. "Her friend Muazzez and the beautiful Lebriz."

"Should I take notice?" asked Abdul Hamid, raising his bushy eyebrows.

"They are beautiful as well. Especially the young Lebriz. She's a stunning girl with beautiful hair and a likeable personality."

"I will take notice," said Abdul Hamid. "If you think she's a good candidate."

"I certainly do," averred Ali, and modestly kept his eye to the ground as the Sultan bent over to smell a rose.

Within a week, a viewing—during which the Sultan would observe the girls through a lattice during their lessons—was arranged. Jafer was furious.

"How dare you!" he shouted at Ali Aga. "You're only doing this to gain further favors from the Sultan. To advance your own position."

"It was inevitable. He was going to see them anyway. And why not? These girls were raised in his harem. He has every right to watch them through the lattice."

"They're friends of his daughter," said Jafer. "They're like his own daughters."

"Why do you want to protect that little girl so much?" asked Ali Aga turning soft now and speaking with a kind voice. "She's a woman now. Let her live her life. It's likely that she will become a wife. Be happy for her. What better honor for a harem girl than to become the wife of the sovereign. Every girl in the harem wants that."

"Not my Lebriz," said Jafer sadly. "She's not like the others."

"Don't fool yourself," said Ali Aga. "They're all the same."

The next week saw a flurry of gossip and rumors in all areas of the harem. The Sultan's "viewing" came and went quietly but reports circulated among the women. For most of them, having been educated and carefully cultivated to capture the Sultan's favor, this viewing was devastating news. It was in the confines of the baths, where they all congregated every Wednesday afternoon, that much of the gossip took place.

"No need to be upset," said one of the women. "That girl is scrawny. The Sultan likes voluptuous women. Like me!" She lowered her towel to reveal her ample breasts and gave them a shake, which made the other women laugh.

The Sultan's subsequent visit to his mother's quarters had caused even more consternation.

"I hear the Sultan's asked for his mother's blessing," said one woman.

"No need to worry about that. She would never give it," said another.

"You never know. Valide Sultan has always had a mind of her own. She may well decide that Lebriz is the perfect next wife for her son. And why not? She's beautiful and elegant. She's talented and smart. She's the perfect choice."

"If only that eunuch would give some indication," moaned another woman, referring to Ali Aga. "He's gotten so stuck up lately."

"Shhh," said her friend. "Do you want to be thrown in the Bosphorus in a bag?"

"That's all a myth," said the first woman. "Nobody's done that in years."

"I heard Valide Sultan has already told the seamstresses to start working on a wedding gown," said someone else.

"How do you know that?" demanded a younger woman.

"One of the seamstresses told me, that's how."

"You're lying. Nobody would have the courage to tell anyone that kind of news."

"Stop it," said a middle-aged woman. "It's all gossip. Best stay quiet and see how things turn out. No use wailing and complaining and speculating. This is out of our hands."

Like many such discussions, this one also resulted in the women's acknowledgment that they had little autonomy or control.

"Yes, she's right," said one of the ladies. "We have no control so why worry about it?"

This reminder was a relief in a way. There was no use in worrying. So why not relax and enjoy the warm water, a cup of soothing tea, and a vigorous massage? The older women lay back while the young odalisques served them beverages and sweets, and played relaxing music, well into the afternoon.

None of them could have ever imagined how the upcoming events would change everything.

Lebriz and her friends had devised several games to occupy themselves during their break after a grueling morning of studies. One of their favorites was what they called the "language game." The rule was that each person had to answer a question, or maintain a conversation, in a different language. The game would often end up in gales of laughter. But today was different, and there were to be no games. The girls had also been subjected to the rumors going around the harem. One of the maids had reported to Muzzy that the Sultan had decided to make Lebriz a wife.

"How does she know this?" asked Lebriz, that familiar feeling of dread arising in her stomach.

"All the women are talking about it," said Muzzy.

"What if he chose you, Muzzy?" asked Lebriz. "Would you want to be the Sultan's wife?"

"Of course," replied the girl. "Why not? I'd be given a nice home, with eunuchs to order about. And also my son would be in line to be sovereign. What would be wrong with that?"

"And what if you didn't give birth to a son," continued Lebriz. "Like Nadide Sultan? What if you fell out of favor like her?"

"I don't think Nadide Sultan minds. She has a beautiful daughter and a beautiful home. What more could she want?"

"The Sultan scares me," said Lebriz in a whisper.

"They say he's gentle," said Muzzy. "And that he hardly talks. He's always in his study. He only comes out for walks and to do his carpentry. Also he's old, so he won't bother you so much."

Suddenly a servant girl ran up to them from the house. "Nadide Sultan wants to see you immediately," she said, trying to catch her breath.

The girls hurried back to the apartments and found Nadide in tears. Güldane was trying to console her while Jafer, looking deeply concerned, stood aside.

"Sit over here," Nadide said, motioning to the girls to sit next to her on the divan. "Güldane has some upsetting news for us."

"Valide Sultan is gravely ill," Güldane sobbed. "She's dying! She wishes to see the three of you."

The girls stood still for a moment. The prospect of someone close to them dying had not occurred to them until this point. They were at once speechless, devastated, and frightened.

"Go at once, before it's too late," urged Nadide.

Jafer escorted the three girls out of the room.

When the girls arrived at Valide Sultan's quarters, they saw that Sultan Abdul Hamid was sitting next to her. Dressed in his usual black jacket with gold braid hanging on his shoulders, the man looked ominous even at this moment of caring tenderness. His large hands, calloused from years of carpentry, rested on his mother's arm. He pointedly observed his daughter and her two companions as they entered the room.

Ayshe ran to Valide Sultan and embraced her. "Oh Grandmamma!"

Valide Sultan opened her eyes and spoke with a frail voice, "Is that my darling? Are the other girls here?"

"Of course they are. We're all here."

"Please approach," Valide Sultan lifted her head slightly. Lebriz and Muzzy crept up to her and kissed her hand.

"These three are my granddaughters," she said to her son. "They are dear to me beyond imagination."

"I understand, Mama," said Abdul Hamid as he surveyed the girls with a discerning eye. He hadn't seen the girls up close before, not even his own daughter, since she was a small girl. Now, he could even smell their sweet perfume. The one called Muazzez was delightful. She had lovely brown hair and an engaging smile. She glanced up for a moment and Abdul Hamid caught the twinkle in her eyes. She was certainly a beautiful addition to the harem but not, he thought, exactly wife material.

But then there was the other girl, the one called Lebriz. For once, Hamid thought, that foolish Ali Aga was correct. Having seen her the other day through the lattice, he'd certainly been impressed. She was lithe and elegant and he could tell that she was demure and modest. Her exceptional beauty was evident even from a distance. Seeing her up close, he couldn't help but be astonished. It wasn't only her appearance that was mesmerizing. Her simple gesture of lowering her head and brushing a strand of hair away from her face was hypnotizing.

"You must be the one called Lebriz," he said finally.

"Yes," she replied with a soft nod, keeping her eyes to the ground.

"Will you lift your head so I can see your face?"

Valide Sultan watched from the bed as the girl lifted her head and met the Sultan's eyes, and immediately recognized the expression on her son's face. She'd seen it only once or twice when he'd considered a bride. She observed young Ayshe curiously watching. Her gentle mother Nadide had been one of those women. Just as he had done with Nadide and all his other wives, Valide Sultan knew that Abdul Hamid would enjoy the girl for a time and then discard her to the recesses of the harem. She knew now that he'd already made up his mind.

"I have something to say," she said straining to sit up on her bed. "Put up my pillow," she ordered. One of the servants quickly propped her up. Now she addressed the room.

"I will tell you what these girls' fortunes will be," she said. "I wish it to be known to all present that these three girls of mine, Ayshe, Lebriz, and Muazzez are to be married to well-educated gentlemen of suitable age and position."

Abdul Hamid stood back, his expression turning from somber to shock. Valide Sultan now looked directly to her son.

"Under no circumstances are any of them to be married into a harem. Whoever marries them must swear never to take another wife or concubine. Is this understood?"

Ladies-in-waiting, servants, and eunuchs respectfully mumbled, "It is understood, Your Majesty."

"Is that understood?" she asked her son directly. Abdul Hamid felt as though he'd been slapped on the face. It was unthinkable that he'd go against his mother's will, especially in front of so many witnesses.

"Bien sûr, Maman," he finally said. "Whatever you wish."

Valide Sultan reached over and took Lebriz's hand. "They are each to have appropriate trousseaus and be accompanied by suitable servants," she continued. "Jafer will accompany Lebriz, as he took an oath to take care of her, long ago. Güldane will be with Muazzez, and Ferah will accompany Ayshe. This is my wish and decree as Valide Sultan, mother of Abdul Hamid, Sultan of the Ottoman Empire," she pronounced with as much strength as she could muster.

"Is this understood and accepted by all?" she asked, looking again at her son.

"Yes, my dear mother, it will be as you wish," he vowed.

"Yes, Your Grace," responded everyone present.

"A treasure lost," muttered Ali Aga. "A treasure lost!"

The girls each kissed Valide Sultan's hand, thanking her for her thoughtfulness.

"You've always been very kind to us, Your Grace. We all love you so very much. Please don't leave us," wept Lebriz.

"My dear little mite, what a beautiful young woman you've grown to be," smiled Valide Sultan. "As you well know, life is not always what we would like it to be. We cannot pick and choose when we are to leave this life, but be assured that I will always be with you in spirit, if not in the flesh."

Abdul Hamid quietly slipped out of the room.

Valide Sultan held on to life for another six months. During this time she selected prospective husbands for each of the girls. She picked the son of a well-known military family of royal lineage for Ayshe Sultan. He was a dashing young man by the name of Nurhan. For Muazzez, she chose a young member of the diplomatic corps. Lebriz was matched with a high-ranking civil servant from an old, well-respected Istanbul family. From her deathbed, Valide Sultan also made sure lavish trousseaus were assembled for all three of her dear girls. Once all these tasks were complete, she died peacefully in her sleep.

All the weddings were put on hold for the following three months of mourning. This was a relief for Lebriz, as she had no desire to get married. She cringed when she even heard the word marriage and the immediacy of the event made her queasy.

"Do you want to get married, Muzzy?" she asked her friend one afternoon after their music lesson.

"What do you mean, Lebriz?" Muazzez was astonished by the question. "Of course I do. Don't you?"

"No, I don't. I never did and I never will want to."

"Why not, what will you do?"

"I don't know. I'd prefer to stay here and serve Nadide Sultan rather than go off to live with a strange man."

"Well you can't do that. You have no choice. A husband has already been selected for you."

"If only I had asked Valide Sultan to spare me this marriage," cried Lebriz. "I think she would have listened to me. But now it's too late."

"I don't think so. Valide Sultan knew we would all be married—it's just the way it should be. She made sure we'd marry important men. You'll have your own home outside of the harem and you'll be free to go anywhere you'd like. Don't you want that? And there will be no second wives, Valide Sultan made sure of that. You will be the master of your own home. You will have children, Lebriz. Surely you look forward to that?"

"I'm not sure," Lebriz said, wiping her face. "I'm not sure of anything."

"You're just scared, but it will be all right Lebriz, I have no doubt about that. With your beauty and lovely presence, no man would ever mistreat you."

Lebriz looked up and tried to smile at her friend.

"Now come. Let's join the others for lunch."

Valide Sultan's death would mark the young companions' passage from girlhood to adulthood. Once they left the gilded confines of Yildiz Palace, nothing would be the same again.

At the house in Bolu, it was a day of rejoicing. Jemil was due to arrive in the afternoon and the household was in frenzy.

Alev and Nanna spent the entire morning trying to keep Nesrin calm. What would he think of her now? Would he recognize her?

Alev attempted to console her. "Of course he'll recognize you, Nesrin Hanim. You look as beautiful and elegant as ever. A child will always recognize his mother. Please don't worry."

"It's a happy day," fussed Nanna, caressing Nesrin's hair. "Don't be melancholy, my dear."

Finally, at two o'clock, the women heard a knock on the door.

"Remain here for just one more moment," said Alev. "Let Kenan greet him first."

The three women listened to the voices as the long lost nephew and his uncle greeted each other. They sounded happy and familiar, even though they'd never met each other before.

Jemil, even though many years younger than Kenan, shook the man's hand instead of kissing it in the traditional manner. Kenan, on his part, treated Jemil like a good friend. They moved to the salon to continue their conversation.

Alev nodded her head to signal to Nesrin that it was time. She gently guided her to the door with Nanna following close behind them.

When Nesrin and Alev first appeared at the portico of the salon, Jemil was in a conversation with Kenan about politics and the state of the declining empire. Jemil was speaking with animated gestures when he realized people had entered the room. He turned to look at them and saw an older woman gazing at him with tears running down her face. She looked familiar, but he couldn't quite place her. Then he noticed the hair. Slightly lighter now, the luxurious burnished copper tint was still as striking as ever. "Mommy?" he said incredulously. "Is that you?"

"My son, my precious son." He walked right into her opened arms. How much he'd grown. How handsome he'd become. She held his head and looked into his eyes. "You're still the same," she said. "You're still my little Jemil."

"Circassian men are not supposed to cry," he choked as tears rolled down his cheeks. He looked behind Nesrin and saw Nanna. She looked remarkably the same. "My God, Nanna," he blurted out.

The old woman hurried to him, caressed his cheeks, and gave him a bear hug. "My boy, my dear boy. Thank almighty Allah for reuniting us."

Jemil turned to Kenan. "Thank you, Uncle Kenan, for this most wonderful gift."

"Your mother has had quite a journey," Kenan explained. "You should all sit together and catch up, enjoy this precious moment."

Alev wiped her own tears and invited everyone into the salon, where tea and savory pastries were served.

Sitting on the couch next to him, Nesrin looked at her son with questioning eyes.

"She's all right," he said gently. She released a huge sigh of relief. She could barely speak.

"Is she? Are you sure?"

"Yes. I have reason to believe she's all right."

"Haven't you seen her?"

"Not since the day we were separated and I was sent to live at the home of Mithat Pasha."

"And what happened to her?"

"I believe she was taken to the palace."

"The palace?" asked Nesrin incredulously. "Which one?"

"I don't know. It could be any one of the Sultan's ten palaces."

"How can we find her? Can we see her?"

"Don't think I haven't tried," said Jemil. "The palaces, and especially the harems, are heavily guarded. Nobody is allowed to go near the gates, or even mention the word harem. I approached one of the palace guards and narrowly escaped being imprisoned. He told me that if I ever made such an attempt again, I could be executed."

Nesrin's eyes widened; she clasped a hand over her mouth.

"How horrible!"

"But things are changing," continued Jemil, now directing his words also to Kenan. "The Sultan is right to be worried. The empire is falling apart and our old ways are starting to give way to newer, more modern ways."

"What does it all mean?" asked Nesrin.

"Time will only tell, Mother. Right now I'm feeling optimistic and happy to be here, with you."

Nesrin finally smiled. "Allah is great. He will show us the way."

Ayshe was married soon after the mourning period was over. By royal standards, her wedding was a modest affair, with only three hundred guests invited. It was to take place in the luxurious salons and elegant terraces of the Chiragan Palace, nestled on the European shore of the Bosphorus.

This grand building was originally built as residence for the Sultan's father, Abdul Aziz. When Abdul Hamid took the throne, he refused to live in it, fearing assassination attempts from the sea. Instead, he built Yildiz Palace on the hill behind Chiragan, and connected the two buildings with a secret bridge. It was via this bridge that the Sultan travelled to attend his daughter's wedding.

Numerous ladies-in-waiting escorted Nadide and the Sultan's other wives. Güldane and Ferah were the only odalisques allowed to attend, and of course Lebriz and Muazzez were among the invited guests. The women were all heavily veiled and would travel in shrouded carriages. Ali Aga, Jafer, and two other eunuchs were engaged to guard the wedding party.

Lebriz had mixed feelings as she watched Ayshe being escorted to the carriage. She was happy for her friend but also sad to see her go. Born within the boundaries of the harem, this was the first time Ayshe Sultan would ever set foot outside Yildiz Palace.

How strange, Lebriz thought, that she walks out of the confines of the palace straight into the confines of her husband's house. Is this to be my fate as well?

Many of the other women had never left the palace since the day they had arrived. Now huddled together in the darkened carriage unable to see anything outside, they listened intently to the clopping of horses on cobbled streets. Soldiers and palace guards silently rode alongside to protect them. Lebriz and Muazzez, giddy with anticipation, sat together and clutched hands. The five-minute ride seemed interminable.

Upon arrival, the harem party was swiftly ushered into a lattice-enclosed room, constructed especially for the wedding. Located just off the main salon, it offered ample views of the party. The women rushed to the lattices, eager to watch the arriving guests, among them many European diplomats and their wives. The European women did not have veils covering their hair and even wore sleeveless gowns that exposed their arms. Lebriz gasped out loud at the sight of a woman wearing a gown that partially revealed her breasts.

"That's called a décolleté," said Nadide. "You've heard about those?"

"Yes, but ..." said Lebriz, blushing with embarrassment. "I didn't think they were so ..." She trailed off.

Other women giggled and snorted in disapproval.

"Have you ever seen anything more shameful? Makes you glad you weren't born in Europe! How outrageous to expose your skin like that. And in public!"

Lebriz wanted to turn away but she couldn't keep her eyes off of the beautiful gowns and elegant hairstyles. Would I be sorry to be born in Europe if I could wear my hair like that? she asked herself.

The Sultan was seated on a throne in the center of the room with the imam seated next to him. Footmen presented the guests one by one. The men bowed, the ladies curtsied, and then were directed to their carved gilt chairs.

Once all the guests were seated, the groom entered, escorted by two military men. Lebriz's heart skipped a beat when she first saw him. The only men she'd seen since being separated from her brother were harem eunuchs and the Sultan. How tall and slender this man was, and dressed so handsomely in his military uniform.

Muzzy and Lebriz held hands and waited anxiously for Ayshe's entrance. When the bride finally emerged, dressed in a stunning white gown designed by her mother, they both gasped. A jeweled tiara held a lace veil that covered Ayshe's face and hair.

The ladies of the harem gushed in praise, agreeing that she looked like a fairy princess. The guests rose and stood in front of a mirrored wall, opposite a virtual army of the groom's uniformed unit. The Sultan's personal guards took position against the third wall.

When the imam stood, the room fell silent. After the initial recitation of Koranic verses, the imam turned to the groom. "Nurhan Bey, do you understand and swear to uphold the conditions set forth by the deceased Valide Sultan for this marriage?"

Nurhan smiled. "I do."

"Ayshe Sultan, do you accept Nurhan Bey as your husband?"

Lebriz held her breath as she waited for Ayshe to answer. After an endless seeming pause, Ayshe finally whispered, "I do."

The two young people turned to face each other. As this was the first time they'd set eyes on each other, the salon went silent with anticipation. The groom slowly lifted the veil from Ayshe's face and they both paused as they stared at one another. Seconds later, the young couple broke into smiles, clearly pleased at what they saw. The guests applauded and an orchestra began to play in celebration of their union.

From behind the gilded lattice rose an audible sigh of relief. Nadide Sultan wiped tears from her cheeks as Lebriz and Muzzy hugged her.

"You see? He is very handsome," said Muazzez to Lebriz.

"But what if he weren't? What if he'd been ugly and mean?"

"Do you imagine our dear grandmother would have allowed that? Absolutely not. You worry too much, Lebriz."

The newlyweds approached the Sultan and kissed his hand. They then turned to Nurhan's parents. His mother, who wore a half veil that revealed her dark hair and brown almond-shaped eyes, was dressed in a stylish gown from Paris. The groom's father proudly wore his full Ottoman Pasha regalia.

"Mama, this is Ayshe Sultan, your new daughter-in-law," Nurhan announced, introducing his bride.

His mother held out her hand and Ayshe kissed it in the usual ritual. She then put a beautiful diamond and aquamarine necklace around Ayshe's neck and slipped a matching ring on her finger.

"My mother Beyza, and my father Selim Pasha," continued Nurhan.

Selim Pasha greeted the young woman with a warm smile. "They told me you were blue-eyed, Ayshe Sultan, but they failed to mention how beautiful you are."

Ayshe stepped forward to kiss his hand. "Thank you, Selim Pasha. You're very kind."

The orchestra began to play as the young couple, accompanied by the groom's parents, followed the Sultan to the dining room. As the guests took their seats around the table, the Sultan, ever fearful of crowds, slipped out quietly to return to Yildiz Palace via his secret bridge. The Grand Vizier took his place.

The feast lasted for hours. The ladies of the harem dined behind the lattice and swayed to the music until Ali Aga finally announced it was time to return. They left the celebrations chatting and giggling, each carrying a guest favor of a crystal bowl filled with chocolate-covered almonds and silver flowers.

The wedding remained the subject of discussion in the harem for weeks. The women chatted endlessly about the lavish gowns and the hairstyles, and relished in gossip about who wore what. They continued to marvel at how stunning Ayshe Sultan looked and how fortunate she was to have such a handsome husband and the kindest of in-laws.

The bride was whisked away only a day after the wedding to make her new home in Paris. Nadide Sultan, although happy for her daughter, struggled to hide her heartache. Her only solace was that Lebriz and Muazzez were still at her side, keeping her company.

A few weeks after Ayshe left the harem, Lebriz and Muzzy sat at the edge of a small pond, watching the goldfish swim through the murky water. Life had been gloomier since Ayshe's departure and even their daily walk around the garden hadn't cheered them up. Lebriz especially was feeling melancholy at the absence of her friend.

"Her humor was infectious," she lamented. "She never failed to make us laugh."

"But she's happy now," Muazzez replied, trying to sound cheery. "Can you imagine? She lives in Paris! She gets to speak French all the time and probably attends the opera at least once a week. She's happy! We should be happy for her too."

"I can't imagine she can be all that happy," mumbled Lebriz. "After all, she must be missing us a little bit too."

Lebriz looked up to see Jafer slowly walking toward them from the house. She noticed that his gait was more measured and deliberate than usual. She wondered if something was wrong. Perhaps it was her own melancholy that made her recognize the man's perpetual sadness more acutely now.

"My dear girl," he said in his soft sotto voice. "You've been looking so unhappy lately."

"I don't mean to," said Lebriz, trying to muster a smile. She realized how much she'd grown to love this gentle man, and how much she'd come to rely on his friendship and wisdom.

"She's missing Ayshe," Muazzez said, placing her hand on Lebriz's arm

Jafer looked down at the pond.

"Is something wrong?" asked Lebriz.

"I have news for you, my girls," he said, without looking at them. "Nadide Sultan has summoned you both."

Lebriz's heart sunk even lower. "What is it?"

"I don't know. You must come with me."

Muazzez took Lebriz's hand in hers. "Let's go. It can't be that bad."

The girls found Nadide near tears in the blue sitting room. Güldane was sitting next to her, trying to console her.

"What's the matter?" Lebriz cried as she and Muazzez rushed to Nadide's side.

"It's time," Nadide sobbed. "The Sultan has ordered that you will both leave me to be married within three months."

Lebriz stiffened and put her hands over her mouth.

"No! I'm not ready," she cried. "I don't want to go."

Jafer moved to her with the instinct to hold her but stopped himself. It was Muzzy who put her arms around Lebriz reassuringly.

"It can't be helped, my child," said Nadide. "It's what Valide Sultan decreed before she died. You both heard her words yourselves."

Lebriz stood erect and stared down at Nadide huddling with Güldane on the divan. "I am certain that if I'd had the chance to talk to Valide Sultan about this, she would have agreed to me not getting married. I'm sure of it."

"I love you girls more than my own heart," said Nadide, her eyes heavy with sorrow. "Please don't make this more difficult than it already is." She took a few deep breaths and then spoke calmly. "Within two weeks, you will both leave me to go stay with your guardian families."

"Guardian families?" said Lebriz. "Why?"

"Your guardian families will allow you to experience the outside world in ways you never could while living in the harem. The Sultan's agents have selected prominent families for you both. They will welcome you into their homes and prepare you for your weddings. Jafer will go with Lebriz and Güldane will accompany Muazzez."

Lebriz despaired at the finality of these words but she also felt oddly optimistic. She hated the idea of leaving Nadide Sultan and being separated from her dear Muazzez and Güldane and she certainly did not want to get married. But the prospect of living outside the harem, even for a few weeks, gave her a glimmer of hope. Perhaps this would give her the opportunity to search and find her mother and brother after all.

The palace seamstresses worked overtime over the next couple of weeks to design and execute the girls' wedding gowns and clothes. They used luxurious fabrics and the highest quality of materials imported from all over the world. In addition to dresses, they made coats, silk veils, peshtemals, soft shoes and undergarments lined with delicate lace. To this were added sets of linens, towels, and mother of pearl inlaid clogs. Dining sets manufactured at Yildiz Palace's very own porcelain factory were added to complete the trousseaus.

Lebriz and Muazzez clung to Nadide as they watched their trunks being loaded onto wagons. Even though they were to travel only a few kilometers from the palace, they all realized that they might never see each other again.

"I feel as though my heart is being torn from me," wailed Nadide. "I cannot bear it."

Muazzez turned to Lebriz and hugged her. "My dear little sister, if you ever need me, just send me a note with Jafer and I will fly to your side."

"What am I to do without you?" sobbed Lebriz. "This is all so wrong!"

Jafer took Lebriz's hand and led her to her carriage. Muazzez climbed into the other carriage where Güldane was waiting for her. A heavy silence fell over both as the great doors of the harem slowly closed behind them.

Sitting across from her, Jafer could barely look at Lebriz, his sadness was so great. She remembered the day she and Muazzez first entered the harem, as though it were only yesterday. They were such frightened little girls. What might fate have in store for them now? Were they leaving one golden cage just to enter another? She muttered a little prayer, then silently repeated, "I will be strong, I will be strong."

Jemil felt strangely energized when he returned to Istanbul. The reunion with his mother had given him an optimistic outlook, not only toward his own future, but oddly, also toward that of his country.

Raised in the home of the venerable General Mithat Pasha, Jemil had joined the military as soon as he graduated from the French Lycée Galatasaray. He'd been sent to boarding school at ten years old, two years after he was introduced to his adoptive family. His formative years were spent traveling between the cold, cavernous buildings of the lycée—from dormitory to study hall, refectory to classroom—always under the stern watch of Jesuit frères. These men seemed to dismiss all the foibles, desires, and hopes of the boys under their care. "Hardship is what will make you a man," was the philosophy, and heavy-handed discipline was its practice.

Jemil excelled in sports and history, but didn't do well in the sciences. He was also a bit of a rebel and his behavioral grades were less than perfect. After each Saturday morning's class, students were given report cards and made to line up at the wall according to their grades. The last student called, the one with the lowest grades, was usually Jemil. He felt humiliated to be the last one to rise from his desk and walk to the end of the line while all other boys watched him. What stung even more was being left behind on Saturday afternoons when other students were sent home to spend time with their families.

For his first two years, the weekends spent alone in the monastic building devastated him. By the third year, he had developed a stoic—if not cold—attitude toward his adopted family. Still, feelings of anger and resentment, particularly directed toward Mithat Pasha and the establishment he represented, continued to fester in his soul.

Joining the military came as a relief. Because he was a member of a prominent household, and a graduate of a prestigious school, he was automatically assigned the rank of corporal and put in charge of five hundred men. This was liberating for Jemil. Not only was he no longer the abandoned boy who suffered the weekly humiliation of failure, he was now in charge of a garrison of men who looked up to him.

His soldiers came mostly from rural peasant backgrounds. They had no formal education and knew little of the world. Even the ones who were raised in cities were illiterate. Army life was harsh, especially for the lower-ranked men. Many officers expected blind obedience from the troops and felt no need to explain or justify their orders. Jemil knew early on that this was not the kind of leader he was going to be.

Even though these soldiers, like Jemil, endured hardship with a stoical outlook, it was evident that morale was low. The empire had suffered heavy defeats on all fronts since the Russo-Turkish war. Coined by the continent as the "Sick man of Europe," it was in steep decline. The military, which the Sultan had made every effort to reform, had become disillusioned and stagnant. The army had grown large and disorganized, and it seemed impossible to create a sense of unity. Jemil did his best to boost his men's self-esteem but the general dissatisfaction directed toward the Sultan and his government continued to grow. Slowly he began to search for paths toward a solution.

Rumors were going around about a group of students and military cadets meeting secretly to discuss government reform. Curious to know more, Jemil decided to go to a meeting. What he found were a group of angry and passionate men, determined to end the Sultan's absolute rule. Jemil found the energy of the group infectious, their anger exhilarating, and their ideas exciting. Fully aware that he could be accused of treason, he began to attend the meetings regularly.

"The Ottoman Freedom Society," as they began to call themselves, was actively recruiting volunteers from the regions. Jemil was heartened to see that people from many ethnicities—Muslims, Jews, Christians, Armenians, Bulgarians, Kurds, and Arabs—stood together around a single cause. Their optimism grew as their numbers increased. Little did they know that these modest beginnings would change the course of history.

As daily amenities of clothes and food began to run even shorter in supply, Jemil realized that most of his men hadn't visited or seen their families in many months. Some of these men had wives and children. Against the advice of his superiors, he introduced a program that would allow small groups of men to take short leaves to visit their families. Even though their turn might not come for a while, the men were overjoyed at the prospect. Many of them stopped by Jemil's tent to offer their gratitude. After the first group of five men left, one of the soldiers gently approached him.

"May I have a word, Jemil Efendi?"

"Of course, soldier. What is your name?"

"My name is Firat, and I want to ask you, sir, since you've been so generous with your men, if you have a family of your own?"

"I don't have a family," said Jemil, surprised at the man's audacity.

"No wife, no children?" asked Firat.

"No," said Jemil, now getting irritated.

"And what about parents? Surely you must have parents waiting for you somewhere?"

"What business is this of yours?" Jemil snapped. "How dare you come in here and ask me such questions? Aren't you aware of your position at all?"

The man seemed unaffected by Jemil's outburst. "You should take some time to see your family also," he continued. "Seeing your family will make you stronger. You must stay strong for your men."

"Get out," said Jemil. "Don't let me see you again."

He dismissed the exchange as insignificant, and went about his daily business, but Firat's words kept echoing in his mind, especially when he lay in bed.

"No family," he muttered to himself. "Not even a wife. Not even a mother and father. And no prospects of marriage or any family life of my own."

He realized he hadn't thought about his mother in quite some time. He'd even given up on any hope of ever reuniting with his sister. When he was old enough he'd started to visit the different palace gates. He was turned away from all of them and given warnings, and once he'd been chased away with guns and sticks.

When he'd approached Mithat Pasha and asked for his help in finding Lebriz the man dismissed the idea:

"It's no use son. She lives in the Sultan's harem; you'll never find her. Be assured she has a wonderful life. She probably wants nothing to do with you."

Even though he knew in his heart that these words were not true, Jemil stopped trying after that.

Tossing around in bed one night, a thought occurred to him. I will travel to Bolu to meet my uncles Kenan and Rafet. I'm sure they can help me to recruit more men for our cause.

PINK MANSION

Once outside the gates of Yildiz Palace, the carriages carrying the young women, along with their accompanying wagons, went their separate ways. Muazzez and Güldane's carriage was headed to Shishli, a district where most of the foreign diplomats had their homes, while the carriage carrying Lebriz and Jafer was to travel half an hour to a house known as the Pink Mansion.

Lebriz, feeling nervous, held on to Jafer's hand as the carriage arrived at the grand house. Ornate gates opened wide and a short driveway led them to the entrance where two well-dressed African slaves met them.

Opening the door of the carriage, the servants bowed and said, "Welcome to Pink Mansion, home of Orhan Pasha and Rengin Hanim."

Realizing that the servants were eunuchs, Lebriz glanced quickly at Jafer. He felt her glance but simply looked away. The two eunuchs removed Lebriz's many chests as the passengers climbed up the steps to the door of the mansion.

A short chubby man with streaks of gray at his temples appeared in the doorway. "Welcome, Lebriz," he said, with a wide smile. "We've been looking forward to your arrival."

He took her hand and kissed it lightly, in the European fashion.

"I am Orhan Pasha, member of the Divan and Adviser to His Royal Highness, the Sultan."

The man's kind gaze helped to put Lebriz at ease. She took his hand, lifted it to her lips and then to her forehead. As she looked up, she saw a petite lady approaching them. She too had a lovely smile and a kind face. Lebriz took notice that her hair was arranged in an intricate style she'd admired so much at Ayshe's wedding.

"This is my wife, Rengin," said Orhan Pasha.

Sensing very quickly that she'd just met a generous mentor, Lebriz bowed, and gently took the woman's hand to show her respect in the usual manner. They were led into the house.

"This is quite an auspicious meeting," said Orhan Pasha as they approached the salon. "You may be surprised to learn that I had the privilege of meeting your grandfather Mustafa Bey many years ago."

Lebriz was startled, unsure how to react to this declaration.

"A group of us were sent to New Manor by the Sultan, to praise the heroic work the Circassian guards had done at the border," Orhan Pasha explained. "Three of those men lived at the Manor. Your father was one of them. This was before you were born, of course, and before your Uncle Bedri was so tragically martyred."

Rengin saw Lebriz's eyes begin to fill with tears. She put her arm around the girl's waist. "What a pleasure to have you here, Lebriz, and what a lovely name for such a beautiful young lady. I hope you'll be happy during your stay with us. I think we'll have a grand time. I'd love to take you shopping and introduce you to our friends and family. Would you like that?"

"I'd like that very much," Lebriz replied, the color now returning to her cheeks.

The mansion was smaller than Yildiz Palace but almost as opulent with its crystal chandeliers and gilt furniture upholstered in silk. Gleaming parquet floors, adorned with luxurious Persian rugs, ran through the house.

Rengin led Lebriz up the curved staircase to her rooms on the second floor. A young lady's maid greeted her as she entered a bright sitting room decorated in yellow and white. Rengin introduced the young woman as Selma.

"She will bathe you and dress you and help arrange your hair. She's very skilled at arranging hair," smiled Rengin.

Selma lowered her eyes. "Welcome, Lebriz Hanim," she said almost inaudibly, clearly in awe of Lebriz's beautiful hair. "I hope I'll be able to please you."

Moved by the girl's modesty, Lebriz smiled. She couldn't have been more than one year younger than she. Then she turned and observed the room. It was lavish and beautiful but there was only one bed.

"Will I sleep here alone?" she asked apprehensively.

"Selma will sleep in the room right next to you," said Rengin, motioning at the girl to open the door to the smaller adjoining room.

"And you also have your private bath."

Lebriz was suddenly struck with the realization that she'd never slept alone in a room before in her life. Her heart sank as she thought Muzzy wouldn't sleep and wake with her anymore, and that Nadide wouldn't wake them with the tinkle of a tiny bell and a "Good morning, my beautiful daughters."

Once the trunks were carried upstairs, Selma carefully opened and began to unpack them.

Lebriz sat down and observed the girl. It was a few minutes later that another maid came and asked Lebriz to join her hosts for lunch.

The dining room, like the salon, was a smaller version of that of Nadide Sultan's at Yildiz Palace. Lebriz took comfort to see that the dining table was almost a replica of the one where she, Muazzez, and Güldane sat around and ate many a meal, listening to Nadide Sultan's stories. When she mentioned this to Rengin, she was told that Orhan Pasha often entertained government representatives as well as foreign diplomats and that the table could extend to seat twenty guests or more.

The next few weeks were a whirlwind of new experiences for Lebriz. One afternoon, Rengin took her to the famous shopping district of Beyoglu where French boutiques lined the street. European visitors as well as wealthy Ottoman families shopped here for many exotic wares including Chinese silk, Belgian lace, Russian furs, and Moroccan leather.

On the way, Lebriz stared at the many fountains, mosques, and churches from within the confines of the carriage. Once the carriage stopped Jafer helped them step gingerly down onto the pavement, Lebriz felt vulnerable. The street was crowded with throngs of people, most of them men. Aside from the eunuchs in the harem—and the gracious Orhan Pasha she'd just met—she'd never been this close to men since she entered the palace. She'd only observed them from a distance through lattice walls, as though they were wild animals. Her heart palpitated as she stepped down and kept her gaze to the ground. Men made way for them as Lebriz followed Rengin down the street. She was struck by a pungent odor emanating from the men as they passed in close proximity—such a striking contrast it was to the sweet perfumed scents of the harem.

Lebriz became all too aware that men took notice of them as she and Rengin walked down the street. Some men even nodded and gave appreciative smiles. Shopkeepers followed them and tried to interest them in their goods and wares. Rengin took it all in stride and seemed to enjoy the attention while Lebriz couldn't help but feel she was surrounded by a pack of wolves.

Rengin stopped by the Italian shoe shop to order the custom-made footwear for her husband, joking lightly to Lebriz that Orhan Pasha had no idea where his shoes came from.

After the customary greetings and offerings of tea were made and politely accepted, Rengin opened her purse to give the man a wad of bills. Lebriz watched curiously, as she'd never actually seen money before, let alone understood what it was for. As they were served tea and sweets in the shop, Rengin explained to Lebriz how money was earned, and what it could be used for. She also told her that the Sultan had endowed Lebriz with a purse of gold—which would be presented to her on her wedding day—and a generous allowance to Orhan Pasha to be spent on the wedding.

Anytime she heard the words "wedding" or "marriage," Lebriz felt the familiar lump rise in her throat. No matter how many outings Rengin took her on, or how many fascinating people she was introduced to, her apprehension over the prospect of marriage never seemed to abate. All she could do was to ignore her worries and hope against hope that the time would never come.

Once a month, Rengin hosted a visitor's day for friends and acquaintances to drop in for tea and refreshments. It was usually a lively affair, with women coming and going throughout the afternoon, engaging in delightful conversation and gossip. They took great interest in Lebriz, commenting on how charming she was, and how elegant and beautiful. They were all amazed that she spoke so many languages.

One woman in particular, Madam Janet, took a special interest in Lebriz. From a well-established Armenian family, Madam Janet had her finger on the pulse of the community. She was charismatic, always knew what was going on, and could always be trusted to bring the latest news and the sweetest gossip. She was a sort of walking newsletter and the ladies loved her.

Madam Janet showered Lebriz with questions. "How were you raised? What was life at the harem like? How did you get to Yildiz Palace?" And, most pointedly, "How did a girl as beautiful as you escape the Sultan's attentions?"

Lebriz blushed and answered as many questions as she could. She explained how she and her dear Muazzez were raised as companions of Ayshe Sultan and were considered granddaughters of the Sultan's mother. And how Valide Sultan had decreed that they be married into good families. "Ayshe Sultan was the first to get married," Lebriz said longingly of her friend.

"How unusual," Madam Janet replied with great interest. "And what happened to the other girl?"

"All I know is that she and her companion were sent to the household of a diplomat where Muazzez will be prepared for marriage. I miss them both so much and hope they are in a home as welcoming as this one."

"Do you know the name of this diplomat?" asked Madam Janet, her curiosity piqued even further.

"I believe his name is Hilmi Bey," said Lebriz.

Madam Janet raised her eyebrows and considered this. She did, indeed, know of a diplomat who went by the name Hilmi, who lived with his mother.

Her eyes wide, Lebriz waited with a glimmer of hope. "I'll see if I can find something out," said Madam Janet, clearly already formulating a plan.

"Thank you, Madam Janet. You're very kind."

That evening, as soon as Madam Janet returned home, she checked her calendar. Just as she'd suspected, Hilmi's mother Suna Hanim hosted her visitor's day on the first Tuesday of each month. She would attend this event the following week and use her best skills to find out as much as possible about Lebriz's friend Muazzez.

While Madam Janet tried to find news of Muazzez, a search for Lebriz was taking place all over Istanbul. Nesrin and Nanna, assisted by Erdal, continued to try to penetrate the sanctum of various royal harems, but to no avail. They parked their carriage close to the harems and pursued anyone—eunuchs or servants—venturing outside the harems' walls.

But no one would talk. They all knew the punishment for revealing any information about the harem to an outsider would be jail or even death. Nesrin still refused to give up.

The following Tuesday, Madam Janet was at the door of house in Ayazpasha, an area on a hill with stunning views of the Bosphorus. Suna lived in a well-endowed house in a respectable neighborhood, though perhaps not as posh as that of the Pink Mansion.

Her visitor's days were popular. When Madam Janet arrived she found many women gathered around in a wide circle in the salon, drinking coffee and tea. She placed herself strategically close to Suna, where she could engage her host in light gossip.

"I met this lovely young girl," she said. "She was brought up in the palace, and now lives with the honorable Orhan Pasha and his wife Rengin. She's a refined and articulate young woman by the name of Lebriz."

At this moment, a young servant asked Madam Janet how she would take her coffee. Madam Janet looked at the young woman's face and noticed her deep blue eyes. She was holding a tray with some plates of sweets and her hand was shaking.

"Plain, please," she said. "No sugar."

The servant nodded and walked away.

"That's unusual," replied Suna. "Most of those girls coming out of the palace are not remarkable creatures. After all, they are the Sultan's leftovers. He has no use for them so he sends them away, like stray cats," she said, waving her hand dismissively. "For the most part, they're good for nothing but ordinary house service."

"Well, that's not the case this time," said Madam Janet, hoping to extract information about Muazzez. "I understand she had a friend with her, but the other girl was sent elsewhere."

"It happens," Suna nodded. "The poor creatures get scattered all around the city and provinces."

Then she promptly changed the subject to the upcoming Cercle d'Orient Ball and wondered if Madam Janet would attend.

Several minutes later Madam Janet was feeling a bit frustrated that she hadn't extracted anything of significance. She resumed light gossip with the woman to her left when the young servant approached her with the tray holding a demitasse of coffee. When Janet reached to pick up the cup that had been offered to her, the girl quickly whispered in her ear: "Please tell Lebriz."

Startled, Madam Janet looked up but the girl averted her eyes, turned and walked away. Madam Janet looked around to see if anyone had noticed. Satisfied that Suna and the others had been oblivious to the servant's message, she tried to calm herself. She had no idea what to do with this turn of events. When she lifted her cup, she noticed a small piece of neatly folded paper on the saucer. Looking around again to make sure nobody saw this, she hastily slipped the note into her handbag.

"The coffee is delicious," she quipped at Suna after taking her first sip. Propriety required her to visit for the rest of the afternoon, which dragged along with news of weddings, engagements, and various other gossip. Dying to read the note in her purse, she didn't dare take it out until she was in the safe confines of her carriage, on her ride home.

Early the next morning, Madam Janet appeared at the door of the Pink Mansion. The servant who greeted her was puzzled because it wasn't visitor's day.

"Get me Orhan Pasha," she commanded.

"He's not available—" the servant began to speak.

"Get him anyway," fired Madam Janet, "and get Lebriz and Rengin Hanim as well. Quickly!"

Less than a minute later Rengin entered the sitting room, closely followed by Lebriz.

"What is it, Madam Janet? Are you all right?"

"Oh my dears, my dears, I'm so distressed!"

Knowing Madam Janet's proclivity for high drama, Rengin was skeptical. "What is it? What's happened?"

"This note is for you, my darling," she told Lebriz as she handed her the piece of paper, with a slight tremble in her hand. "Please read it first, and then I'll tell you what happened."

Lebriz held the note delicately for a second before she very carefully opened it. A look of fright came over her face as she read it in silence. She turned pale as tears gathered in her eyes.

"What does it say?" asked Rengin as Orhan Pasha entered the room and stood aside.

"Oh my God!" Lebriz cried, her hands now also beginning to tremble.

"What does it say, my darling?" Rengin urged.

"Read the note," Orhan Pasha said with a firm tone.

"Please help us," Lebriz read with difficulty. "We're in danger. Help us, please!" She broke into tears.

"Do you recognize the handwriting?" asked Madam Janet, grasping for the note.

"Yes. It's Muzzy's hand."

Madam Janet explained how she had come to receive the note at Suna's house.

"I'm afraid Valide Sultan's people did not do a good job researching this family, Orhan Pasha," Madam Janet said, her voice rising with emotion. "Clearly these young women are in great distress, perhaps even enslaved and tortured or, god forbid, even raped!"

Lebriz let out a cry. "What can I do? What can I do to help them?"

"Madam Janet, please come with me, we will get to the bottom of this matter," said Orhan Pasha. She quickly followed him out of the room, leaving Rengin to try to console Lebriz.

Orhan Pasha and Madam Janet spent half an hour behind closed doors. During that time he questioned her closely on what she knew about the family. He asked which district the house was in and whether there were any guards protecting it.

"I hope you can help them," pleaded Madam Janet in her overdramatic way.

"I will do what I can," said Orhan Pasha. "Thank you for bringing us this difficult news."

Within hours, Orhan Pasha was at the door of Suna's home in Ayazpasha, accompanied by two policemen. Suna seemed agitated when she met them at the door.

"I want to see your son Hilmi," said Orhan Pasha.

The woman immediately retreated, then returned with Hilmi at her side. The man looked disheveled, with uncombed hair and bags under his eyes, dressed in a dirty shirt.

"What is it?" he asked. "Who wants to see me?"

"You've betrayed your promise to Valide Sultan," said Orhan Pasha. "What have you to say for yourself?

"I've done no such thing," said the man belligerently. "Tell me your business and get out of my house."

"The two girls who were sent here to be under your care until they're married," said Orhan Pasha. "We want them back."

"Oh, them," said Hilmi dismissively. "You can have them. They were more trouble than they're worth anyway."

Orhan Pasha could barely control his temper. He could have strangled the creature with his bare hands if he hadn't more important business to take care of. "Bring them to me at once. Before my men arrest you."

"As you please," Hilmi snorted as he left the room.

Suna glared defiantly at Orhan Pasha, who wouldn't even deem to look at the woman.

Minutes later, Orhan Pasha sat in the carriage across from Muazzez and Güldane. Both wrapped in blankets, the girls clung to each other. They shook with fear, unsure of what was in store for them next.

"You're safe now," said Orhan Pasha. "Lebriz is waiting for you at the Pink Mansion."

The girls continued to cling to each other, saying nothing. They held up their hands to shield their eyes from the light.

Lebriz could hardly believe her eyes when she first saw her friends. Their faces were dirty and their clothes were in tatters. She saw none of Muazzez's smile and optimism she'd admired so much in their early days. Güldane looked worn and defeated. The girls hugged Lebriz without speaking a word. They seemed to be in shock that they'd been rescued.

After a moment, Rengin spoke gently. "Why don't we take the girls upstairs and give them a bath and find them some clean clothes. I'm sure they're hungry and in need of rest."

Muazzez and Güldane looked at Rengin's gentle face for the first time. "Thank you," Muazzez finally said. "Thank you so much."

Güldane had a remote look in her eyes and remained silent. Muazzez took her by the hand as Lebriz accompanied the girls up the stairs to take their baths.

Lebriz was shattered to hear the story Muazzez had to tell. She gently wiped the dirt from the girls' faces and helped them dry their hair after their baths. The three friends sat together for a long time.

"We were beaten," Muazzez uttered between sobs, "and forced to dance, half naked, in front of many men. We were told that if we didn't obey orders we would be sent to a brothel."

"A brothel!" Lebriz cried out, remembering the horrible fate of the girls from the harem.

"I was spared being raped because I was told I'd bring a higher price as a virgin." Muazzez sobbed harder.

Terrible thoughts ran through Lebriz's mind as she looked at her two friends. Güldane remained still, with no visible emotion. Had she also been spared, Lebriz wanted to ask. But then, seeing Muzzy glance at Güldane and shake her head, it dawned on her that Güldane had not been as fortunate.

Lebriz's anguish was so great that she had to avert her eyes. She wondered if Güldane would ever recover her lovely smile.

Two days passed before the young women felt safe enough to leave their room. Lebriz stayed with them the entire time, just sitting with them quietly. There were no words to describe the utter sadness she felt for her friends, and the anger that was brewing in her heart.

It was on the third day that Güldane and Muazzez finally joined the family at the dinner table. Orhan Pasha had arranged for them to move to his good friend Semih Pasha's house where he knew the family would be safe and well treated. Lebriz was already worried about putting her friends through another change.

The usual feast was served, starting with chicken soup, and followed by a variety of vegetables and meat. Lebriz watched Muzzy take a sip of her soup and was reminded of the innocent days the three of them had spent at Nadide's apartments. Tonight's dinner was certainly more sober. Everyone remained quiet. Only the clinking of silver against porcelain broke the silence. Lebriz felt if she even attempted to say a word, she'd break down in tears. She was grateful for Orhan Pasha's generosity and open heart—but why did her friends have to be moved away so soon after they'd been reunited?

Rengin decided to break the silence. "Preparations for Lebriz's wedding are well under way." She glanced at Lebriz who was looking down at her plate. "Of course, we'd like you girls to participate, as part of the family. I would think that would be most appropriate," she said, looking at her husband, hoping for him to back her up.

"Certainly," Orhan Pasha agreed. "We wouldn't have it any other way."

Everyone turned to Lebriz for a reaction but she remained staring down. Then in a raspy voice she muttered, "I don't want to get married."

"What did you say, my darling girl?" asked Rengin, even though she'd heard Lebriz perfectly well.

"I don't want to get married," Lebriz repeated, this time looking up and speaking with a clear voice.

"What do you mean, my dear?" said Rengin, now panic rising in her voice. "Preparations are well under way! Your trousseau is complete, the guests have all been invited, and we've reserved the most beautiful ballroom in all of Istanbul."

"No!" Lebriz shouted, raising her voice for probably the first time in her entire life. She pushed her chair back and rose. "I don't want to get married! If you have a heart, you won't make me do this. Please. Don't make me do this!"

She ran out of the room, leaving Orhan Pasha, Rengin, and the two girls stunned into silence.

Lebriz ran through the halls in search of Jafer. She found him in his room, in the far reaches of the mansion, where he spent most of his time in quiet solitude. He rose when Lebriz burst desperately into the room.

"What's the matter, Lebriz Hanim?" he asked, alarmed. "What's happened to you?"

"I can't bear it," she sobbed. "I can't bear the cruelty of men! My own father was a beast and now this? I can't bear what they've done to my friends, Jafer Efendi. I don't know what to do. I told Rengin Hanim I refuse get married. Please help me. You've always helped me. Please tell me what to do," she sobbed.

"Sit here, my child," he said, motioning her to join him as he sat on the bench..

"The cruelty of men is the way of the world, my dear. Most people cannot escape it. The only remedy to this curse is time. All it takes is time."

She looked at the man's face. He hadn't changed at all since she had seen him for the first time on that awful night. He'd looked so frightening to her then, but was such a comfort to her now.

"When I look at you," she said, "all I think about is the horrible thing that happened to you. But you won't talk about it. You don't acknowledge it. How can you be silent over such an injustice?"

"You mustn't weep for me, my lady. My life is what it is. There is no point in complaining about it now."

"But I weep all the time! Whenever I think about it, I weep."

"I don't think anyone's ever wept for me," Jafer said, now deeply moved. He took a pause and then continued. "For many years, all I dreamed of was revenge." His voice grew harsh. "My father, who sold me for a few pieces of silver, knew full well what would happen to me."

Lebriz heard hatred in his voice. "The pain over that betrayal was a hundred times worse than any physical pain I endured after that. For many years I could think of nothing but finding him and cutting him into small pieces—just like what those men had done to me—and to watch him suffer."

"Then what happened," she asked. "Please don't tell me you forgave him."

"No," he continued. "I didn't forgive him. A few years ago I learned that he'd been caught in a fire. He burned to death and suffered horribly. Perhaps it's wrong, but I rejoiced in his suffering and death. And now I am at peace."

"I could never forgive my father," she said. "For what he did to me and my mother and brother."

"Life will take turns you never suspected," said Jafer. Then he spoke reassuringly:

"There is only one thing you can be certain of in this life, Lebriz Hanim," he said. "And that is that I will never abandon you. I will always be there and will protect you from any harm. I will always follow you wherever you go and whatever decisions you may make. You can be certain of that."

Rengin was near devastated. She had no idea what to do. Orhan Pasha had already rented the fashionable Pera Wedding Salon for the reception and dinner. Invitations had been delivered. Should all of that be canceled? And worst of all, what would they tell the groom's family?

"Idil will be shattered," she told Orhan Pasha. "This is the one thing she was looking forward to after the loss of her husband. And what about the boy?" she cried. "These people have been friends of ours all these years. How will we face them ever again?"

"We are not canceling the wedding," Orhan Pasha replied. "It's out of the question. This wedding will go forward."

"But how?" she wailed. "Will you force the poor girl to do this?"

"You must talk with her. She's afraid, but she doesn't understand what's at stake. Tell her about Nazif and his family, and warn her of the consequences if she refuses this marriage."

"What about the other girls?" Rengin demanded. "What are we to do with them?"

"The three girls comfort each other. They're welcome to stay as long as they'd like."

She rose to leave.

"And please make them eat something," he added before she left the room. "They must be starving up there."

Lebriz had been shut up with her friends in their room in the far west pavilion of the house since dinner the night before. Güldane had still not uttered a word and Lebriz remained distraught. It was Muazzez who became the emotional caretaker for both of them. She stroked Güldane's cheek and brushed Lebriz's hair.

"I wish it were always like this," she said. "Just like at the harem. I wish we would never be separated again."

There was a soft knock on the door. Quietly, Rengin opened the door and entered, followed by a servant carrying a tray of food.

"You must be so hungry," she said. "Please allow us to bring you some food."

Lebriz and Güldane didn't answer but Muazzez nodded at Rengin, indicating that it was all right for her to join them.

A small side table was brought to the middle of the room on which the servant placed the tray of bread, various cheeses, olives, and fruit. Rengin motioned to the servant to leave and then sat on the edge of the bed.

Muazzez placed slices of bread on plates and gave one to Güldane and the other to Lebriz. She took a plate for herself and began to eat. Güldane ate a little, but Lebriz left her food untouched and refused to take her eyes off the floor in front of her.

"Eat something, Lebriz, please," urged Rengin. "At least have a piece of cheese."

The girl spoke without looking up. "I'm so ashamed. I've ruined everything. You and Orhan Pasha have been so kind to me and I've betrayed you. I'll never forgive myself."

"I realize you're afraid," said Rengin softly. "Terrible things have happened to your sisters. But I assure you, these are not what will happen to you."

"How can you be so sure? I don't even know this man. What if he is cruel, like the others? What if he's just like my father?"

"We have known Nazif since he was a boy. Idil Hanim is a personal friend of our family. She and Nazif have been in grief since Nazif's father died, three months ago. They are very much looking forward to this wedding and I assure you, they are good people. Orhan Pasha and I both made sure of that."

"Do I have a choice?" Lebriz asked, after a moment.

Rengin took a pause. "My darling, Valide Sultan was very careful to make a decree before she died. Unfortunately, it was not for the best for Muazzez and Güldane, but she did this to protect you from her son. The Sultan had his eye on you, and if it hadn't been for Valide Sultan's decree, you would be a concubine at the harem, preparing to be one of his wives. Is this something you'd have wanted? Do you think the Sultan will stand aside once he finds out this wedding is called off? He will surely come after you. What will you do then?"

"I will escape," said Lebriz, through her tears. "Jafer will help me. We will go away together. All I've ever wanted was to find my mother. He will help me find her. I know he will."

Rengin took another long pause. "Neither Orhan Pasha, nor I, will stop you from making your choice, but for your own sake, please think about this very carefully. Consider the alternatives and what will happen to you, then make a decision, my darling, that you are prepared to live with."

She stood up to leave. "Orhan Pasha and I will be waiting."

The three girls sat quietly for a few moments. Muazzez ate some more food. This time it was Güldane who served Lebriz, making sure to include some black olives, which she knew Lebriz liked very much.

She spoke hesitantly. "Do you want to have children Lebriz?"

These were the first words Güldane had uttered since she'd arrived at the Pink Mansion. Lebriz looked at her friend and started to cry.

"I know you've always wanted to have children of your own," continued Güldane.

"Have I ever said that to you?" Lebriz asked, wiping the tears from her cheeks.

"No, you haven't. But you didn't have to. I've watched you yearn for your family over the years. You should think about the beautiful children you will have, and how happy they will be."

Lebriz continued to cry.

"Eat," said Muazzez, holding an olive up to Lebriz's lips.

She accepted the olive between her slender fingers and considered it for a moment before finally eating it.

As the date for the wedding approached, Orhan Pasha and Rengin continued to be concerned about Lebriz. She seemed to have become resigned to getting married but was clearly downtrodden and afraid. Since it was out of the question for her to meet her future husband before the nuptials, Rengin suggested that they invite Nazif's mother Idil to come and meet the new bride. Orhan Pasha agreed with this plan. He also decided to invite his friend and colleague Semih Pasha and his wife Filiz to visit on the same day so they could meet Muazzez and Güldane, whom they'd agreed to host.

Semih Pasha and Filiz arrived first and greeted Muazzez and Güldane with warm smiles. The young women kissed the elders' hands to convey their respect and gratitude and Lebriz followed suit. Idil arrived just as the guests were getting settled in the salon.

Idil looked around the room and spotted Lebriz. "My goodness," she exclaimed, clasping her hands.

Lebriz blushed and looked down.

"Lebriz, this is your future mother-in-law Idil Hanim," said Rengin. "Won't you go over and greet her"

"You are more beautiful than I imagined," Idil gushed as Lebriz kissed her hand. "Everyone said you had very unusual hair, but I didn't believe it. How lovely you are, my dear."

The guests sat down to catch up as the three younger women retired to the kitchen to prepare coffee and sweets. An essential test for any bride-to-be in an Ottoman household was her ability to make a perfect cup of coffee. Prepared in a tiny brass pot for a single serving, achieving the subtle variations in taste—between bitter, sweet, or very sweet—as well as the perfect aroma and body, was an art to master.

Lebriz carried a single cup and saucer on a tray and gracefully bent down to offer it to Idil. Seeing her delicate composure, the woman smiled at the girl, and delicately lifted the coffee off of the tray, careful to hold it only by the edge of the saucer. The etiquette of receiving a cup of coffee was just as essential to the ritual as the preparation. After observing how lovely the cup was, she raised it to eye level and inspected the foam. She nodded at Rengin in approval, and sat back to prepare to take the first coveted sip. Lebriz stood back and held her breath. The entire room fell silent. While still balancing the saucer on one hand, Idil reached to the cup's tiny handle and held it as though it was a delicate butterfly. Then she raised the cup to her lips and, with a barely discernible sound, took her first sip. She took a pause, and then smiled.

"Very nice, my dear."

In the meantime, Muazzez and Güldane had prepared coffee for Filiz and Rengin.

Filiz also inspected the foam before her first tiny sip.

"A wonderful cup of coffee! Best I've ever had."

"Güldane made it," said Muazzez. "She was the best of all the girls at the harem."

Filiz nodded at Güldane with a smile.

The girl looked down but was obviously pleased.

Muazzez was gathering up the coffee cups and plates when Filiz turned to Rengin and said, "We're very much looking forward to the upcoming event. All of Istanbul is abuzz, you know. It's such a wonderful match."

All eyes turned to Lebriz.

"We're very sad to lose our three young ladies," Rengin replied. "Lebriz has been like our own daughter for the last few months."

"You're not losing her," said Idil. "You will always be welcome to visit her, and she will come to you as well."

"And Muazzez and Güldane," chimed in Filiz.

Idil now addressed Lebriz directly. "I will never be able to replace your own mother, my dear, but I promise you this, I will be the best mother to you that I possibly can. It will be an honor to call you my daughter."

"Thank you. You're very kind," said Lebriz, barely holding back tears.

The following few days were spent completing the lavish preparations for the nuptials. Güldane embroidered additional articles for the dowry, as well as ornaments for the groom's house, while Muazzez embroidered napkins for the guests.

Orhan Pasha's chief concern was to orchestrate an unforgettably extravagant wedding. Anything less would be an embarrassment to his family name. And even though Lebriz wasn't his true daughter, since she was being given away from his household, he would give her all the attention a true daughter deserved. He'd become fond of the girl and shared a profound connection to her past. His efforts came out of pure love.

Valide Sultan's gift to his family had been considerable, but Orhan Pasha did not hesitate to spend his own money to rent the most luxurious wedding salon in Istanbul. An abundant feast and many gifts were planned for the more than three hundred anticipated guests, yet Orhan Pasha insisted on calling the event a "modest affair."

Idil's home, in Taksim, received its share of attention as well. Friends and relatives, including Muazzez and Güldane, were given the job of decorating the home. Pillows and covers were embroidered for the divans, and sashes, towels, and panels were made to hang from the walls. The day the driver came to carry Lebriz's trousseau to Taksim, Muazzez and Güldane were discussing how beautiful the wedding would be.

"There won't be any lattices," said Muazzez. "We'll be in the same room with the men."

"How do you know this?" asked an astonished Güldane.

"Orhan Pasha has rented the Pera Wedding Salon. It's a European-style room with no divisions. The men and women are all allowed to walk about together! I also heard there will be an orchestra!"

"An orchestra for what?"

"For music, silly, so people can dance."

After a pause, Güldane added, "I hope they won't make me dance."

"Oh no, it's not like that," Muazzez assured her. "Rengin Hanim said the European people will probably dance, but not us. And you're going to look beautiful."

"I don't care if I look beautiful," said Güldane. "I only care that you stay with me, always."

Muazzez caressed her friend's hair. "Don't you worry, my precious. Nobody can separate us now."

Nesrin and Nanna continued their tireless search for Lebriz through the mazelike streets of Istanbul. Jemil had returned to active duty and it was Erdal who drove them back and forth between the eleven palaces of the city. They made a small han near Topkapi Palace their home and often stayed for two weeks at a time.

On this particular day, a light rain was coming down. Both women had left the carriage and were walking toward the gate of the Beylerbeyeri Palace when Nanna spotted a black man, most likely a eunuch, leaving the gate and crossing the street. She and Nesrin rushed to follow him. After a few steps, Nanna shouted to get his attention. "Hello! Hello! Stop, please. Please!"

The man didn't turn around.

"He must be deaf," said Nesrin. "Let him go." But Nanna wouldn't let up. For an old woman, she had remarkable stamina and could have probably outrun Nesrin any day. She started to walk faster and soon was trotting and shouting at the same time. Suddenly she slipped and lost her balance. Nesrin watched in horror as Nanna tripped over and fell on the cobblestone street.

"Nanna!" she cried and ran over to the old woman. "Are you all right?

"I'm fine," Nanna replied, trying to get to her feet. "Go! Get the man!"

"No! Let him go. Are you hurt?"

"Just a little bruise, don't worry."

"Don't move," said Nesrin. "I'm going to get Erdal Efendi."

Erdal was right behind them with the carriage. When he saw Nanna on the ground, he immediately secured his horse to a pole and ran over to her.

"Thank God Erdal Efendi," said Nanna. "Follow the black eunuch. He went down the street!"

"No," shouted Nesrin. "Erdal Efendi, help me get her to the carriage."

Nesrin and Erdal held Nanna under both arms and pulled her up. She had clearly hurt her left ankle and had trouble standing on it. Despite all her protestations, they carried her to the carriage and secured her inside. All three of them were soaking wet.

They rushed to the han and helped Nanna into a chair by the fire. Erdal propped her leg up on a stool.

"Erdal, go get yourself dry," commanded Nesrin, as she rushed to get towels and dry clothes for Nanna.

"She should stay off the foot," said Erdal just before heading to his own room for the night. "I believe she's twisted her ankle."

"No such thing," grumbled Nanna. My ankle is fine. Good night.

The next morning, Nesrin woke up later than usual. She noticed that Nanna was already up and hobbling about the room.

"What are you doing, Nanna? Sit down. Rest that ankle."

"Nonsense, my ankle is fine. You're late. Erdal will be here soon."

Nesrin clambered out of bed and crossed the room. "Sit down. Let me take a look at that."

"Leave me alone," protested Nanna, but she sat down anyway.

Nesrin gently touched Nanna's ankle. "It's very swollen, you can't walk around on that today. You must be patient or it will get worse."

"Get dressed," ordered Nanna. "It's nearly the middle of the day. You should be ashamed!"

Nesrin quietly put on her clothes and started to comb her hair.

"Give me that comb and sit," Nanna snapped.

Despite her gruff tone, she lovingly combed through Nesrin's still long and beautiful hair. "I've been doing this ever since you were a small girl growing up in Bolu. I'm not about to quit now."

Nesrin let Nanna groom her, aware that this was one ritual that always calmed them both down.

"There you go," said Nanna after a few minutes. "You're as beautiful as ever."

"I've gotten old," Nesrin said, staring at her reflection in the small oval mirror. "We both have."

"What nonsense! You're barely in your thirties. What have you got to complain about?"

Nesrin looked at her for a moment. "I think it's time to give up," she said, quietly.

"Give up what?" Nanna was getting impatient again.

"I've looked high and low for my babies for years. I found one of them, and I'm eternally thankful to Allah for that, but I despair that we'll never find Lebriz."

Nanna set down the comb and leaned against Nesrin's chair, taking the weight off her swollen ankle. "You want to give up on our beautiful Lebriz?"

Nesrin's eyes glistened with tears. "I can only hope that she's forgotten that she had a mother at all."

"Now you're talking crazy," scolded Nanna. "Lebriz has not forgotten us. And we will not give up on her, never!"

"How many more doors will we knock on? How many more years will we search?"

"As long as it takes, until my dying day."

Nesrin stood and stared out the window. "If Allah had wanted me to find my daughter, he would have granted that by now."

"Allah told you where she is," Nanna replied. "He led us to Istanbul. We know she's at one of the palaces here."

"Perhaps, but which one? I can't have you knocking at gates all over the city, in the rain. You're too old for that, and I'm getting too tired."

Glaring at the door, Nanna tried to stand but her ankle buckled under her weight. "Where's that blasted Erdal Efendi? If he'd just get in here he'd set you straight."

"It's time to give up, Nanna," Nesrin said with finality. "I will instruct Erdal to drive us home to Bolu, today."

Erdal was heard climbing the stairs.

"Thank God you're back, Erdal Efendi," Nanna called through the opened door.

"What are you doing?" he asked, staring at Nanna. "You should be sitting with your foot propped up on a pillow."

"You too?" exclaimed Nanna incredulously. "You should listen to Nesrin here and all the nonsense she speaks."

"I want you to drive us back to Bolu," Nesrin said, collecting her things into her bag.

"Have you ever heard such nonsense?" Nanna scoffed.

Erdal looked serious. "I have some news."

"What news?" demanded Nanna.

"I met an old man this morning in the coffee house, a former courier for the Sultan, called Haluk. He told me that he'd brought a young girl to Istanbul, many years ago. She was the most beautiful creature he'd ever seen, with hazel eyes and hair the shade of copper. I asked him if he remembered her name. And he said, yes, I've never forgotten her. Her name was Lebriz."

Nesrin collapsed onto the bed beside Nanna. "Allah is great"

"Where did he take her?" Nanna demanded. "Did he say which palace?"

"Yildiz Palace," Erdal replied.

Nesrin looked up in surprise. "We've been there so many times! Banged at that gate and yelled our questions to the wind, but nobody would ever tell us anything."

"At least we now know where to look," said Erdal.

On the day before the wedding, Rengin pulled Lebriz into her bedroom for a private talk.

"Every girl will be nervous before her wedding. Your case is not unusual. What can I do to put your mind at ease, my darling?"

"I'm not sure what it will be like," said Lebriz. "I mean on the first night … I'm told what will happen but I'm so afraid."

"My poor girl, it is completely normal for you to feel that way. Only rest assured that intimate relations between men and women can be most pleasurable, especially if you love your husband."

"But what if I don't love him? I've never even met him and I have no idea what love means. All I can think about is my mother. Even when I was a small girl, I saw how horrified she looked when my father approached her. She seemed so helpless and afraid. And after what happened to Güldane…"

Rengin took her hands. "My darling put your trust in Allah. Know that even if it is painful the first time, you will learn to enjoy it as you get to know your husband."

"But what if I don't? I will be stuck with this man for the rest of my life! I will never do what my mother did, even if he takes in a kuma. And besides, once I am married, I will never have the chance to find my mother and brother."

Rengin held Lebriz tight as the girl continued to cry. After a few moments the tears subsided. Lebriz looked at the woman's face.

"You've been so kind to me," she said. "I'll be eternally grateful "

"Your sisters are ready to perform the cleansing ritual. Are you ready for that?" Lebriz nodded. Rengin wiped the tears off her cheek.

A few moments later, Rengin came out and signaled to Muazzez and Güldane that Lebriz was ready. The two girls entered the room with a bowl of hot wax. Muazzez undressed Lebriz while Güldane kneaded the wax in her hands to achieve the right consistency. She then tenderly applied the hot wax to Lebriz's underarm. When she pulled it off, Lebriz flinched.

"I'm sorry," Güldane apologized. "Did that hurt?"

"Only a little," said Lebriz. "It's all right."

Both women proceeded to gently wax the unwanted hair off of Lebriz's body. Having only been touched by women and girls before, Lebriz wondered what it would be like to be touched by a man.

On the morning of the wedding, Erdal was once again at the gates of Yildiz Palace. This time he would not be polite. Nesrin and Nanna waited in the carriage while the old man shouted and hammered on the gate with his whip. "Ho, there! Ho, there! Anyone! Ho!"

Two men heard the commotion and hurried out of the guardhouse, brandishing their guns. "What do you think you're doing, you crazy old man?" demanded the first guard. "Don't you realize this is the Sultan's home? Stop your racket or I'll shoot you right now."

"Please," Erdal implored, "hear me out."

"What do you want?" growled the other man. "If you're a beggar, nobody has any money to give to you here. So scram!"

"I carry two ladies from Bolu. One of them is the daughter of the Circassian Rashit Bey, and the daughter-in-law of Mustafa Bey, of the Circassian border guards. She's accompanied by her lady-in-waiting."

"Circassian border guards?" asked the first man, lowering his gun to his side as he approached the gate.

"Yes. Her name is Nesrin Hanim."

"I've served with the Circassian Border Guards," the man replied. "They are honorable and well-trained men. What does Nesrin Hanim want?"

"News of her long-lost daughter," said Erdal. "I know you are not allowed to talk to me about the ladies of the harem, but if you have any mercy, you will tell us how she is. Her name is Lebriz."

"Ah yes, the famous beauty," said the guard, smiling now. "There is nothing wrong with my telling you this, because she's no longer here. She has been sent away to be married."

Nesrin heard the conversation from the carriage and could no longer contain herself. She flung open the door and stepped out, covered in the usual a black charshaf. "I beg of you, sir, in Allah's name, can you tell me where my daughter was sent? Please!"

"You have no need to worry my lady," said the guard gently. "Your daughter was sent to the Pink Mansion, near Bebek, home of the honorable Orhan Pasha."

"Thank you so much," cried Nesrin through the black shroud. "May Allah's blessings be upon you both."

Nesrin climbed back into the carriage as Erdal nodded at the guards in appreciation. "You've won a place in Heaven this day, kind sirs."

He then jumped back in his cab to drive the carriage down the shore of the Bosphorus.

Over her wedding gown, Lebriz wore a deep red kaftan and gold belt that circled her waist. Muazzez and Güldane helped her dress, and then escorted her to the door of the Pink Mansion. Jafer was waiting there to wish her well.

"I wish you could come to the ceremony, Jafer Efendi," Lebriz said.

"It would not be appropriate," Jafer replied. "But you can count on me to be waiting for you at your new home."

Lebriz joined Orhan Pasha and Rengin in the carriage. The vessel lurched forward toward Pera with Muazzez and Güldane following in a second carriage behind.

An hour after the family left, Erdal arrived at the Pink Mansion with Nesrin anxiously peering out the window of the carriage. Once again, Erdal banged on the gates and shouted, "Ho, there. Ho there!"

A black eunuch came to the gate. "What do you want?"

"We seek Lebriz Hanim, from the palace of Abdul Hamid and guest of Orhan Pasha."

"You're a little late," the guard replied. "They left an hour ago to take Lebriz Hanim to Pera for her wedding."

"Where in Pera, man? Where exactly?"

"I don't know. Some big, fancy wedding salon."

In the meantime, the wedding party had arrived at the salon to find lines of carriages waiting at the gate. Ladies in their finery appeared, accompanied by men dressed in uniforms or formal attire. Once inside, the ladies were shown to the dressing rooms where their coiffures were retouched and skirts straightened. Then they joined the men and were led to the tables to be seated according to military and social rank.

Inside the carriage, Rengin gave Lebriz's hand a quick squeeze. "Bon courage, my lovely. You're the shining star of this day."

She kissed the girl on both cheeks and climbed out of the carriage, leaving Lebriz with Orhan Pasha, and joining Muazzez and Güldane to enter the salon.

"What a pity Nadide couldn't be here," Muazzez said, as they entered the building, "or all the other women from the harem."

Muazzez and Güldane were greeted by their future hosts, Semih Pasha and Filiz. After the compulsory hand-kissing ritual, the group was seated together at a side table. Fingers were not pointed, but a buzz of conversation went up among the guests, including Madam Janet, who was seated on the side with a full view of the head table. She had much to whisper to the ladies sitting nearby.

The groom entered, following the Imam. Muazzez and Güldane quickly appraised Nazif and exchanged glances. He wasn't particularly handsome, but stood upright with a strong carriage. Muazzez observed that he seemed nervous, perhaps just as nervous as Lebriz. His slightly graying uncle accompanied him.

Next entered Idil, who was seated at the head table with her son and brother-in-law.

Once all the guests were situated, a servant approached the carriage and gently knocked on its door.

"It's time, my darling," said Orhan Pasha. His heart broke as he watched her lift her veil and gently lower it over her face.

"I'm ready," she said.

Orhan Pasha assisted her out of the carriage.

A gasp rose from the guests when Lebriz entered the salon. Idil was so moved by the girl's appearance that she started clapping. The crowd followed suit and began to applaud.

Orhan Pasha led the bride to be seated next to Nazif. She caught a sidelong glance of her future husband through the veil, but kept her gaze down. Nazif avoided looking at her altogether. Orhan Pasha took his seat next to his wife at the end of the table.

As the Imam began to chant the Koran, Muslim guests held their palms up in prayer, while the non-Muslims simply bowed their heads.

The ceremony was well under way when Erdal, having taken a few wrong turns through the labyrinth of Pera, finally found his way to the Pera Salon. He jumped off his box, helped Nesrin and Nanna out of the carriage, and led them to the entrance, where two servants greeted them.

"May I see your invitation?" asked one of the servants.

"These women don't need an invitation," said Erdal firmly. "This is the bride's mother and her lady-in-waiting."

The guard hesitated for a moment.

Nesrin threw off her charshaf and pleaded, "Please, sir. I haven't seen my daughter in years. I just want to see her! I won't make a sound. Please allow us in."

The guard was moved by Nesrin's words. He looked at the other guard who gave him a nod of affirmation. The two men stood by to let Nanna and Nesrin enter the salon. Erdal watched them disappear behind the ornate doors before he turned to tend to his horses.

The building was silent when Nesrin and Nanna entered. As they neared the wide doors that opened to the main room, Nesrin heard the voice of the Imam reciting the Koran. She removed the charchaf, then she and Nanna approached quietly and paused in the doorway.

When Nesrin looked at the couple in the middle of the room and caught a glance of the young woman standing before the Imam, she choked. Her face was covered in a veil but Nesrin still recognized her. She quickly assessed the young groom standing next to her. He stood tall and seemed like a gentle soul.

The Imam completed the passage from the Koran and asked, "Who is the witness for the groom?"

The words – the same words she'd heard at her own wedding so may years ago - echoed in Nesrin's mind.

Nazif's Uncle Sami stood up. "I am."

"Do you accept and guarantee the terms of marriage as put forth by His Highness Sultan Abdul Hamid, and Her Grace, Merhume Valide Sultan, Sami Bey?"

"I do," replied the uncle.

The Imam turned to Nazif. "Do you, Nazif Bey, understand and swear to uphold the terms of marriage as put forth by His Highness Sultan Abdul Hamid, and Her Grace, the dearly departed Valide Sultan?"

"I do," replied Nazif, in a clear voice.

"Who is witness for Lebriz Hanim?" the Imam asked next.

Nesrin choked when she heard her daughter's name.

Orhan Pasha stood. "I, Orhan Pasha, am witness and guardian, by special order of His Highness Sultan Abdul Hamid."

The Imam turned to Lebriz. "Lebriz Hanim, do you accept Nazif Bey as your husband?"

Through her veil, Lebriz looked at the man standing in front of her. This was the moment she'd dreaded and had tried to avoid her whole life. It was fate that brought her here, and it was fate she had to put her trust in now. Güldane's words echoed through her mind. Think of the children you'll have. Think how happy you'll be.

With a stronger voice that surprised even herself, Lebriz spoke the words, "I do."

A cry was heard from across the salon.

Rengin turned to see a tall woman dressed in a blue kaftan, standing near the door with her hand over her mouth, trying to suppress further sounds.

She immediately knew who it was. "For the love of Allah," she muttered.

The Imam closed the Koran and announced, "I now pronounce you man and wife."

Rengin couldn't take her eyes off the woman, whose face was distorted with a mix of devastation and joy. Unsteady on her feet, she held onto an older woman beside her, who did her best to keep her propped upright.

All other eyes were on the couple facing each other in the middle of the room. Nazif gently reached over and lifted the veil to uncover his bride's face. At first, she wouldn't look at him. But then he simply said her name, "Lebriz Hanim."

She looked up to meet his eyes. For the first time in her life, she was face to face with a man. She recognized something in his eyes that was comforting. A rush of relief ran through her. She couldn't be certain, but she felt that perhaps she could trust this man.

Guests gathered around the couple with words of congratulations. Men patted Nazif on the back and shook his hand. Madam Janet was the first to reach Lebriz to grab her and kiss her on both cheeks. Rengin stepped forward and grabbed Lebriz rather firmly by the shoulders. This startled the bride.

"What is it?" Lebriz asked, aware that Rengin had something urgent to tell her.

"Lebriz, my dear," Rengin said as she turned the girl to face the entrance of the room.

Through the crowd, Lebriz spotted the tall woman at once. Their eyes met. For a moment Lebriz was disoriented. Then realization struck her. She choked on a cry and then stumbled. Rengin held her to prevent her from falling. Without taking her eyes off her daughter, Nesrin began to make her way through the crowded room. Lebriz was shaking uncontrollably. Rengin let her go only at the moment her mother reached her and Lebriz fell into Nesrin's arms.

Mother and daughter embraced and held each other for several moments.

Lebriz finally spoke. "You found me."

"I found you, my darling. I always prayed I would."

Güldane and Muazzez had both witnessed the reunion. They stood aside as other guests began to realize what had happened. The room quieted down. The men who were congratulating Nazif drew away. He was left facing mother and daughter.

"Nazif," said Lebriz. "This is my mother, Nesrin Hanim."

The rest of the evening was a blur. In spite of everything, the wedding had to go on.

Nesrin whispered to her daughter, "It's your wedding, my darling. Enjoy your wedding."

"Jemil?" asked Lebriz uncertainly.

"He is fine," Nesrin smiled.

Lebriz shut her eyes for a moment to hold back the tears.

"And Nanna is with me too."

"Nanna is here?"

"Yes!"

"Where?"

Nesrin turned toward the door but Nanna was gone. "She must be waiting outside. Now go. We'll have lots of time to catch up."

Lebriz turned to her husband, who'd been waiting patiently while admiring his new wife. She looked at him and their eyes met.

"Would you mind if I introduced you?" he asked. "People are dying to meet you, Lebriz Hanim."

"Of course," she said.

He offered his arm and escorted his bride around the room, introducing her to friends, family and colleagues.

Lebriz's mind was reeling. How could life change so completely in one day! Her mother, and Nanna, and her beloved Jemil! It was all too much to comprehend. She went through the motions of meeting the guests who showered her with congratulations and compliments. She responded as graciously as she could, but kept turning to look at her mother, just to be sure that she was really there. She couldn't believe it had actually happened.

Nesrin couldn't keep her eyes off of her daughter. What an elegant young woman she'd become! She was refined and intelligent, and navigated the room with restrained confidence.

Orhan Pasha approached her and introduced himself and his wife. "Rengin and I have embraced Lebriz as our own," he said. "We're so glad to meet you, and elated that the two of you are finally reunited. Would you give us the honor of joining us"

Before Nesrin had a chance to accept the offer, Idil joined them and Orhan Pasha showed them all to the head table.

"We have so much to talk about, Nesrin Hanim," she said. "We're family now."

Their eyes met with the mutual recognition of mothers who deeply love their children.

Muazzez and Güldane approached Nesrin and expressed their love for their dear Lebriz.

"It warms my heart to know that my Lebriz has been surrounded by so much love," Nesrin replied as she was seated next to Idil at the family table.

Much of the conversation over dinner revolved around Nesrin and her search for her children. Idil listened attentively to the stories of how Nesrin and Nanna had spent many years knocking on doors all across the country. She was quite moved by the woman's countenance and bravery.

An orchestra played softly in the background during dinner. After the dessert plates were taken away, the man leading the orchestra—Muazzez whispered to Güldane that he was called a "conductor"—became more animated and led the orchestra to play a lovely waltz. The diplomats' wives, who'd all had their share of wine, began to sway their well-coiffed heads.

All eyes turned to Nazif when he stood and offered Lebriz his hand.

With a look of panic in her eyes, Lebriz turned to Rengin. She, in turn, smiled and nodded encouragingly.

The crowd was captivated by the couple taking up the dance floor. People were stunned to see how elegantly the newlyweds fit together and swayed across the floor to the music.

Nesrin couldn't help but remember her first dance with Nejmi, and how beautifully they too had fit together. "Dear Allah," she prayed, "Please make it right. Make it right this time."

Soon, Orhan Pasha and Rengin joined the couple on the dance floor, followed by several diplomats and their women. Idil and Nesrin were left together at the table.

"I was never much of a dancer," Idil admitted. "Were you?"

"I used to dance the Circassian kafe," said Nesrin, "but that was a very long time ago."

"My husband enjoyed dancing," Idil smiled. "I used to dance with him sometimes. I can't tell you how lonely I am since he's been gone."

"I'm sorry to hear that. How long has it been?"

"Only three months. It's just Nazif and me in the house now. Of course, with Lebriz joining us, we'll be a family again."

Idil paused for a moment, considering again Nesrin's thoughtful and wizened visage. "I wonder if you would ..." she said.

Nesrin looked at her.

"Would you consider staying with us, Nesrin Hanim? I know you and Lebriz would like to spend time together, and Nazif and I would love to have you."

Nesrin was struck by the generosity of this offer. "I couldn't possibly. You see I have Nanna with me—"

"Please bring her with you! There's plenty of room. We'd love it if you'd accept."

At this moment, Lebriz and Nazif left the dance floor and returned to the table.

"I've asked Nesrin Hanim to stay with us," said Idil to her son. "Don't you think that's a good idea?"

"I'd be delighted," Nazif replied, smiling widely at his new mother-in-law. "Has Nesrin Hanim accepted?"

Nesrin looked at her daughter who was beaming with happiness. "How can I say no? Of course I accept your gracious offer. Thank you."

The hour grew late and guests began to leave. Lebriz and Nazif, along with their mothers, Orhan Pasha and Rengin, stood at the door and shook hands with their departing guests.

Once they were all gone, the family stepped into the cool night air. Nanna, who'd been waiting in the carriage with Erdal, clambered out as she saw Lebriz come through the door.

Still cloaked in her black charshaf, her veil parted to reveal her pure white hair, Nanna limped up to Lebriz and held her tight. "My child," she cried, "My beautiful child!"

Erdal joined the wedding party outside the salon. His face was creased in a large grin, unable to hide his delight at seeing Lebriz again.

"I could never have survived these many painful years, nor could I have found you, my darling," said Nesrin, "without the devotion and aid of Nanna and Erdal Efendi."

Smiling through tears of joy, Lebriz hugged Nanna, and taking Erdal's hand, whispered, "Thank you, thank you both!"

Nazif pointed to his carriage. "We're driving to Taksim, not very far from here. Will you follow us, Erdal Efendi?"

"I will follow most carefully," Erdal replied.

"I will ride with Nesrin," said Idil as she caressed her son's cheek. "You and your bride should ride alone."

Nazif and Lebriz stood still, silently watching their mothers climb into Nesrin's carriage. Idil's driver held the door open for them. Nazif offered his hand and helped Lebriz get in the carriage. He then got in and sat next to her.

TAKSİM

The ride to Taksim took all but ten minutes. The newlyweds sat side by side in silence. The evening's events had put Lebriz into a trance. Thoughts of her mother and Jemil swirled through her mind. Was she dreaming or had these events actually happened? And who was the man sitting next to her? She couldn't conceive of being married.

Nazif, shy by nature, didn't say a word, let alone touch his new wife. He kept both hands firmly on his lap and stared ahead until the carriage came to a stop. The driver stepped down to open the carriage door.

Nestled at the end of a lane on the grounds of a small park, the Taksim house was not as luxurious as Pink Mansion, but ample enough to house the family and their guests. A separate apartment on the third floor had been prepared for the newlyweds.

A manservant named Hayri opened the door. Idil walked in first, followed by Nesrin and Nanna. She quickly ordered Hayri to alert the maids.

"Please tell them to prepare the yellow bedroom, and the pink room next to it for our guests," she said, smiling at Nesrin. "And tell them to hurry up. We're all very tired."

"Right away," Hayri replied and hurried up the stairs.

"We don't want to cause any trouble…." Nesrin started to say, but Idil interrupted her.

"Don't even mention it, my dear," she said. "It is our pleasure to welcome you." She gestured grandly toward the door. "And look who's here."

Lebriz and Nazif were just entering the house.

"My darling girl," Idil cooed as she rushed to hold Lebriz's hand. "Muazzez and Güldane have worked tirelessly to prepare your rooms. I think you'll be pleased."

Lebriz smiled and looked beyond her to see Nesrin and Nanna watching her. It's not a dream, she thought. They're both really standing there.

"Thank you," she said, distractedly. "Muzzy and Güldane have been the most wonderful of friends."

Idil motioned to a girl who was waiting by the stairs. "This is Selin," she said. "She will assist you with every need you may have. She will accompany you to your bedchamber and prepare you for the night."

Lebriz drew her eyes away from her mother and considered the girl. She felt the tears well up in her eyes.

"What's the matter, dear?" asked her mother-in-law. "Are you all right?"

Before Lebriz could say anything, she heard Nanna's voice:

"Idil Hanim, if I may?"

This was the first time Nanna spoke since she met the family at the wedding salon. All eyes turned to her. She reached out for Lebriz's hand.

"I wonder if I could have the honor of preparing Lebriz myself," she said. "It would mean so much to me after not seeing her for all these years."

"Of course," Idil nodded. "Lebriz, is this what you would like?"

"Yes, please," said the girl.

"Very good. Selin will accompany you both to your apartments." She embraced Lebriz. "Welcome to our family, my daughter."

Nesrin watched as her daughter started to follow Selin up the stairs. Then her attention turned to the groom. Nazif stood on the side, curiously observing the women as though a mere spectator. He seemed mild-mannered to Nesrin, but who could be certain? She wanted so much to pull him aside and tell him to be gentle with his new bride. It was Idil who articulated Nesrin's exact thoughts.

"Be gentle with her," she said to Nazif. "Be as gentle and loving as your father, God rest his soul. Then you will have true happiness, my dear son."

As Nazif kissed his mother's hand and turned to follow his bride up the stairs, Idil turned to Nesrin with a sigh of relief.

"Come along, my dear. What a long night we've all had. We could both use a few minutes at the hearth."

She led Nesrin by the arm to the drawing room where they each sat in one of several plush chairs. Nesrin sat back in her chair and watched a servant stoke the fire. Twenty years' worth of tension and worry seemed to drain out of her body. She extended her feet toward the flames. Finally, she thought. Finally there is hope.

Selin took Lebriz and Nanna into the room adjacent to the couple's bedroom, where a jug filled with hot water and a washbowl sat on a table with several towels. The room had been lovingly decorated by Muazzez and Güldane. Lebriz recognized the sashes and towels Güldane had embroidered with her own hands.

Nanna helped Lebriz take off her wedding dress with a gentle hand. She hung the dress, then waited for Lebriz to undress completely before wrapping her in a towel.

"You're just as beautiful as your mother was on her wedding day," she said.

Lebriz sat quietly as Nanna sponge-washed her arms and legs. She dressed Lebriz in a nightgown, also sewn and embroidered by her sisters, and then she began to comb Lebriz's hair.

"All I remember," said Lebriz softly, "are the nights when my father would come home and my brother and I would hide behind your skirts. I can never forget the look of fear on my mother's face."

"That's all in the past," said Nanna, smoothing out her hair with her fingers. "We must forget the past now."

"But can we?" Lebriz asked. "I can't seem to be able to forget the past."

"I made a mistake twenty years ago," replied Nanna. "I won't make that mistake again with you."

"What do you mean?"

"On her wedding night, I told your mother that everything would be all right. I assured her that she'd learn to live with and to love her husband. I told her that even though the first night might be painful, she'd get over the pain and eventually enjoy being with her husband. Little did I know."

"It wasn't your fault." Lebriz touched Nanna's hand.

"Perhaps not, but I still feel responsible. I was the one who prepared her, just as I'm preparing you now."

"Don't you have any words of comfort for me?" asked Lebriz.

"No words, my darling. I only have love and my best wishes for you."

Nanna continued to brush her hair as the young bride became lost in her thoughts.

Minutes later, Nanna accompanied her to her bedchamber. She carried with her the nuptial sheet, which she carefully placed under the covers.

"I will wait outside, my darling. Once the nuptial sheet is soiled, you must bring it to me so that I can take it to Idil Hanim."

"I know," Lebriz replied, sitting in a chair next to the window. "It's such a beautiful moonlit night. I can see the park from here."

"Won't you lie down, my darling?" asked Nanna.

"In a little while."

Nanna caressed Lebriz's cheek. "I'll tell Nazif you're ready for him."

She left the room, leaving Lebriz gazing out of the window.

Lebriz was startled when the door slowly creaked open. She turned to see Nazif, dressed in pajamas and a robe, quietly enter the room.

Seeing his wife seated by the window he took the chair opposite her. They looked at each other. Neither one of them knew what to say.

Lebriz didn't know what to make of this stranger. She finally stood, took off her robe and placed it on the chair. Pulling back the covers, she lay on the bed.

Mesmerized, Nazif's eyes followed her every move.

Lebriz pulled up the covers and shut her eyes tight.

"Lebriz Hanim," Nazif said, still addressing her formally.

"I'm ready, Nazif Bey."

He sat on the edge of the bed and reached over for her hand.

She cringed. He held her hand anyway.

"It's been a long night," he said. "We're both very tired. I will sleep in the other room tonight. Let's get some rest."

She opened her eyes as tears started to well up. "Thank you."

He squeezed her hand then let it fall gently on the bed cover. "Sleep well."

Feeling the night's tension lift off of her, Lebriz's entire body relaxed. She began to doze off.

Nazif sat back in the chair and watched her fall asleep. Once her breathing got heavier, and he felt sure she was in a deep slumber, he reached under the covers and gingerly pulled the nuptial sheet from under her. He gathered it up and took it to the bathroom.

Lebriz tossed in the bed and thought she saw a dark figure next to the door, but then fell right back to sleep.

Nanna received the nuptial sheet handed to her through the door. She inspected it, saw the stain of blood, and uttered a short prayer.

It was well after Lebriz had fallen asleep that Nanna left to deliver the sheet to Idil's room. She decided to take the long way and cross the courtyard to get some fresh air. As she walked by the oak tree in the middle of the yard, she saw the shadow of a large man coming toward her. Startled, she looked up and tried to make out the man's face. She screamed and fell to the ground.

Lebriz sat straight up in bed. Both Idil and Nesrin heard the scream and ran outside. Nanna was lying on the ground with Jafer leaning over her.

"What's happened?" cried Nesrin. "What's wrong with her?"

"Who are you?" she demanded, looking up at the large-framed man. "What have you done to Nanna?"

"Nothing," Jafer replied. "She took one look at me and fainted."

Lebriz had come out by now, closely followed by Nazif.

"Mother, this is Jafer Efendi, a dear friend who has protected me through all these years. Jafer Efendi, meet my mother Nesrin."

"An honor," said Jafer, taking a bow just as Nanna started to regain consciousness.

"It's him! I'd recognize that face anywhere," she cried. "He's the man who took away my babies."

"It's all right, Nanna," Lebriz said. "I can explain everything."

"He's a monster!"

"No, he's not. He's a gentle, kind man."

"I'm sorry I startled you." Jafer turned to Idil. "I didn't mean to startle her."

Idil smiled at the man. "It's quite all right, Jafer Efendi."

She'd noticed that Nanna had dropped the nuptial sheet on the ground and leaned down to pick it up. Lebriz saw her quickly tuck away the sheet in her sleeve and was puzzled for a moment. Then she looked at Nazif. Had he really done this for her? He noticed her gaze and looked away. She saw that he kept one hand in the pocket of his robe. A feeling of gratitude rose up in her heart.

Lebriz and Nesrin helped Nanna to her room and stayed with her until she felt calm. It was early morning when Lebriz finally returned to her bedroom and slipped back under the covers.

Lebriz woke with a start. She sat up in bed, her eyes flashing around the room, taking in all the furniture and the heavily draped windows that were so unfamiliar to her. The events of the previous night began to dawn on her. My mother! she thought. Nanna. And that man in the next room—my husband!

She climbed out of bed to use the toilet. When she came back to her bedroom Selin was waiting for her. "Have you rested well, Lebriz Hanim?" The girl opened the heavy drapes to let the sun stream into the room.

"Yes, thank you. How did you know I was awake?"

"I was waiting right outside the door."

"What time is it?"

"Well after noon," Lebriz heard the man's voice coming from the side door. She turned to see Nazif standing there, fully dressed. "I hope you slept well."

"Very well, thank you."

"You must be starving. Shall we have breakfast?"

Selin held out Lebriz's dressing gown. She slipped into it then followed Nazif into the salon, where a breakfast table was already set up for them. He offered her his right hand and led her to a chair. A samovar was brewing on the sideboard.

"Can I get you some tea?" asked Nazif.

"Yes, please."

"How do you take it?"

"Not very strong with one lump of sugar."

"That's exactly the way I like my tea," smiled Nazif as he poured two glasses, put them on a small tray, and delivered them to the table.

"Shall I serve you some cheese?" he asked.

"I'll do it," she said, reaching over to put a slice of bread on a plate along with some cheese, olives, butter, and jam. She put the plate in front of Nazif.

"Thank you," he said.

As Lebriz made a plate up for herself, she noticed Nazif was using his left hand to hold the bread he was buttering. His forefinger was heavily bandaged. Nazif noticed Lebriz looking at it.

"It's nothing," he said. "Just a scratch."

"I know what it is," she said.

He finished buttering his toast and looked at her affectionately.

"I wish I could spend the entire day with you but I must go to work. I'm ashamed that I'm not able to take you on a honeymoon just yet. Things are complicated at the moment, but this will give you some time to spend with your mother."

"I don't know what you do."

"I'm the Deputy Undersecretary for the Ministry of Foreign Affairs."

"Oh," she smiled.

Nazif smiled back. "I know, it sounds awfully complicated."

"Yes, it does."

"How lovely you are when you smile."

Lebriz blushed and lifted her piece of toast.

"Afiyet olsun," he said.

"Bon appétit," she replied with a smile.

"I hope we will find a common language," he said in Turkish.

"Oui, moi aussi," she said, which made him grin.

He reached over and took her hand. "Lebriz Hanim."

"Nazif Bey," she replied.

"I do hope we will get to know each other better in the next few days."

"I hope so too."

He finished his toast, wiped his hands and bid her farewell. Selin was there immediately to clear the table. She then accompanied Lebriz back to her bedroom to help her dress and brush her hair, and then to the main house to join her mother, Nanna and Idil.

Lebriz spent the next two days with the women in the salon of the main house, joining them after Nazif left for work. They had a lot to catch up on. Idil and Nesrin were both fascinated to hear about Lebriz's days at the harem, the long hours she'd spent with her dear friends Muzzy and Güldane, and how at home they felt with Nadide. Idil was especially moved when she heard how Valide Sultan made a decree concerning Lebriz and her friends, and how, because of this, Lebriz escaped the clutches of the sultan.

"So we have Valide Sultan to thank for this gift of Lebriz in our family," she said. "Allah bless her soul."

Nanna teased Nesrin while telling everyone how Erdal had forced her out of her melancholy. She imitated Erdal's voice.

"You're a Circassian woman! Pull yourself together. Sadness does not become you!'"

Nesrin laughed at the memory, but Idil simply smiled. She was saddened to hear how much Nesrin had suffered while searching for her children over the years.

"And what about Jemil?" she asked. "When will we get to meet him?"

"Allah only knows," Nesrin sighed. "Last we heard, he was stationed in Eastern Anatolia, not far from our old home. I can only pray that he's okay and will return to us soon."

On her visitor's day, women came in throngs to Idil's Taksim home. Among them, of course, were Rengin and Madam Janet. Everyone had been discussing the beautiful wedding and the heartrending reunion between mother and daughter. Madam Janet was hungry for gossip. She absorbed every bit of information she could gather.

It was nearing midafternoon when Muazzez and Güldane arrived. Lebriz was overjoyed at seeing her friends. All three embraced and sat in a corner to catch up.

"I am getting married," Muazzez declared. "And I already met my husband!"

"Really?" said Madam Janet, who'd been shamelessly eavesdropping on the conversation. "How unusual."

"Semih Pasha was very generous," Muazzez gushed. "He invited the groom and his family for lunch. We all sat at the lunch table together and I sat next to my intended!"

"Goodness."

"Semih Pasha says the old ways are changing and that a new world is coming upon us. He says the archaic customs are no longer valid."

"Archaic?" asked the now-astonished Madam Janet.

"Yes, that's the word he used," said Muazzez. "The best part is that Güldane will go with us. That was the deal we made. That Güldane and I shall never be parted."

"That's wonderful," said Madam Janet. "Wonderful indeed."

Nazif returned home every afternoon, usually right after teatime. As spring was approaching, and the days were getting longer, he and Lebriz would take a daily stroll in the park. Nesrin sometimes watched them through the window and thought how tender he was with her. He held her hand while they walked and it looked like they were in deep conversation.

Nazif wanted to know everything about Lebriz's past. He was furious to know how cruel Nejmi had been to Nesrin, and how heartbreaking it was for she and Jemil to be separated.

Lebriz wanted to learn all about his work. He said he hobnobbed with tedious diplomats, but he seemed troubled.

"What troubles you?" Lebriz asked one evening. "Whenever you start talking about your day at work you get somber."

"Our country is going in a bad direction," Nazif replied. "I'm worried about what may be in our future. But…." he took his wife's hand, "we will not worry about that now. I'm determined to take one day off next week to spend with you. I want to spend the entire day with you and never let you out of my sight."

Lebriz blushed and looked down.

"I grew up believing the world was full of cruelty," she said. "But now I believe I was wrong."

Nazif kissed her tenderly on the cheek.

"On the day we'll be spending together," he asked, "is there something special you'd like to do?"

"Actually, yes," said Lebriz. "There is something I've always wanted to do."

Nesrin continued to watch from the window as the couple held hands and continued their stroll. How happy she was that her daughter seemed so content. She had no idea, and neither did Nanna or Idil, that Nazif slept on the couch in the next room every night.

Nazif took off from work on the following Saturday. Erdal drove the couple to the wharf at Beshiktash, the spot where Lebriz had first landed in Istanbul, all those years ago. She remembered how shocked she was when she first saw such a large body of water—and how she was startled by the loud horns, and charmed by seagulls diving for food. Nothing, it seemed, had changed. Once again the waves, the gulls, the foghorns, and the fishermen mesmerized her. She could sit here forever, she thought, and just watch the fishermen tow their lines off their fishing boats.

"Is this what you had in mind?" asked Nazif.

"Yes," she said. "Can we go on the ferry, please?"

"I have an even better idea," he said, and guided her down to a small pier that jutted off of the main wharf. Several small rowboats were docked there. He jumped onto one of the boats and held out his hand to her.

"Come on."

She was at once terrified and thrilled. The boat was unsteady. She'd never done anything like this before. What if she fell in the water?

"Are you sure?" she said. "I can't swim."

"Don't worry. I'm here. I won't let anything happen to you."

She held onto his hand and gingerly stepped off the pier onto the boat. She immediately felt unsteady and thought she was going to fall. He held onto her.

"Sit," he said. "It will be all right."

She sat on a bench-like plank on the far end of the dinghy and faced him. He lifted two oars that had been lying on the floor and secured them on the side of the boat, letting the ends hang in the water. Erdal was on the pier with a smile and a wooden bucket. He handed the bucket to Nazif, who had to stand and reach up to take it. This made the boat sway and Lebriz let out a cry. She held on even harder to the bench.

Nazif put the bucket on the floor of the boat. "Our supplies," he said.

Erdal released the rope that kept the vessel fastened to the pier and tossed it on board.

"Enjoy yourselves," he shouted as Nazif dunked the ends of the oars into the water and, with one swift move, propelled the boat away from shore.

Lebriz remembered the first time she'd been on the Bosphorus. Then the heavy vessel seemed to take command of the water, slicing through it confidently. This little dinghy had no authority at all. It seemed they were floating in any direction the waves would push them. She was surprised at how little anxiety she felt. Now it was Nazif who kept command with his strong stroking of the oars.

"Relax," he said. "We're going fishing!"

How astounding, she thought. We're going fishing.

After about twenty minutes of steady rowing, the boat came to a stop. They were in the middle of the water now and the shore seemed remote. Lebriz looked back at the majestic view that was Istanbul. The minarets of the grand mosques reached out to the sky, while people on shore were mere specks running to and fro. The dinghy swayed back and forth like a crib. Nazif pulled the oars out of the water and sat there for a moment, facing her. Lebriz felt at peace.

"Take off your veil," he said.

Startled, she looked at him. What did he mean?

"Uncover your hair," he said. "No one can see you here. Except me. Feel the breeze."

Lebriz gently unraveled the fabric that had hidden her hair. The last time she'd uncovered her hair out of doors was by the pool at the harem. But this was different. Now there were no walls inhibiting the wind and no shrubs for shelter from others' eyes. Her hair fell on her shoulders for an instant but then the wind picked it up and blew it all over. She tried to control it with both hands, but it was as though her hair had taken flight. She saw Nazif smiling at her. She let go of her hair and let it sweep across her face and blow up in the air. She laughed, which made him laugh too.

My hair is free, she thought, and so am I.

Suddenly he stood up. The boat rocked back and forth. Lebriz laughed again and held on.

"Let's fish!" he proclaimed. Erdal had already prepared fishing lines for them. Nazif took out one line with a hook and a piece of lead tied at the end. He held something he took out of a small container and pierced it with the hook.

"What is that?" she asked.

"It's a worm," he said. She looked at him in mock horror. "Fish find them irresistible."

He flung out the end of the line as far as he could. The piece of lead splashed into the water and sunk down.

"Here," he said, and handed her the line. He then threaded the second line with bait and threw that one out as well.

"Now we wait," he said. "You'll feel it if you catch anything."

He was the one who made the first catch. "I got one!" he shouted, and started to pull the line out of the water. At the end of it, there was a fairly large fish, jumping and squirming. He grabbed it and pulled the hook out of its mouth. He held up the squirming creature for her to see. "It's a sea bass," he said. "It will make a wonderful meal."

Soon she felt her line tug as well.

"Let me help you," he said.

"No," she replied. "I'll do it myself."

It wasn't long before she caught her own sea bass. He took the fish off the hook and threw it in the bucket.

"Your first catch," he said. "I'm proud of you."

They continued to fish until the late afternoon. Catching fish didn't seem to be the point after a while. They sat back and enjoyed their surroundings and their intimacy. It was almost sundown when he rowed them back ashore. Fishermen were lined up along the pier, standing over barrels containing hot coals, cooking their fish.

"This is where we'll have dinner," said Nazif. He approached one of the fishermen.

"My friend," he said. "Would you mind sharing your fire with me and my wife?"

The man immediately stood aside and let Nazif place two of his own fish on the grill. He and another fisherman pulled together a small barrel and two stools to create a makeshift-dining corner for the couple. Lebriz thanked them and sat down, charmed by the kindness of the fishermen and her own husband who stood there cooking their dinner. Finally he finished, put the fish on some paper the fishermen provided and brought it to the table. She felt this was the most delicious meal she'd ever had.

"What brought you to me, Lebriz Hanim?" he asked. "How did you get here? How did you escape the Sultan?"

"It's a long story, Nazif Bey," she said, smiling at the formality they still pretended to maintain.

"I want to hear all of it," he told her.

Lebriz started to explain how she'd escaped becoming a concubine because Valide Sultan had adopted her, but Nazif stopped her.

"I want to hear your story from the beginning," he said.

He listened intently as she told him about her grandfather and the Russian persecution, and how her father had taken a kuma causing his wife to leave her children behind. She described to Nazif her early days in the harem and how she could not have survived without Jafer's protection. She also spoke affectionately about Nadide, and Muazzez and Güldane. By the time she finished her story evening was well under way.

"I'm honored that you were reunited with your mother at the very moment you married me," he said.

"I know," she agreed. "God does indeed work in mysterious ways."

They had finished their supper and sat together for a few minutes, watching the glimmer of light reflected off the Bosphorus at sunset. It was a melancholy and beautiful moment. Nazif reached over and held her hand.

"I'm grateful that you ended up with me, Lebriz."

Erdal, who had been sitting against a wall only a few yards away, watched the couple as they rose and walked toward him.

"We're ready to go home, Erdal Efendi," Nazif announced.

"Right away," smiled Erdal as he jumped up on his box.

Nazif helped Lebriz mount the carriage. Soon, they were on their way back to Taksim.

Nazif accompanied Lebriz to her bedroom. Then, in his usual fashion, he bid her goodnight. "Thank you for such a lovely day, Lebriz Hanim." He kissed her tenderly on the cheek and turned to leave the room.

"Nazif," she said quietly.

He turned to look at her.

She walked to him and held out her hand.

"I will never touch you unless you're ready," he said, taking her hand in his.

"I'm ready."

He held her close and kissed her on the mouth. She trembled at the sensation that coursed through her body. Nazif caressed her hair and her cheek then kissed her again, this time with more urgency.

He stood back and unbuttoned his shirt and took it off. He watched her as she undid her dress and dropped it on the floor. She stood in front of him in a silk slip, her arms bare. He embraced her. The feeling of his flesh against hers sent shivers through her once again.

Nazif sat on the bed and held out his hand. She joined him and lay down next to him. Pulling her close, he continued to kiss her. It wasn't much longer until they were both naked and he was ready to enter her. He looked into her eyes. She looked back and nodded. He entered her gently. Soon, she was able to completely let go and let him make love to her freely. She understood, right then, that it was just a matter of trust.

The following two years were a time of happiness for the young couple. The more they got to know each other, the more they fell in love. Nazif took delight in observing how his new wife became increasingly accustomed to life outside the harem. She absorbed news and information, and read voraciously. She delighted in making even the most minute of decisions. They attended the theater and opera together, and Nazif always took pleasure in taking his wife shopping.

Lebriz was fascinated by street life; the shop windows, the peddlers, fruit and vegetable stands, the butchers, and even the beggars were an endless source of fascination for her. For Nazif, it was like watching a young child discover a new universe. Her innocence and curiosity, combined with her elegance and beauty, made his heart ache with love. She, in turn, was beginning to realize what a gift it was to be truly loved by her husband.

Rengin and Idil continued hosting their visitor's days as usual. Except now, these lively afternoons usually turned into evenings for the whole family to get together. If Idil was hosting at Taksim, Orhan Pasha would arrive shortly after the guests went home; and if Rengin was hosting at Pink Mansion, Nazif would arrive and join the women for the usual feast. Güldane also attended often, as did Muazzez, along with her new husband.

Pink Mansion, with its lush gardens, was the ideal setting for summer parties, while in the winter, the family loved sitting in front of the fireplace in Taksim, telling stories and playing games. Rengin continued to be fascinated by Nesrin's tales of her childhood and Circassian lore. Orhan Pasha, on the other hand, loved holding court and talking about his life in the military and his many adventures in far-flung areas of the empire.

Even during the happiest of occasions, Nesrin would sometimes grow quiet and thoughtful. Lebriz always noticed this and knew what her mother was thinking. She too felt her happiness could not be complete until Jemil was with them. They were at least grateful to be told that he was alive. Orhan Pasha reported that he was stationed in the Balkans. This was a delicate area in a politically precarious time, but since no battles were currently fought, Orhan Pasha was convinced Jemil was safe. Any news of her son came as a relief for Nesrin.

"Can't he take time off to come see his family?" she asked.

"As soon as things settle down," Orhan Pasha replied. "I know that he misses you as much as you miss him."

"How do you know that?" asked Nesrin.

"I've been a soldier all my life. I know what it's like to be away from loved ones."

Nesrin would grow quiet again and Lebriz knew she wasn't quite convinced. She wouldn't believe her son was alive until she saw him in the flesh.

On a sunny spring morning, Lebriz told her husband that she was expecting a child. Nazif dropped his paper and jumped off his seat. He grabbed his wife by the waist and held her tight. He looked into her eyes.

"Look at you. You're glowing."

"I'm happy. I'm the happiest I've ever been."

"Have you told anyone?"

"Only my mother and Nanna."

"May I tell my mother?"

"Yes, please do!"

Soon, Nesrin, Idil, Nanna, and even Erdal had gathered in the salon.

Idil was overjoyed. "My first grandson!" she exclaimed as she squeezed Lebriz with her hefty arms.

"We don't know if it's a boy," said Lebriz with a smile.

"It's a boy," Idil affirmed. "I'm sure of it."

"But what if it's a girl, Madre?" Nazif asked.

"We will love the child as a most precious gift, whether it's a boy or a girl." She smiled and added mischievously, "But it's a boy."

This made Lebriz laugh.

"Congratulations, Nesrin Hanim," Idil exclaimed. "Congratulations, Nanna!"

"Why congratulate me?" retorted Nanna. "I'm not the one who's pregnant, God forbid!"

"Yes, you are," said Idil, grasping Lebriz's hand. "We all are."

"Erdal Efendi, please take the news to Rengin Hanim and Orhan Pasha. Let's all gather together tonight to celebrate."

"Right away," said Erdal, and went straightaway to Pink Mansion.

The gathering that night was jubilant. Nanna had made sure that all of Lebriz's favorite food was served, including duck a l'orange, which Lebriz remembered from Nadide Sultan's table. A recent experiment for Idil's cook, the dish tasted nothing like the original Lebriz so fondly remembered, but she said it was *comme il faut*, just as it should be. The women showered her with questions and advice.

"I craved pickles when I was pregnant with Nazif," cooed Idil, "but not just any pickles--purple carrot pickles from Afyon! Do you crave pickles, Lebriz?"

"No. I crave green plums, but I always crave those."

"They're almost in season," said Nanna. "I will go out to look for them next week!"

Nazif and Orhan Pasha were both amused to listen to the women. When the subject turned to preparations for the newborn, Orhan Pasha turned to Nazif. "Why don't we go have a smoke, Nazif Bey?"

"I'd be delighted," said Nazif, relieved at the chance to escape.

Nazif shut the door to the smoking room, produced two finely aged cigars, and offered one to Orhan Pasha. The men settled back in their comfortable chairs. Orhan Pasha, who was normally talkative, seemed thoughtful.

"Is there something that concerns you, Orhan Pasha?"

"Indeed there is," said the older man, somberly. "It seems our world is falling apart."

"Are you taking about the trouble in the Balkans?"

"I understand the troops are frustrated," Orhan Pasha replied. "They just assassinated the police commissioner in Salonika. These are our own troops, committing such crimes."

"I hadn't heard about that."

"The sultan is at a loss. His aides are telling him it's an organization of rabbles called the Committee of something or other...."

"Committee of Union and Progress."

"Yes! You know about them?"

"Of course, everyone's talking about them. What they want is something simple, Orhan Pasha."

"They want to decry the authority of the government, the supreme authority of the sultan. That's what they want!"

Nazif shook his head. "What they want is the restitution of the constitution that the sultan abolished illegally thirty years ago."

"Do you agree with them, then?" Orhan Pasha looked surprised.

"I agree with their motives. I'm not sure I agree with their methods."

"Well they're not going to get it by causing uprisings and assassinating people! We have enough trouble as it is. The Russians, Italians, Greeks, and even the British are threatening our borders. These rabblerousers are betraying our own country."

"Is there something I can do to help, Orhan Pasha?"

"Yes! There is something. I've asked my lawyers to draw up papers to have all my property transferred to you: the Pink Mansion, the house at Shishli and my bank accounts. I've put all my gold sovereigns under the name of Rengin, with the provision of your supervision."

"I don't understand. Why would you do such a thing?

"Because I can see a revolution brewing. As a servant of the Sublime Porte, I will be most at risk. I will be sent to exile or be executed."

"Nothing like that will happen, Orhan Pasha. Rest assured—"

"It's nice of you to try to appease my fears, but this is what's happening, my boy. Please tell me you accept my offer and promise me one thing."

"Anything."

"Promise me that you'll take care of Rengin. She will be lost without me."

"God forbid, Orhan Pasha. Nothing's going to happen."

"Do I have your word?"

"Of course."

"There is one more thing, and I'm only telling you this because I think you should know, and also because I trust your discretion."

"Of course."

"One of the leading members of the rabble-rousers in the Committee of…."

"Committee of Union and Progress."

"Yes. One of their leaders is an officer assigned to the fifth regiment in Macedonia and is known by the name of Jemil."

"Jemil?"

"Yes."

"Lebriz's brother?"

"The one."

Nazif took a pause. He wasn't quite sure what to do with this information. "Why are you telling me this?"

"Because you and this man are related, my boy. Your paths will no doubt cross one day. I trust you won't speak a word of this to Lebriz or Nesrin Hanim."

"Why not? She and her mother both crave information about Jemil. They would be relieved to know that he's alive. Nesrin Hanim would be proud to hear that her son has risen to the rank of officer."

"Are you sure about that?" asked Orhan Pasha with a stern tone of voice. "Wouldn't it be embarrassing to know that your son is a rabble-rouser? Why not let them believe that he's a hero? Why let them know that he's a criminal and a traitor to his country?"

Nazif stood up from his chair, stunned at the man's tone of voice and what he was saying.

After a moment, Orhan Pasha finally said, "I would advise you to not tell them anything at all. There is no good ending to this. You know very well that as soon as he's caught—and you know he will be—he will be hanged. Is that what you want them to know?"

Nazif left the meeting, his mind reeling with thoughts. Should he not tell Lebriz and Nesrin that Jemil was found and that he is still alive? Was Orhan Pasha right in not wanting to tell them? He realized that the only reason not to tell them would be to protect them from the worry of what might happen to Jemil if he were caught.

That night, Nazif held his wife as they both lay in bed. She'd been falling asleep in his arms lately, her head pressed against his shoulder.

"My only wish," Lebriz muttered, right before drifting off to sleep, "is that Jemil is here for the birth of my child."

Nazif felt he was holding two souls against his bosom.

Lebriz's pregnancy progressed without incident. As her tummy grew, her cheeks got rosier, and her eyes seemed even brighter than before. She was unrelentingly pampered by both Nanna and Nesrin, and ate enough green plums to make her sick more than once. She loved the attention, but enjoyed a quiet moment once in a while to sit in the garden, smell the roses, and feel the fresh air against her skin.

On a Sunday afternoon, Lebriz headed out to the garden, leaving Nazif in the study to pore over the latest newspapers. She was now in her fourth month of pregnancy and it was rare that she escaped her mother and Nanna. Just as she got settled down on the bench facing the bush of yellow roses, Erdal opened the gate.

"There's someone here to see you," he said.

Lebriz looked up at Erdal and saw a man standing behind him, on the other side of the gate.

It was right at the moment when she began to utter the words "Who is it?" that recognized him. Her heart jumped up in her chest. "Jemil?" she asked uncertainly.

He smiled but remained by the gate, looking at her.

Erdal stood aside.

Lebriz rushed to him and he opened his arms for her. Locked in his embrace, she stared up at his face. How tall he'd grown and how handsome. He wore a mustache, and his jet-black hair was beginning to show signs of gray in the temples.

She kissed his cheeks, he kissed her forehead and her hair, then he held her at arms' length.

"How lovely you look. You're pregnant!"

Tears flowed down her cheeks as she caressed his face. "My only wish was that you be here for the birth of my child. Look at you. You're a man! The last time I saw you, we were only children."

Nazif was now standing by the gate.

"Nazif," she said as she motioned at him to approach. "Look who it is. My brother Jemil has arrived. Jemil, this is my husband Nazif Bey."

"It's a pleasure to meet you, Nazif Bey." Jemil shook Nazif's hand.

"The pleasure's mine, Captain," Nazif replied.

"Captain?" exclaimed Lebriz.

Jemil smiled modestly and ignored the remark. "I'm sorry to say I can only stay for a short time."

"How short?" cried Lebriz.

"A few hours. I have to go join my unit."

"Your unit?" asked Nazif simply. Jemil looked at him and their eyes met. "Of course, your unit," Nazif said.

"At least spend the night," Lebriz protested. "Mother will be devastated if you don't stay at least one night!"

"How is mother?"

"She's fine! She will be so happy to see you! She and Nanna both!"

"I hope you'd consider staying overnight," said Nazif. "Or at least stay for dinner."

"I'll stay as long as I can."

"Let's ask Erdal Efendi to fetch Orhan Pasha," Lebriz suggested.

"Maybe that's not a good idea," said Nazif.

"Why not? He and Rengin Hanim are dying to meet Jemil!"

"Perhaps your brother wants to spend some time alone with you, your mother, and Nanna. He's here for such a short time."

"Thank you," said Jemil. "I'd appreciate that."

"Of course," said Lebriz, running back to the house. "I'll get Nanna and my mother right away!"

"Thank you," Jemil said to Nazif.

"Why are you here? Aren't you putting yourself in danger?"

"I wanted to see my sister and my mother. And I wanted to meet you. I'm happy to see that Lebriz is well and thriving. I can tell that you love her."

Nazif spoke in a low voice. "She's very precious to me. I'd do anything to protect her."

"Rest assured that whatever happens, you and your family will be safe. No harm will come to you or your home."

"Orhan Pasha and his home?"

"I know how lovingly they've taken care of my sister. They will be protected as well."

"Welcome home, Captain," said Nazif, as he offered Jemil his hand.

At the dinner table that night, Nesrin was overcome with a sense of relief combined with the sorrow of lost years and the uncertainty of the future. Here was her son, finally, sitting at the table. Their little family was together at last. He looked healthy and dignified in his uniform, but also seemed remote, like a guest. Nesrin couldn't fathom where he came from, what his life was like, or where he was headed. Vague words about soldiers and wars and governments meant little to her. When she'd found Lebriz, she felt she was still her little girl, just older. But Jemil seemed a stranger to her.

Nanna was overjoyed to see Jemil again. She sensed Nesrin's apprehension and gave her a hard look, as if to tell her: be grateful he's here. Nesrin maintained her elegant composure and thanked Idil once again for hosting her family. Even Erdal and Jafer were invited to sit at the table for the occasion.

"Erdal Efendi is our hero," Nesrin announced. "None of this would have been possible without him."

Not accustomed to sitting at the table with the family, Erdal was embarrassed. "I would do anything for you, Nesrin Hanim, you know that."

Jafer refused to sit, aware that Nanna still couldn't look at him.

The family stayed at the table long after dinner was finished, telling stories and reminiscing.

"You probably won't remember this, you were so small," said Jemil to Lebriz, "but I used to hide you behind Nanna's skirts. Mother would always pretend she couldn't find us and then you'd jump out and surprise her. We all laughed so hard!"

"I do remember," Lebriz smiled. "I remember it very well."

"You look like you could use a good night's rest, Jemil Bey," said Idil finally. "Why don't you spend the night?"

"Yes," said Lebriz. "Why not? Your unit will wait for you."

"I suppose you're right," Jemil replied sheepishly. "Thank you for your hospitality, Idil Hanim."

"You're always welcome. This is your family."

Idil ordered the maid to prepare a room for Jemil.

"I'll take you to your room," Lebriz offered, standing up from the table.

Jemil bid everyone good night. He kissed his mother on the cheek and did the same to Nanna, promising to see them in the morning.

Lebriz accompanied her brother to the guest room in the east wing of the house. It was a small room with fresh sheets spread on a modest bed.

"I wish you could stay longer. Promise me you'll come back soon."

"As soon as I can, I promise."

She kissed him on the cheek. "Good night, my sweet brother."

Just as she was walking out the door, Jemil asked, "Do you remember our father at all, Lebriz?"

"No," she lied. She had no intention of spending these few precious moments talking about him. "I don't remember him at all."

"I do. Sometimes I wonder whatever happened to him."

"Who knows?" she shrugged. "I'll see you in the morning."

Lebriz woke early the next day and went straight to the east wing to invite Jemil to breakfast. The maid told her that he'd left before dawn.

It was only two nights later, on a Wednesday, that Orhan Pasha and Rengin met the family at the Taksim house after Idil's visitor's day. They were all gathered around the table after a leisurely dinner of leg of lamb, and the wonderful cheese pastry Idil 's kitchen was famous for. Coffee was being served when gunshots and shouting men were heard outside.

Erdal and Orhan Pasha's driver, Aziz, both ran into the dining room to alert the family that an attack was taking place. Jafer also rushed into the dining room.

Orhan Pasha immediately barked orders. "Jafer Efendi, take the ladies upstairs to the salon that overlooks the garden. There must no lights on in the front of the house, and stay away from the windows!"

Nazif consoled the women. "Most likely there's nothing to worry about, but please stay upstairs until Orhan Pasha or I come to you."

"Take care," said Rengin as she was being shuffled out of the room with the others. "May God's protection be with you all."

Idil, heavier now than before Nazif's wedding, and having just devoured a healthy portion of roast lamb, huffed as she tramped up the stairs.

"Probably another rabble demonstration against some new law or tax imposed on them. It's been happening more and more these days."

The women got settled in Nazif and Lebriz's apartment. Nesrin and Idil retired to the bedrooms while Lebriz, Nanna, Rengin, and some of the servants remained in the salon with Jafer, who pulled the drapes shut and lit one small lamp.

Sounds of gunshots and shouting voices continued throughout the night. At times, it sounded like men were fighting right in front of the house. Rengin and Lebriz stayed up while the others slept. It was right around dawn that the noise finally subsided. At ten o'clock Nazif strode into the apartment. The acrid smell of smoke still hung in the air.

"It seems safe to come out," he announced. "Orhan Pasha left the house to get some news and to check the Pink Mansion for damages."

"Did he leave alone?" asked Rengin.

"Of course not," Nazif replied. "Aziz and Erdal both went with him. We've all had a rough night. Why don't we gather together in the dining room and have something to eat?"

The family was just finishing lunch when Orhan Pasha returned, looking defeated and ten years older.

"Mobs have sacked and burned the homes of many prominent supporters of the sultan," he said somberly. "They've also pillaged both the Chiragan Palace, and Yildiz Palace."

Lebriz exclaimed, "The harem!"

"I don't have all the details yet. As far as I know, only a few lives were lost."

Lebriz looked at Jafer, who looked equally concerned. What could have happened to all their friends, Nadide, and the other women? They must be terrified, she thought, her mind racing. Were they safe?

"We will know more, later in the day," Orhan Pasha continued. "In the meantime, Rengin and I must return home."

"Has there been any damage to Pink Mansion?" asked Rengin anxiously.

"None whatsoever," replied Orhan Pasha. "Our home and this one are the only two that have been spared." He and Nazif exchanged a glance.

"Now let's go and start putting the pieces back together. These are mobs in the service of foreign powers. They're traitors. We will not let them win."

Nazif accompanied Rengin and Orhan Pasha to the Pink Mansion. He then went around the city, surveying the damage and getting reports from various witnesses. It was late afternoon by the time he returned to Taksim.

"The sultan has been deposed," he declared. "Our country is in tatters. We have no idea what the future will hold."

"What about Yildiz Palace?" asked Lebriz. "What's the news from the harem there?"

"I'm told the sultan will be sent to exile," Nazif replied. "One can only assume that the women will be sent with him. It appears most of the Divan and the royal associates of the sultanate will be sent abroad as well."

"And Orhan Pasha?" asked Lebriz.

"I don't know."

"Why was our house not attacked?"

"I have no answer to that." He answered looking down.

"Does this have something to do with Jemil?" Lebriz was becoming anxious. "I could tell there was something happening that you weren't telling us."

"I can't say anything, my dear," said Nazif.

"And how did you know he was a captain?" she pressed. "You knew things about him before he even showed up. What did you know? What didn't you tell us?"

Nazif sighed. "Orhan Pasha had found out that Jemil was involved with the Committee of Union and Progress. They are the group largely behind the uprising."

"When?" she asked, now visibly agitated.

"When what?"

"When did Orhan Pasha tell you this?"

"It was perhaps two months ago," he answered, running his hands through his hair.

"We thought he might be dead!" shouted Lebriz. "My mother had given up on him. You knew he was alive and you didn't tell us?"

"It was on the advice of Orhan Pasha," Nazif said, his voice controlled but his eyes flashing with exasperation. "I had to do what he told me."

"I will not forgive you for this, Nazif!" Lebriz stomped out of the room.

Minutes later, Lebriz was knocking on Jafer's door. "Open up, Jafer Efendi, please open up!"

Jafer looked bewildered when he opened the door. He'd been asleep since he'd stayed up the entire previous night. "What's the matter, Lebriz Hanim? What's happened?"

"Please come with me," she said, turning away and striding back into the house.

"Where are we going?"

"To Yildiz Palace. I've already asked Erdal Efendi to bring up the carriage."

"Yildiz Palace, why? What will we do there?"

"Just come with me," she commanded, "and don't ask questions. You promised me you'd stand by my side, no matter what!"

"There are limits to my loyalty, Lebriz Hanim," Jafer argued. "You must calm yourself. Remember that you're pregnant!"

They were at the foyer by now and Erdal had pulled up to the door in the carriage.

"I will be pregnant for another month," she said. "We'll be back way before then."

"You're very upset, Lebriz Hanim. You're behaving rashly. Please, let's be reasonable," Jafer pleaded. "What will your mother say? Where is Nazif Bey?"

"I don't care," Lebriz cried out. "I want to see my friends. Our old friends! I want to see Nadide Sultan before it's too late!"

"Too late, for what?"

Nazif had entered the foyer and was now standing at the door, a concerned look on his face.

Jafer glared at him in despair. "Nazif Bey, she wants to go to Yildiz Palace. What can I do? This is outrageous. She can't do this, sir. Not in her condition."

Nazif looked at Lebriz. She glared back at him with fiery, piercing eyes. Never had he seen her so angry before.

"We're going," Lebriz said to Jafer. "You gave me your promise. We'll be back by evening."

Jafer looked at Nazif again.

"She can go," said Nazif helplessly. "Just bring her back to me safe and sound."

Lebriz was out the door before Nazif finished speaking. Erdal helped her mount the carriage and Jafer reluctantly followed her.

When Lebriz and Jafer arrived at the gates of Yildiz Palace they were astounded to see that there were no guards. It was unheard of to have the gates of the palace unguarded. They drove up to the harem with no intervention whatsoever, climbed out of the carriage, and walked straight up to the door.

A black eunuch recognized Jafer and Lebriz immediately. "Why would you come back?" he asked. "It's crazy here."

"I want to see Nadide Sultan," said Lebriz firmly.

The eunuch stood aside.

The harem was in chaos. Women were running all around the place trying to gather up supplies. They'd been told that the sultan was to travel abroad and that they were to follow him. They had no idea where they were going, nor did they know when. The sultan's wives—all ten of the twelve still living—were frantically gathering up their jewelry and other valuables and packing them in trunks and bags. Concubines and servants were swarming around, taking orders and doing their best to meet all the wives' demands.

Jafer and Lebriz headed straight to Nadide's apartments. Unlike the rest of the harem, these rooms appeared to be quiet and calm. Nadide was reclined on the divan, looking relaxed and enjoying her coffee. Her trunks were already packed and placed in the hallway. She looked serene until the very moment she saw Lebriz enter the room followed by the eunuch Jafer.

Nadide broke down in tears. "My girl, my beautiful girl, what are you doing here?"

Lebriz rushed to her side and threw her arms around her. "I wanted to see you, Nadide Sultan. I couldn't bear to think you'd leave without saying goodbye."

Nadide saw Lebriz' swollen belly and caressed it. "You're pregnant! How lovely you look. I have missed you so much. I'm so grateful that you've come to see me."

"Do you know where you'll go?" asked Lebriz, also shedding tears.

"Oh, it's such a mess. Nobody knows anything. They're all running about like chickens with no heads. You know I have no tolerance for chaos. Whatever happens will be Allah's will. I have to trust in that."

Lebriz sat beside her on the divan.

"But you must leave, my dear girl. The chaos will only get worse."

"I will stay a little while longer," Lebriz said, wiping her face.

"Then tell me everything. Who is your husband? Where is your home? How are Muazzez and Güldane? Do you ever see them? Do they remember me?"

"My husband is the most loving man you can imagine. He's nothing like I feared."

Nadide listened intently as Lebriz answered all of her questions. Jafer stood by the door, observing.

"What a life you've had, my dear Lebriz. Soon you'll have a child and that will change everything."

Nobody noticed the passage of time. It had been a full hour and Jafer was becoming nervous.

"You must go," Nadide said. "Please get back before sundown. Who knows what will happen when darkness descends. God bless you and protect you and your family, my darling Lebriz. Now go!"

Lebriz kissed Nadide's hand in the traditional fashion. "I'm so grateful for all you've done for me and I'll always remember you and love you."

The two women held each other for a long time.

"Go with God, sweet girl," said Nadide. "Jafer Efendi, you have my deepest gratitude for taking such good care of our treasure."

The sun was setting when the carriage pulled up to the house in Taksim. Nazif was anxiously waiting at the door. Lebriz walked past him, barely acknowledging him, and headed straight for her room.

Crestfallen, Nazif looked at Jafer.

"She'll be fine," said the old man. "Just give her some time."

"I have patience, if nothing else," Nazif nodded.

His wife's anger devastated him. He could only wait for half an hour before going to their rooms. He found her seated by the window, looking out at the park.

He took a chair across from her. He remembered the first time he'd sat with her on their first night together, and how patient he'd been back then. Even though he was aching to touch her, to caress her hair and kiss her luscious lips, he'd held back.

"Forgive me," he said. "Please forgive me."

Lebriz still wouldn't look at him. "I spent my whole life in confinement. I was protected from everything. Now that I'm free, I see the world around me and all I want is to learn about it. I don't want to be protected. I want to know everything. I want to know what's happening in the world. Is that so wrong?"

"Of course not," he said.

For the next two hours, Nazif spoke and Lebriz listened. He explained that Jemil was part of a group that was fighting against the absolute autocracy of the sultan. In the beginning, they were students and intellectuals, but the movement had spilled into the military, which was how Jemil had become involved. It was now a group of all ethnicities involving Turks, Greeks, Armenians, and Arabs, all united in fighting the sultan.

"Their intentions are good," Nazif explained. "They want to reinstate the constitution. But they are seen as rebels and criminals and they face great odds."

Lebriz listened intently, then asked, "Do you agree with this group?"

"As I told Orhan Pasha, I agree with their ideology, but I disagree with their methods. They have no qualms about assassinating anyone who opposes them. I hope they won't continue in that vein."

"Is Orhan Pasha in danger?"

"He is vulnerable because of his close relations with the sultan's government."

"What about you? You work for the government too."

"I'm a mere clerk in an office so I pose no threat to them. I'm not an outspoken loyalist, like Orhan Pasha is." He took her hand in his.

"I want our child to know he has a mother who is not just a doll from a harem," she said, "but is someone who understands our changing world. Whether it's a boy or a girl, I want our child to be proud of her mother."

Unlike Lebriz, Rengin had little interest in learning about politics and world affairs. Her main concern was her home. She scurried around inspecting everything to make sure there was no damage, and that nothing had been stolen.

Aziz explained that he and the servants had guarded the house and were ready to fight. "But nothing happened," he said. "They pillaged other houses nearby, but passed our house without even taking notice. It was very odd."

This news was remarkable for Rengin, but not pertinent. To her, it made sense that they wouldn't touch Orhan Pasha's house. He was a well-respected and admired pillar of the nation. They wouldn't dare harm his home or family.

When she glanced into the foyer and saw Orhan Pasha welcoming a visitor, she didn't make much of it. She assumed it was a local citizen, giving her husband a report about what had happened. Surely it was nothing that would concern her.

She busied herself with dinner arrangements, leaving the men to talk. When the maid announced there was no meat in the house, and no way to go shopping today, Rengin was outraged but thought it best to control herself. These were unusual and difficult times, after all.

The man at the door introduced himself to Orhan Pasha.

"I am Jemil Bey, son of Nejmi Bey and grandson of Mustafa Bey of New Manor, granted by the sultan, for the seven villages of the Circassian and for guarding the borders against the Russians."

"I know who you are," said Orhan Pasha. "I met your grandfather many years ago. Please come inside."

The conversation began with the usual formalities but soon heated up.

"You and your men are naive," said Orhan Pasha angrily, pacing the floor of the study. "You have no idea what you're doing. Do you understand the consequences of these attacks? You'll change the entire world! You've upset the balance of power by deposing the sultan. It puts the entire nation in danger. Who amongst you knows anything about running an empire? Who do you think you are?"

"All has not changed," said Jemil, calmly. "We've deposed the sultan and replaced him with another."

"Yes, Murat the Fifth," sneered Orhan Pasha. "He's a mere symbol, an ineffectual, powerless man. He's exactly what the British and the Russians want—a puppet sultan." Orhan Pasha's face was red with anger.

"I regret that you feel this way. It is indeed a new world. But we're optimistic that this will be a new and better chapter in our nation's history. We intend to make the empire part of the modern, civilized world."

"Ah. An idealist," Orhan Pasha groaned. "I suppose you're here for my assistance or advice? I'm sorry that I won't be able to offer you anything."

"Actually, no. I'm here to thank you for all you've done for my sister and mother. I'm very grateful for your generosity and kind heart," Jemil said, his eyes heavy with emotion. "I'm also here to tell you that for your own protection, we feel it's best that you leave the country."

"You're sending me to exile, in other words."

Jemil nodded. "Yes."

"I suppose I should be grateful I won't be executed."

"I'm afraid you'll be in danger if you stay here. We will provide you with protection while you prepare to leave. We hope this can happen as soon as possible."

Orhan Pasha looked earnestly at the young captain. "How soon?" he asked.

"Tomorrow," replied Jemil.

Orhan Pasha paused for a moment and surveyed the man standing in front of him. He was still young, handsome and strong. He almost felt sorry for him for being so optimistic about the empire's future. He had no idea what lay in store. How brave and foolish he seemed.

"Do you realize I also knew your father, Nejmi Bey?"

"Yes," Jemil replied, flinching at the sound of his father's name. "I think you knew him better than I did. I was only a child when I was separated from my parents. My mother refuses to speak about him."

"He was one of the bravest soldiers I knew. An upstanding, noble man who fought for his country. A true patriot. He would be ashamed to see you now."

Jemil looked down, barely able to digest these words.

"Now if you'll excuse me," Orhan Pasha concluded, "I will alert my wife as to what will happen to us."

Orhan Pasha turned and left the room, leaving Jemil alone to stare at the gaping door.

At first, Rengin took the news in stride. "Just another trip abroad," she said. "You'll return soon enough."

"I think not, my dear wife, love of my life. I beg of you to be strong through all of this. If God wills, I will return. If not, I will die with honor, and in the certainty of your love."

He held her tight in his arms and kissed her gently.

"What will I do without you?" she cried. "How will I live?"

"Nazif will take care of all our affairs. I've put all my property in his trust. You will take care of yourself and our family, and you'll always remember that you're more precious to me than life itself."

She held his face in her hands.. "You will come back to me, my husband. No man, nor God, can take you out of my heart."

Muazzez, Güldane, and other friends joined the family the next day to send Orhan Pasha abroad. Nazif and Lebriz both kissed Orhan Pasha's hand and he wished them well. Rengin mustered all the strength she could as she said goodbye to her husband. He smiled at her, admiring her courage.

Two uniformed men arrived to escort Orhan Pasha away. Aziz was bewildered to watch his master mount a carriage driven by other men. After he was gone, the family receded deep into the house, where they spent the rest of the day grieving and reminiscing. To everyone's surprise, Rengin was the one who retained her courage and optimism.

"One era is over," she announced at the dinner table. "But the future is right here," she said, indicating Lebriz's swollen tummy.

It wasn't until everyone went to bed that she fell apart.

With her mother and Idil at her side, Lebriz gave birth to a healthy baby boy in the early fall. As soon as Nanna clipped the umbilical cord and Nesrin handed her the baby, Lebriz knew her life would never be the same again. The three women smiled and stroked Lebriz's cheek, saying "God bless and give a long full life to you both."

Nazif was overcome with emotion as he watched mother and baby together. He too found his son mesmerizing. Idil couldn't resist the temptation to gloat. "I told you it would be a boy!"

The birth was just the tonic to distract Rengin from her husband's exile. She was deeply moved when the couple decided to name the baby Orhan.

Lebriz was captivated by the baby's every move and gurgle, yet also found her attention shifting to other matters. Still affected by the conversation she'd had with her husband about the state of the country, her thoughts turned to politics for the first time in her life.

She began to imagine what the future might hold for her child. Questions flooded her mind. What kind of world had her baby come into? How safe would he be? How could she protect him? Would there ever be peace in his lifetime? Political events like the uprisings, the wars in the Balkans, elections, and even Orhan Pasha's exile, took on more significance for her as she thought about her own child's prospects. Would he be lucky enough to find love, as she had found herself?

She questioned her husband daily about what was happening in the country at large, demanding where the political movements stood, and what issues were currently discussed. This new side to Lebriz intrigued Nesrin. Nanna was mystified by it, and Idil dismissed it as an interesting but passing phase.

Nazif met Lebriz's questions with equanimity. He would bring home the newspapers so they could read them together, and then discuss the issues. One afternoon he brought home a publication named Tanim and showed her that a woman had written one of the articles.

Lebriz was astounded.

"First time in our history that we have a woman's words in print," Nazif said with a grin.

The writer, Halide Hanim, became a regular contributor to the paper. Her articles were usually about education and the status of women, which Lebriz devoured as soon as they appeared.

Weeks after his departure, Orhan Pasha's absence was felt ever more deeply in the household. News came that his old friend and colleague Semih Pasha had also been exiled. Nesrin, Idil, Rengin, and Nanna were all bewildered but required no information other than when the man would be allowed to return home. Lebriz, on the other hand, wanted to understand everything. She couldn't quite grasp what the so-called Committee of Union and Progress was out to accomplish, why Jemil was involved with them, and why on earth did such a good-hearted man as Orhan Pasha pose any threat to them.

"He symbolizes the old order," said Nazif.

"Has he committed a crime?" asked Lebriz despondently. "Has he done anything wrong?"

"Yes and no," replied Nazif to his even more befuddled wife. "Some of what he did—some of his actions in the past—may not have been considered illegal at the time, but are seen as criminal in the new era."

"How can that be?" she cried out. "The man is innocent. He deserves no punishment!"

"Even his existence poses a threat to the new regime," said Nazif. "It's unfortunate but that's the way it is."

"How could Jemil do this to us? How could he do this to our family?"

"Don't blame him," said Nazif. "It's not his choice."

"I do blame him," she said. "I think he did have a choice."

"He came to deliver the news to Orhan Pasha personally," said Nazif. "Because he cared. He was as gentle and considerate as possible."

"How cruel that two men that I care so much about would be cast against each other in such an unthinkable way!"

Nazif had some suspicions about where Orhan Pasha had been sent, and some investigation through government acquaintances confirmed his fears. Orhan Pasha was on his way to Fezzan, a city in the southern edges of the desert in Libya, so far from Istanbul that it took more than a month to reach. It was well known that Abdul Hamid sent political agitators there, sometimes for life.

Nazif certainly didn't want to share this information with the family. It was likely that Orhan Pasha would suffer torture, starvation, and illness in the place deemed by many as "hell on earth." In spite of his promise to keep his wife informed of everything, he thought it best to pretend he knew nothing at all.

Meanwhile, Orhan Pasha himself was in the dark about where the convoy was headed. He was saddened to see that his dear friend Semih Pasha was in the same carriage as he, but also felt comforted. The two men acknowledged each other with a nod, as no one was allowed to speak. It was well into the second week of the journey that both men felt their suspicions had probably come to pass. When they were both given a moment of privacy while they were urinating against a bush by the side of the road, Semih Pasha muttered under his breath, "Fezzan."

Just hearing his friend's voice was a relief and Orhan Pasha could not help but smile.

"I suspect so," he said.

As sultan's deputies, both Orhan and Semih had, at one point or another, been instrumental in sending political agitators to Fezzan. The purpose was to keep them as far away from Istanbul as possible. Both men also knew that these political dissidents, contrary to what the public thought, were not imprisoned at all. Instead, they were left free to roam about as they pleased as long as they did not leave the region. In most cases, the Sultan even granted them a monthly salary. Now, as they buttoned up their pants, the two men smiled not only at the irony of the realization, but also because this intimate moment reminded them of their days serving together as young soldiers. They both knew well that the trip to Fezzan would take at least another miserable three weeks. But the realization that they'd meet whatever fate awaited them together gave them comfort.

For the next several years, the Ottoman Empire experienced the most democratic era of its history. A myriad of political parties were up for election and several secular and liberal reforms came to pass. Many voices belonging to different ethnicities—including Muslims, Jews, Armenians, Arabs, and Christians—were now being heard. Even women were more vocal about their rights and positions in society.

In spite of the sorrow over Orhan Pasha's fate, both Lebriz and Nazif felt energized by these changes. Nazif had long dreamed of a liberal, democratic nation aspiring to European standards and Lebriz was getting increasingly involved in women's causes. She and Muazzez banded together with several other women to host meetings in their homes. Unlike Idil and Rengin's visitor's days, which continued to thrive, these meetings addressed serious subjects: women's changing roles in Ottoman society, educational reform, and the literary and artistic expression of women's concerns.

Just as Orhan Pasha had predicted, the new Sultan, Mahmud V, was left essentially powerless under the leadership of the Committee of Union and Progress, and stood more or less as a symbol. While social life became relatively modernized in Istanbul and other large cities, serious trouble plagued the empire abroad and in the provinces. The unrest in Macedonia was compounded further by a forceful Ottoman military response. Bulgaria won its independence and Bosnia was lost to Austria-

Hungary, leaving Istanbul vulnerable to European attacks.

In the East, matters were just as bleak if not worse. The age-old conflict with Russia continued with the eastern borders under continuous threat. A short war with Italy lost Libya and effectively ended the empire's 340 year-long presence in North Africa.

Over the course of two years, thousands of refugees flooded the city. Internal politics went into further turmoil as Christian and Jewish minorities, along with the progressives, questioned the unity of the government. A subsequent coup put the three leaders of the Committee of Union and Progress—Pahsas Enver, Talat and Jemal—in charge. Established to defend Istanbul, the triumvirate would soon drive the country into a misguided and catastrophic war.

Back at the Taksim house, Nazif was all too aware of the danger rising in the streets. More and more bandits and rebels were causing trouble in neighborhoods that had once been thought safe. Taksim, being so centrally located, felt especially exposed. It was Erdal, along with the driver Aziz, who would stay up and guard the house all night.

The family was grateful to be safe within the confines of the home and soon there was more good news. Lebriz gave birth again, this time to a baby girl named Nil. Orhan was three years old now, and with two small children in the house, Nesrin, Nanna, and Idil had much to occupy themselves. Lebriz continued to pursue her political aspirations but clearly nothing was more important to her than the safety and health of her children.

Energetic and curious, little Orhan was always ready to ravage every corner of the house. Jafer was his chief guardian and best friend. Nazif being away at work all day and the women constantly occupied with the baby, Jafer was the one always available for fun. Lebriz was especially glad to see this friendship unfold. Joined by Nesrin and Nanna, she often sat in the garden with the baby on her lap and watched Orhan's mischief with Jafer.

The old man would lift the boy off the ground with one hand and act as though he was going to fling him across the lawn, which would send Orhan into convulsions of laughter. Other times, Orhan would climb up Jafer's arm like a tree and holler with delight as he wrapped his arms around the man's bald head. Jafer simply stood still and grinned. It warmed Lebriz's heart to see the smile in the old man's eyes. Even Nanna would chuckle on the sidelines.

In calmer moments, the two of them would sit together quietly and observe things in the garden: the fish in the pond, the bugs and ants and other crawly insects that fascinated Orhan. Jafer had spent many a year with young girls at the harem, but never with a boy as energetic and curious as this one. It was as though he was discovering the world through Orhan's young eyes.

One evening Nazif returned from work and asked to speak to his mother in private.

"Things are looking precarious in the city, Madre," he said. "There is too much burglary and violence going around. I have an offer from a British firm to buy this house. With your permission, I'd like to sell it and move the family to Sariyer."

"Sariyer?" she asked despondently. "You're asking me to leave my house and move to the hinterlands?"

"It's not the hinterlands, Madre. It's very nice. It's peaceful and safe."

"It's all the way up north. It's where people go to have picnics. What do you think your father would think about abandoning his precious house and moving to the boondocks?"

"Only think about it, Madre," said Nazif. "But remember I'm in charge of the family now. It's my job to keep us safe."

"I can't bear the thought," she said, almost in tears. "I can't bear the thought of leaving my beautiful house."

Nazif spoke to his wife late that evening. The couple was enjoying a rare moment alone together. They were lying in bed, having just finished making love. She caressed her husband's brow.

"You're so worried all the time," she said. "And I'm worried about you."

"You're my shelter from the storm," he said, and kissed her lips.

"What's worrying you so much?"

"Everything, "he said. "Our country is in great danger. Everything Orhan Pasha said is coming to pass."

"How do you mean? What did he say?"

"He said the committee wouldn't be able to run the country. That they didn't have the experience or the vision to handle internal and external affairs…."

"The country was in trouble before they took power," said Lebriz.

"Yes, and they were certain they could improve things but they've made it only worse. It looks like we're headed toward war."

"War. It seems like there is always a war going on in this place or another."

"I'm afraid this one will be bigger than the rest."

"I wonder where my brother is. And what's happened to Orhan Pasha."

"Your brother is stationed in the East, fighting the Russians."

"In the East? How do you know this?" she asked, surprised.

"I get sporadic reports, Lebriz. I'm sorry I don't tell you everything."

"Fighting the Russians just like our father."

"And Orhan Pasha is in Fezzan."

"Fezzan?" she said with horror in her voice. "He's been in Fezzan all this time?"

"I'm hoping we'll get some news of him soon. Whether it will be good or bad I don't know. But now that Italy's occupied that area, I hope he will be released and free to come home."

"I know why you don't tell me everything," she said while caressing his cheek. "It's because you want to protect me."

"Yes," he said sadly. "I don't want you to worry about anything."

"But when you keep it inside," she said, "it's even worse. Because I know you're preoccupied and I want to help, don't you see? I want to be useful, I want to help you."

"There is actually something you can do," said Nazif.

"Tell me what it is."

"I've told Madre I want to sell this house and move the family to Sariyer."

"Why Sariyer?"

"Because we will be safer there. All I want is to keep our family safe."

"You would like me to talk to her."

"Yes, with your gentle way, I think only you will be able to convince her."

Lebriz didn't have to approach Idil to convince her. Late that night a band of five men attacked the house. They came from all directions and both Aziz and Erdal were caught off guard. Aziz immediately grabbed his rifle and started to shoot. He shot one of the men dead and injured another. The men shot back and Aziz was able to cower behind a half wall. Erdal remained exposed and was hit with a bullet in the head. He died instantly. Aziz kept shooting and the men, realizing they wouldn't get any further, dispersed and ran down the street. Lebriz and Nazif were both awakened by the shots and ran downstairs.

"Stay back," warned Nazif. Lebriz waited in the foyer in her nightgown while Nazif gently opened the door to find the heartbreaking sight. Lebriz heard him gasp. She immediately knew.

"Who have we lost?" she asked.

"It's our old friend Erdal Efendi," said Nazif. "Please stay inside. Please don't come out."

Lebriz stood there trembling and covering her mouth to keep herself from screaming.

How cruel, she thought, to kill such a gentle and loving man. How would she tell her mother? How would she tell Nanna?

SARIYER

The entire house went into mourning after Erdal's death. Nesrin was grieved beyond words. This was a man who'd been her protector and mentor all these years. All his life he'd served selflessly. How senseless it was that this kindest of men should be victim to one bullet. She and Lebriz held each other and cried. Nazif, as protector of the family, was at a loss. He felt utterly helpless because there was nothing he could do. Only Nanna remained stoic.

"We're all going to die," she said. "At least he didn't suffer. I hope my death is as sudden and painless as his."

She reminded Nesrin of how Erdal would not have wanted her to grieve so much.

"He'd be the first to tell you to look at your children and take consolation in them," she said. "And look! Look at him!"

Little Orhan had entered the room with Jafer. Wide-eyed and inquisitive, he knew something had gone wrong. When he saw both his grandmother and mother in tears, his small face got distorted and he started to cry as well. Nesrin waved at Jafer to indicate to take the boy away. She couldn't bare the child's sadness and confusion at what life had in store. "Let him not see it," she said.

Jafer swept the child up and took him to the window.

"Look," he said to the boy. "Look at those squirrels. Look how they're chasing each other. Look! Look!"

Soon the child stopped crying and even smiled at the sight of the creatures jumping from branch to branch. How easy it is to distract the young, thought Jafer.

Idil was aggrieved as well. Not only for Erdal, whom she didn't know so well, but also for her home, which she now knew she must give up.

"I'm sorry I resisted you," she told her son. "Maybe if I hadn't, maybe if we'd moved earlier, this wouldn't have happened."

"No use blaming yourself, Madre. Nothing could've been done. Let's let go of this old place and welcome the future."

The Taksim house was sold in a few short weeks. The new dwelling in Sariyer, big enough to accommodate the family, their servants, and guests, was made of three wings surrounding a lush garden. The top two floors had generous views of the ships, ferries, and fishing boats eternally sailing the Bosphorus.

The balcony jutting out of Idil's salon became a favorite place for the ladies to congregate for tea. The visitor's days, now overlooking the garden and majestic view, resumed as usual but the conversation was subdued. Petty gossip felt less than enjoyable in these troubled times. Even Madam Janet had lost her passion for talk. Sometimes the ladies sat in silence and gazed at the view.

In the back of the property were stables and four small cottages. One of these cottages was reserved for the gardener Riza and his wife, and the other for Idil's spirited cook, Ali, and his family. The third cottage was occupied by Aziz the driver and the stable boys.

These were frustrating times especially for Ali since he had to make do with shortages of food. All varieties of vegetables—including potatoes, green peppers, cabbage, and aubergines—thankfully came from Riza's meticulously kept garden, but meats, rice, and bulgur were in short supply. With more than twenty mouths to feed, Ali had to use his skills to stretch what provisions he could find. The stable boys would go fishing on the Bosphorus, and their catch always made a delicious soup. Sometimes they would catch palamut, a large variety of sea bass, and that would make a feast for the family.

With Orhan Pasha still absent, Rengin grew increasingly desolate at Pink Mansion. She had an open invitation to visit Sariyer anytime she wanted, and was always warmly welcomed by the family, but living in a large house alone, under the threat of rebels and thieves, was becoming untenable. Nazif knew that it fell on him to approach her.

"Dearest Rengin Hanim," he said during one of her lengthy visits. "You know how much Lebriz, my mother, and I love you. We regard you as family. There is enough room at Sariyer to accommodate you. In fact, you can have your private apartments. Would you consider coming to live with us permanently?"

"And leave Pink Mansion?" she asked incredulously. "What about when my husband returns? Don't you think he'll ever return?"

"I have every hope that Orhan Pasha will return," said Nazif. "But in the meantime, I think he would feel much better if you were safe among friends, rather than being alone in a big, vulnerable house."

Rengin wouldn't show it, but this offer had actually come as a relief to her. Nazif was right. Nights had become unbearable in the big house, and it was worse now since Idil and her family had moved away.

"We will not let Pink Mansion go," said Nazif. "It will always be there if you ever want to return to it."

As the family grew accustomed to their new home in Sariyer, Europe went into further chaos. Austria-Hungary's invasion of Serbia provoked Russia to step in, which in turn drew Germany into the war. Soon, the battle lines were drawn between the Allies, made up of Russia, United Kingdom, and France, and the opposing Central Powers of Germany and Austria-Hungary. The three Pashas leading the Committee of Union and Progress, now known in Europe as "The Young Turks," realized that remaining neutral would be disastrous for the Empire. They were convinced that only an alliance with Britain and France could guarantee the survival of what remained of Ottoman lands. This proved impossible and in the end, despite all objections of the military and political and intellectual elite, the triumvirate formed an alliance with Germany and entered the war.

A month after Rengin moved to the house in Sariyer, news came that Orhan Pasha had been released and that he was heading back home. Italy had already occupied Libya, and all Ottoman political exiles were now being released. Rengin was beside herself with joy but also worry.

"I must get back to Pink Mansion!" she said. "I must get it ready for his arrival."

It was Nesrin who interfered this time.

"Don't you think he would be more comfortable here among friends?" she asked. "He's been through so much. He will be glad to have friends greeting him and soothing him after such difficult times."

"It's his house," said Rengin. "That's where he'll want to be!"

"But the house is in disrepair," stressed Idil in turn. "It will take time and much work to get it back in shape. I think he would be much more comfortable here, as Nesrin Hanim says, among friends."

"Let's just be happy," said Nesrin, "and not worry so much. Let's all be happy Orhan Pasha is coming home."

"I can't express my happiness in words," said Rengin, and broke down in tears.

Orhan Pasha, with Semih Pasha by his side, arrived at the newly built Haydarpasha train terminal on the Anatolian shore of Istanbul. Filiz and Rengin were there as the train pulled up. Muazzez had also come with Güldane, who had recently gotten married and bore a child. Even though they now lived in separate houses, they were still the closest of friends. They both came with their husbands and children.

When Rengin first saw Orhan Pasha as he emerged from the train, she almost didn't recognize him. He looked smaller and didn't stand erect like he used to. He was unshaven and instead of his usual military uniform, he was dressed in tattered civilian clothes. He seemed disoriented and tentative.

Semih Pasha, who seemed in better shape, stepped down to the platform and extended his hand to help his friend. Once on the ground, Orhan Pasha moved gingerly and deliberately, hesitating with each step.

Both men seemed so fragile that the greeters were hesitant to touch them at first. It was Semih who spotted his wife first. He looked at her and she came straight into his arms. Orhan Pasha squinted as though daylight bothered his eyes. When he finally spotted Rengin, his face lit up.

"Oh my husband, my dear husband," she sobbed as she made her way over to him.

Semih Pasha, realizing what a shock it was for the family to see Orhan Pasha, said:

"He's all right. He's just tired right now. It will be all right."

Orhan Pasha's eyes seemed to adjust as everyone came up to him one by one and kissed his hand and hugged him. First it was Nazif who went up to him, and then Lebriz. Muazzez and Güldane took their turns as well. Everyone also greeted Semih Pasha the same way. Orhan Pasha looked at every face with a hesitant smile, as though he was seeing them for the first time. When Orhan and little Nil, accompanied by Jafer, approached him, his smile grew wider. Both children reached over and kissed his hand in the traditional fashion. Orhan Pasha uttered his first words since getting off the train.

"Who are these little rascals?" he asked.

"This is your namesake Orhan," said Nazif, "and the little girl is his sister Nil. They're Lebriz's and my children."

At the mention of her name, Orhan Pasha looked up.

"My Lebriz," he said. "My beautiful Lebriz."

Nesrin watched as Lebriz embraced him.

He's the father she never had, she thought. Thank God he's back.

"Come along, old friend," said Semih Pasha, offering Orhan his arm. "Let's get you home."

After a twenty-minute carriage ride, the family arrived at the house at Sariyer. Idil had prepared a suite for the couple on the east end of the house. Rengin was a bit agitated when they first entered.

"It's only temporary," she said. "We'll return to the Pink Mansion as soon as it's cleaned up and the windows are fixed."

The apartment's lush living room had a spectacular view of the Bosphorus. The garden was also accessible from the front, with two small steps.

Orhan Pasha sat on the couch facing the window overlooking the strait.

"Come sit next to me," he said.

"I'm so sorry," she said, as she sat down. "I didn't want to move out of the Pink Mansion. But it got so lonely without you."

He wrapped an arm around her shoulder and continued to gaze out the window.

"I like it here. I like being here."

It took Orhan Pasha nearly a month to regain his strength. The sweltering heat of the Libyan Desert had aged him considerably but the long, treacherous trip back had worn him out even more.

"Other than the heat," he said during one of the long dinners, "life was fine, amenable even. Semih Pasha and I spent many hours taking walks and reminiscing. The worst part was not knowing what was happening in the outside world, what was happening to our country."

"Was that really the worst part?" asked Rengin suggestively, delighted that her husband was returning to his old self—holding court at the dinner table.

"Actually no, my dear," said Orhan Pasha affectionately. "The worst part was being away from you."

The more he recovered, the more Orhan Pasha became aware of the absolute disaster the country was headed for. The monumentally wrong-headed decision of joining the Germans was leading the empire toward defeat and dismemberment. Nazif, still employed at the Ministry of Foreign Affairs, gave daily reports to Orhan Pasha of what he heard was going on in the country and kept Lebriz abreast as well. The war with Russia raged on and an Armenian uprising was taking place in the East. Word came around that Armenian friends, even in Istanbul, were being arrested and sent to exile.

Madam Janet arrived in a state of panic.

"Avram was arrested," she lamented. "We don't know what's going on or what his crime was. Other friends are leaving Istanbul. My sister is urging me to go with her to Bulgaria. To Bulgaria! What will I ever do there?"

Nesrin, Idil, and Rengin could hardly console her.

"Take heart, my friend," said Rengin. "Remain hopeful. Surely he will return one day, just like my own Orhan. You must be patient and stay strong amongst friends."

Madam Janet remained for a whole afternoon. Two days later news came that she and her sister had left the country.

Despondent, Nesrin began to ask questions.

"I don't understand anything anymore," she said. "What's happening? What's all the turmoil about? Why is there so much war? What do people want?"

Orhan Pasha, Nazif, and Lebriz were all gathered around for tea when Nesrin had her outburst. None of them knew quite what to say.

"What about my son? Can anyone tell me where he is? Is he still alive? Is he fighting as well?"

"We understand he's stationed in the East," said Nazif gently. "As far as we know, he's still alive."

"Fighting the Russians, no doubt," said Nesrin spitefully. "Just like his father. Just like Nejmi."

A silence fell across the room. This was the first time anyone had heard Nesrin utter the name of the man.

"Curses on those Russians," she said. "They've ruined our lives. They've ruined everything."

That evening, after the men retired and Lebriz took the children to bed, Idil and Rengin stayed up late with Nesrin and heard her life story. Starting with her first visit to Yeniköy as a young Circassian girl, then her misguided marriage to Nejmi and how disillusioned and miserable she'd become, Nesrin poured out the story of her life. The two women listened to her intently, learning things about their friend they'd never known before. Rengin had heard some of these stories when Lebriz came to live with them before her marriage, but certainly not in this kind of detail. Idil had been ignorant to all that Nesrin was telling her. She said she couldn't imagine what it must have been like to search for her children all those years, with no real hope in sight.

"My children are all that mattered to me," Nesrin said. "I made it my life's purpose to find them and make sure they were safe. But now they slip away from me. I'm so grateful to you, my dear Idil, for providing my Lebriz such a warm, wonderful home. I can't tell you what a comfort it is to see my daughter so happy, with such a fine husband and wonderful children. I will forever be grateful for that."

"You know how much I all love your daughter," said Idil. "She's like my own child."

"And now it's my son that I continue to worry about. I'll never forget the day we lost our dear Bedri to war. I'm so afraid the same will happen to my Jemil."

"Jemil sounds like a fine and courageous soldier," said Idil. "He's putting up a brave fight for his country. With Allah's help, he will return to you safe and sound."

Rengin nodded in agreement, not daring to mention Jemil's role in sending her husband to exile. How strange it is, she thought, that the man I thought was enemy is someone I hope will survive for the sake of this dear friend.

Instead, she spoke softly.

"What about the other man you mentioned? Whatever happened to him? The one in Yeniköy. Your husband's brother."

"You mean Sadi?"

"Yes."

"I don't know," said Nesrin absently. "I never heard from him and don't know what happened to him."

"Such a strange twist of fate," said Idil.

"It wasn't fate. I made a decision. I didn't listen to my heart."

The empire continued to suffer losses on all fronts. Muslims considered the disastrous defeat against the Russians in the East as a war between Islam and Christianity. While the main thrust of the Committee of Union and Progress had been to unite all ethnicities and religions together as one nation, the war in the East became a fight between the Muslim Turks and Christian Armenians. The Ottomans were failing in the South and East as well. Lands in Libya and Egypt were lost to the British, and Greek forces were taking over large swaths of the Aegean coast.

By the middle of winter, the situation grew even worse.

"The British and French are poised to invade Istanbul," said Nazif to Orhan Pasha. "Don't you think we should move the family away?"

"Where would we go?"

"They've gathered battleships at the strait of the Dardanelles. If that strait falls, it's the end for us."

One bright moment of triumph came at Gallipoli, where a young general named Mustafa Kemal drove the allies from the peninsula and defended the capital. In spite of that victory, the German-led effort continued to fail.

An armistice signed in Mudros in October of 1918 spelled disaster for the Turks. It granted the Allies the right to occupy both the Dardanelles and the Bosphorus and also to occupy any Ottoman territory in case of a threat to security. The Ottoman army was demobilized, and the Allies made all ports, railways, and other strategic points available for their own use. The first French troops entered the city of Istanbul on November 12, 1918, followed by British zrmy the next day.

Early on that November morning, the family woke to an eerie silence. For the first time in many months, there was no yelling in the streets, no gunshots, no police whistles. They came out to the balcony and looked out to the Bosphorus. A myriad of British warships were anchored all along the strait, some of them close enough to be at their doorstep.

What a relief it is to have quiet again, Rengin thought, but at what price?

Orhan Pasha held her hand. "It's over, my darling," he said. "It's finally over."

As usual, Aziz drove Nazif to the office. These short drives to work were usually when Aziz and Nazif caught up on the daily events. Aziz would tell Nazif about his latest argument with his wife and would take delight in hearing what shenanigans Orhan and Nil had been up to. This morning, however, both men were silent. When they arrived at the building that housed the Ministry of Foreign Affairs, they found the gate flanked by British soldiers. After being searched, Nazif was allowed inside but was politely told by a British officer that the office was now closed, and if he had any personal items, he was welcome to gather them and take them home. It took Nazif only a few minutes to gather articles that had graced his desk for all those years: his trusted fountain pen which was a gift from his father, his ink blotter, paper weight, and, of course, the certificates, awards, and photos of his children that hung on the wall.

He had mixed feelings. Unlike many men of his generation, he had not joined the fight. He remained in Istanbul, working in a dusty office that became increasingly ineffectual over the years. While many men perished, he remained alive to nurture and protect his family. He was not a hero. Could anybody blame him for that?

Aziz was waiting in the carriage in front of the building. One soldier quickly inspected Nazif's box of belongings and allowed him to pass with a nod. Aziz helped Nazif load his things into the carriage, shut the door, climbed up to his post, and took up his whip. Right as the phaeton was starting off a man knocked on the door and peered inside.

"Hold on, Aziz Efendi," said Nazif.

"Don't mind him, Nazif Bey. He's only a beggar," said Aziz and snapped his whip. The carriage lurched forward, leaving the man behind.

"Stop!" shouted Nazif.

Puzzled by the tone in Nazif's voice, Aziz pulled the reins and brought the carriage to a halt. The man's face appeared at the window again. He certainly did look like a beggar. He was drawn, dirty, and unshaven. He looked desperate and hungry. But there was something else. It took Nazif one second to recognize the man's deep, blue eyes. He opened the carriage door.

"Jemil Bey," he said. "Please climb in."

It took a few minutes for Jemil to settle down on the seat across Nazif. Even though it was a bright fall day, he was shivering in his tattered clothes.

"You're not well," said Nazif. "Let's get you home at once."

"I only ask for shelter for a few days," said Jemil. "Please don't tell anyone I'm here. May I trust you to keep this a secret?"

"Of course," said Nazif. "There is a cottage in the back of the house generally reserved for summer guests. No one will know you're there."

"Thank you," said Jemil. "I didn't know where you and my sister lived. All I knew was where you worked. Forgive me for the abrupt approach."

Nazif's mind was reeling with questions and strategies. What would he do now? How would he handle this disturbing turn of events?

"I'm glad you found me," he told Jemil.

The carriage pulled up to the cottage hidden behind the woods in the back of the main house. Aziz was sworn to secrecy and he and Nazif ushered Jemil inside. It was a small wooden structure with a comfortable bed, two chairs and a desk, a lavatory, and even a small kitchen. Jemil sat heavily in one of the chairs.

"Forgive me but I'm very hungry," he said. "I'd be grateful for any morsel of food you might spare."

"Of course," said Nazif and ordered Aziz to go fetch some food.

"I'm considered a fugitive. The last thing I want is to jeopardize you and your family."

"You're safe here," said Nazif. "But please don't talk now. Wait until you've rested a bit and had something to eat. We will have many hours to catch up."

Jemil looked at him skeptically but agreed.

Aziz brought over whatever scraps of food he could find. There were slices of day-old bread, some cheese and olives, and even a slice of roast lamb, which Ali had reserved for the children. Jemil ate with great appetite. Nazif just sat there and waited until he was finished. Finally Jemil pushed the plate aside and looked up.

"Thank you, Nazif Bey," he said. "God's grace be upon you."

He had by now stopped trembling and color had returned to his face.

"You need some rest," said Nazif. "Why don't you get some sleep and we can talk early tomorrow morning."

"You are right," said Jemil and lay on the bed. He was fast asleep by the time Nazif got up and left the cottage.

The following day, the entire city was weighted under the gravity of the invasion. The household remained calm until midafternoon when Orhan Pasha returned from a tour of the city. He had inspected various neighborhoods and made contact with several colleagues, including Semih Pasha.

"It's an outrage," he shouted. "There are soldiers everywhere. All British and French! And they've taken over Pink Mansion! Don't tell Rengin," he told Nazif. "It will break her heart."

"I heard that!" shouted Rengin from the hallway.

She entered the room. "I don't care about Pink Mansion or the invasion or all that nonsense," she said. "I want you to calm down."

She turned to Nazif and Lebriz who were both standing aside. "His heart!" she said.

"There's nothing wrong with my heart!" Orhan Pasha spat out.

"The doctor said—" started Nesrin.

"Why would you believe that quack? Don't you see our city is under siege? We've lost everything, our country is gone."

He turned to Nazif. "Didn't I say this would happen? Didn't I tell you those idiots had no idea what they were doing? They're the ones that got us into this mess. They're the ones that got us into this damned war."

"Please calm down, please," pleaded Lebriz.

Lebriz's voice seemed to relax Orhan somewhat. He sat down.

"Send me some tea," he ordered after a few minutes. "And where are the children?"

Nazif had spent the entire morning in the back cottage with Jemil. When Lebriz asked him where he'd been, Nazif said he'd been doing some carpentry in the back.

"Carpentry?" asked Lebriz, "Since when?"

"I always wanted to pick it up," said Nazif. "And now that I no longer have a job…"

Lebriz knew how important his job was to Nazif, how dedicated he'd been to his work and how passionately he embraced the daily challenges. She wondered what he'd do next. He was not the kind of man who'd be happy spending the whole day at home.

"I'm glad you're taking up carpentry," she said and caressed his cheek.

Jemil had showered and shaved by the time Nazif had gone to see him. Aziz had provided him with towels and soap. Nazif brought over two suits of clothes—shirts, ties, pants, jackets, and one pair of shoes.

"I can't wear these shoes," said Jemil. "They're much too nice. I'm not used to such things."

"They are nice shoes," said Nazif. "French made. I want you to have them. Please try them on."

The shoes fit Jemil perfectly.

"I'm grateful," he said, trying to swallow his pride. "But these shoes, nor all these clothes are of any use to me. It's inevitable that they'll track me down. In fact I shouldn't be here at all. All I want is, with your permission, to see my mother and sister one last time."

Nazif remained quiet for a moment.

"Do you think it's possible," Jemil asked finally, "to see my mother and sister even for a short time? And then I'll turn myself in before they hunt me down like a dog."

Nazif gave this some thought. Whether he turned himself in or not, he knew what Jemil's fate would be.

"The best way to do this," he said, "is to give you a hero's welcome."

"A hero's welcome?" Jemil asked, astonished.

"This will be a favor I will ask of you," said Nazif. "I can't bear the thought of them seeing you while knowing they'll lose you once again. I will have Aziz drive you to the house as though you're arriving for the first time. We will tell them that you've served your country well and that you will continue to do so. You may stay as long as you'd like. Then, if you choose, you may leave and meet your fate. Is that agreeable to you?"

Jemil paused while considering this.

"Aziz will take you out later in the afternoon and drive you back before dinner."

"I understand," said Jemil and nodded his head.

The household was jubilant that afternoon. Nazif had announced that he'd got news that Jemil was returning, and that Aziz would pick him up at the train station later in the day.

"I want to go," said Lebriz. "We should all go to greet him."

"He'll most likely be exhausted," said Nazif. "Let's let the man come to a warm welcome at home."

Idil began to shout orders about what to fix for dinner, and for a bedroom to be prepared.

"No need for a bedroom," said Nazif. "He can stay in the cottage in the back."

"Nonsense," said Idil. "He's family. He will have his own bedroom and he'll stay as long as he'd like."

Even though Lebriz and Nesrin were both ecstatic that Jemil was coming, Lebriz had caught a glimpse of the quick look Orhan Pasha and Nazif exchanged moments after her husband made the announcement. She couldn't help but get that familiar knot in her stomach as she sensed that things were not exactly the way Nazif had portrayed them. Out of respect for him, she decided to remain quiet and keep her doubts to herself. She involved herself with the preparations with the other women. Nesrin could hardly sit still.

"He's finally coming back, Nanna," she said to the old woman. "He's coming back and he'll stay this time. There is no war to take him away from us!"

Nanna nodded and caressed Nesrin's hair, just like old times.

"After this," she said, "I can go to my grave with a happy heart."

"Hold that tongue!" said Nesrin. "I won't have any of that kind of talk today."

Just as Nazif had planned, Jemil arrived to the warmest of welcomes later that day. Lebriz, Nesrin, and the children ran out to the carriage as it pulled up. Jemil was dressed in one of the suits Nazif had lent him, and was wearing the French shoes. He was hugged, kissed, and lovingly shoved and prodded all the way into the house. Nanna wouldn't stop grabbing him, kissing and squeezing his cheeks.

"My boy," she cooed. "My handsome boy all grown up."

Jemil grinned and hugged everyone in turn, including Idil. Even Orhan Pasha came up to him and shook his hand.

"Welcome home, Jemil Bey," he said cordially. Jemil took the man's hand and kissed it to express his respect. Rengin watched from the side with mixed feelings.

I'm happy, she said to herself. Of course I'm glad this man is saved.

Little Orhan, now nine years old, had grown to be a dignified and intelligent boy. He shook Jemil's hand like a true gentleman.

"Come here," said Jemil and wrapped his arms around the boy. "I was there right before you were born. I was there to welcome you into the world."

"Welcome home, Uncle Jemil," said the boy with a blush.

Six-year-old Nil was not nearly as reserved as her brother. She hugged Jemil unreservedly and even climbed on his lap as soon as he sat down.

"I can dance the Circassian kafe," she said, "just like my mother and grandmother."

"I'm sure you can," said Jemil with a grin.

"Do you want to see?"

"Of course!"

Lebriz jumped in. "Not now, Nil. Let your uncle rest for a while."

"No, please," said Jemil. "I'd be delighted to see Nil dance the kafe now. Will you dance for me, Nil?"

The little girl looked at her mother. Lebriz smiled and nodded.

"Who will provide the music?" asked Jemil.

"I will," said young Orhan, and left the room to fetch his violin.

Soon everyone had spread out to make room for the dance. As soon as the boy started up with the violin, Nil jumped up without hesitation and began to gyrate to the music. Jemil began to clap. As young Orhan picked up the rhythm and Nil continued to dance, Jemil gazed at Lebriz, and his mother next to her. Both women were clapping, swaying to the music and watching the girl with adoring eyes. Jemil and Lebriz's eyes met. Jemil nodded with an encouraging smile. She smiled back and turned to her mother. She held her mother's hand to lead her to dance. Nesrin blushed and resisted at first. Lebriz joined Nil on the floor and started to dance. Soon enough, Nesrin had joined them, recreating the elegant moves that made Nejmi fall in love with her all those years ago. Lebriz danced with a freer spirit. She let her arms loose, reaching high and wide like a swan in flight. Little Nil watched carefully and imitated her mother best she could. Orhan picked up the tempo and the others began to clap. Nanna stood on the side hooting, hollering, and clapping. Even Orhan Pasha was now swaying to the music. Tears ran down Jemil's cheeks. Even if for one short moment, he forgot everything and felt happy.

Dinner that evening went late into the night. The family remained around the table, talking, reminiscing, telling jokes, and laughing. Lebriz told everyone how Muazzez had to learn her way around dinner utensils. She picked up her own fork to show how awkward her friend had been using a fork for the first time.

"Amazing how far we've come, isn't it" said Idil after everyone had a good laugh. "So much has changed within our lifetime."

By now, Nil had nodded off in her mother's lap and young Orhan was looking tired. Lebriz bid everyone goodnight. She kissed her brother's cheek. Jemil caressed Nil's hair and gave young Orhan a hug. Soon Nesrin, Idil, and Nanna had all risen to go to bed. Nesrin wrapped her arms around her son.

"Thanks to Allah you're back with me, my boy," she said. She and Nanna retreated together.

Orhan Pasha stood. Normally, this would be when he and Nazif would retreat to the smoking room to enjoy that last smoke of the day.

"Well, gentlemen," he said, addressing both Nazif and Jemil, "it's time to kill that last cigar. You're both welcome to join me, if you'd like." He left the room, leaving Jemil and Nazif alone.

"I can't thank you enough," said Jemil, "for what you've done for me."

"You will stay for a while, will you?"

"What would be the point?"

"The war is over. There is no more need for more carnage. People forgive and forget. We have a nation to nurse back to health. There is a whole new movement gaining momentum…."

"I know Mustafa Kemal," Jemil said. "He and I were comrades in Macedonia. He's a fine soldier."

"Why don't you join him then?" asked Nazif. "They can use a soldier like you. At least lie low for a while. You never know which way events will take us."

Jemil paused for a moment.

"I don't think they will forgive me," he said.

"Have a word with Orhan Pasha," said Nazif after a pause. "He will offer you a fine cigar and perhaps talk some sense into you."

Jemil went to shake the man's hand. Nazif pulled him for a hug.

"We're brothers," he said before he left the room. "Take care of yourself, please."

Orhan Pasha had left the door ajar. "Come in!" he called to Jemil rather jovially. He'd helped himself to a considerable amount of wine over dinner and was feeling relaxed. "Where's Nazif?"

"He went to bed," said Jemil.

"Oh. I see. Well, come in. May I offer you a cigar?"

"No, thank you," said Jemil.

"Come on," said Orhan, extending Jemil the cigar. "Best cigar you'll ever have, I assure you. You have to give it a puff."

"Thank you," said Jemil and accepted the cigar. Orhan Pasha lit it for him, then sat back on his chair. "Please sit down."

Jemil sat awkwardly and took a puff off the cigar. After a moment he said, "I owe you many apologies, Orhan Pasha."

"No need for regrets," said Orhan. "I should be thanking you. You actually saved my life. If I hadn't been sent to exile, my fate could've been worse—like others we knew."

"You said my father would be ashamed of me," said Jemil, his voice shaking now. "You said he was a hero. But I know now that he was no hero. He might have been a courageous fighter on the battlefield but he was a coward at home."

Jemil's body was trembling and tears were starting to come.

"He destroyed his own family. He destroyed the house and land left to him by his father. He died a miserable drunk. So you were wrong about that. I am like my father after all. I too am a coward and a criminal."

"Your comrades are the true cowards," said Orhan Pasha. "Both Enver and Jemal Pashas have escaped the country. They're the ones that caused this mess we're in, not you."

"I've seen the most horrific events imaginable," said Jemil. "People driven to hunger and death, innocent people suffering inconceivable losses and pain. And I stood by," he said. "Like the rest of my men. We did nothing. That's the most despicable crime."

Jemil sat there with the lit cigar hanging between his fingers, tears rolling down his cheeks. Orhan got up, gently removed the cigar and offered him a handkerchief. Then he sat back down, facing Jemil.

"I can help you," he said. "You don't have to turn yourself in. I can help you escape."

"I haven't slept in days," said Jemil finally. "I'll never wake from this nightmare."

"A hero one day is a criminal the next," said Orhan. "Do you think I'm free of guilt? Do you think I've not sent men to death because of their convictions? You did what you thought was right. You shouldn't be punished for that."

"Then we're all criminals," said Jemil. "All of us."

"Come to me in the morning," said Orhan. "Let me help you. No need for senseless sacrifice."

Jemil stood.

"I'll see you in the morning then?"

Jemil nodded. "Good night, Orhan Pasha."

He felt a great sadness as he watched the young man leave the room. He knew Jemil wouldn't come to him the next day. He also knew that his effort to save this man had everything to do with trying to save himself. Jemil's words rang in his head:

We're all criminals. All of us.

The room felt warm all of a sudden. The cigar smoke hung in the air. He opened a window and loosened his tie. He took a deep breath.

Jemil walked up the stairs to go to the room Idil had prepared for him. Jafer was waiting for him on the landing.

"I wanted to take a look at your face again," said Jafer. "You haven't changed much, you know."

"Neither have you, Jafer Efendi."

"That little face of yours, looking up at me all those years ago, and asking me to make a promise. I've never forgotten that. I look at you and I see it like it was just yesterday. Do you remember asking me to make a promise?"

"Of course I do."

"Have I kept my promise, Jemil Bey? Have I carried through my duty?"

"You've done that and more," said Jemil. "I can't thank you enough for taking such good care of my sister."

"Thank you. That's all I wanted to know."

After leaving Jemil with Orhan Pasha, Nazif went for a stroll to clear his mind. It was a cool, crisp fall night. He sat on a bench under the birch tree and lit a cigarette. His wife would be in bed by now, he thought. If he spent some more time out here, she would surely be asleep by the time he got to the bedroom. He couldn't stand facing her right now. Not tonight. He wanted, for once, not to discuss anything, and to let events unfold naturally. All he ever wanted was to protect his wife and children from pain—from the cruelty of life. What could he do now, other than stay silent and hope for the best?

When he got to the bedroom, he saw that Lebriz was sitting, waiting for him.

"What are you doing up?" he asked. "You need to get some sleep."

Her voice stung with anger. "Is it because I'm a woman?"

"What are you talking about?"

"The reason why you continue to lie to me. Do you think I'm too tender, too helpless to handle the truth? Do you think I'll betray you, that I won't be able to keep a secret? Do you think because I'm a woman, I'm weak, helpless, a coward?"

"Of course not!"

"Then why? How stupid do you think I am? Did you think I wouldn't recognize the shoes, the shirt? He didn't come straight from the train at all. You put together an entire scenario, made fools out of all of us! Why?"

"I have my reasons," he said with difficulty.

"What reason could you have to lie to your own wife," she spat out in contempt.

Suddenly he exploded.

"Why do I have to explain this to you?" he shouted. "Why can't you accept that, once and for all, it's not appropriate for me to tell you everything? I don't tell you because… because I can't bear it, don't you see? Why can't you accept that for once and stay quiet. Just stay quiet! Because I can't bear it. So shut up!"

She froze. His eyes met hers, and they stood suspended for a moment with their gaze locked upon each other. Suddenly a scream was heard tearing across the house. The couple remained standing, facing each other and looking deep into each other's eyes. Another scream shot through.

"What is that?" she said finally.

"It's Rengin Hanim," he said, and turned and left the room. Lebriz waited a moment before she cautiously started down the stairs, afraid of what she would find. The entire household was gathered in the smoking room. Orhan Pasha was sprawled on the floor, his eyes open, gazing up at the ceiling. Rengin was on the floor, holding on to his lifeless body and sobbing. Lebriz reached to her and held her shoulders. Nazif shut Orhan Pasha's eyes.

Lebriz sat up with Rengin all night. According to Muslim law, the body would have to be buried the very next day. Nazif, Aziz, and Jafer prepared Orhan Pasha for his final journey early the next morning. They conducted the "washing ceremony" in which male members of the family wash the body to rid it of all impurities and wrap it in a white shroud.

Nobody noticed as Jemil quietly slipped out and left the house. It was two weeks later that he turned himself in at the sultan's army's headquarters at Galata.

The following four years would bring staggering changes across the country as well as in the household. The occupation of Istanbul was only the beginning of a series of devastating invasions. French troops occupied lands on the Southern Anatolian coast, while Britain took over Syria. Italy invaded the Antalya region and the Greeks were poised to occupy the entire Aegean coast. The Sultanate lost all governing power as the Allies divided the country amongst themselves.

In the meantime, an underground resistance movement was gathering steam. The young general Mustafa Kemal, who was appointed by the sultan with the hopes that he would establish peace in Anatolia, instead arrived with different intentions. Traveling across the country, he met with regional representatives to gather forces toward building a resistance to the occupation.

Jemil was immediately put on trial, found guilty of treason, and was condemned to death. Locked up in a cell for what seemed like an eternity, he was left alone with his thoughts. His nightmares continued to haunt him. He would occasionally fall asleep and then wake up screaming in the middle of the night. Someone would slip a slop of food into his cell each morning and another man would accompany him to relieve himself twice a day. He asked for a pen and some paper just to keep track of his thoughts but was refused. He lost count of the number of days but was determined to remain sane.

I want my mind to be clear when I meet my maker, he thought. I want to be aware of my gifts and faults, my good deeds and bad.

His greatest regret was that he'd never fallen in love.

That would've been a memory that could have sustained me, he thought.

Even though Mustafa Kemal was declared a traitor and condemned to death by a military tribunal, his nationalist movement continued to grow in numbers and strength. Modest successes were achieved in the east: French troops occupying small towns were driven out, and parts of the Black Sea region were rescued from Britain. In the west, however, the Greeks continued their assault on the Aegean coast. The beautiful city of Izmir was the only remaining holdout but the enemy was closing in fast. The Greeks entered the city in May of 1919 after having evacuated their own citizens. The Turkish population was left behind to face a bleak fate.

Early one morning, two soldiers came to Jemil's cell and told him to get up and follow them. He had no idea what month, day of the week, or even what year it was. They took him to the showers, undressed him, and washed him. It took several men to rub off the months' worth of stink from his body. Then he was shaved, dressed in civilian clothes, and his hair was combed. All this just to get hanged, Jemil thought.

"How many are invited to watch?" he asked.

The soldiers remained quiet. They held him by the arms and walked him down a long corridor. He thought it odd that he wasn't shackled.

They arrived at the massive door of a military office. They took him inside and placed him on a chair.

"Wait here."

Jemil surveyed his surroundings. He took in the plush leather chairs, the elaborate desk with many objects on it, and the large windows that looked out to a lush garden. The sunlight made his eyes hurt.

The door opened, a soldier walked in, and stood at attention. An older man in uniform came in. Jemil stood up. The man shook Jemil's hand.

"State your name, soldier," he said.

"I'm Jemil. Grandson of Mustafa of New Manor, granted by the sultan himself, for the seven villages of the Circassian. I served with the ninth garrison in Eastern Anatolia. I'm aware of my crimes. I'm ready to receive my punishment. "

"Sit down," ordered the man and motioned to the soldier to leave the room. Surprised, Jemil took a seat again.

"My name is Sadettin Pasha," he said. "I see you've inherited your mother's eyes."

Days later, Jemil was riding southbound toward Izmir with a unit of the nationalist army. He'd joined anonymously as a private and was relieved to not be in charge of other men. Unlike the modern Allied forces, his unit had no motorized vehicles. Instead, the artillery and other supplies were carried on ox carts. Once again Jemil was enthralled by his comrades' passion for a cause. Sadi's words echoed in his mind:

"You come from a family of Circassian fighters," he'd said. "You're no ordinary criminal. You'll fight for your country. You will make all of us proud."

The journey to Izmir took ten days. The Greeks had by now retreated to a defensive line that stretched 700 kilometers along a hilly terrain. Even though they thought their position easily defensible, the one railway that was their main supply route was compromised and this left the army of 220,000 Greeks unexpectedly vulnerable. The morale of the Greek troops was low. They were occupying unfriendly territories and no end to the war was in sight. Mustafa Kemal took advantage of this breathing space and organized a major offensive.

The Turkish attack opened on August 26,1922 with two army divisions attacking simultaneously. A devastating and accurate artillery barrage caused heavy casualties to the frontline Greek infantry battalions. The Turks had cut off telegraph lines as well as the railroad, rendering communication between Greek forces in the region impossible. By the third day, the situation for the Greeks became even more critical when they experienced heavy pressure from the east, the south, and the north. Soon Greeks troops were retreating to the west.

Nazif arrived one afternoon with the happy news.

"The Greeks are defeated," he announced. "The war is coming to a close!"

Nesrin, Lebriz and Nanna huddled together and cried tears of joy. They had lived through four years of shortages, curfews, and the family had suffered heartbreaking losses. Rengin had passed away shortly after Orhan Pasha's death and Idil had died of pneumonia only three months after that. The large house had lost its central personages. Gone were Orhan Pasha's evenings in the smoking room. No longer were Idil and Rengin's lively visitor's days. Only Jafer and Nanna remained of the older generation, and they were both well into their old age. Aziz and the gardener were still there but most of the other servants had to be let go. Even with two growing children, the house seemed like an empty shell compared to the grandeur of its past years. But now, once again, there was hope.

"Do you think we'll see Jemil again?" asked Nesrin.

"I don't know, Mother," said Nazif gently. "It's still chaotic out there. We can hope that he will emerge, but it might not be for a long time."

She knew Nazif was being kind and she forgave him for not telling her the truth. She had long resigned herself to the loss of her son. Still, it was comforting to retain even the slightest bit of hope. What if he did show up? If that happened, her life would be complete. After that, she could go to her death in peace.

"What do you mean, go to your death?" scolded Nanna. "You're only 53! I will be gone long before you, and I certainly don't intend to go yet!"

Nesrin smiled and gazed out the window.

"Look at her," she said. "Isn't she the loveliest thing you've ever seen?"

Little Nil was in the garden, reading a book under the shade of the fig tree.

"Stunning," said Nanna. "Just like her mother and grandmother. With all that beauty, I don't know why she always has her nose in one of those books!"

Nesrin found great comfort whenever she was with her grandchildren. Nil was now an elegant ten-year-old, interested in literature and fashion. Her favorite book, she told her grandmother, was Alice's Adventures in Wonderland. She and Nesrin would sit together after school and Nil would read some passages out loud. Nesrin delighted in the wonders of the book alongside her granddaughter. No matter how many times she heard the story, she always laughed when the White Hare ran past with his pocket watch, and gasped each time the foul-tempered Queen of Hearts pronounced: "Off with his head!"

By now Orhan was a handsome and thoughtful thriteen-year-old. Even though he still harbored his childhood dream of becoming a pilot one day, his thoughts had turned to the more serious subjects of history and politics.

Within one year after the liberation of Izmir, Mustafa Kemal abolished the Sultanate and formed a new democratic republic. Modeled after western democracies, he built a new constitution, introduced many social and political reforms, and was elected its first president. Along with his parents, Orhan followed these dramatic events with great interest.

"I'm going to be president one day," he announced boastfully. "Jafer Efendi says so!"

Nesrin laughed at such declarations but also thought it could very well be true. She nodded and smiled at Jafer, who proudly stood by.

"Orhan is studying the French Revolution at school," said the eunuch with a wide grin. "We're studying together!"

As a new age dawned upon the nation, Nesrin found herself at a happy time in her life, perhaps happier than she'd ever known. Everyone seemed so optimistic, including her glorious daughter. Nesrin admired Lebriz but also envied her a little. She seemed so independent and confident. She was always outside the house, going to meetings and pursuing what she called "women's causes."

With the new republic came many reforms, some of them directly concerning women. The new civil code forbade polygamy, ended divorce by renunciation, and introduced civil marriage. The Islamic sharia law was abolished, affording women many social freedoms. Now women were free to walk in the streets alone and own property, and some of them even started to work outside the home.

One of the striking reforms that came with the advent of the new republic was the modification of headgear and dress. Men were now forbidden to wear the fez—considered a symbol of Islam—and encouraged to wear western hats. Women, on the other hand, were encouraged to stop wearing the veil and to dress in the European fashion. Nil was mesmerized by the many outfits—including blouses, skirts, dresses, and even ball gowns—her mother had especially tailored for her.

It was Nanna who had little tolerance for all these changes.

"I've seen too many changes in my life," she said grumpily. "I don't have to see any more."

She thought Lebriz's newly fitted tailleur was distasteful and pretentious.

"She looks ridiculous," she would complain to Nesrin. "Who is she trying to be? Why can't people just be themselves? That's not my darling Lebriz. That's an uppity French woman."

"I think she's beautiful," said Nesrin with a serene smile. "I'm so proud of my daughter."

One horrific moment for Nanna came when Lebriz returned from an afternoon of shopping with a European-style hat upon her head. Nanna watched from the window as Aziz opened the carriage gate and let Lebriz out. Nanna gasped at the sight.

"Nesrin Hanim, come here, quick!" she cried out.

Nesrin rushed over, expecting to face disaster, but instead met her daughter as she came through the door, followed by Aziz carrying several packages. Both women looked at Lebriz in a kind of stupor. It wasn't the hideous hat that was the issue. What caused great dismay was that it appeared that Lebriz's hair was all but gone. Nanna nearly had a stroke.

"What have you done with your hair, my darling," Nesrin asked apprehensively.

"It had to be done," answered Lebriz. "It's the modern times. What do you think of my hat? Don't you think it's elegant? It's called the cloche."

"It's revolting," said Nanna. "It looks like a pinhead."

"I'm sorry, Nanna. I had to do it."

"Why? Why did you have to do something so ridiculous?"

"Because I'm going to have a job."

There was stunned silence.

"What?" Nesrin finally asked. Had she actually heard those words?

"What job?" demanded Nanna.

"I'm going to be a teacher. I'm going to teach the new alphabet."

The older women took a pause as they considered this declaration. The new alphabet reform was yet another radical change that Nanna found ridiculous and confounding.

"Does your husband know this?" Nanna asked.

"Of course," said Lebriz. "He's the one who got me the job."

"I don't know what the world is coming to," griped Nanna and walked away. "I need to go lie down."

"I'm so proud of you," said Nesrin to Lebriz. "And you look beautiful."

"Thank you, Mother. I'm very happy."

The old Ottoman writing, which required more than five hundred Arabic letters, had been replaced overnight by the new Turkish alphabet, consisting of only twenty-one Latin characters.

"The Turkish language has been a prisoner for centuries and is now casting off its chains," Mustafa Kemal had declared. He himself enthusiastically studied the new alphabet and even taught classes with his ministers and officials as his students. He opened schools all across the nation and made it mandatory for everyone between the ages of sixteen and forty to learn to read and write using the new alphabet.

Teaching a whole nation how to read and write all over again required an infrastructure not only of schools, but also government agencies, contractors and, most essentially, qualified teachers. Nazif, having worked at a government ministry before the war, was immediately assigned to a position at the Ministry of Language. His job was to oversee the new language schools that were opening across the country. He and his wife, both fluent speakers of French, had no trouble mastering the new alphabet. It only made sense that Nazif would propose that Lebriz take a teaching position as well.

Lebriz was thrilled to have a job outside the home, but what made her even happier was that this allowed her to reconnect with Muazzez. The two friends hadn't seen each other in many months, and even then, had met only in passing. Both had been involved in raising families, and the war had interfered with all social events. Now they both had jobs teaching at the prestigious Robert College, the school founded by American philanthropists.

Their initial meeting was jubilant, full of giggles, stories and gossip.

By now Muazzez had two boys, Sait and Omar, and a husband who worked as an engineer for the railroads. They lived in a mansion on the Asian side of Istanbul.

"Look at us, we're two grown women, acting like girls," giggled Muazzez when she first saw her friend. "You look beautiful, Lebriz. Motherhood becomes you."

"I'm so happy to see you, Muzzy. I've missed our friendship so much. Now we can see each other every day again, just like old times. The only thing missing is Güldane. Have you seen her? How is she?"

"She's very well. Her husband is a rising politician, preparing to run for election. They live in Ankara."

"How delightful," said Lebriz. "You know my husband works for the government as well."

"I know! It's so impressive!"

"I'm very proud of him. And he's very happy. Unfortunately his job might require us to relocate to Ankara soon."

"How soon?" asked Muazzez, her smile quickly giving way to a look of concern.

"I don't know. He's been traveling back and forth quite a bit. He hasn't been able to spend much time at home. I'm just waiting for him to announce that we will have to move."

"Well, let's not think about that now," said Muazzez, turning cheery again. "How is your mother?"

"She's all right. She and Nanna keep to themselves. My mother says she's proud of me but I don't think she really likes my clothes or my working outside the house. She's been pretty much a recluse lately."

"We should do something about that," said Muazzez. "I'd like so much to see her!"

Nesrin was glad to see Muazzez at her daughter's side again.

"Look at these two, Nanna. They look so happy to be together."

"Yes they do," said Nanna as Lebriz served coffee on a tray. "If only they were dressed better!"

"We should take both of you out shopping," said Muazzez enthusiastically.

"Don't think I haven't tried," said Lebriz.

Nanna muttered, "Shopping for what? Those ridiculous European skirts? I wouldn't get caught dead in one of those."

"And what about you, Aunt Nesrin," asked Muazzez. "Wouldn't you like to buy some new clothes? I think you'd look wonderful."

"I don't think so," said Nesrin softly and with a smile. "Nanna is right. We're two old women set in our ways. We have no business trying out the new fashions."

"Speak for yourself," Nanna snapped. "I don't know about you but I don't feel old. I'm just stubborn!"

"I'm very happy in this house," said Nesrin, as though in a dream. "I've never been happy in a house like this before. I love my grandchildren and spending time in the garden. The world has changed too much and I don't feel I fit in anymore. I never want to leave this house."

"What if we have to move to Ankara?" said Lebriz. "What will you do then?"

Nesrin gazed at Nanna for a moment, as though her whole girlhood flashed before her eyes.

"I don't want to think about that now," she said. "Let's all enjoy being together on this lovely afternoon.

Sure enough it was only a few days later that Nazif brought up the subject. The couple was basking in the glorious moment after having just made love when Nazif gently asked, "How would you feel, my darling, about spending the summer in Ankara?"

"The summer?" asked Lebriz.

"Just as a trial. I know how much you love this house and how much your mother and the children love Istanbul. So I thought we might try being there only for the summer and see how we like it."

"Do you want to move there?"

"It's just that I've been spending so much time there—away from home and apart from my family. I thought it might make life easier for all of us if we found a nice home there. We wouldn't have to give up Sariyer."

"It will be difficult," said Lebriz. "But I will bring it up with my mother."

Just as Lebriz predicted, Nesrin didn't take the news very well.

"Why do we all have to go?" she asked. "Nanna and I can stay here. The two of you should take the children and go."

"I won't leave you, Mother. You know that."

"I can't even set foot outside the house. How do you expect me to go to Ankara? And by train? All these things scare me. I'm better off here at home."

"What's wrong, Mother? Why won't you leave the house?"

"I don't think I belong out there, that's why."

Later that afternoon, Jafer came into Nazif's study.

"Pardon me for bothering you, Nazif Bey," he said softly. "May I have a word?"

"Of course, Jafer Efendi. Please sit down."

Jafer stepped in and sat awkwardly on the chair closest to the door. He'd just finished helping Orhan with his history homework.

"Your boy has a big exam coming up," he said tentatively. "In Socratic philosophy!"

"Is that right," said Nazif, feeling a little bit embarrassed that he didn't know much about the subject. "How is he doing? Are you worried that he might not do well?"

"Not at all," said the old eunuch. "Quite the contrary. Orhan is excelling in his studies. He is very smart and works very hard. And Nil as well. She's first in her class in arithmetic. Very unusual for a young girl. Her teachers are impressed. Both of your children are wonderful, Nazif Bey."

"Thank you," said Nazif. "And we owe much of that to you."

Jafer stared at the floor.

"Is there something I can do for you?" asked Nazif. It was unusual for Jafer to come into his office, let alone ask for a favor.

"I thank Allah every day for those children," said Jafer finally. "I wake up every morning with love in my heart. No man can ever ask for a greater gift than that."

"I appreciate that. The children love you as well."

"I understand you will take the family to Ankara."

"It's a possibility. And you're part of our family. If we go, we'd like you to go with us."

Jafer took another pause, carefully weighing what he was about to say.

"So I regret very much," he finally said, "to ask to be relieved of my duties."

"Your duties?" exclaimed Nazif, trying to hide his surprise. Life at the house without Jafer was unthinkable. "There are no duties, Jafer Efendi," he said gently. "You are not a servant. You may do as you please."

Jafer tried to hold back the tears.

"Thank you. It breaks my heart to do this."

"What will you do? Where will you go?"

"I've been hearing of a group of eunuchs who've set up a community in Cairo. I wrote to them recently and received an invitation to join them. It's my chance to live my last days among men like myself. People who understand my predicament and my fate."

"Of course," said Nazif, fighting back tears himself. "I understand. Lebriz and the children will be sad, but they too will realize that this is the best choice for you."

The thought of losing Jafer devastated Lebriz. She spent the next morning crying in her mother's room. Even Nanna was upset.

"Foolish eunuch!" Nanna spat out. "He thinks he will be happy among other eunuchs? Those people fight like cats and dogs. Jealousy among them in harems is legendary."

"Hush, Nanna," chided Nesrin. "Leave the man alone. He's never done anything for himself his entire life. He needs to live freely just like everyone else."

"And at what expense? Doesn't he realize what he's leaving behind? These beautiful children need him. He owes them his loyalty and love."

"The children will be fine," said Nesrin. "They're young. They'll soon get over it."

She caressed Lebriz's hair.

"And so will my beautiful Lebriz," she said, looking into her daughter's eyes. "Won't you, my dear?"

Lebriz sniffled back the tears and sat up.

"Yes I will," she said. "For the sake of Jafer's happiness, I will be all right."

Jafer used what little savings he had to buy passage to Egypt. He refused any financial help Nazif begged to give him.

On the morning of his departure, Nanna was in Nesrin's room.

"You have to go with us to see him off. The man's devoted his life to your daughter and grandchildren. You must give him your blessing and respect."

"I don't feel well," said Nesrin, still lounging on the couch in her house clothes.

"No excuses," said Nanna. "The Nesrin I know is proud of who she is. She will get up, get dressed, and go without shame. You have nothing to be ashamed of Nesrin Hanim."

Nesrin finally got up. As usual, Nanna helped her into her traditional white chemise and an embroidered silk coat that reached to her feet, and handed her the veil.

"I must look ridiculous," said Nesrin. "People will laugh at me."

"Nonsense," said Nanna. "Drape the veil on your shoulders. Not everyone is following the European fashions."

Aziz drove the carriage with Jafer, Lebriz, Nazif, and the children. Nanna and Nesrin followed in a smaller carriage behind. They arrived at the Karakoy pier, where a large boat was docked, waiting for the passengers to embark. All of Jafer's possessions were contained in one small, black suitcase. Nanna and Nesrin watched from the carriage as the family followed him to the dock. The old eunuch put down his valise and turned to the family to say goodbye.

"Come on," said Nanna. "Let's bid the old fool adieu."

Nesrin followed Nanna and came out of the carriage. She left the veil draped around her shoulders. The sea breeze against her hair felt strange, like a revelation.

"I'd forgotten what the breeze feels like," she murmured. She and Nanna approached the group.

Jafer hugged Nazif and thanked him for his kindness. Then he turned to Nesrin and kissed her on both cheeks.

"I've always admired you for your courage and resilience, Nesrin Hanim," he said. "You're a lucky woman to be surrounded with such love. I wish you many more years of happiness. You deserve all of it."

"I will never forget you, my friend," said Nesrin through her tears.

Jafer paused in front of Nanna and looked into her eyes. Now she was nearly in tears as well.

"I leave this family in your charge, Nanna," he said. "I can't think of anyone I could trust more."

"God's speed, you old fool," said Nanna. "Nobody can ever replace you. Not even I."

Jafer hugged the children one by one. Nil was crying but Orhan remained stoic. Jafer squeezed him in his arms just a little while longer.

"You're a brave boy," he said. "You make your parents proud."

When he finally turned to Lebriz, tears were rolling down his cheeks. She was no longer crying. She looked at him with gratitude in her eyes.

"You're my treasure, Lebriz Hanim. My beautiful little girl, I told you

I'd never abandon you and now I'm breaking my promise."

"You've been my protector, Jafer Efendi. You were always there for me" she said. "I owe you everything. But now it's time for you to go and it's all right. Go with love and always remember you have a home here."

She reached up and wrapped both arms around his neck and held him tight for one last time. Then she let him go.

Jafer turned and walked up the plank. Dressed in his freshly pressed secondhand suit, he looked proud yet vulnerable. He turned back to wave goodbye for one short moment, and then was gone.

When the family returned to the house, Nesrin approached her daughter.

"I think it's time, my dear," she said. "Will you take me shopping?"

The Beyoglu district was bustling as always. Pubs, patisseries, and upscale clothing shops still lined the streets, except now telephone wires hung overhead and several of the buildings housed major European consulates.

It was a rainy day. Nesrin, Lebriz, and Nanna huddled under a single umbrella before entering one of the fashionable clothing shop called Maison Etiquette.

An effete middle-aged man, dressed in a tailored suit with a foulard around the neck, immediately approached them and offered tea and cakes. Then, with the help of two female assistants, he presented a line of fabrics and fashions. A dizzying variety of frocks, contemporary afternoon wear, footwear, hats, and accessories—all inspired by the fashions of Hollywood film stars—were paraded in front of them. Nanna was appalled, Nesrin had to sit down, and even Lebriz was overwhelmed.

At first the man's attention was automatically focused on Lebriz since she seemed to be the one most invested in current fashions. But once Lebriz announced, to her mother's chagrin, that it was her they were shopping for, the man's attention shifted, albeit more reservedly, to Nesrin.

"How wonderfully this silk blouse highlights your eyes," he fussed as he held up a garish garment. "And we must also consider some makeup, Madame. Nothing too extreme, some lipstick to emphasize your beautiful skin," he said as he held up a stick of red lipstick for Lebriz—not for

Nesrin—to approve.

After more then twenty minutes of a display that seemed like it could last the whole afternoon, Nanna interfered.

"Nesrin is tired," she said. "It's time to go home."

Lebriz realized that, spellbound by the merchandise, she had neglected to observe her mother. Now she saw that, although she tried to maintain a feeble smile, Nesrin looked particularly fatigued.

"Let's go home," she said, and asked the man to order their carriage.

Nesrin spent the rest of the day in her room. She came down for dinner but said she felt too tired and went back to bed soon after. The next morning, she was late to rise. Since Jafer was gone and Lebriz had to teach, it came to Nanna to prepare the children for school. When Lebriz returned in the afternoon, she found that her mother was still in her room. When she went to her side, Nesrin assured her that the previous day's outing had been too stimulating and that she was only catching up on some rest.

"Do you really think I should dress in the new fashions, my daughter?" she asked.

"Not if it's going to distress you so much, Mother."

"Good. Because I find the whole thing to be so much work!"

"I agree. Just get some rest. And we won't have to talk about this ever again."

In the meantime, the preparations for the trip to Ankara were well underway. Nazif had reserved two sleeping compartments on the newly anointed Ankara Express and the family was scheduled to depart in one week. That night after dinner, when the couple retreated to the bedroom, Lebriz said she would have to cancel the trip if her mother didn't feel well.

"I'm sure she'll feel much better in the morning," Nazif reassured her. "She hardly ever leaves the house. She's likely caught a mild cold."

Nesrin seemed more energetic the following morning but by afternoon she was feeling fatigued again and went back to lie down. When Lebriz returned from teaching in the afternoon, Nanna pulled her aside.

"She hasn't been feeling well for a while," she said. "I didn't say anything because she didn't want me to."

"Shall I call the doctor?"

"Absolutely not. You know she wouldn't be happy about that. And please don't tell her I said anything."

"Don't worry, Nanna. I won't."

At teatime, Lebriz and the children visited Nesrin in her room. She was dressed and sat up in a chair and enjoyed her grandchildren.

That night, however, there was a turn for the worst. Nesrin was up in the middle of the night, vomiting and complaining of abdominal pain.

"It's her gallbladder," diagnosed Nanna. "I've seen it before. She will have to have an operation."

Nesrin fell asleep by early morning and when she woke up she seemed to be somewhat better.

"Only plain rice and fruit," ordered Nanna, and the maids followed her instructions.

By midafternoon, however, Nesrin was feeling sick again. Lebriz urged Nazif to get in touch with Mahmut Bey, their family doctor, and Nazif immediately sent the gardener's son Mehmet to deliver a message. One hour later Mehmet returned with a message saying the doctor was unable to leave the hospital that night, but to please let him know how things were the following morning. He advised that Nesrin continue to rest and drink lots of tea.

After another agonizing night of pain and vomiting, Dr. Mahmut was summoned first thing in the morning. After his initial examination, he thought it would be best to take Nesrin to the American Hospital where they would do more tests. Nanna was still convinced.

"It's her gallbladder, isn't it?"

"It may be, Nanna. But I'd like to rule out any other possibilities."

Nesrin was admitted and prescribed medication to ease her pain and vomiting. She was to spend the night at the hospital under supervision while various tests would be performed. Lebriz sent Nazif home and spent the night on a chair, sitting next to her mother.

Nesrin woke from a deep slumber at one point and, seeing her daughter next to her, smiled.

"I had a most wonderful dream," she said. "My dear mother and father were there, welcoming me with open arms. And Jemil was there too. They're all waiting for me."

Lebriz squeezed her mother's hand.

"You're not going anywhere, Mother. It's only your gallbladder like Nanna says. You'll have an operation and be back home in only a few weeks."

After the flurry of tests and examinations, Dr. Mahmut invited Lebriz and Nazif to his office.

"I'm afraid the news is not good," he said. "There is a large lump in your mother's abdomen, pressing against her pancreas."

"Is it cancer?" asked Nazif.

"Very likely," said the doctor simply.

Lebriz, devastated, remained quiet.

"Can nothing be done? Can she have an operation?" asked Nazif.

"I'm afraid removing the tumor won't do much good. We suspect the cancer may have spread to other organs. Perhaps the stomach or lungs."

Nazif held Lebriz's hand. The doctor let them digest the devastating news.

"What do you recommend that we do?" asked Nazif finally

"Take her home and keep her comfortable, "said Dr. Mahmut. "We will do everything we can to ease her pain. Let her enjoy her home and her family for her last days. It's up to you whether you want to tell her or not."

"We don't have to tell her anything," said Lebriz. "She knows."

The family trip to Ankara had to be canceled but Nazif's traveling for work was unavoidable. He hated to leave Nesrin and his family but nothing could be done.

"I'll return as soon as I'm able," he promised before leaving for the train.

The following few weeks were a series of ups and downs for Nesrin. One day she'd be experiencing severe pain and the next morning she'd be sitting up in her chair, enjoying a laugh with her grandchildren. Lebriz reduced her teaching hours considerably. Now she left the house only two days a week and was gone for half the day. Nesrin scolded her.

"Staying at home is not going to make me get better! You should go be with your students."

"I want to spend as much time with you as possible. How can you complain about that?"

Nanna, in the meantime, was determined to find a cure for Nesrin's illness. She had heard that a mixture of black seed oil and honey was the definitive treatment for cancer. She ordered the purest grade of honey from a bee farm she knew in Bolu and had Aziz bring cumin oil from the spice bazaar. She made sure Nesrin ingested a healthy dose every morning before breakfast.

"On an empty stomach," she insisted. "That's when it's the most potent."

On the days that she felt relatively well, Nesrin was happy to receive visitors. Semih Pasha and Filiz were her regulars, and Muazzez came on the weekends along with her daughter Ipek. Ipek and Nil were close in age and were classmates at the American School for Girls.

Güldane would occasionally travel from Ankara and join Muazzez on the weekend visit. Having her dear friends nearby, especially during Nazif's long absences, was hugely comforting for Lebriz.

Despite all of Nanna's efforts, Nesrin's health did not improve. None of her remedies, or her efforts to get Nesrin out of bed and move around, seemed to pay off. Nesrin seemed serene and resigned to her fate.

"I'm afraid it's no use, Nanna. This is God's will."

"Nonsense! God's will is that I'm supposed to go first. Now you drink your medicine and get up and move."

Lebriz couldn't bear to see her mother deteriorating before her eyes but tried her best to keep a hopeful attitude. She was especially grateful that Nanna was so determined that Nesrin would recover.

In the beginning of fall, when leaves were just starting to turn, a carriage arrived at Sariyer and an older gentleman got out. Using a cane, and carrying a bouquet of flowers, he slowly made his way to the front gate and pulled on the string to ring the bell. The gardener's son Mehmet came and opened the gate.

"I'm an old friend of the family," said the man. "I'm here to visit Lebriz Hanim."

Mehmet accompanied the gentleman to the foyer.

Nazif had returned from his latest trip to Ankara just the day before. He'd gotten up early and seen the children off to school. He had just finished his breakfast and was still at the table enjoying the morning paper and his tea when Mehmet came to summon him. Nanna and Lebriz were upstairs with Nesrin. Nazif came to the foyer to greet the man.

"Good morning, sir. I understand you're asking for my wife. May I ask why?"

"Actually it's her mother I was inquiring about. I understand Nesrin Hanim lives here? I'm an old friend."

"My mother-in-law is not feeling well. Shall I tell her who's calling?"

"I will only leave these flowers for her. There is a card with them."

"No, please… If you're an old friend, perhaps she'd like to see you as well."

"If she remembers me at all, she'll know me by the name of Sadi."

"Sadi Bey. If you would kindly wait here, I'll go tell her right away."

Nesrin couldn't believe her ears when Nazif told her Sadi was waiting downstairs.

"Sadi? Dearest Sadi? How can that be? I didn't even think he was still alive! Nanna!"

Nanna rushed in from the next room.

"What is it, Nesrin?"

"Nazif says Sadi is here. Dear old Sadi. Unbelievable!" She was in near panic when Lebriz walked in.

"Lebriz, my dear. You must go down and meet him. He's such a lovely man. A very kind heart."

"Who is he?" asked Lebriz incredulously.

"Don't ask, my darling, just go and meet him."

"He's your uncle," Nanna blurted out.

"My uncle? I have an uncle?"

"Go down and greet him," said Nesrin. "And thank him for coming."

"He wants to see you," said Nazif. "He came here to find you."

"Then tell him I'm dead! I won't see him like this. I can't. Just tell him I've died and he'll go away."

"I'm not going to do that," said Lebriz.

"Why? What difference does it make? I'll be dead in a week anyway. Thank the man and tell him to go away."

"Get up!" ordered Nanna.

"I can't. I won't."

"Yes you can. Lebriz, help me get your mother dressed. Nazif, please tell the gentleman that Nesrin will see him shortly."

Nazif looked doubtful but finally said, "All right, I will," and left the room.

Lebriz and Nanna propped Nesrin up. Nanna immediately started to work on her hair while Lebriz went to the wardrobe to pick out an outfit.

"Look at you," said Nanna. "You're so excited that the color has returned to your cheeks!"

She tried to help Nesrin up from the bed.

"Let go of me," snapped Nesrin. "I can get myself up!" She held onto the bedpost and stood on her two shaky feet.

Nazif kept Sadi company while they waited. Sadi was interested in the work Nazif had been doing with schools across the country.

"We've opened them in every corner of the nation," said Nazif. "The challenge has been to find teachers but we've nearly accomplished that as well. In fact, I hope to be I'll be able to stop traveling to Ankara soon."

"Wonderful. That means you won't have to leave your family behind."

"My wife teaches as well. She's a remarkable woman. You'll enjoy meeting her."

"I know I will," said Sadi. "Now if you don't mind, I'll wait in the garden. It's such a lovely day."

Sadi remained in the garden for more than an hour. Finally, when he was invited upstairs, he found Nesrin sitting in a chair, lovely as ever. His heart nearly sank.

"My dear lady."

"Dearest Sadi," she said with a smile. "Life has its way of playing tricks, doesn't it? Who would have thought you and I would meet each other again after all these years. Please sit down. This is my devoted friend Nanna. Nanna will you take the beautiful flowers?"

"Very nice to meet you Nanna," said Sadi and shook Nanna's hand.

Then he saw Lebriz. "And this must be your daughter, Lebriz." He gazed at her with wonder in his eyes. "I'd recognize you anywhere," he said.

Nanna grumbled something unintelligible. She had already arranged the flowers in a vase.

"And thank you for the beautiful flowers," said Nesrin.

"Come on, Nanna," said Lebriz. "Let's see what Ali Efendi can drum up for lunch."

Again, Nanna grumbled and followed Lebriz out of the room.

"The nerve," she said. "The nerve of him coming to her after all these years without communicating with her at all. And now he shows up when she's ill and needs to rest."

"But you're the one who made her get up and get dressed," said Lebriz with a laugh. Nanna was not amused.

"Well of course, she had to!" she said. "She's Circassian. She must be cordial."

"It's all right," said Lebriz. "The man means well."

In the bedroom, Sadi held Nesrin's hand.

"I want to report," he said, "that I had the honor of serving alongside your son Jemil Bey during the war."

"My son. We haven't heard a word about him in years."

"Your son was a brave man," he said and paused as he saw the tears welling up in her eyes. She looked at him expectantly.

"He was a true hero," he said gently. "We lost him to the Greeks in Izmir."

Tears were running down her cheeks, yet she smiled at him and squeezed his hand.

"Thank you," she said. "Thank you for telling me."

"I wanted to bring you the news personally. And also I wanted to tell you how sorry I was to hear your story. Jemil Bey told me about how you were separated from your children, and the years you spent searching for them. If I had known at the time, I probably would not be sitting here now, but would have been hung for the violent death of Nejmi. For whatever it may be worth, I would like to apologize for his unforgivable and criminal behavior."

Sadi spent the rest of the morning and the afternoon with Nesrin. They sat on the veranda and enjoyed the lunch Lebriz and Nanna served them. He told her about his life as a soldier. How devoted he'd been to his country and how proud he was to have taken part in its resurrection. "I gave away my life," he said. "All my hopes and chances for love and a family. But I'm proud of what I've helped accomplish."

He told Nesrin that now that he was retired, he was living in small house not far from Sariyer. "We're within walking distance of each other," he said with a smile. "Could you ever have thought that possible? Would you mind," he asked gently, "if I came to visit you frequently?"

"I would welcome it," said Nesrin, feeling the odd sensation that her heart had just been lifted. She looked into Sadi's eyes and saw the young man she knew so many years ago.

As promised, Sadi visited Nesrin every day for the next two weeks. The two of them sat together reminiscing, observing, and contemplating the strange turns their lives had taken. And sometimes they just sat quietly together.

Nanna was cautious but also amazed that Nesrin's illness did not advance as anticipated. She still stayed in her room, but seemed livelier and more interested. Each morning she got up and got dressed and waited for Sadi. They always had lunch on the veranda, even though the fall weather was fast approaching.

Nazif had gone to Ankara again, but assured Lebriz that this would be the last time.

"We won't ever have to be apart, my darling," he said. "I will never leave your side."

Two weeks after he'd started his visits, Sadi came in the morning to Nesrin's room, sat next to her, and held her hand.

"How would you like, my lady," he asked, "to take a walk with me?"

"A walk?" His hand felt firm yet warm and comforting. Nesrin felt a kind feeling course through her body.

"The leaves are just starting to turn, and it's a warm, sunny morning."

"I'd love to come," said Nesrin.

Nanna and Lebriz watched from the porch in front of the house as the couple made their way through the garden to the gate. They both walked slowly and deliberately, he with his cane, and she holding on to his arm.

They seemed to contemplate each step as though it were a significant and miraculous event. She stopped for a moment to touch a rose.

"Are they going to go out the gate?" asked Lebriz with wonder.

"I believe they are," said Nanna. "You know it's the black seed and honey concoction. I told you it would work."

"And you were right," said Lebriz, her eyes tearing up.

They watched as Sadi slowly opened the gate. Then he held Nesrin's hand and the two of them walked out. As they made their way down the street, Nanna looked at Lebriz's face. How glowing, how beautiful, how happy she looked.

"My girl," she said. "My precious girl."

"Oh Nanna, my heart is so full right now," said Lebriz. "I don't want to think about the future, and I don't want to think about the past, I don't want to think about anything else."

THE END

ACKNOWLEDGMENTS

This novel would not have been possible without the evenings I spent listening to the musings and remembrances of my formidable mother-in-law Enise Ünel and her life-long friend and helper, Ayşe Koçer.

When I first arrived in Turkey in 1959, I didn't speak a word of Turkish. My husband was quickly whisked away to fulfill his military service while my one-year-old son and I were left to live with my in-laws in Istanbul. After the child had gone to bed, and the dinner table was cleared, I would sit with the ladies, eat sweets and fruit, and try to piece together what little I could comprehend of the stories they told. As time passed, and my Turkish improved, I got a fuller account of the life of Enise's mother Lebriz Hanim. Stunningly beautiful, with fair skin and hazel eyes, she had indeed been given away by her father to be raised in the Sultan's Harem. Her mother searched for her high and low for many years until the two of them were finally reunited at Lebriz' wedding. These two events – Lebriz' separation from her family and her marriage – profoundly affected me and formed the backbone of my novel. The rest is pure fiction.

I was also moved by Ayşe Abla's story. She was orphaned at five years old when her parents fell victim to Cossack attacks. Discovered in the courtyard of a mosque in Eastern Anatolia by Lebriz' older brother, she was brought to Istanbul to be raised by Lebriz and her husband Nazif, as a companion to their daughter Enise. Even though she was an *evlatlık* (adoptee,) by all accounts, she was raised as a member of the family. She adored and respected Lebriz Hanım and remained a devoted friend and servant to Enise. She served as nanny to her children and grandchildren, including my son Sinan and my beautiful daughter Aylin.

Both women served as mentors to me. When I was confronted day by day by a culture that surprised and baffled me, when I was confused, lost or amazed, they embraced me, held me by the hand, supported and reassured me. My mother-in-law was in competition with me, determined to master the English language before I learned Turkish. She had little chance of winning that race, however. Once my son spoke his first Turkish phrase, which I couldn't understand, there was no question that I would be proficient in the language as quickly as humanly possible. As a foreign *gelin*, or bride, I was curious, enthusiastic, but also stubborn and not always easy to handle. I will forever be grateful for the generosity, love and direction these two dear women gave me not only during those early days, but for the rest of their lives.

Further thanks go to playwright Sinan Ünel who collaborated with me on this book. He not only encouraged the writing from the very beginning but he checked all of the dates and data, and is completely responsible for getting the book published.

John Andert has been so kind as to design and lay out the front and back covers beautifully.

Nicki Burnell, Kate Kennedy and Sonia Pabley have edited and provided valuable feedback and support.

The early readers, Jackie Kelly, John Keller, Nili Bilkur, Mary Neufeld, Lisa Lambert were all generous with their excellent comments and encouragement.

A special thank you to my family Aylin, Erhan, Mete, John and Sinan for not only nurturing me but also for giving me space, love and inspiration to write the book.

Visit www.lebriznovel.com to learn about Yildiz Palace, Sultan Abdulhamid and the women and eunuchs of the harem. You will also find information about the author and the woman whose story inspired the book.